STAR TREK®

VOLUME 10

Story Consultant:

ROBERTO ORCI

Cover by

CAT STAGGS

Collection Edits by

JUSTIN EISINGER and ALONZO SIMON

Collection Design by

CLAUDIA CHONG

Star Trek created by Gene Roddenberry.
Special thanks to Risa Kessler and John Van Citters of CBS Consumer Products for their invaluable assistance.

www.IDWPUBLISHING.com
IDW founded by Ted Adams, Alex Garner, Kris Oprisko, and Robbie Robbins

Ted Adams, CEO & Publisher
Greg Goldstein, President & COO
Robbie Robbins, EVP/Sr. Graphic Artist
Chris Ryall, Chief Creative Officer/Editor-in-Chief
Matthew Ruzicka, CPA, Chief Financial Officer
Alan Payne, VP of Sales
Dirk Wood, VP of Marketing
Lorelei Bunjes, VP of Digital Services
Jeff Webber, VP of Digital Publishing & Business Development

Facebook: facebook.com/idwpublishing
Twitter: @idwpublishing
YouTube: youtube.com/idwpublishing
Tumblr: tumblr.idwpublishing.com
Instagram: instagram.com/idwpublishing

Originally published as STAR TREK issues #41-45.

STAR TREK®

VOLUME 10

Written by
MIKE JOHNSON

BEHEMOTH	EURYDICE
Art by	Art by
CAT STAGGS	**TONY SHASTEEN**
Colors by	Colors by
WES HARTMAN	**DAVIDE MASTROLONARDO**

Letters by
NEIL UYETAKE

Series Edits by
SARAH GAYDOS

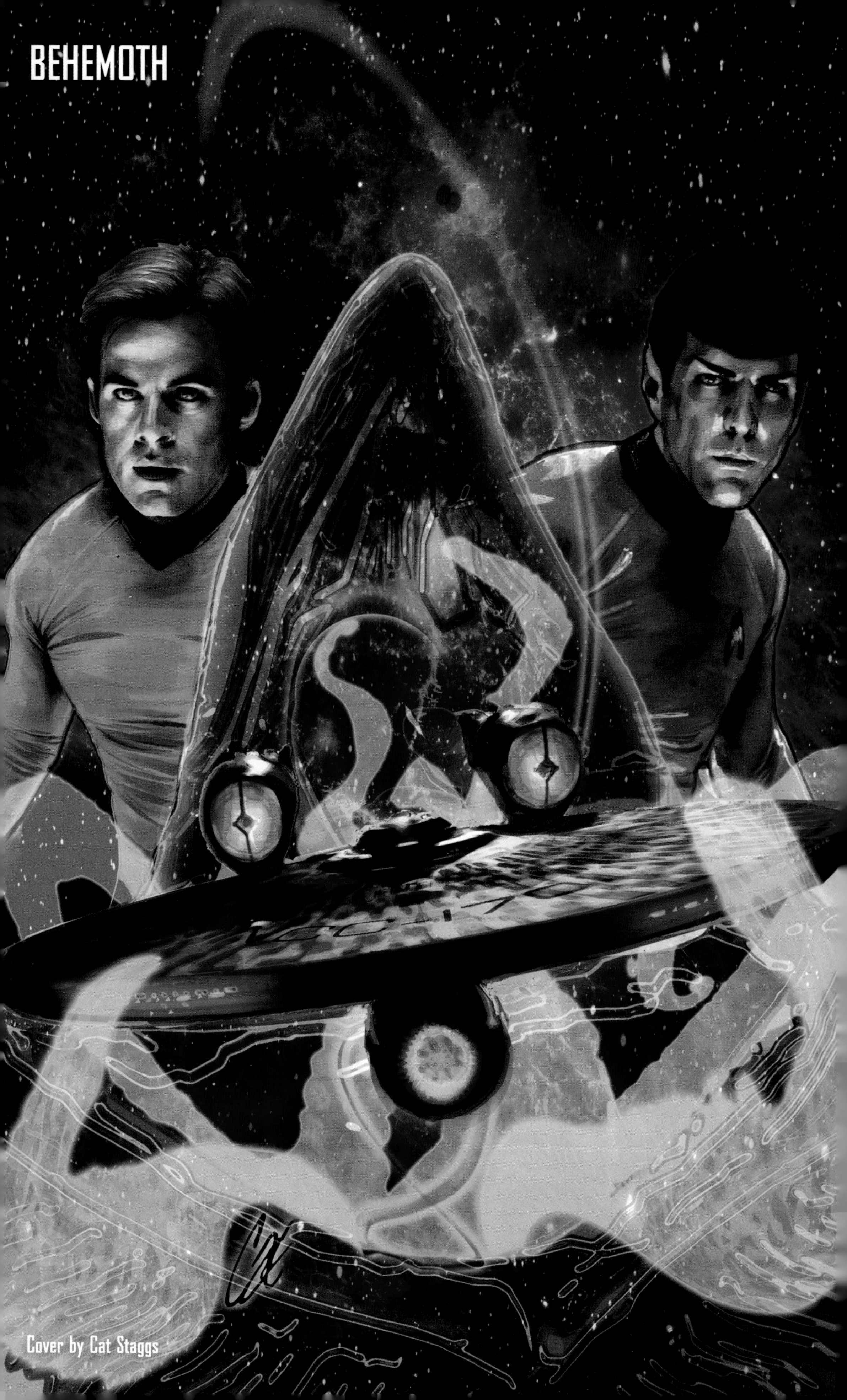
BEHEMOTH
Cover by Cat Staggs

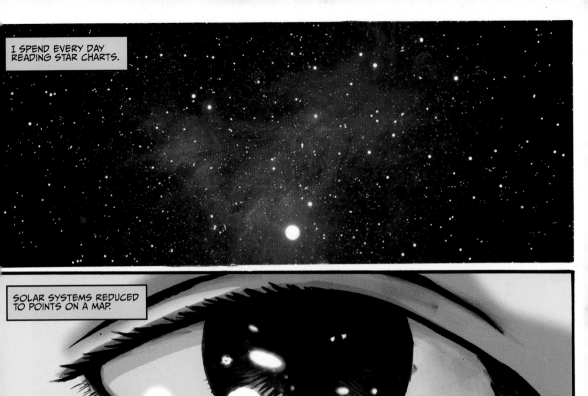

I SPEND EVERY DAY READING STAR CHARTS.

SOLAR SYSTEMS REDUCED TO POINTS ON A MAP.

EVERY SO OFTEN I NEED TO STEP AWAY. CHANGE MY PERSPECTIVE.

SO I COME TO ONE OF THE OBSERVATION DECKS AND SPEND A FEW HOURS JUST LOOKING OUT...

...TO REMEMBER HOW *BEAUTIFUL THE UNIVERSE IS.*
"AMAZING, ISN'T IT?"
TO THINK THAT NOBODY'S EVER TRAVELED THIS FAR FROM EARTH BEFORE?
DA, IT IS...
...AMAZING, UH...
IRINA.
YES... YOU...
YOU DON'T REMEMBER ME, DO YOU, LIEUTENANT?
O-OF COURSE, YOU'RE...
FROM RUSSIA. LIKE YOU. WE MET BRIEFLY AT THE ACADEMY, JUST BEFORE YOU WERE ASSIGNED TO THE *ENTERPRISE.*

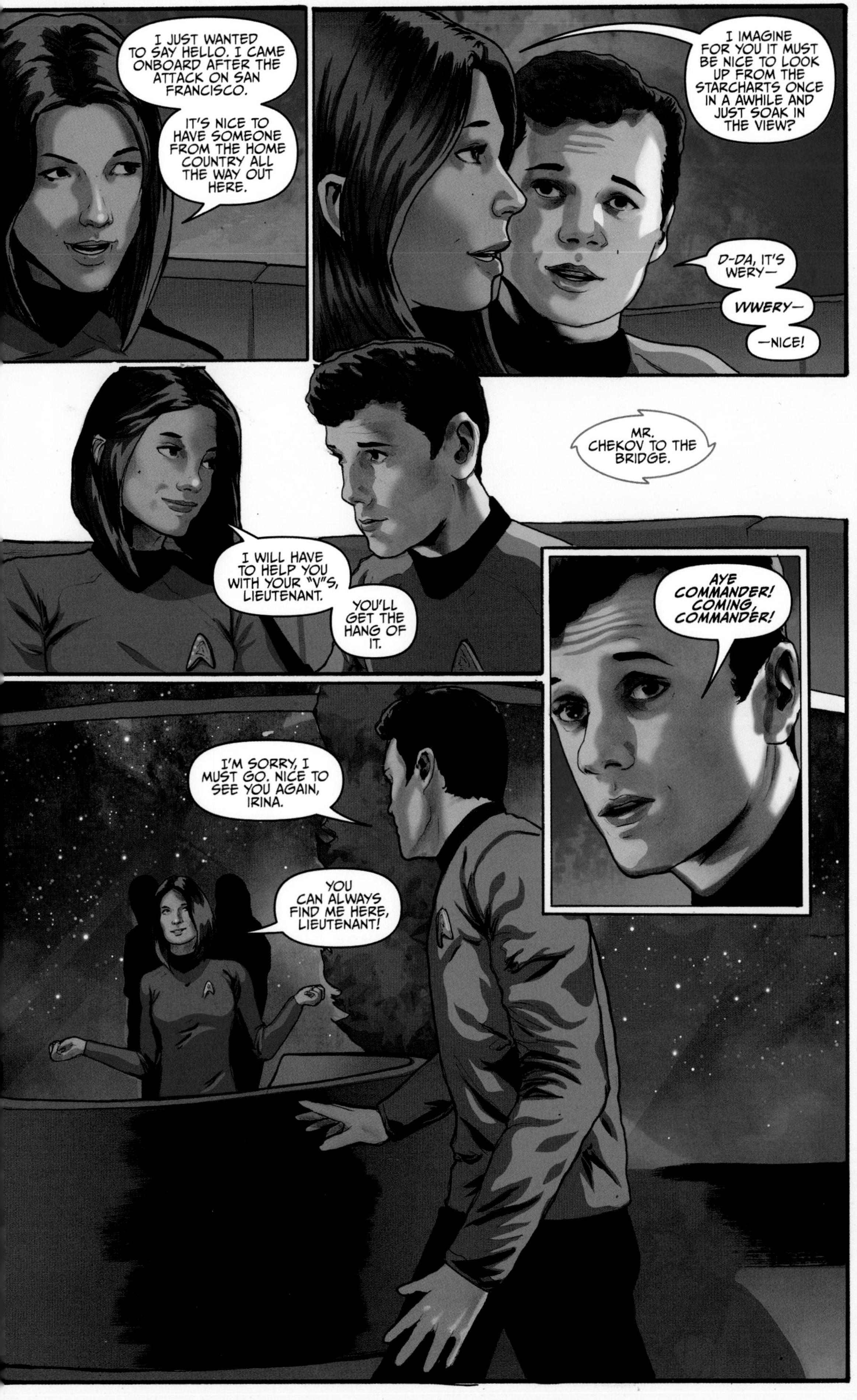
I JUST WANTED TO SAY HELLO. I CAME ONBOARD AFTER THE ATTACK ON SAN FRANCISCO.
IT'S NICE TO HAVE SOMEONE FROM THE HOME COUNTRY ALL THE WAY OUT HERE.
I IMAGINE FOR YOU IT MUST BE NICE TO LOOK UP FROM THE STARCHARTS ONCE IN A AWHILE AND JUST SOAK IN THE VIEW?
D-DA, IT'S WERY—
VVWERY—
—NICE!
MR. CHEKOV TO THE BRIDGE.
I WILL HAVE TO HELP YOU WITH YOUR "V"S, LIEUTENANT.
YOU'LL GET THE HANG OF IT.
AYE COMMANDER! COMING, COMMANDER!
I'M SORRY, I MUST GO. NICE TO SEE YOU AGAIN, IRINA.
YOU CAN ALWAYS FIND ME HERE, LIEUTENANT!

WHAT WAS IT YOU WANTED TO DISCUSS, CAPTAIN?

TECHNICALLY WE'RE OFF THE CLOCK, CAROL. YOU CAN CALL ME JIM.

WE MET UNDER LESS-THAN-IDEAL CIRCUMSTANCES. I'VE BARELY HAD A CHANCE TO GET TO KNOW MY NEW WEAPONS SPECIALIST.

I'M GLAD YOU'RE ONBOARD.

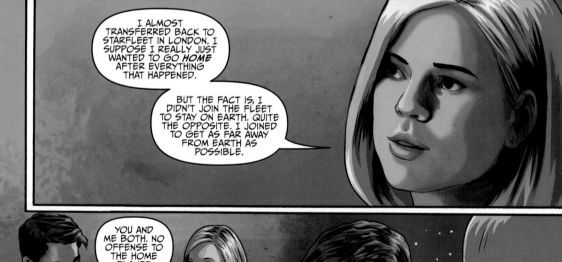

I ALMOST TRANSFERRED BACK TO STARFLEET IN LONDON. I SUPPOSE I REALLY JUST WANTED TO GO *HOME* AFTER EVERYTHING THAT HAPPENED.

BUT THE FACT IS, I DIDN'T JOIN THE FLEET TO STAY ON EARTH. QUITE THE OPPOSITE. I JOINED TO GET AS FAR AWAY FROM EARTH AS POSSIBLE.

YOU AND ME BOTH. NO OFFENSE TO THE HOME PLANET.

TO THE BLUE MARBLE.

THE BLUE MARBLE.

SO, WHY *WEAPONS SYSTEMS*?

CURIOSITY, I SUPPOSE. IT SEEMED LIKE SUCH A BOYS' CLUB AT THE ACADEMY. I WANTED TO CRASH IT.

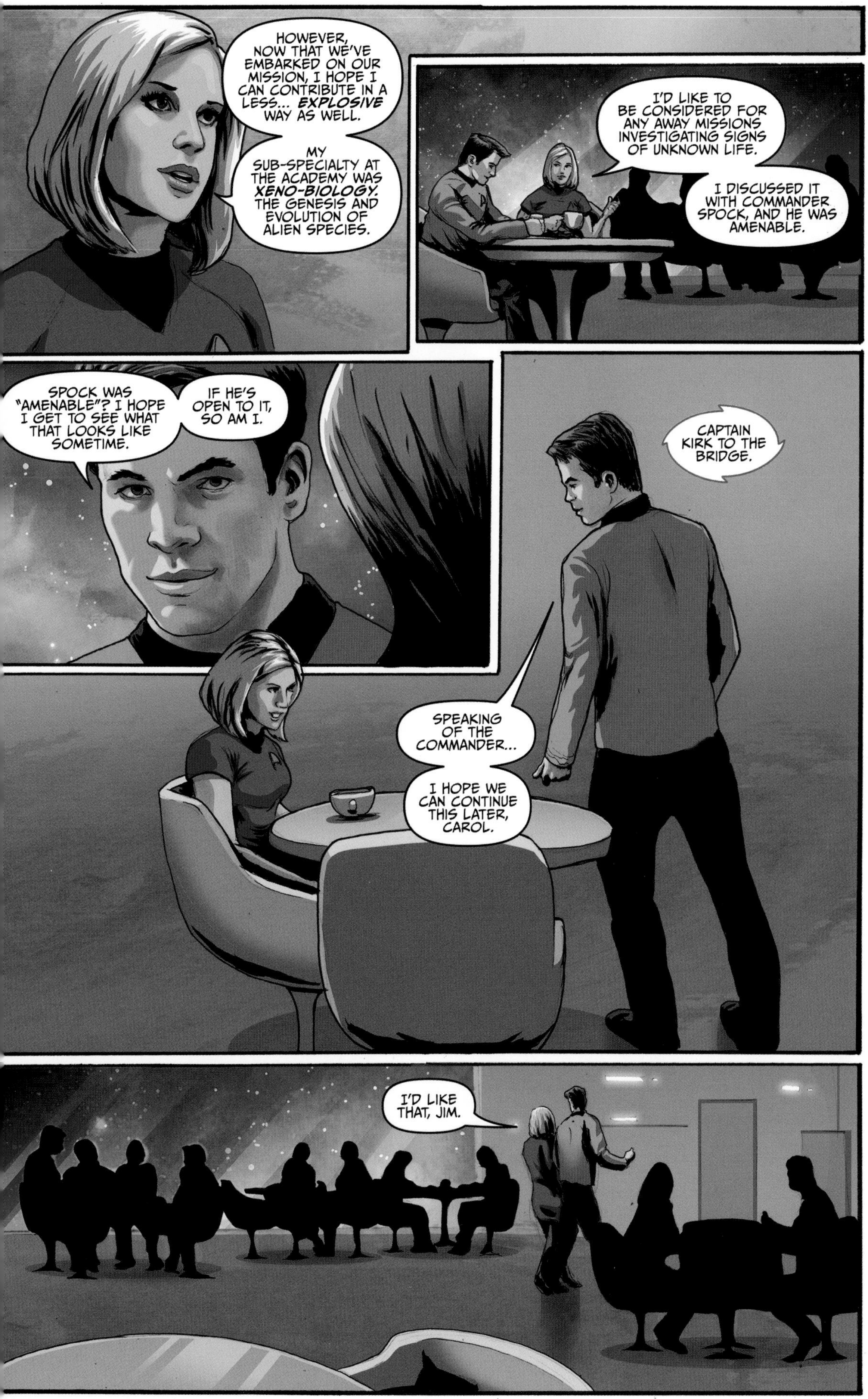
HOWEVER, NOW THAT WE'VE EMBARKED ON OUR MISSION, I HOPE I CAN CONTRIBUTE IN A LESS... EXPLOSIVE WAY AS WELL.
MY SUB-SPECIALTY AT THE ACADEMY WAS XENO-BIOLOGY. THE GENESIS AND EVOLUTION OF ALIEN SPECIES.
I'D LIKE TO BE CONSIDERED FOR ANY AWAY MISSIONS INVESTIGATING SIGNS OF UNKNOWN LIFE.
I DISCUSSED IT WITH COMMANDER SPOCK, AND HE WAS AMENABLE.
SPOCK WAS "AMENABLE"? I HOPE I GET TO SEE WHAT THAT LOOKS LIKE SOMETIME.
IF HE'S OPEN TO IT, SO AM I.
CAPTAIN KIRK TO THE BRIDGE.
SPEAKING OF THE COMMANDER...
I HOPE WE CAN CONTINUE THIS LATER, CAROL.
I'D LIKE THAT, JIM.

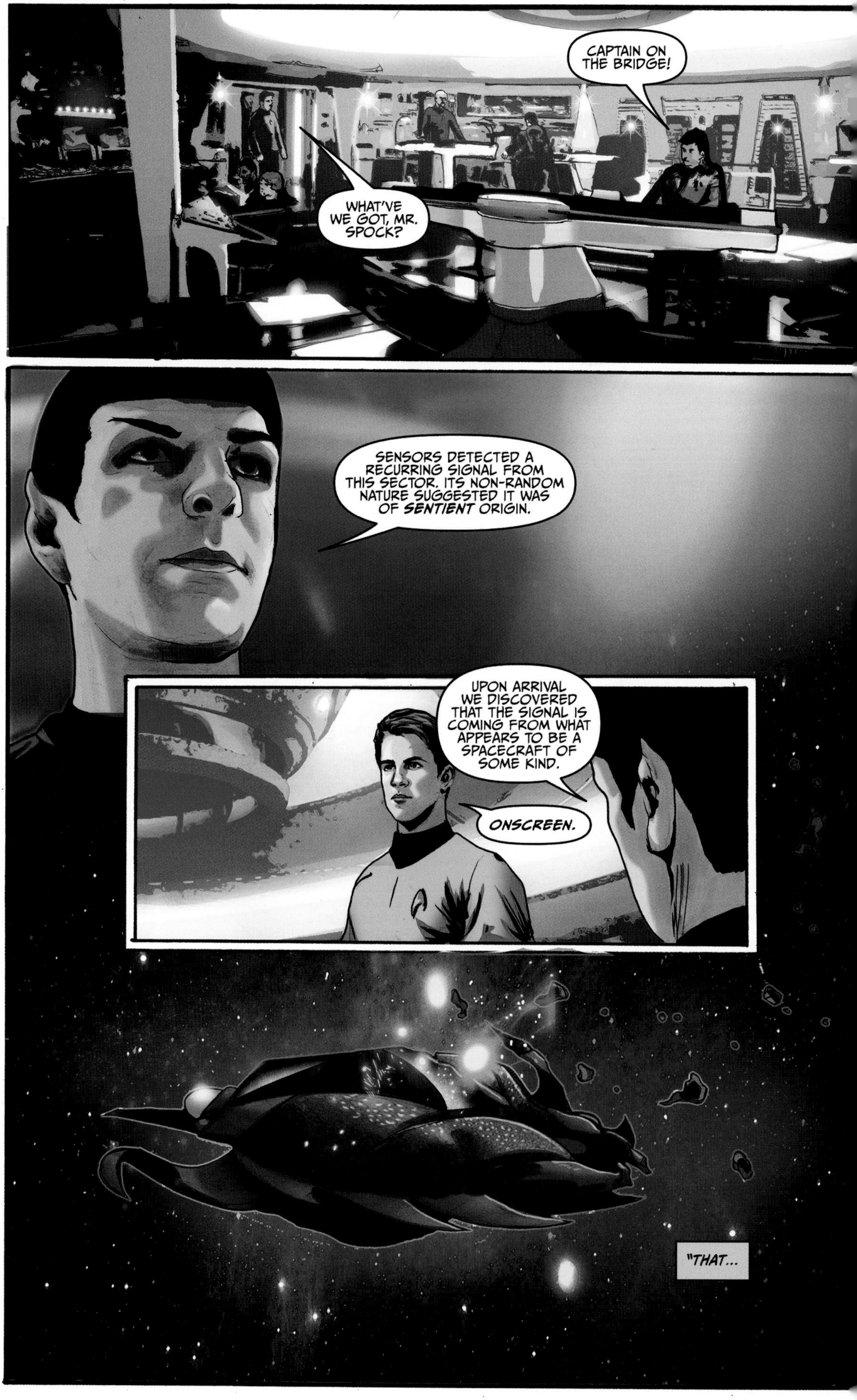

CAPTAIN ON THE BRIDGE!
WHAT'VE WE GOT, MR. SPOCK?
SENSORS DETECTED A RECURRING SIGNAL FROM THIS SECTOR. ITS NON-RANDOM NATURE SUGGESTED IT WAS OF SENTIENT ORIGIN.
UPON ARRIVAL WE DISCOVERED THAT THE SIGNAL IS COMING FROM WHAT APPEARS TO BE A SPACECRAFT OF SOME KIND.
ONSCREEN.
"THAT...

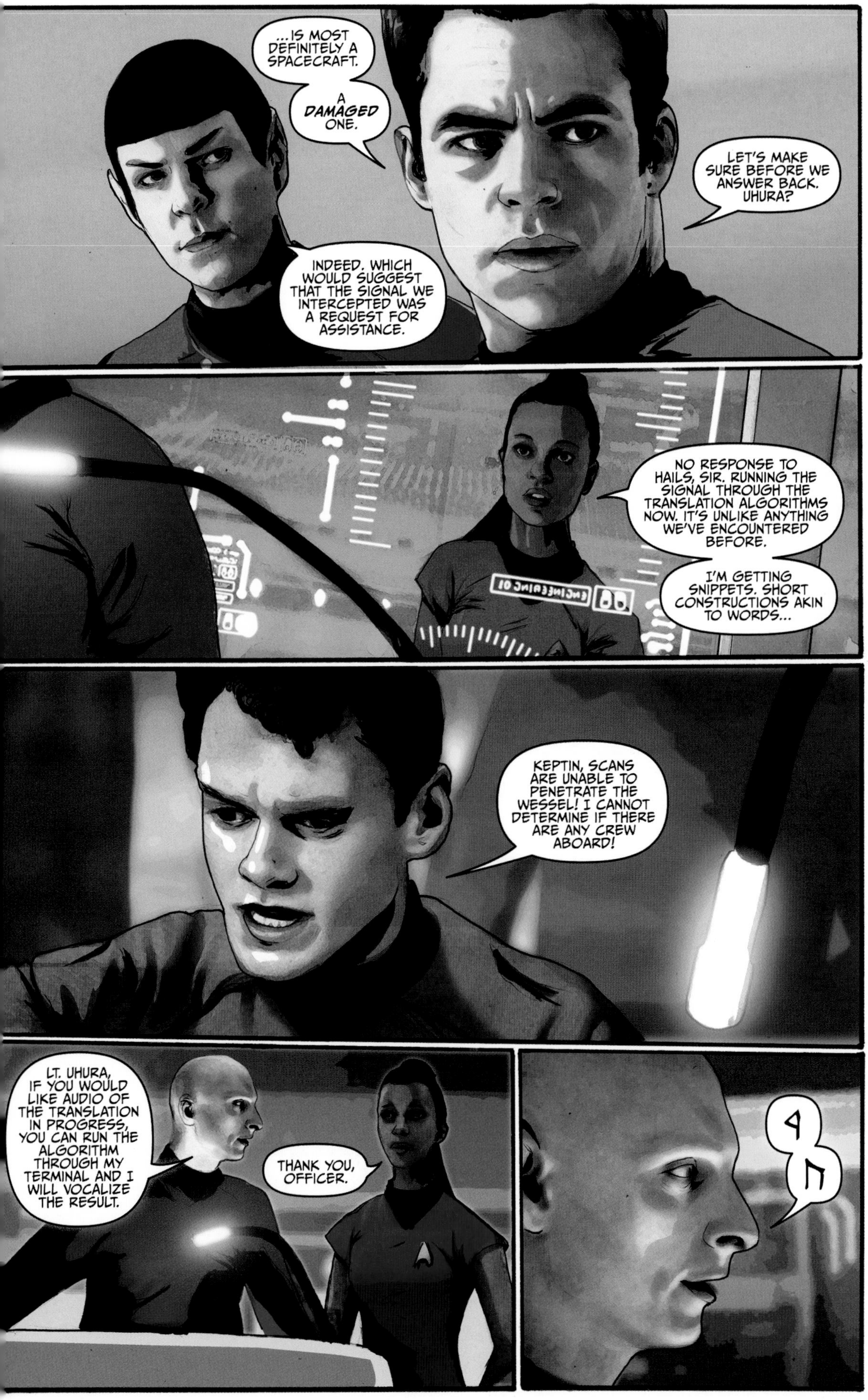
...IS MOST DEFINITELY A SPACECRAFT.
A *DAMAGED* ONE.
LET'S MAKE SURE BEFORE WE ANSWER BACK. UHURA?
INDEED. WHICH WOULD SUGGEST THAT THE SIGNAL WE INTERCEPTED WAS A REQUEST FOR ASSISTANCE.
NO RESPONSE TO HAILS, SIR. RUNNING THE SIGNAL THROUGH THE TRANSLATION ALGORITHMS NOW. IT'S UNLIKE ANYTHING WE'VE ENCOUNTERED BEFORE.
I'M GETTING SNIPPETS. SHORT CONSTRUCTIONS AKIN TO WORDS...
KEPTIN, SCANS ARE UNABLE TO PENETRATE THE WESSEL! I CANNOT DETERMINE IF THERE ARE ANY CREW ABOARD!
LT. UHURA, IF YOU WOULD LIKE AUDIO OF THE TRANSLATION IN PROGRESS, YOU CAN RUN THE ALGORITHM THROUGH MY TERMINAL AND I WILL VOCALIZE THE RESULT.
THANK YOU, OFFICER.

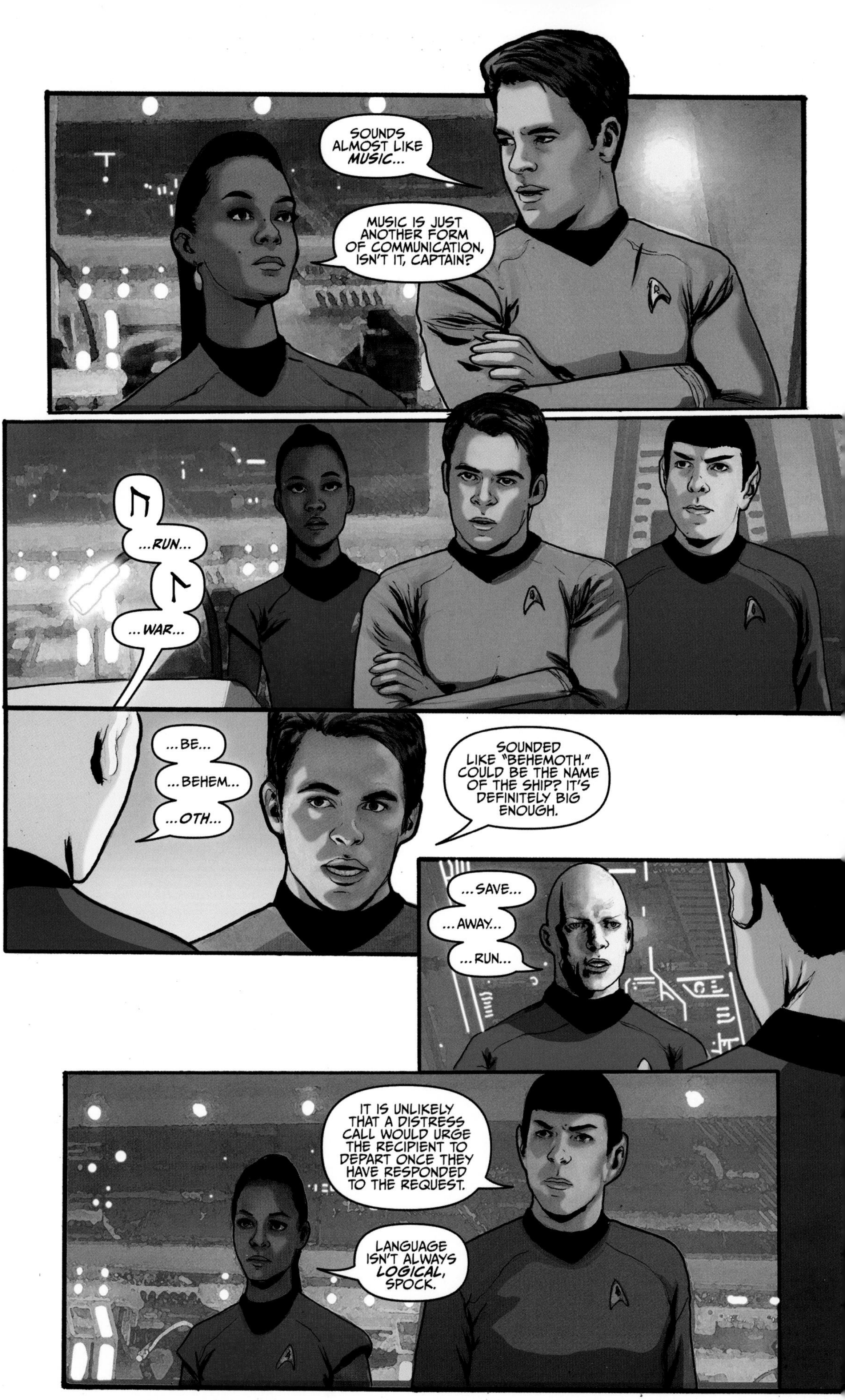
SOUNDS ALMOST LIKE MUSIC...
MUSIC IS JUST ANOTHER FORM OF COMMUNICATION, ISN'T IT, CAPTAIN?
...RUN...
...WAR...
...BE...
...BEHEM...
...OTH...
SOUNDED LIKE "BEHEMOTH." COULD BE THE NAME OF THE SHIP? IT'S DEFINITELY BIG ENOUGH.
...SAVE...
...AWAY...
...RUN...
IT IS UNLIKELY THAT A DISTRESS CALL WOULD URGE THE RECIPIENT TO DEPART ONCE THEY HAVE RESPONDED TO THE REQUEST.
LANGUAGE ISN'T ALWAYS LOGICAL, SPOCK.

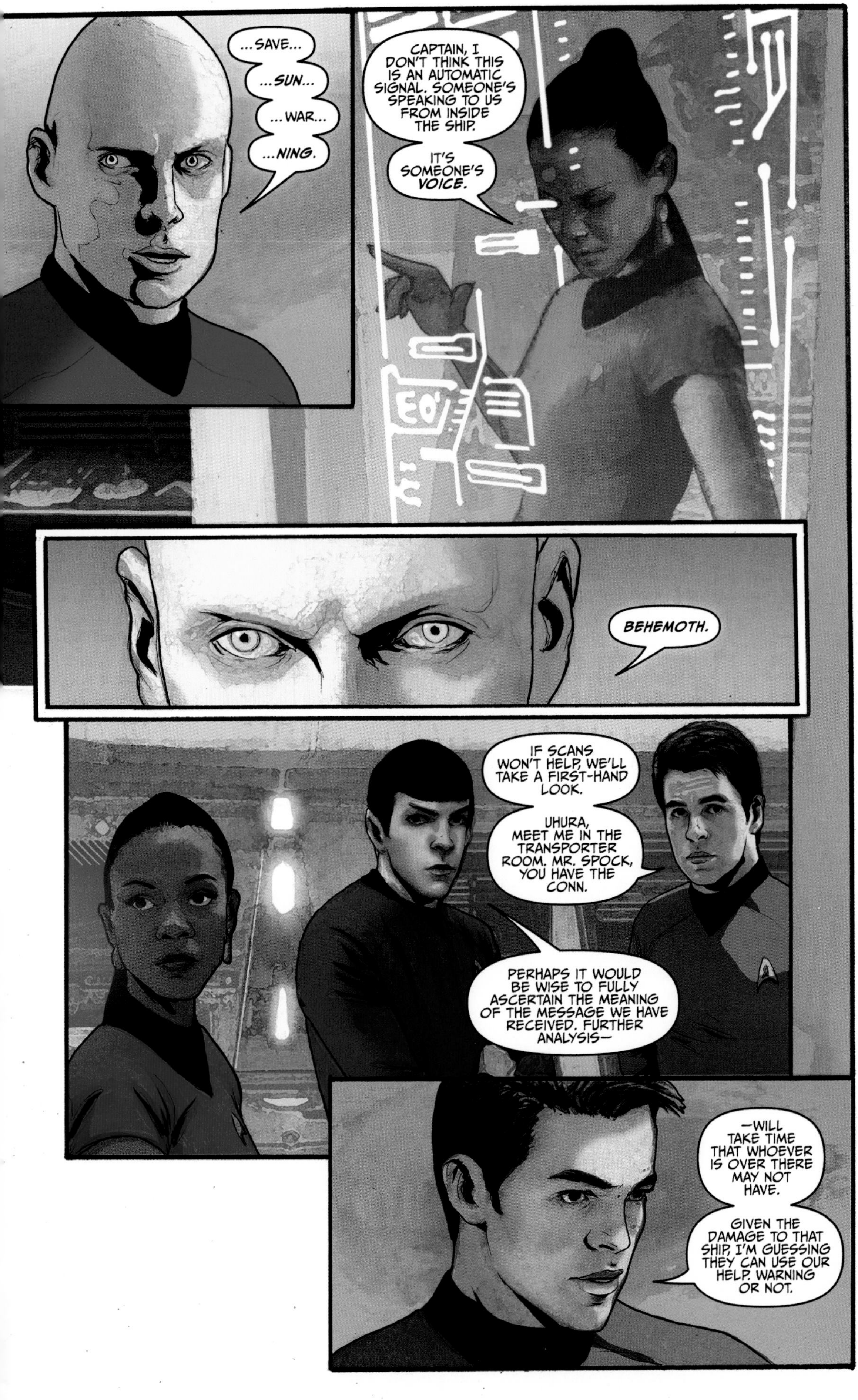
...SAVE...
...SUN...
...WAR...
...NING.
CAPTAIN, I DON'T THINK THIS IS AN AUTOMATIC SIGNAL. SOMEONE'S SPEAKING TO US FROM INSIDE THE SHIP.
IT'S SOMEONE'S VOICE.
BEHEMOTH.
IF SCANS WON'T HELP, WE'LL TAKE A FIRST-HAND LOOK.
UHURA, MEET ME IN THE TRANSPORTER ROOM. MR. SPOCK, YOU HAVE THE CONN.
PERHAPS IT WOULD BE WISE TO FULLY ASCERTAIN THE MEANING OF THE MESSAGE WE HAVE RECEIVED. FURTHER ANALYSIS—
—WILL TAKE TIME THAT WHOEVER IS OVER THERE MAY NOT HAVE.
GIVEN THE DAMAGE TO THAT SHIP, I'M GUESSING THEY CAN USE OUR HELP. WARNING OR NOT.

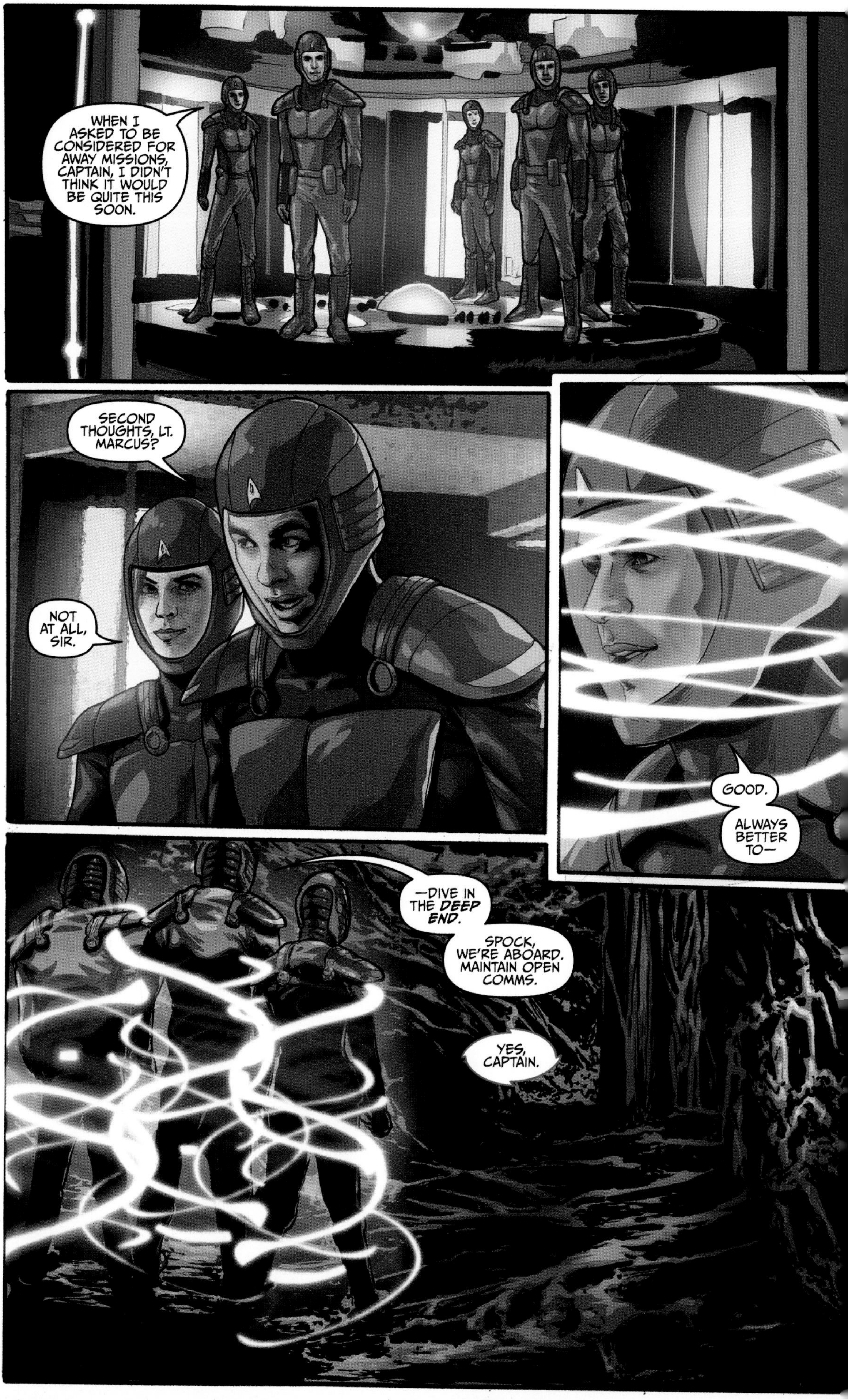
WHEN I ASKED TO BE CONSIDERED FOR AWAY MISSIONS, CAPTAIN, I DIDN'T THINK IT WOULD BE QUITE THIS SOON.
SECOND THOUGHTS, LT. MARCUS?
NOT AT ALL, SIR.
GOOD.
ALWAYS BETTER TO—
—DIVE IN THE *DEEP END*.
SPOCK, WE'RE ABOARD. MAINTAIN OPEN COMMS.
YES, CAPTAIN.

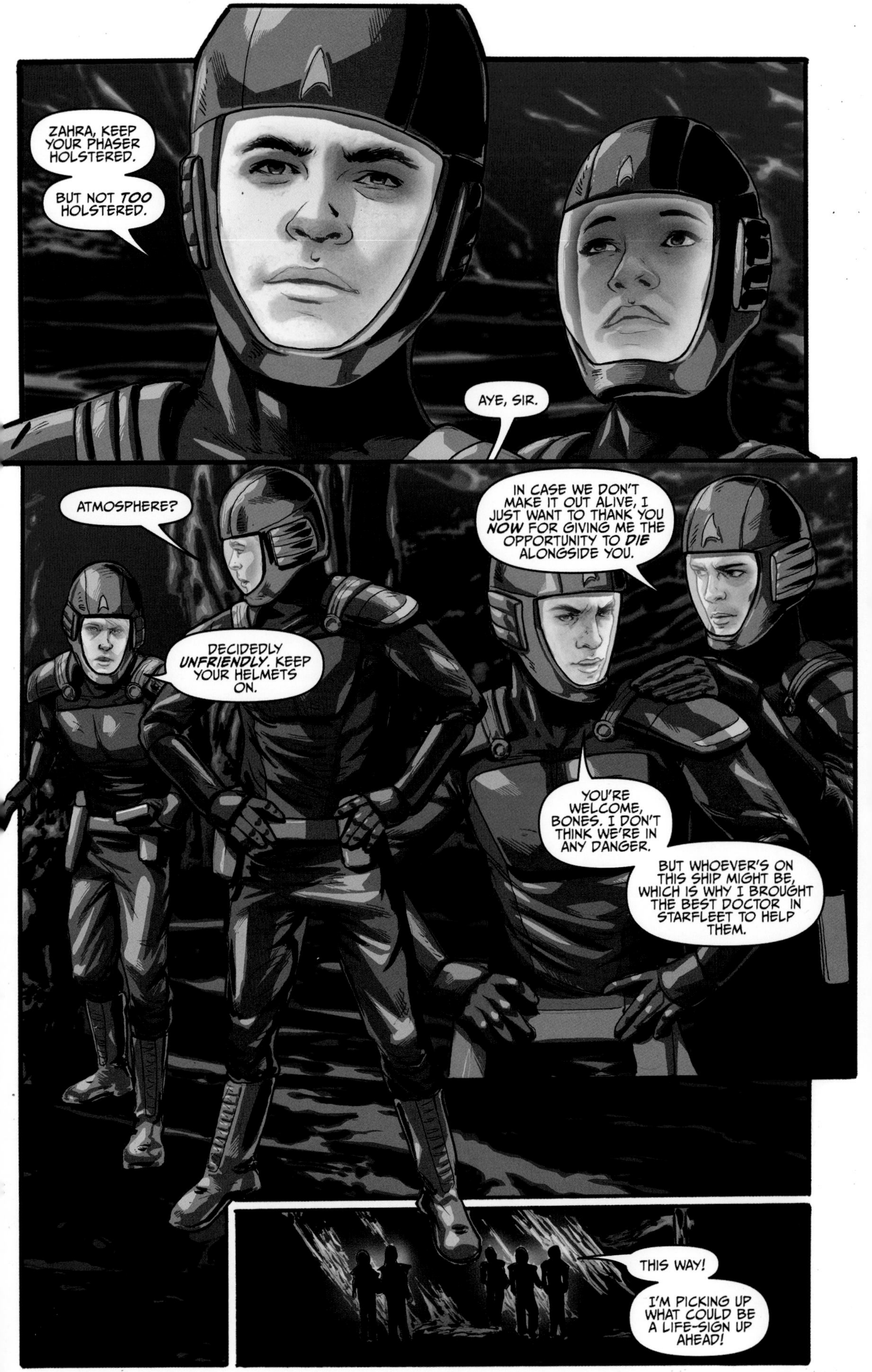
ZAHRA, KEEP YOUR PHASER HOLSTERED.
BUT NOT *TOO* HOLSTERED.
AYE, SIR.
ATMOSPHERE?
DECIDEDLY *UNFRIENDLY*. KEEP YOUR HELMETS ON.
IN CASE WE DON'T MAKE IT OUT ALIVE, I JUST WANT TO THANK YOU *NOW* FOR GIVING ME THE OPPORTUNITY TO *DIE* ALONGSIDE YOU.
YOU'RE WELCOME, BONES. I DON'T THINK WE'RE IN ANY DANGER.
BUT WHOEVER'S ON THIS SHIP MIGHT BE, WHICH IS WHY I BROUGHT THE BEST DOCTOR IN STARFLEET TO HELP THEM.
THIS WAY!
I'M PICKING UP WHAT COULD BE A LIFE-SIGN UP AHEAD!

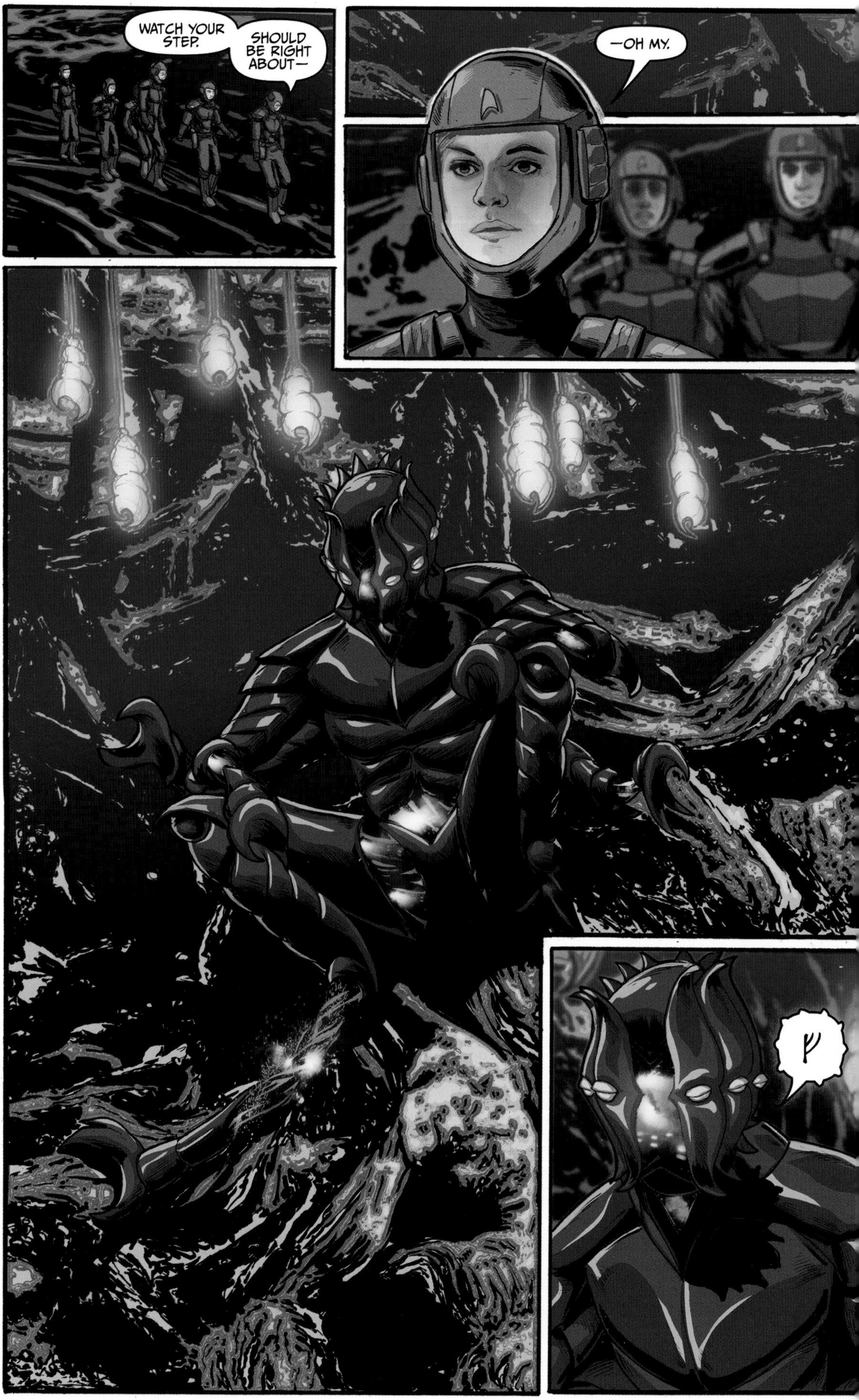

WATCH YOUR STEP.
SHOULD BE RIGHT ABOUT—
—OH MY.

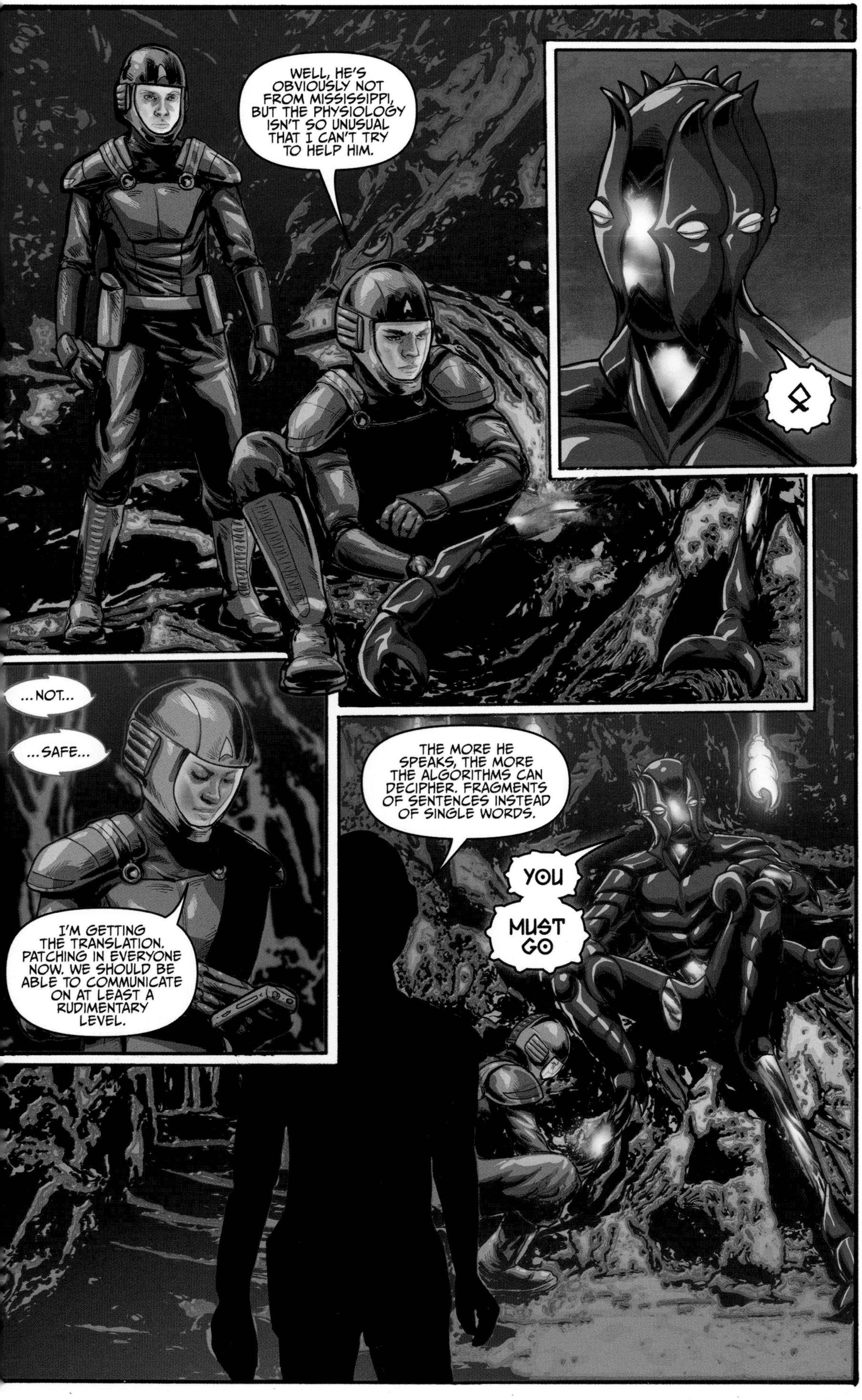
WELL, HE'S OBVIOUSLY NOT FROM MISSISSIPPI, BUT THE PHYSIOLOGY ISN'T SO UNUSUAL THAT I CAN'T TRY TO HELP HIM.
...NOT...
...SAFE...
I'M GETTING THE TRANSLATION. PATCHING IN EVERYONE NOW. WE SHOULD BE ABLE TO COMMUNICATE ON AT LEAST A RUDIMENTARY LEVEL.
THE MORE HE SPEAKS, THE MORE THE ALGORITHMS CAN DECIPHER. FRAGMENTS OF SENTENCES INSTEAD OF SINGLE WORDS.
YOU
MUST GO

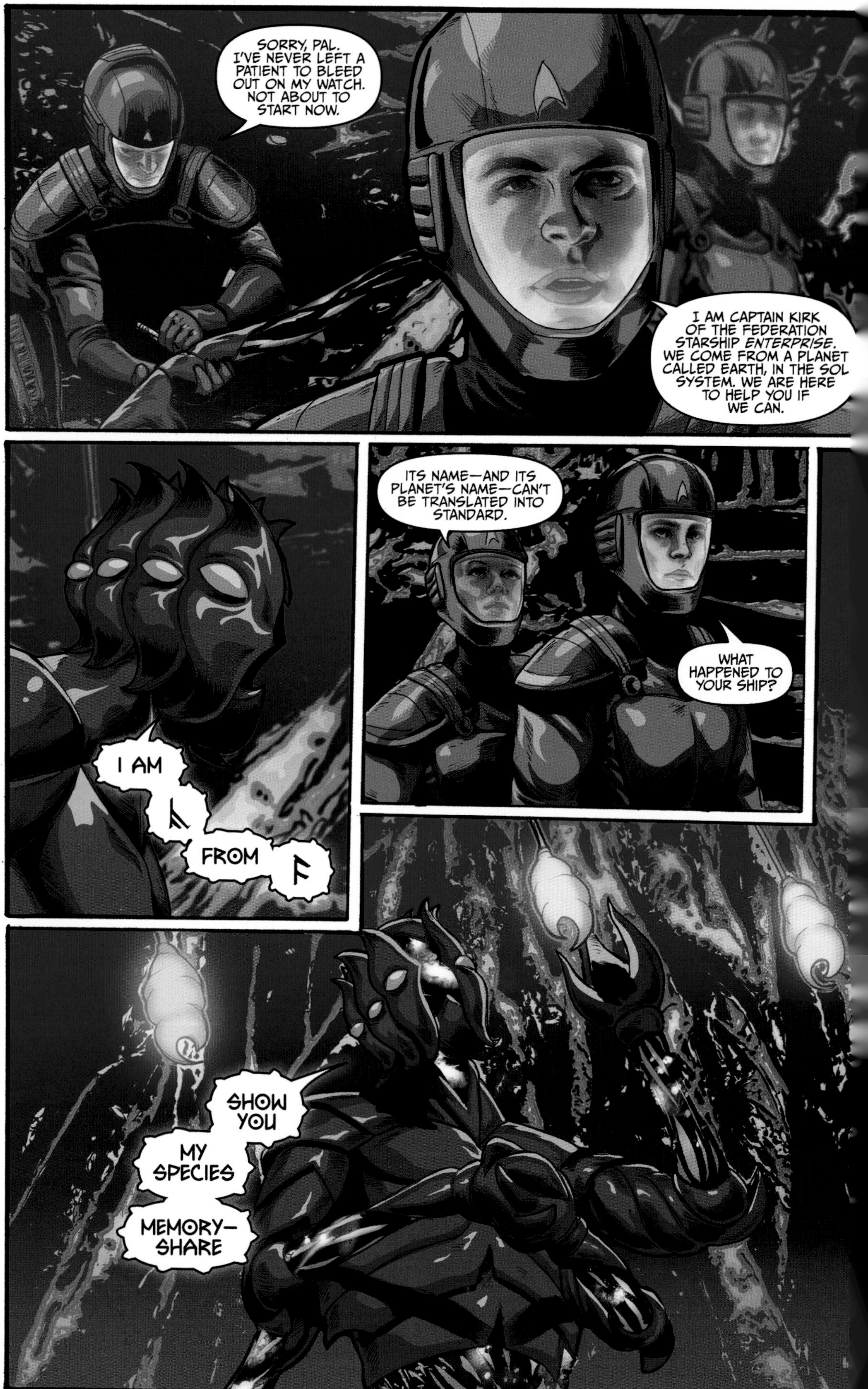

SORRY, PAL. I'VE NEVER LEFT A PATIENT TO BLEED OUT ON MY WATCH. NOT ABOUT TO START NOW.
I AM CAPTAIN KIRK OF THE FEDERATION STARSHIP *ENTERPRISE*. WE COME FROM A PLANET CALLED EARTH, IN THE SOL SYSTEM. WE ARE HERE TO HELP YOU IF WE CAN.
I AM
FROM
ITS NAME—AND ITS PLANET'S NAME—CAN'T BE TRANSLATED INTO STANDARD.
WHAT HAPPENED TO YOUR SHIP?
SHOW YOU
MY SPECIES
MEMORY-SHARE

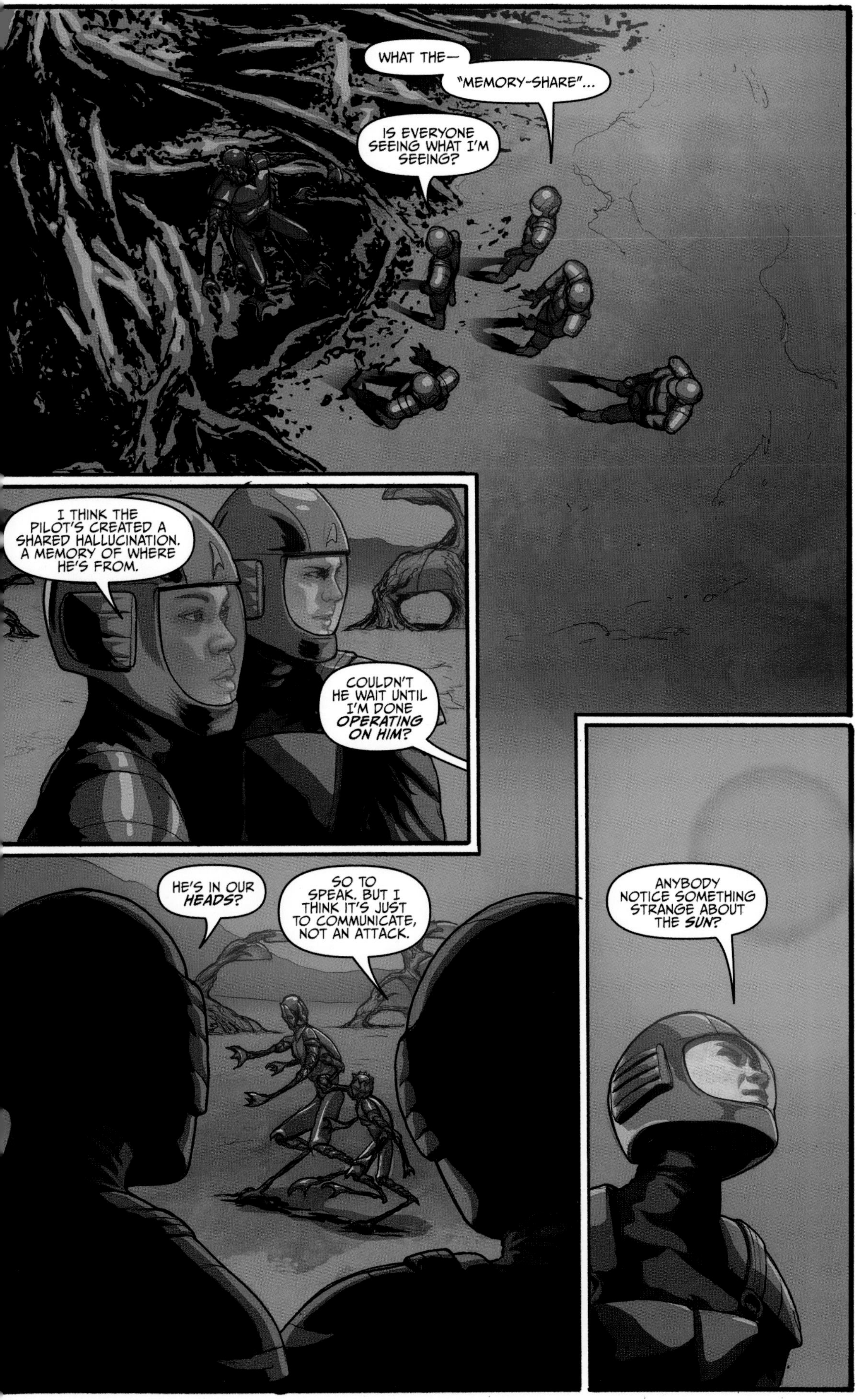
WHAT THE—
"MEMORY-SHARE"...
IS EVERYONE SEEING WHAT I'M SEEING?
I THINK THE PILOT'S CREATED A SHARED HALLUCINATION. A MEMORY OF WHERE HE'S FROM.
COULDN'T HE WAIT UNTIL I'M DONE *OPERATING ON HIM?*
HE'S IN OUR *HEADS?*
SO TO SPEAK, BUT I THINK IT'S JUST TO COMMUNICATE, NOT AN ATTACK.
ANYBODY NOTICE SOMETHING STRANGE ABOUT THE *SUN?*

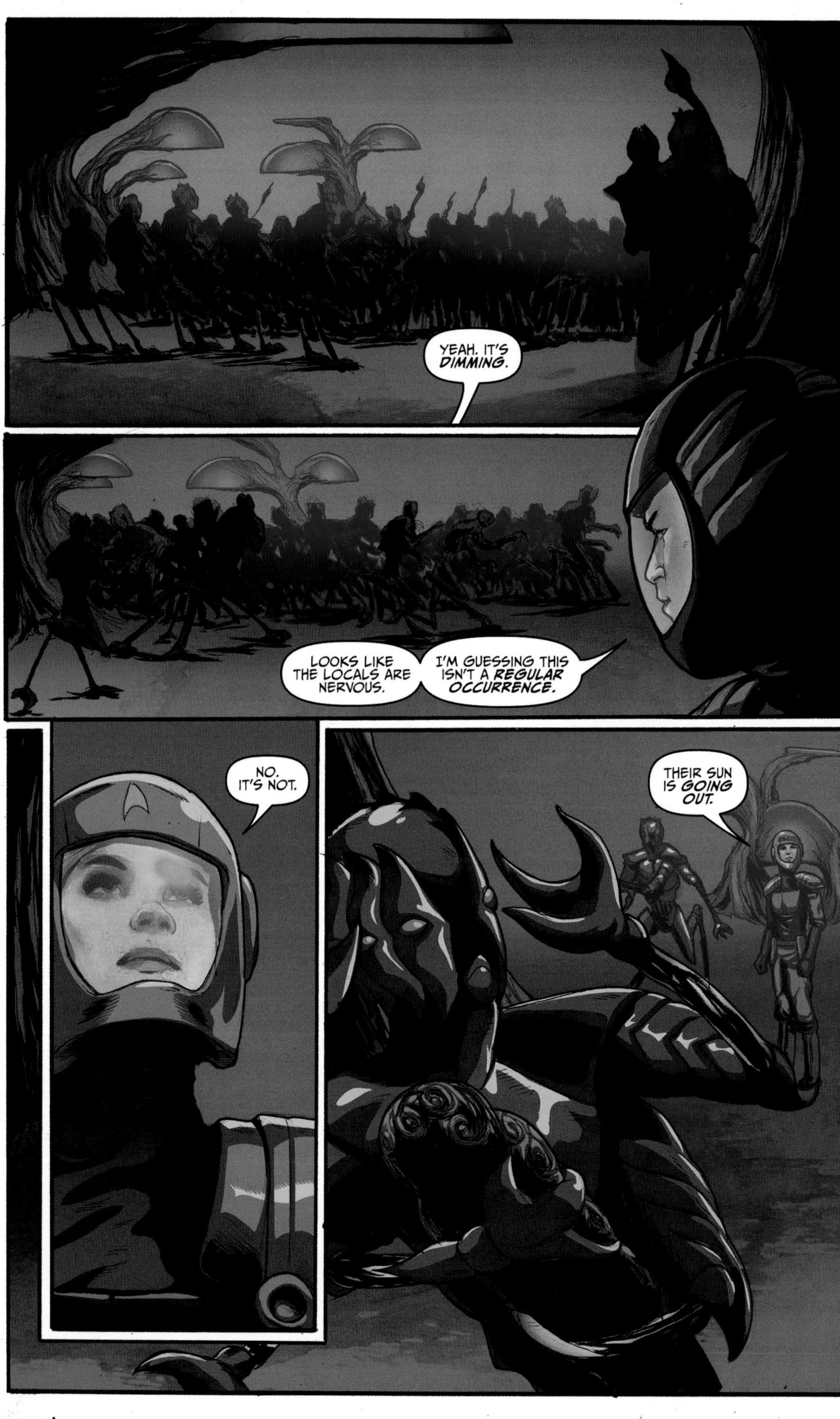

YEAH. IT'S DIMMING.
LOOKS LIKE THE LOCALS ARE NERVOUS.
I'M GUESSING THIS ISN'T A REGULAR OCCURRENCE.
NO. IT'S NOT.
THEIR SUN IS GOING OUT.

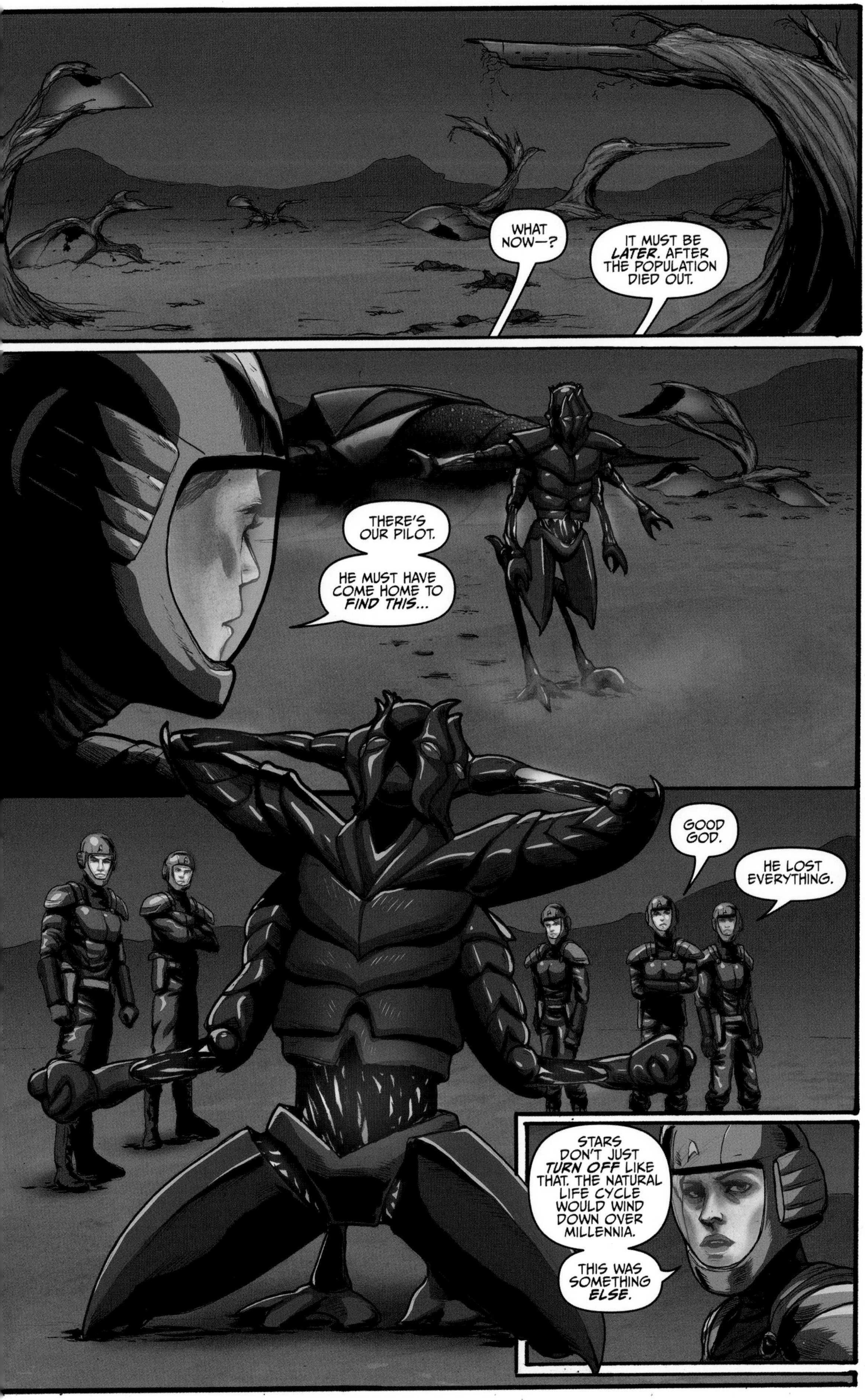

WHAT NOW—?
IT MUST BE LATER. AFTER THE POPULATION DIED OUT.
THERE'S OUR PILOT.
HE MUST HAVE COME HOME TO FIND THIS...
GOOD GOD.
HE LOST EVERYTHING.
STARS DON'T JUST TURN OFF LIKE THAT. THE NATURAL LIFE CYCLE WOULD WIND DOWN OVER MILLENNIA.
THIS WAS SOMETHING ELSE.

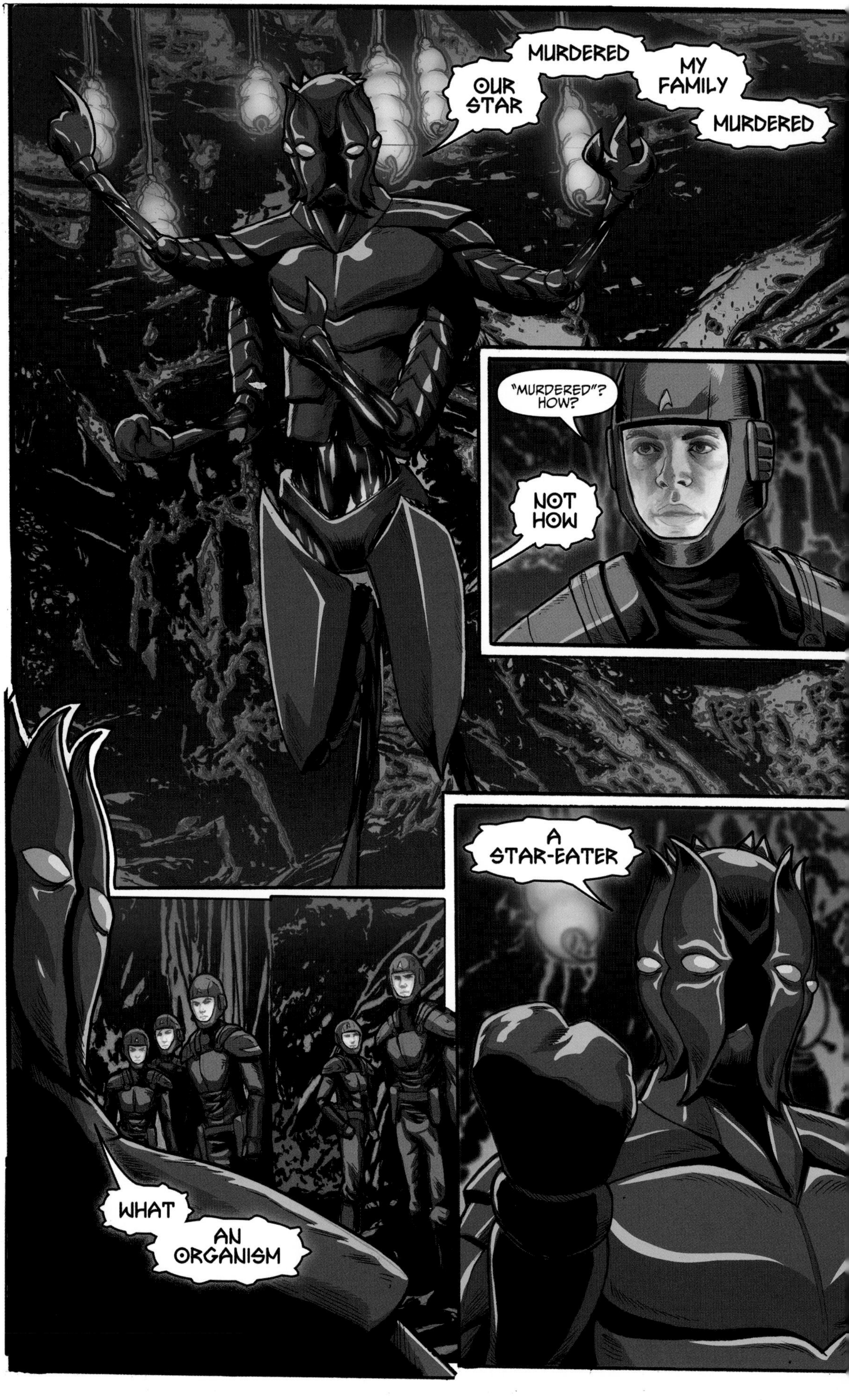
OUR STAR
MURDERED
MY FAMILY
MURDERED
"MURDERED"? HOW?
NOT HOW
A STAR-EATER
WHAT
AN ORGANISM

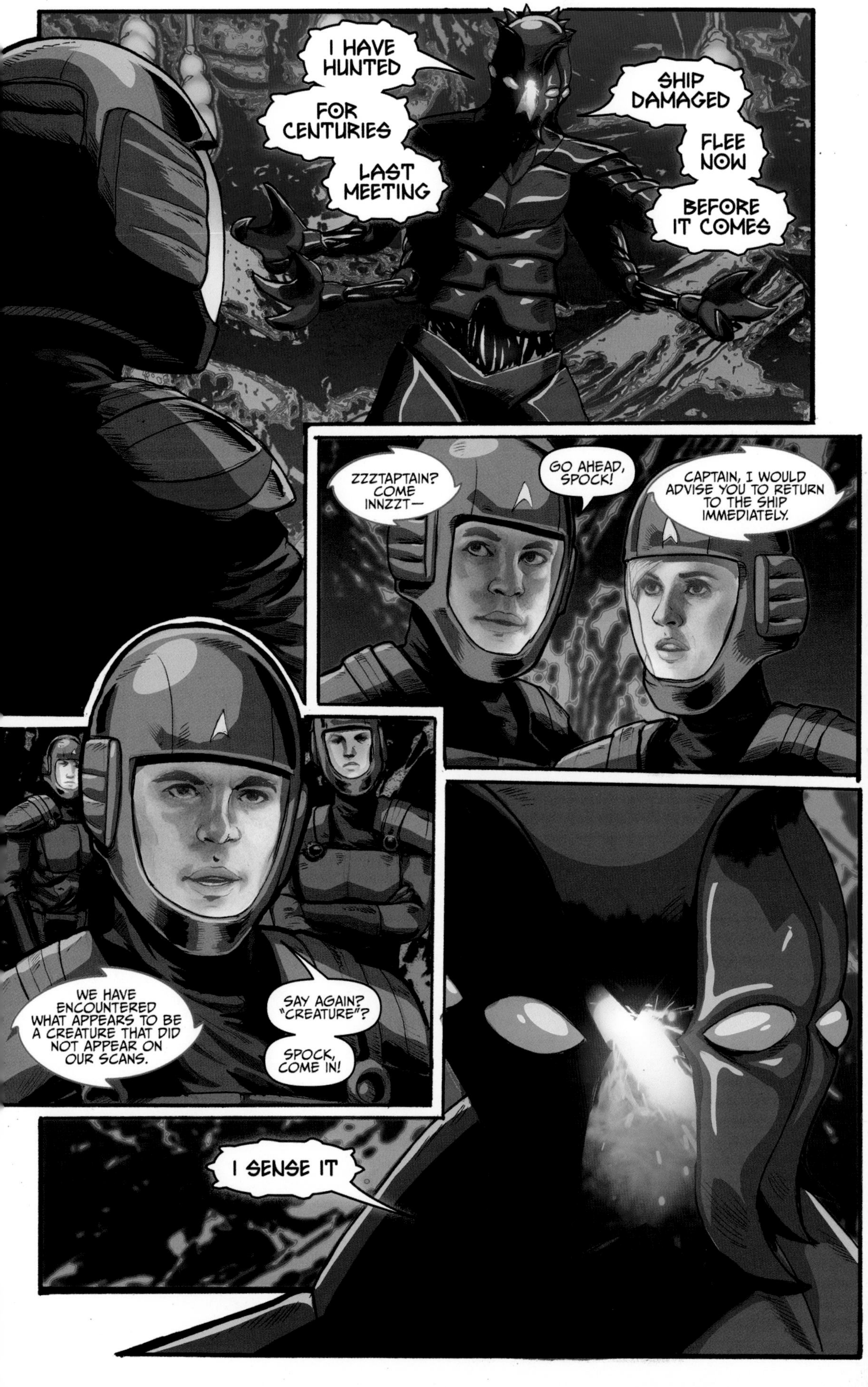
I HAVE HUNTED
FOR CENTURIES
LAST MEETING
SHIP DAMAGED
FLEE NOW
BEFORE IT COMES
ZZZTAPTAIN? COME INNZZT—
GO AHEAD, SPOCK!
CAPTAIN, I WOULD ADVISE YOU TO RETURN TO THE SHIP IMMEDIATELY.
WE HAVE ENCOUNTERED WHAT APPEARS TO BE A CREATURE THAT DID NOT APPEAR ON OUR SCANS.
SAY AGAIN? "CREATURE"?
SPOCK, COME IN!
I SENSE IT

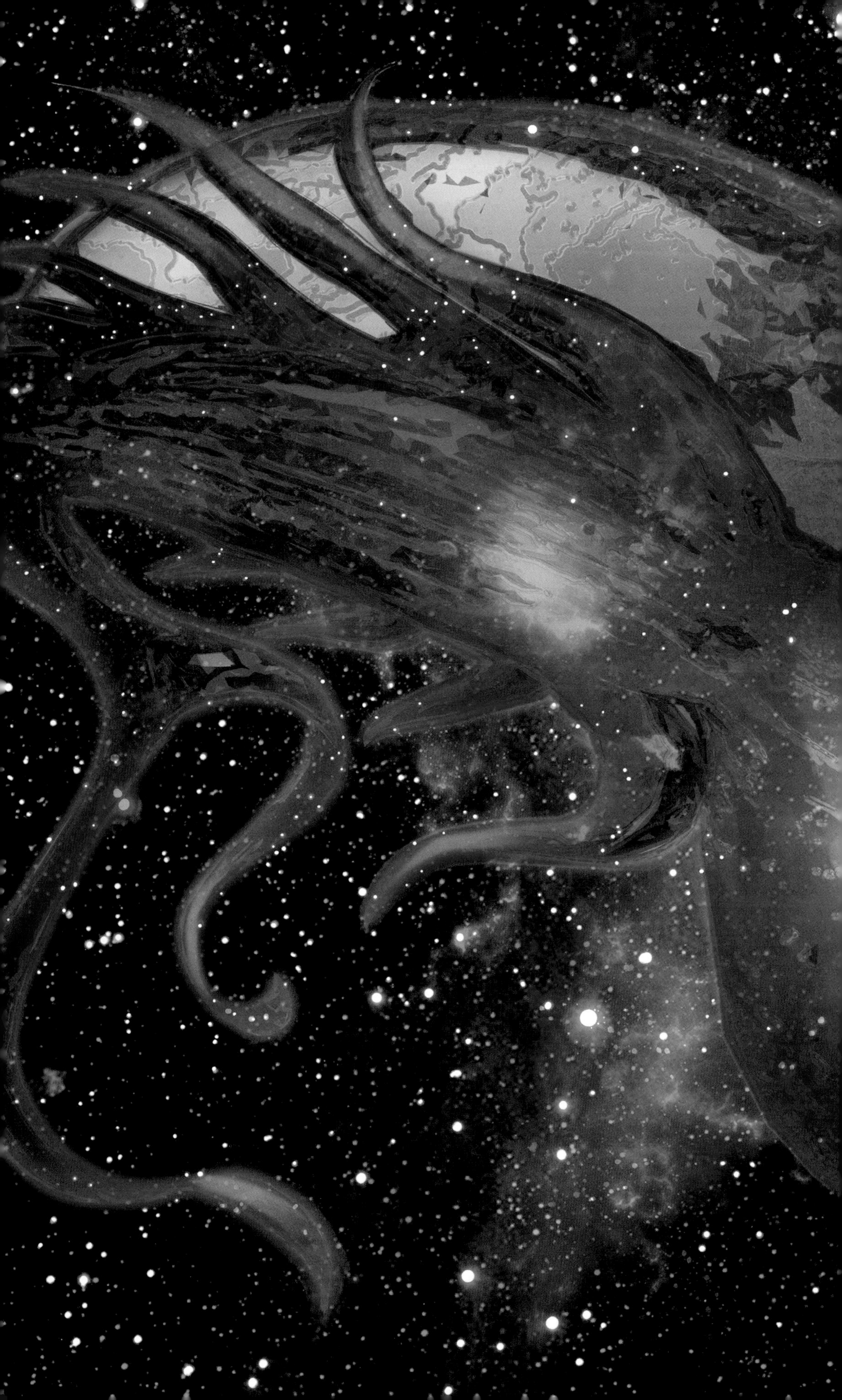

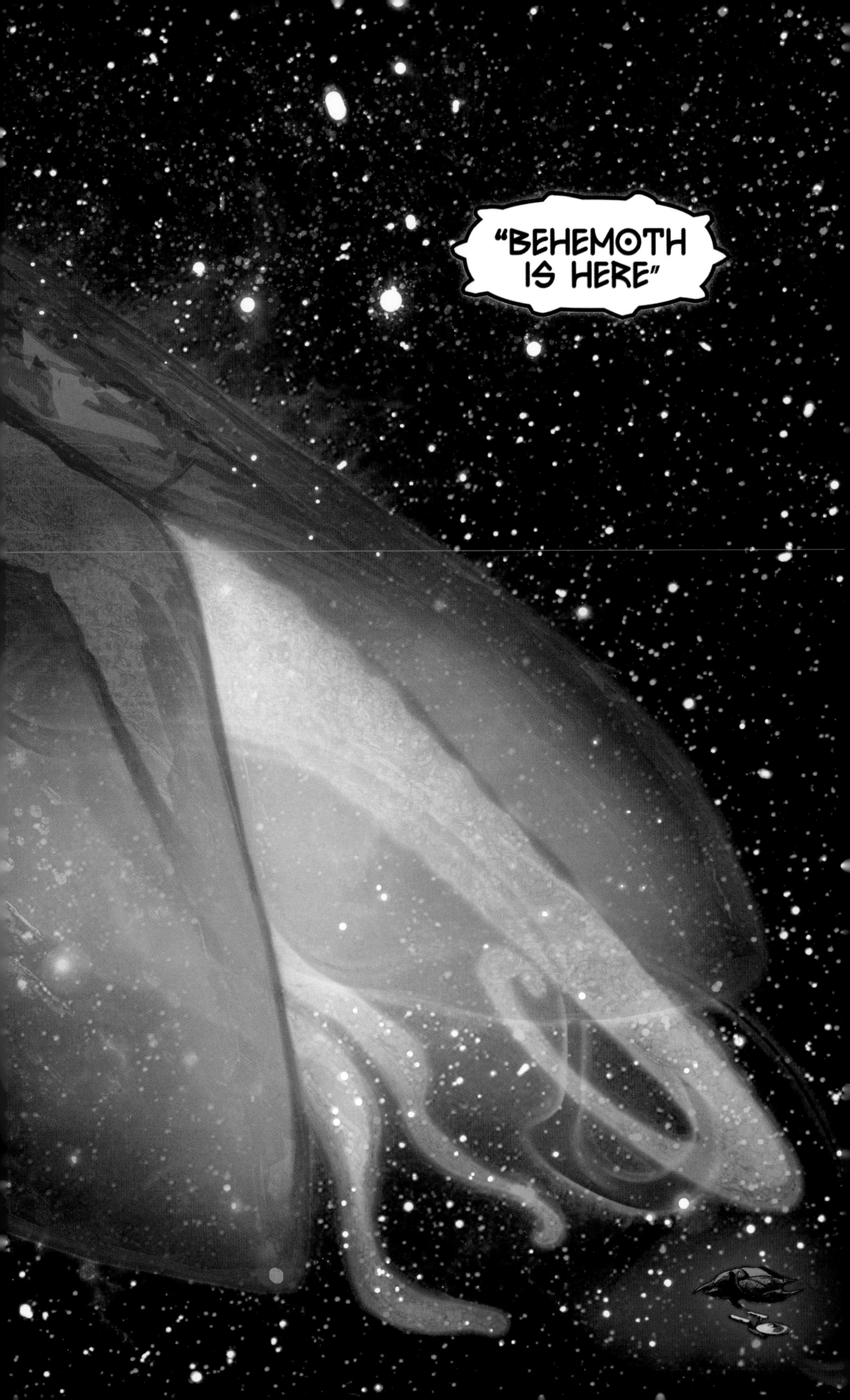
"BEHEMOTH IS HERE"

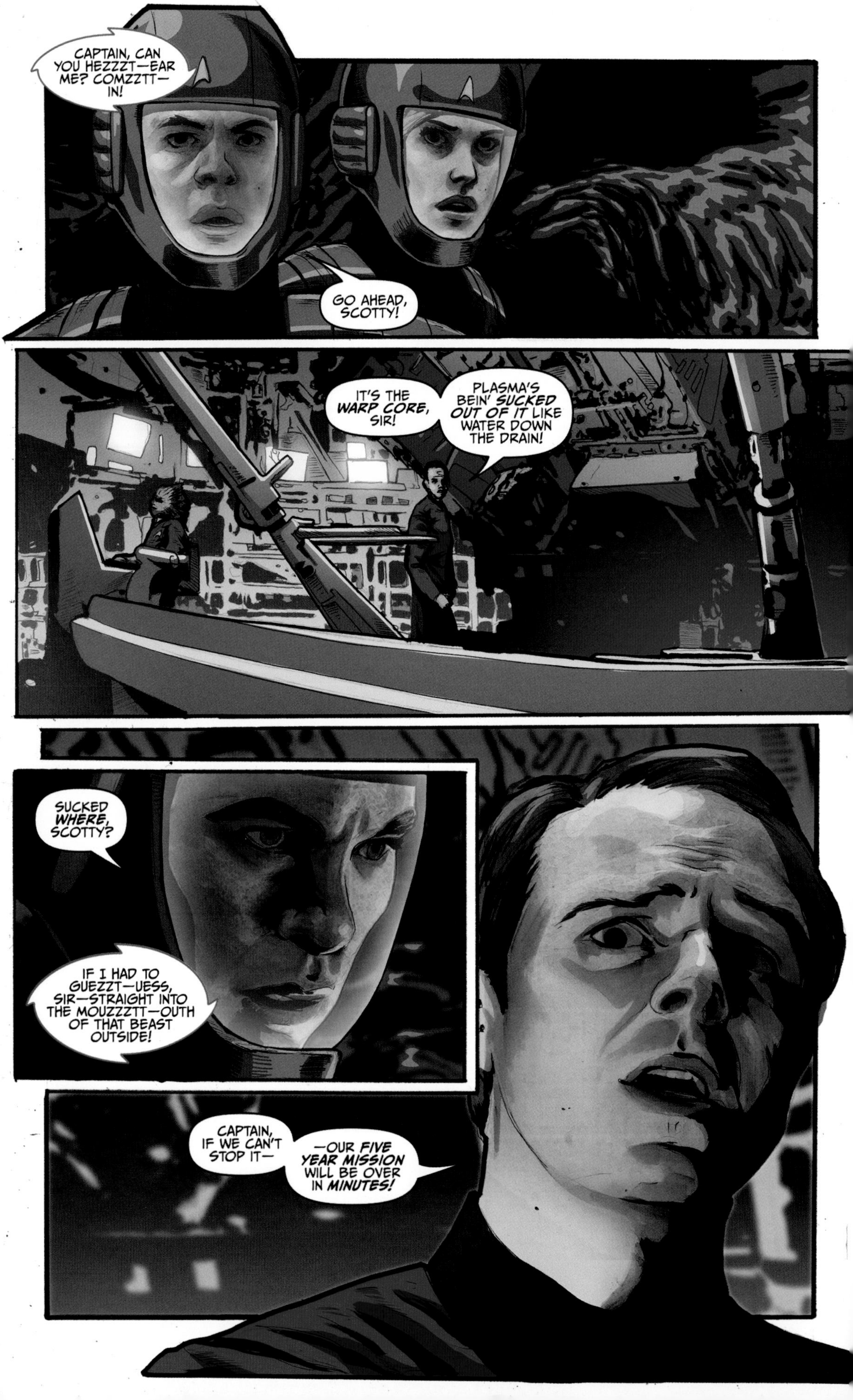
CAPTAIN, CAN YOU HEZZZT—EAR ME? COMZZTT—IN!
GO AHEAD, SCOTTY!
IT'S THE WARP CORE, SIR!
PLASMA'S BEIN' SUCKED OUT OF IT LIKE WATER DOWN THE DRAIN!
SUCKED WHERE, SCOTTY?
IF I HAD TO GUEZZT—UESS, SIR—STRAIGHT INTO THE MOUZZZTT—OUTH OF THAT BEAST OUTSIDE!
CAPTAIN, IF WE CAN'T STOP IT—
—OUR FIVE YEAR MISSION WILL BE OVER IN MINUTES!

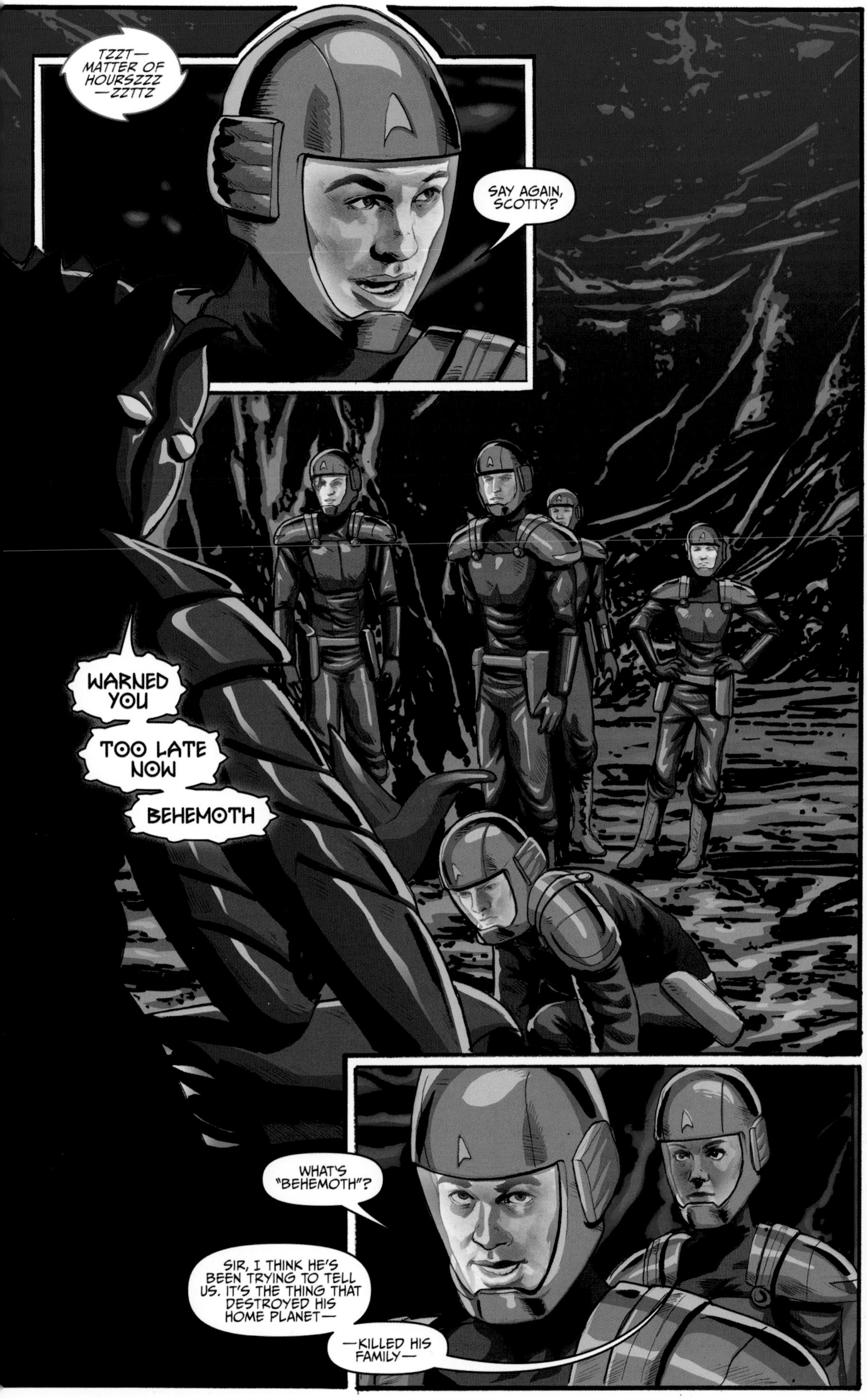

TZZT—MATTER OF HOURSZZZ—ZZTTZ
SAY AGAIN, SCOTTY?
WARNED YOU
TOO LATE NOW
BEHEMOTH
WHAT'S "BEHEMOTH"?
SIR, I THINK HE'S BEEN TRYING TO TELL US. IT'S THE THING THAT DESTROYED HIS HOME PLANET—
—KILLED HIS FAMILY—

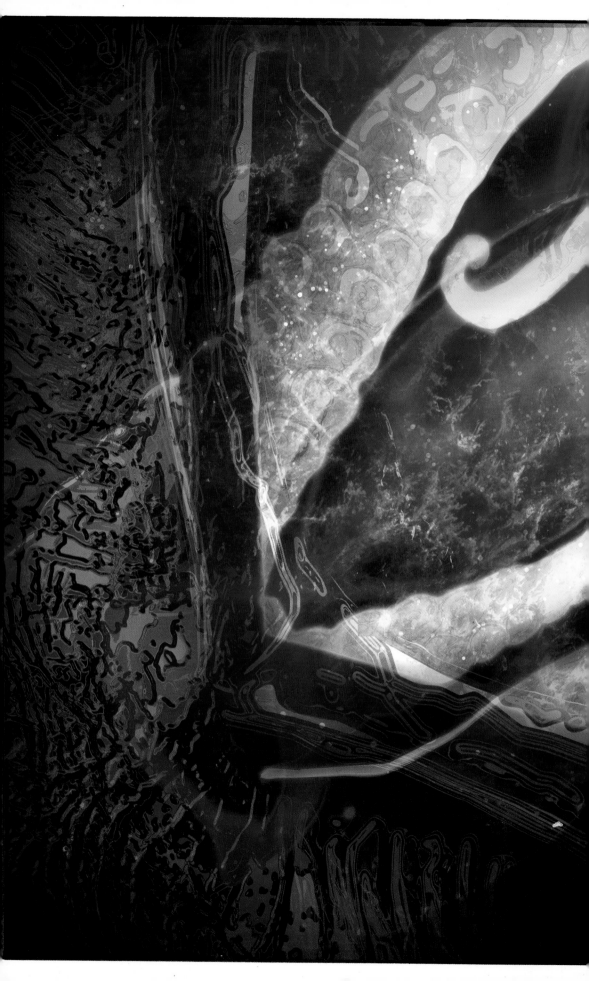

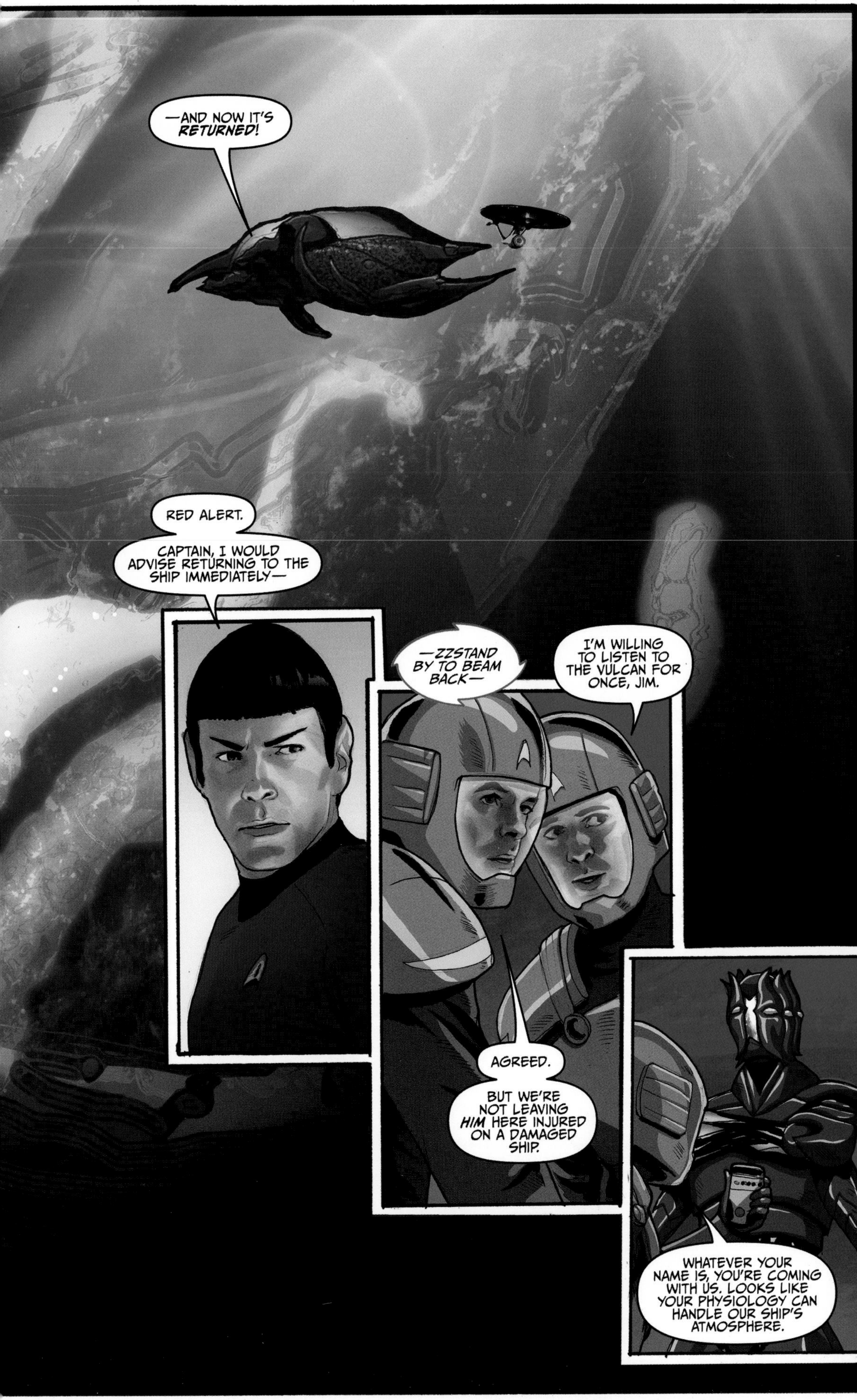
—AND NOW IT'S *RETURNED!*
RED ALERT.
CAPTAIN, I WOULD ADVISE RETURNING TO THE SHIP IMMEDIATELY—
—ZZSTAND BY TO BEAM BACK—
I'M WILLING TO LISTEN TO THE VULCAN FOR ONCE, JIM.
AGREED.
BUT WE'RE NOT LEAVING *HIM* HERE INJURED ON A DAMAGED SHIP.
WHATEVER YOUR NAME IS, YOU'RE COMING WITH US. LOOKS LIKE YOUR PHYSIOLOGY CAN HANDLE OUR SHIP'S ATMOSPHERE.

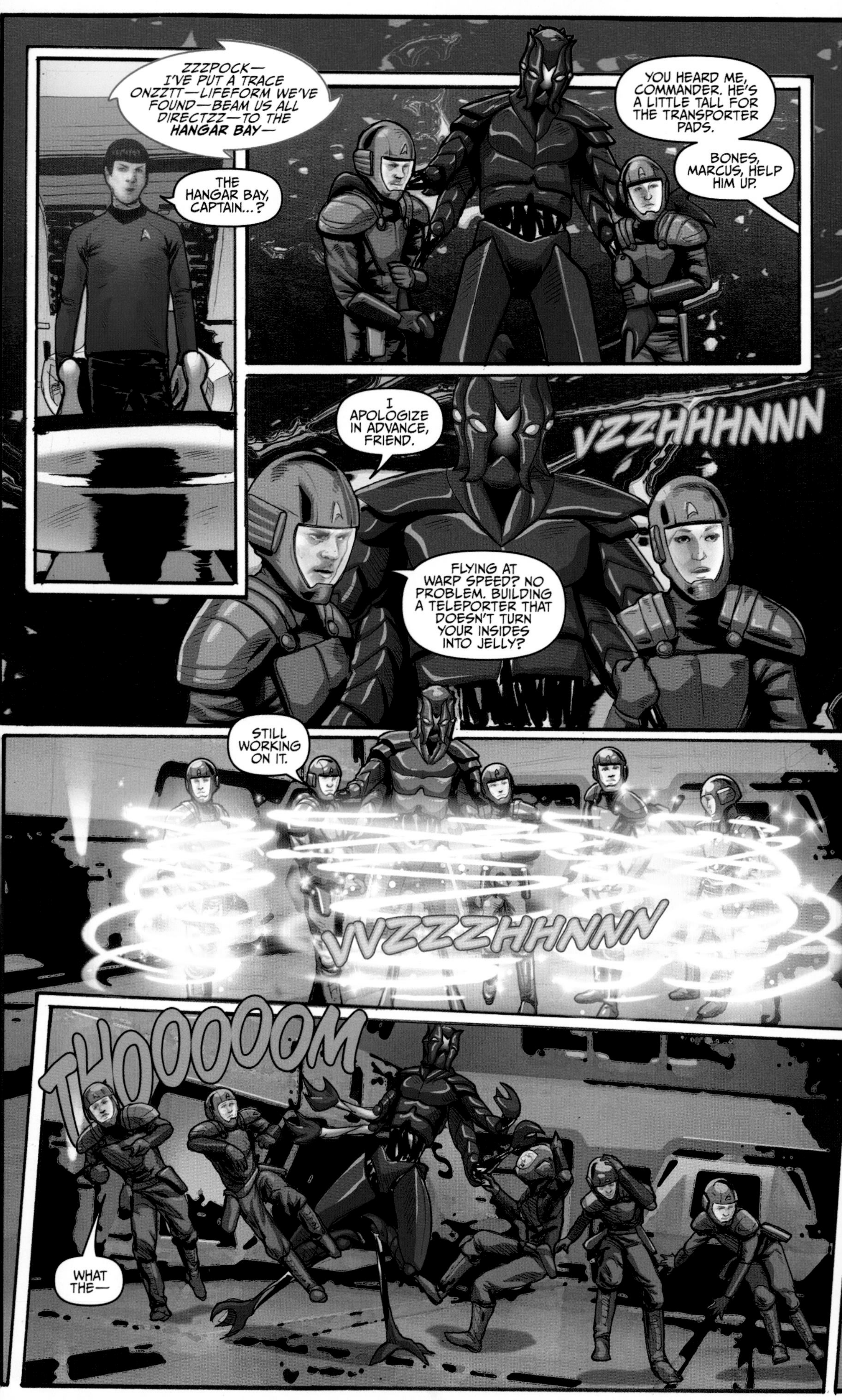
ZZZPOCK—
I'VE PUT A TRACE ONZZTT—LIFEFORM WE'VE FOUND—BEAM US ALL DIRECTZZ—TO THE HANGAR BAY—
THE HANGAR BAY, CAPTAIN...?
YOU HEARD ME, COMMANDER. HE'S A LITTLE TALL FOR THE TRANSPORTER PADS.
BONES, MARCUS, HELP HIM UP.
I APOLOGIZE IN ADVANCE, FRIEND.
VZZHHHNNN
FLYING AT WARP SPEED? NO PROBLEM. BUILDING A TELEPORTER THAT DOESN'T TURN YOUR INSIDES INTO JELLY?
STILL WORKING ON IT.
VVZZZHHNNN
THOOOOOM
WHAT THE—

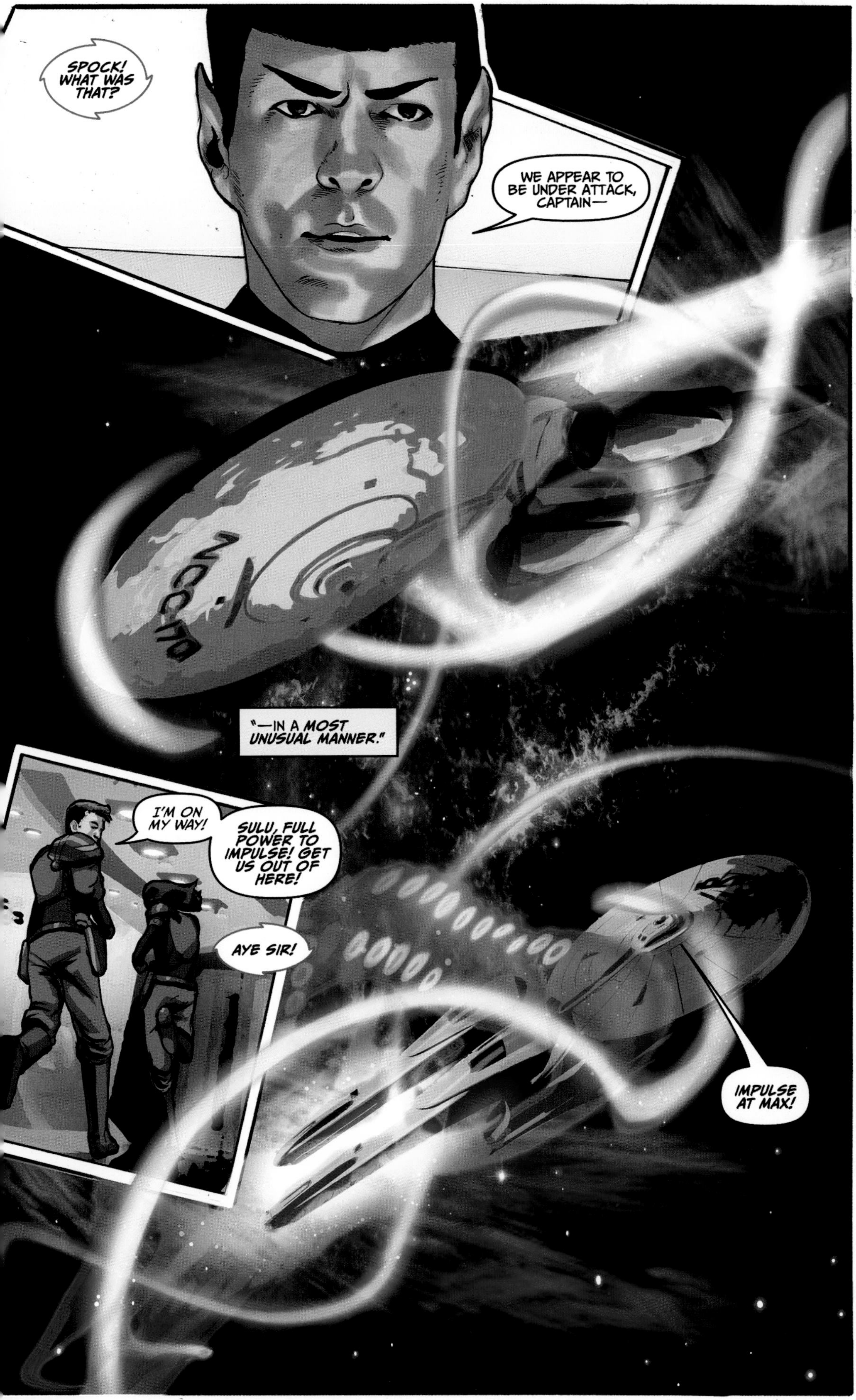
SPOCK! WHAT WAS THAT?
WE APPEAR TO BE UNDER ATTACK, CAPTAIN—
"—IN A MOST UNUSUAL MANNER."
I'M ON MY WAY!
SULU, FULL POWER TO IMPULSE! GET US OUT OF HERE!
AYE SIR!
IMPULSE AT MAX!

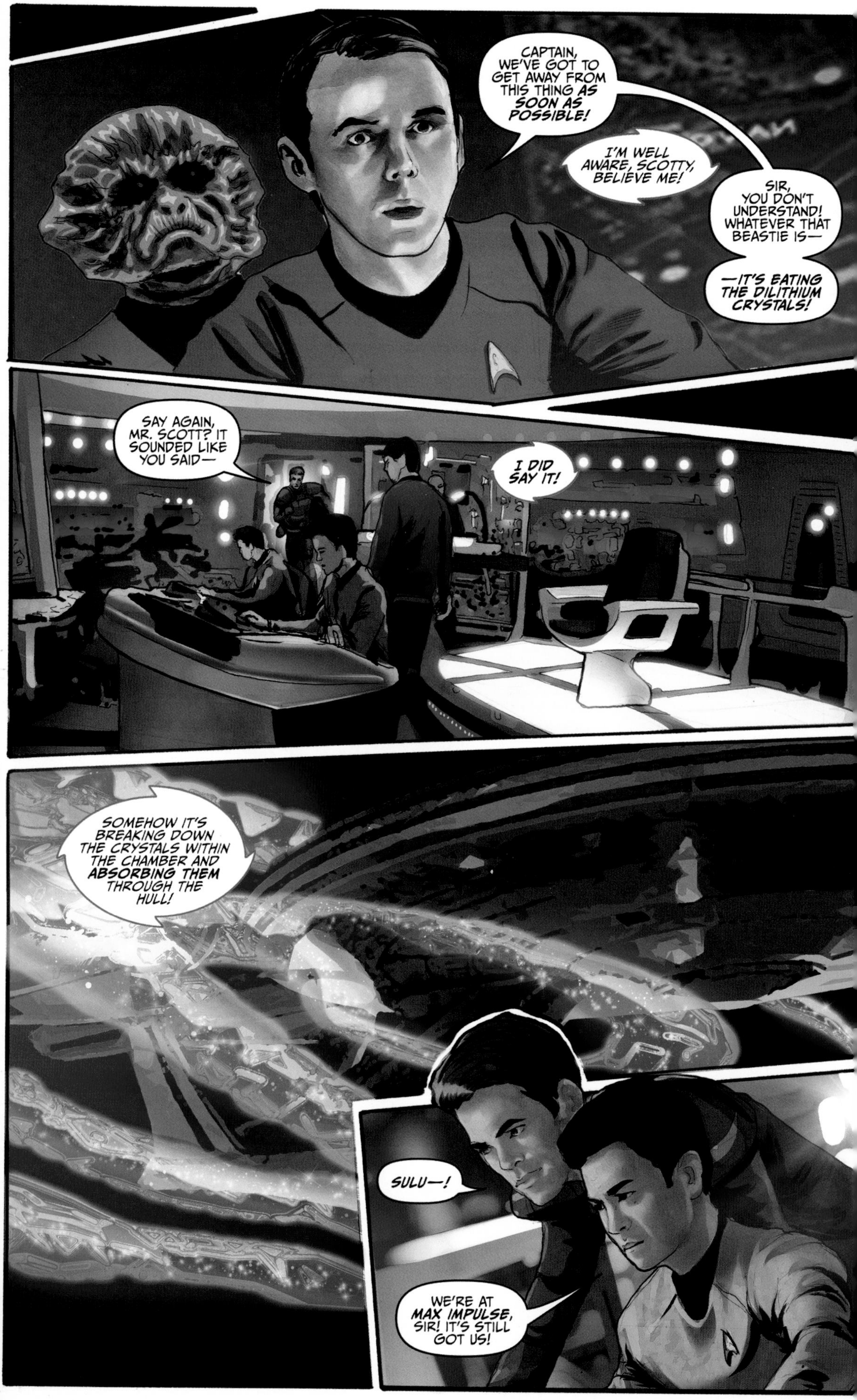
CAPTAIN, WE'VE GOT TO GET AWAY FROM THIS THING AS SOON AS POSSIBLE!
I'M WELL AWARE, SCOTTY, BELIEVE ME!
SIR, YOU DON'T UNDERSTAND! WHATEVER THAT BEASTIE IS—
—IT'S EATING THE DILITHIUM CRYSTALS!
SAY AGAIN, MR. SCOTT? IT SOUNDED LIKE YOU SAID—
I DID SAY IT!
SOMEHOW IT'S BREAKING DOWN THE CRYSTALS WITHIN THE CHAMBER AND ABSORBING THEM THROUGH THE HULL!
SULU—!
WE'RE AT MAX IMPULSE, SIR! IT'S STILL GOT US!

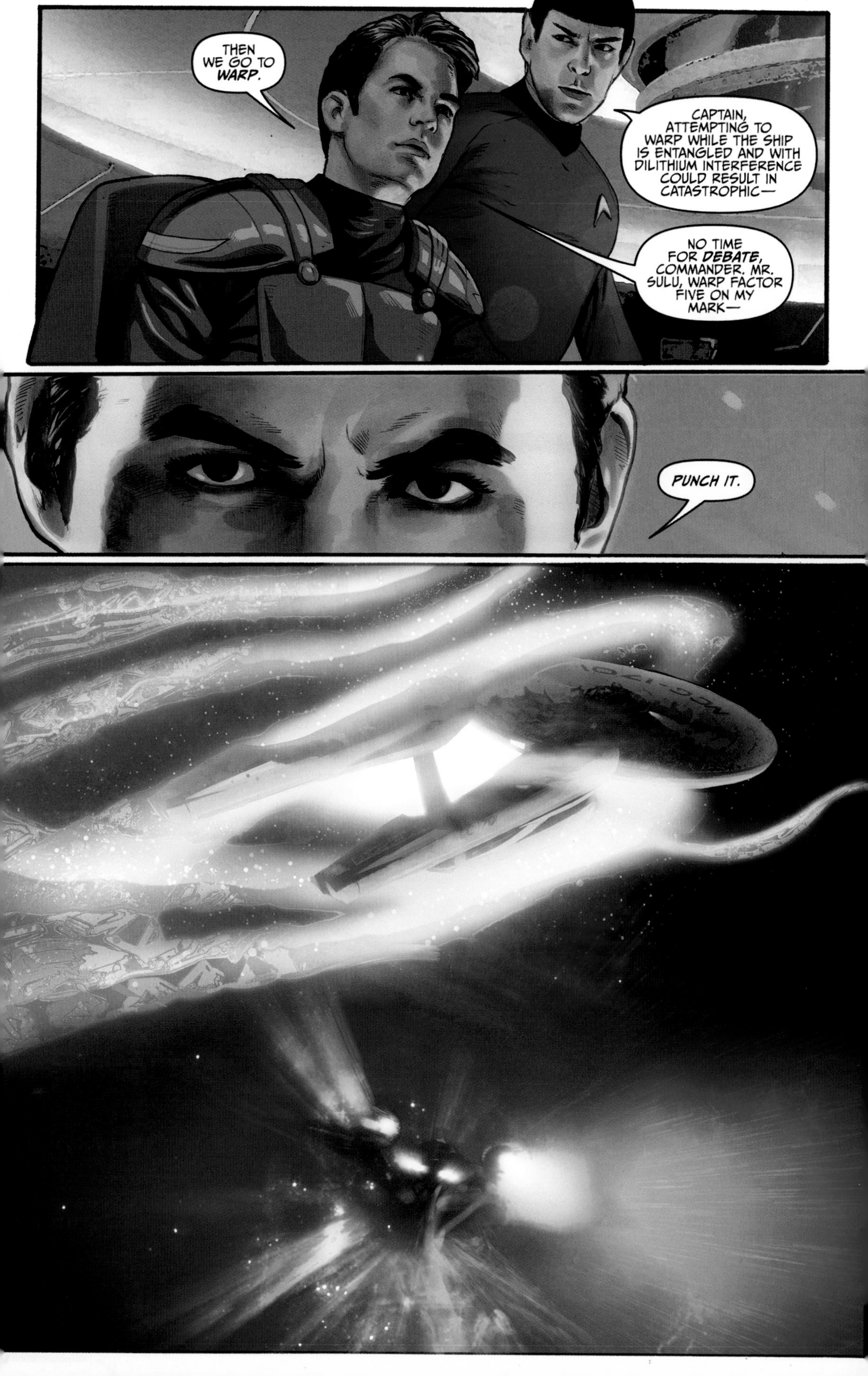
THEN WE GO TO WARP.
CAPTAIN, ATTEMPTING TO WARP WHILE THE SHIP IS ENTANGLED AND WITH DILITHIUM INTERFERENCE COULD RESULT IN CATASTROPHIC—
NO TIME FOR DEBATE, COMMANDER. MR. SULU, WARP FACTOR FIVE ON MY MARK—
PUNCH IT.

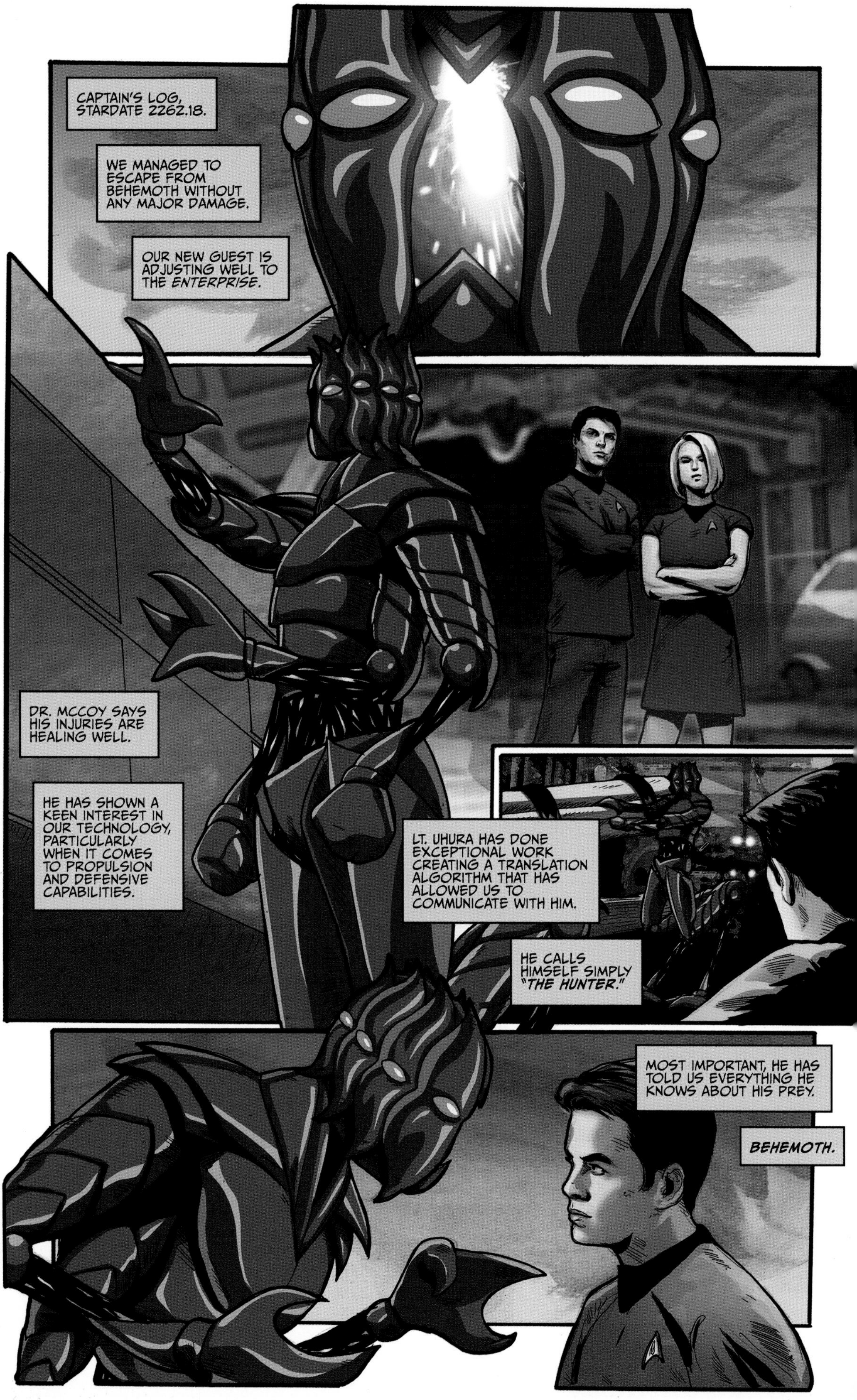
CAPTAIN'S LOG, STARDATE 2262.18.
WE MANAGED TO ESCAPE FROM BEHEMOTH WITHOUT ANY MAJOR DAMAGE.
OUR NEW GUEST IS ADJUSTING WELL TO THE *ENTERPRISE.*
DR. MCCOY SAYS HIS INJURIES ARE HEALING WELL.
HE HAS SHOWN A KEEN INTEREST IN OUR TECHNOLOGY, PARTICULARLY WHEN IT COMES TO PROPULSION AND DEFENSIVE CAPABILITIES.
LT. UHURA HAS DONE EXCEPTIONAL WORK CREATING A TRANSLATION ALGORITHM THAT HAS ALLOWED US TO COMMUNICATE WITH HIM.
HE CALLS HIMSELF SIMPLY *"THE HUNTER."*
MOST IMPORTANT, HE HAS TOLD US EVERYTHING HE KNOWS ABOUT HIS PREY.
BEHEMOTH.

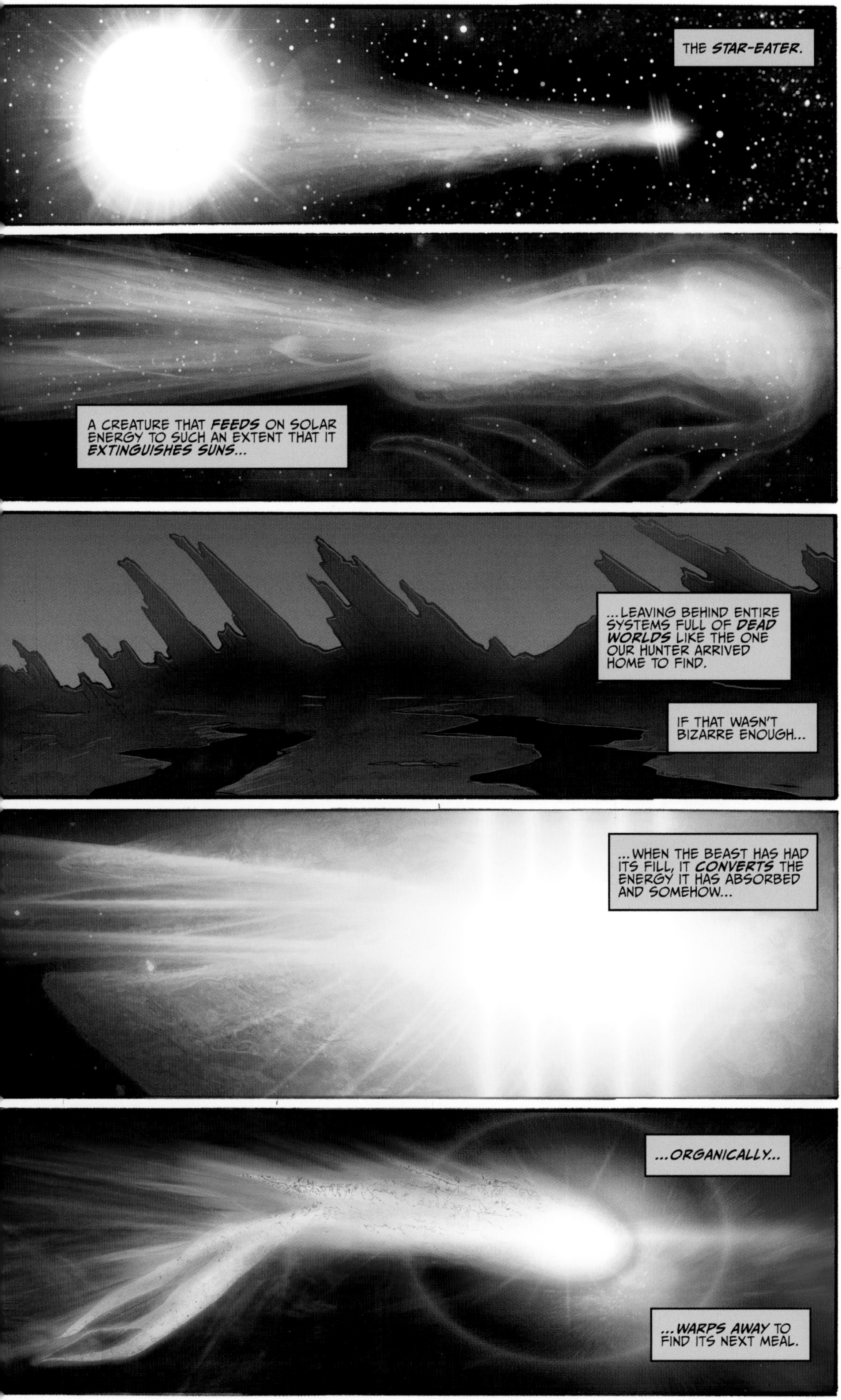
THE STAR-EATER.
A CREATURE THAT FEEDS ON SOLAR ENERGY TO SUCH AN EXTENT THAT IT EXTINGUISHES SUNS...
...LEAVING BEHIND ENTIRE SYSTEMS FULL OF DEAD WORLDS LIKE THE ONE OUR HUNTER ARRIVED HOME TO FIND.
IF THAT WASN'T BIZARRE ENOUGH...
...WHEN THE BEAST HAS HAD ITS FILL, IT CONVERTS THE ENERGY IT HAS ABSORBED AND SOMEHOW...
...ORGANICALLY...
...WARPS AWAY TO FIND ITS NEXT MEAL.

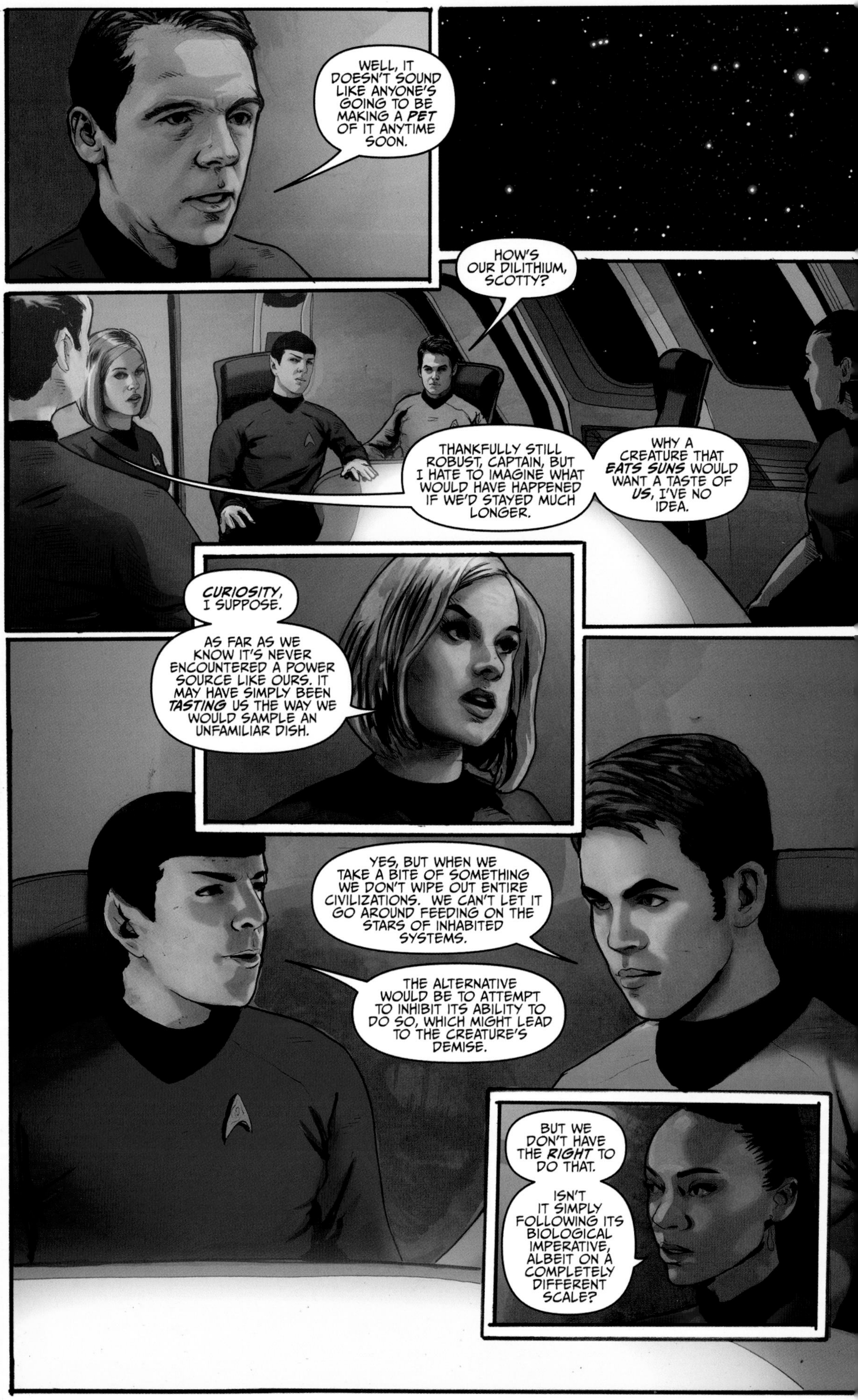
WELL, IT DOESN'T SOUND LIKE ANYONE'S GOING TO BE MAKING A *PET* OF IT ANYTIME SOON.
HOW'S OUR DILITHIUM, SCOTTY?
THANKFULLY STILL ROBUST, CAPTAIN, BUT I HATE TO IMAGINE WHAT WOULD HAVE HAPPENED IF WE'D STAYED MUCH LONGER.
WHY A CREATURE THAT *EATS SUNS* WOULD WANT A TASTE OF *US*, I'VE NO IDEA.
CURIOSITY, I SUPPOSE.
AS FAR AS WE KNOW IT'S NEVER ENCOUNTERED A POWER SOURCE LIKE OURS. IT MAY HAVE SIMPLY BEEN *TASTING* US THE WAY WE WOULD SAMPLE AN UNFAMILIAR DISH.
YES, BUT WHEN WE TAKE A BITE OF SOMETHING WE DON'T WIPE OUT ENTIRE CIVILIZATIONS. WE CAN'T LET IT GO AROUND FEEDING ON THE STARS OF INHABITED SYSTEMS.
THE ALTERNATIVE WOULD BE TO ATTEMPT TO INHIBIT ITS ABILITY TO DO SO, WHICH MIGHT LEAD TO THE CREATURE'S DEMISE.
BUT WE DON'T HAVE THE *RIGHT* TO DO THAT.
ISN'T IT SIMPLY FOLLOWING ITS BIOLOGICAL IMPERATIVE, ALBEIT ON A COMPLETELY DIFFERENT SCALE?

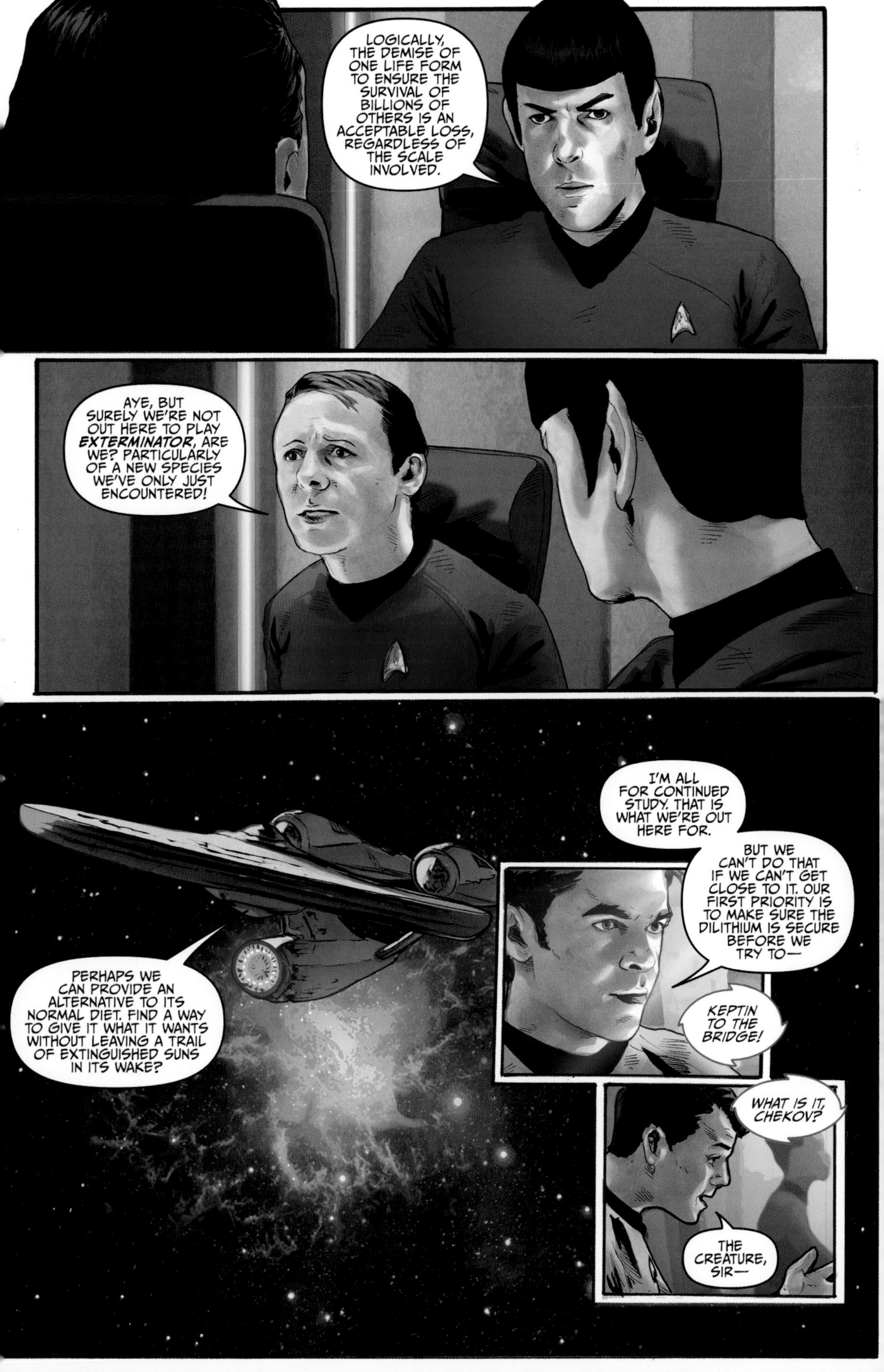
LOGICALLY, THE DEMISE OF ONE LIFE FORM TO ENSURE THE SURVIVAL OF BILLIONS OF OTHERS IS AN ACCEPTABLE LOSS, REGARDLESS OF THE SCALE INVOLVED.
AYE, BUT SURELY WE'RE NOT OUT HERE TO PLAY **EXTERMINATOR**, ARE WE? PARTICULARLY OF A NEW SPECIES WE'VE ONLY JUST ENCOUNTERED!
PERHAPS WE CAN PROVIDE AN ALTERNATIVE TO ITS NORMAL DIET. FIND A WAY TO GIVE IT WHAT IT WANTS WITHOUT LEAVING A TRAIL OF EXTINGUISHED SUNS IN ITS WAKE?
I'M ALL FOR CONTINUED STUDY. THAT IS WHAT WE'RE OUT HERE FOR.
BUT WE CAN'T DO THAT IF WE CAN'T GET CLOSE TO IT. OUR FIRST PRIORITY IS TO MAKE SURE THE DILITHIUM IS SECURE BEFORE WE TRY TO—
KEPTIN TO THE BRIDGE!
WHAT IS IT, CHEKOV?
THE CREATURE, SIR—

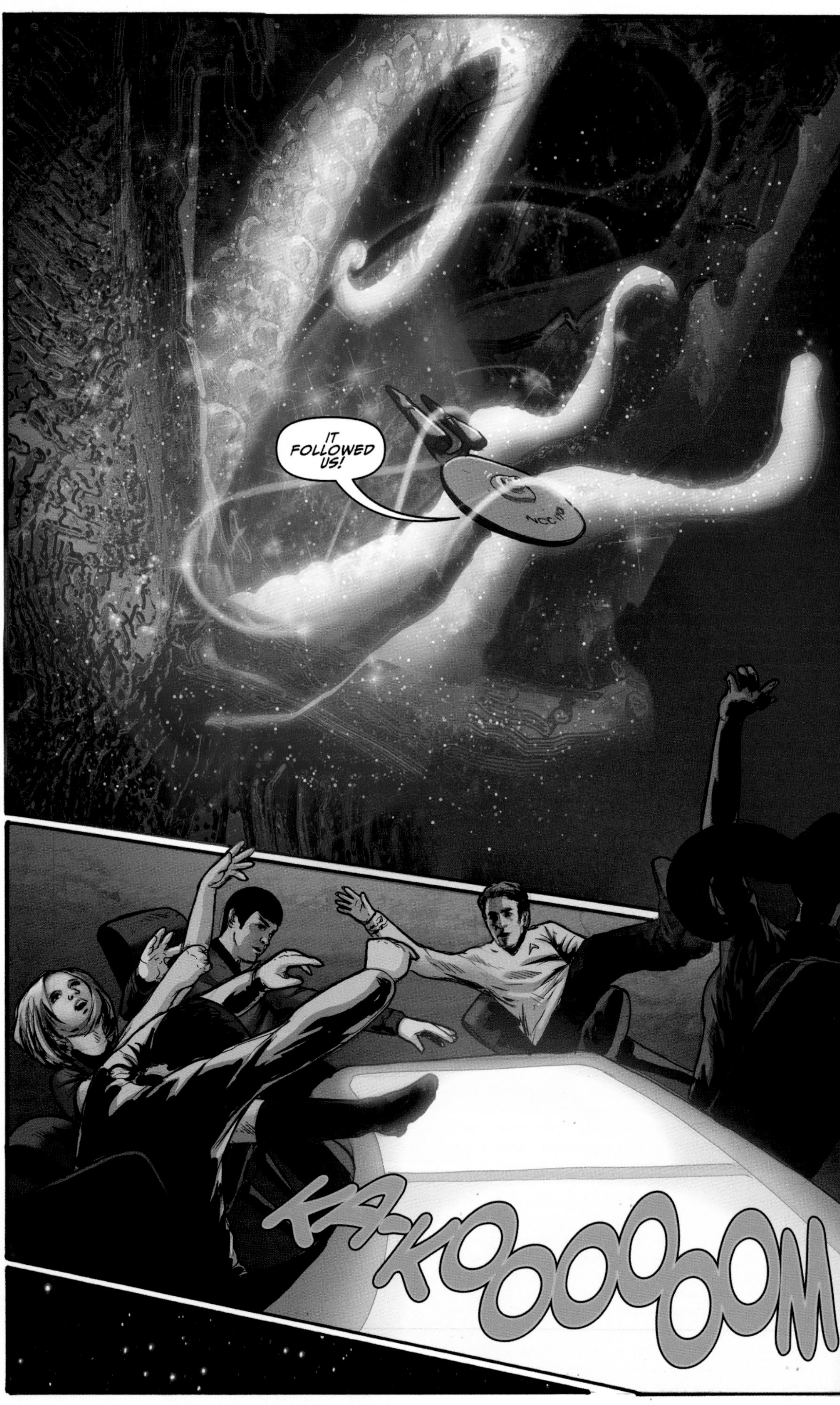
IT FOLLOWED US!
KA-KOOOOOOOM

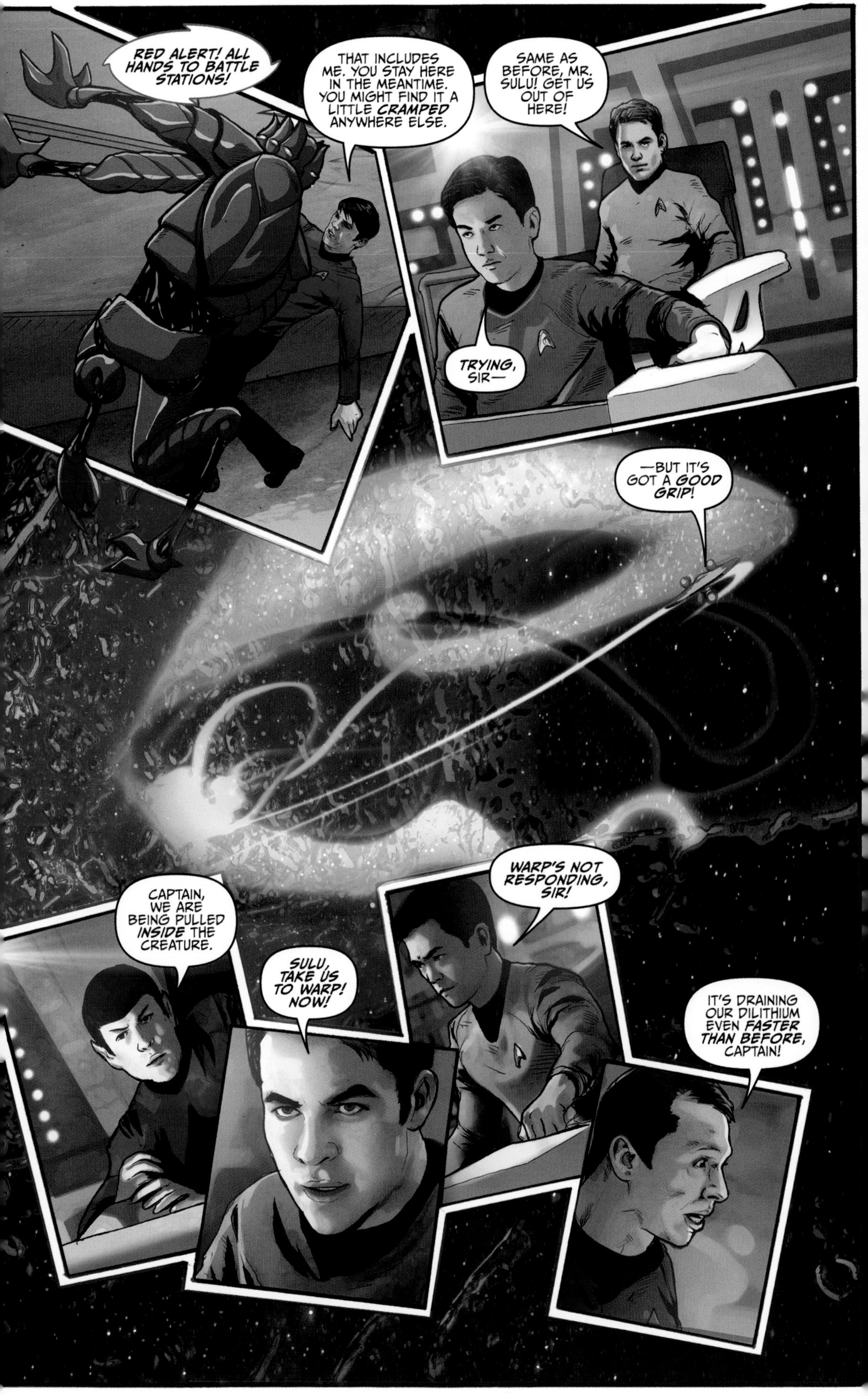

RED ALERT! ALL HANDS TO BATTLE STATIONS!
THAT INCLUDES ME. YOU STAY HERE IN THE MEANTIME. YOU MIGHT FIND IT A LITTLE *CRAMPED* ANYWHERE ELSE.
SAME AS BEFORE, MR. SULU! GET US OUT OF HERE!
TRYING, SIR—
—BUT IT'S GOT A *GOOD GRIP!*
CAPTAIN, WE ARE BEING PULLED *INSIDE* THE CREATURE.
SULU, TAKE US TO WARP! NOW!
WARP'S NOT RESPONDING, SIR!
IT'S DRAINING OUR DILITHIUM EVEN *FASTER THAN BEFORE,* CAPTAIN!

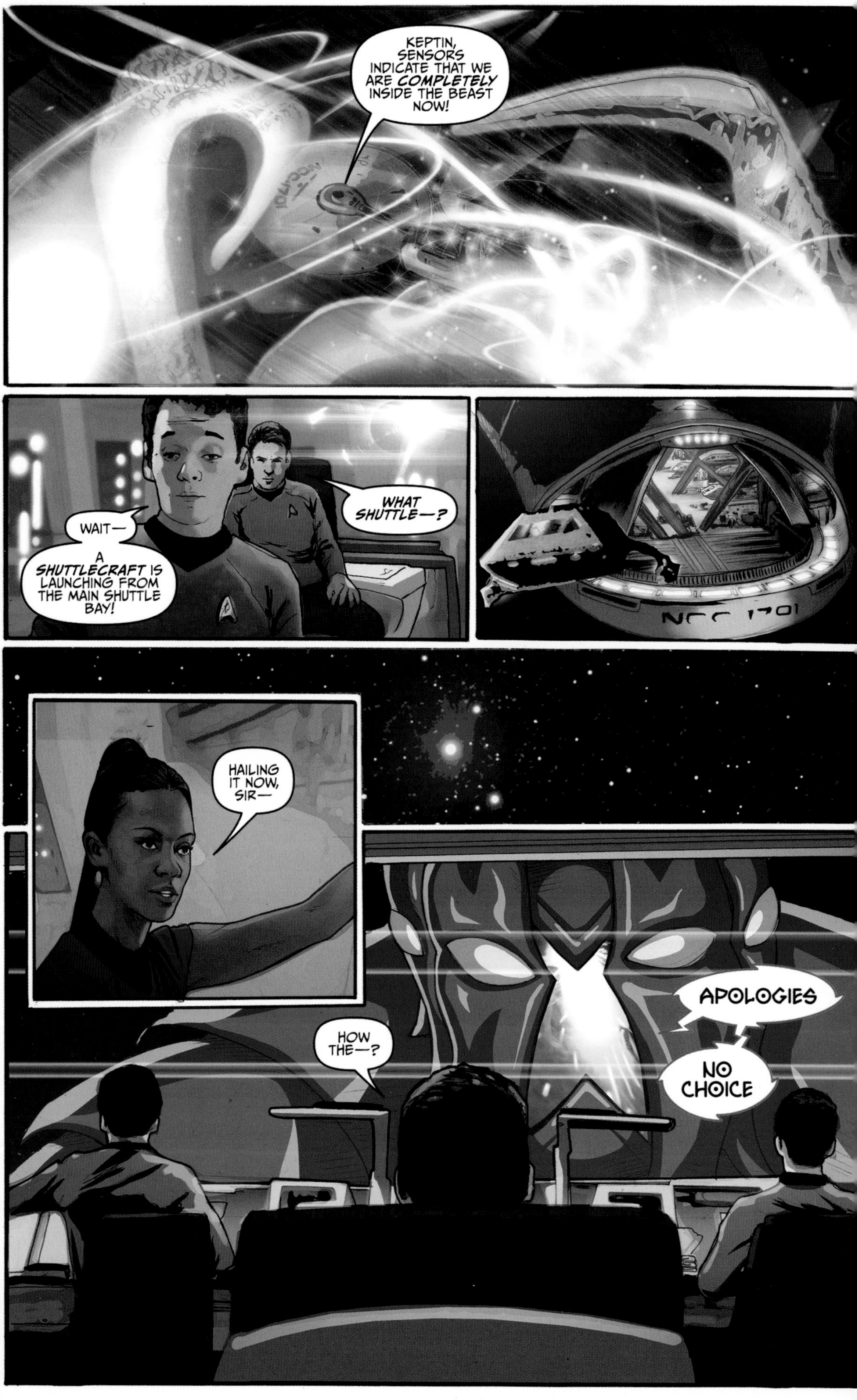
KEPTIN, SENSORS INDICATE THAT WE ARE COMPLETELY INSIDE THE BEAST NOW!
WAIT—
A SHUTTLECRAFT IS LAUNCHING FROM THE MAIN SHUTTLE BAY!
WHAT SHUTTLE—?
NCC 1701
HAILING IT NOW, SIR—
HOW THE—?
APOLOGIES
NO CHOICE

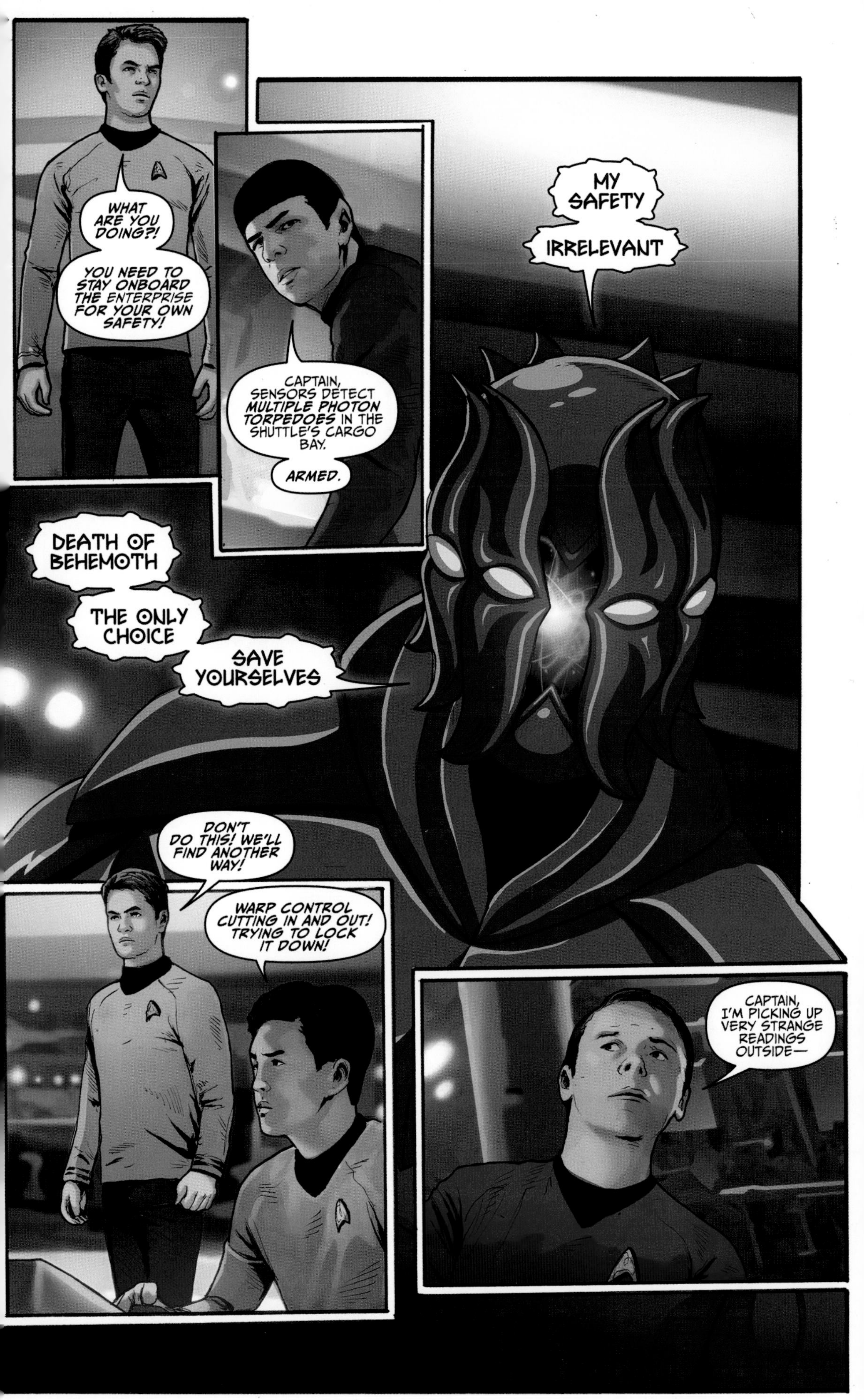
WHAT ARE YOU DOING?!
YOU NEED TO STAY ONBOARD THE ENTERPRISE FOR YOUR OWN SAFETY!
CAPTAIN, SENSORS DETECT MULTIPLE PHOTON TORPEDOES IN THE SHUTTLE'S CARGO BAY.
ARMED.
MY SAFETY
IRRELEVANT
DEATH OF BEHEMOTH
THE ONLY CHOICE
SAVE YOURSELVES
DON'T DO THIS! WE'LL FIND ANOTHER WAY!
WARP CONTROL CUTTING IN AND OUT! TRYING TO LOCK IT DOWN!
CAPTAIN, I'M PICKING UP VERY STRANGE READINGS OUTSIDE—

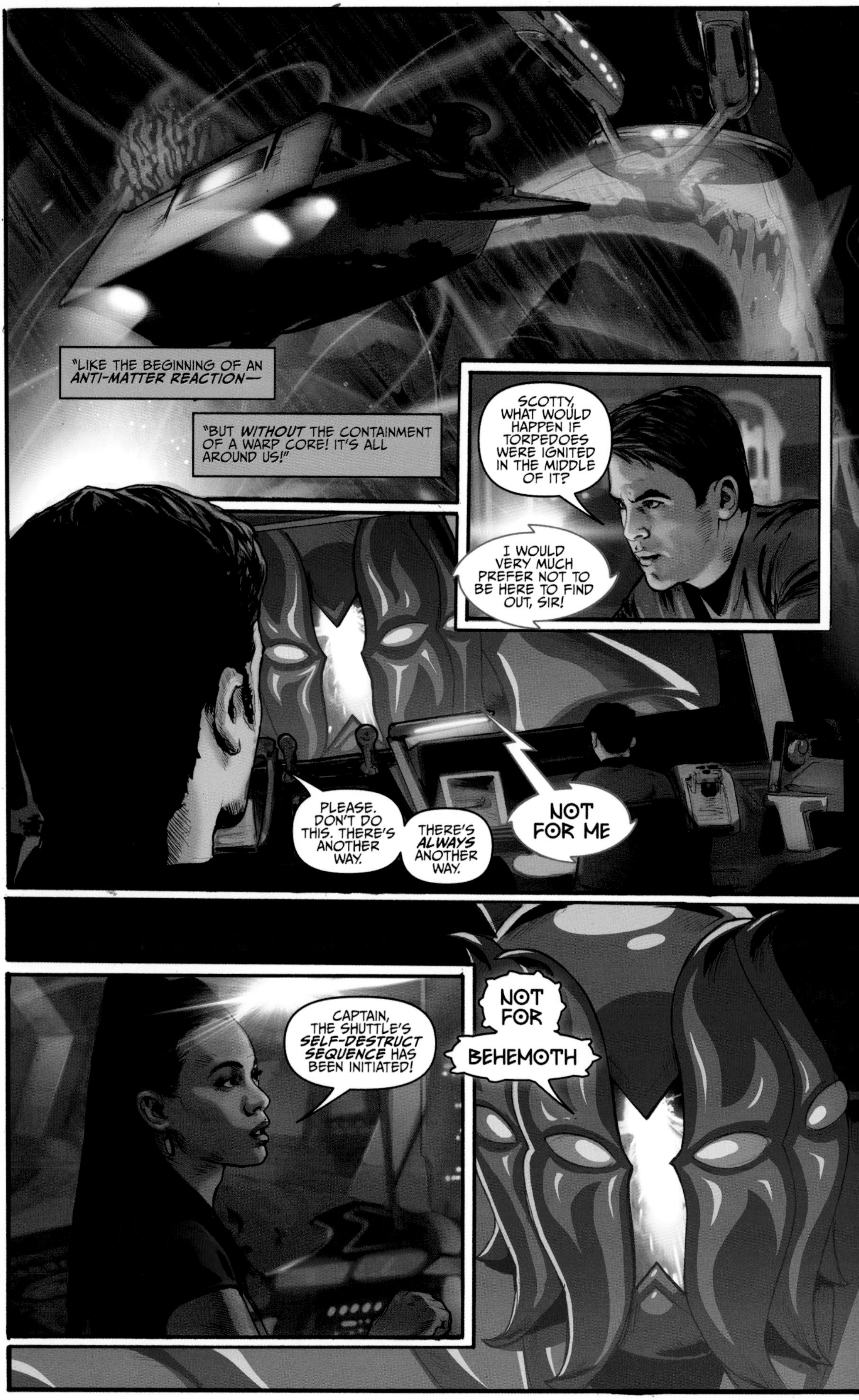
"LIKE THE BEGINNING OF AN ANTI-MATTER REACTION—
"BUT WITHOUT THE CONTAINMENT OF A WARP CORE! IT'S ALL AROUND US!"
SCOTTY, WHAT WOULD HAPPEN IF TORPEDOES WERE IGNITED IN THE MIDDLE OF IT?
I WOULD VERY MUCH PREFER NOT TO BE HERE TO FIND OUT, SIR!
PLEASE. DON'T DO THIS. THERE'S ANOTHER WAY.
THERE'S ALWAYS ANOTHER WAY.
NOT FOR ME
CAPTAIN, THE SHUTTLE'S SELF-DESTRUCT SEQUENCE HAS BEEN INITIATED!
NOT FOR
BEHEMOTH

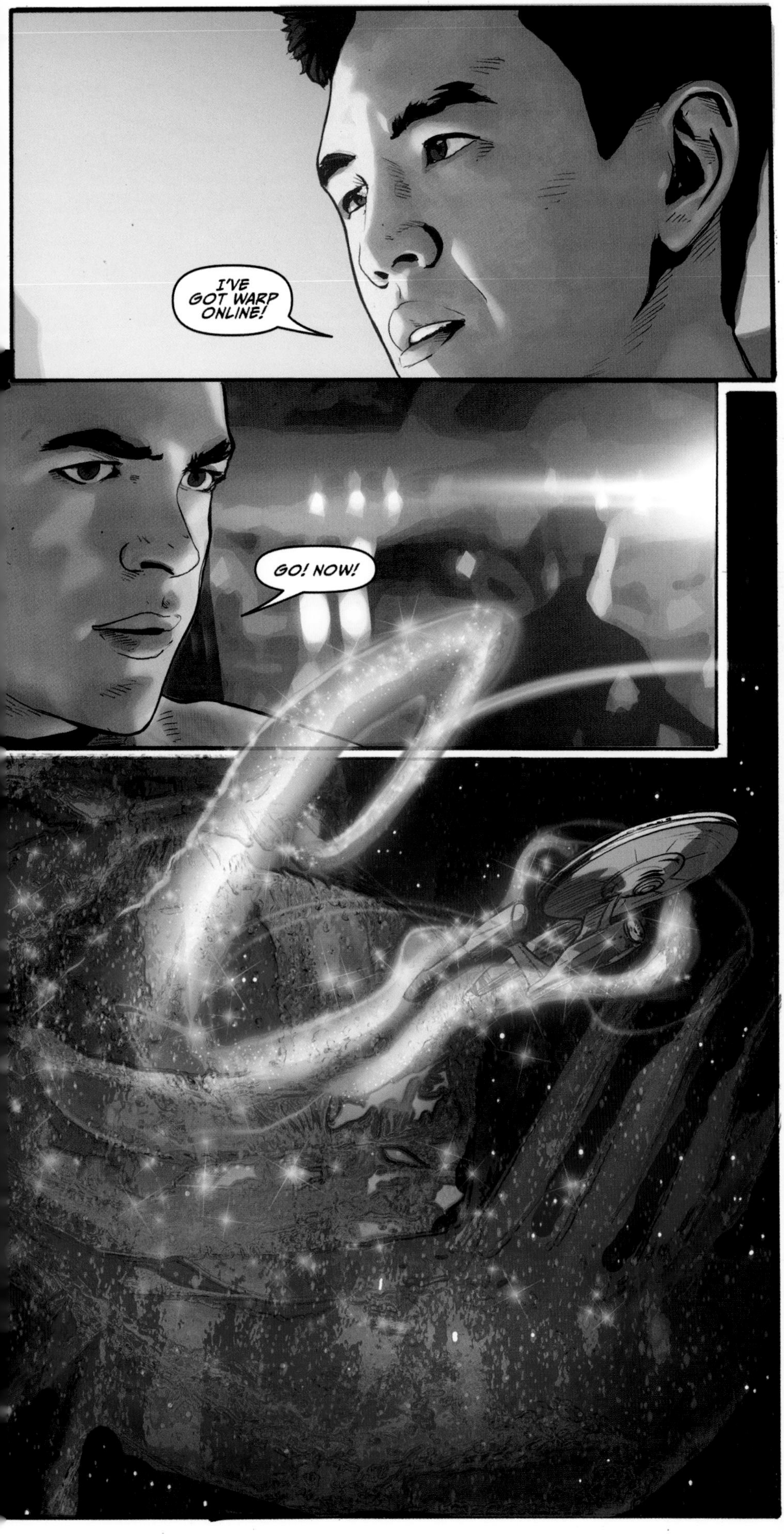
I'VE GOT WARP ONLINE!
GO! NOW!

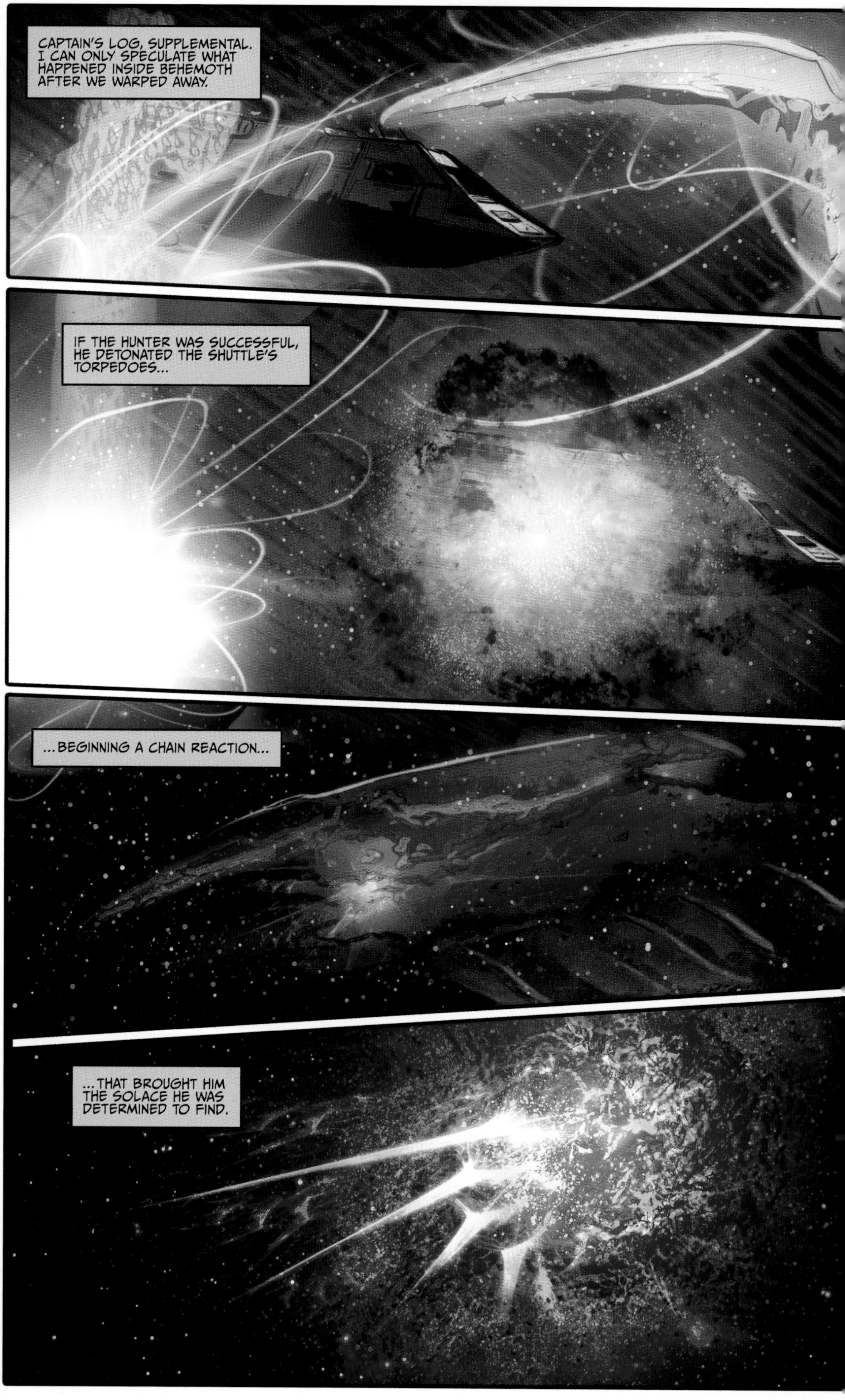
CAPTAIN'S LOG, SUPPLEMENTAL. I CAN ONLY SPECULATE WHAT HAPPENED INSIDE BEHEMOTH AFTER WE WARPED AWAY.
IF THE HUNTER WAS SUCCESSFUL, HE DETONATED THE SHUTTLE'S TORPEDOES...
...BEGINNING A CHAIN REACTION...
...THAT BROUGHT HIM THE SOLACE HE WAS DETERMINED TO FIND.

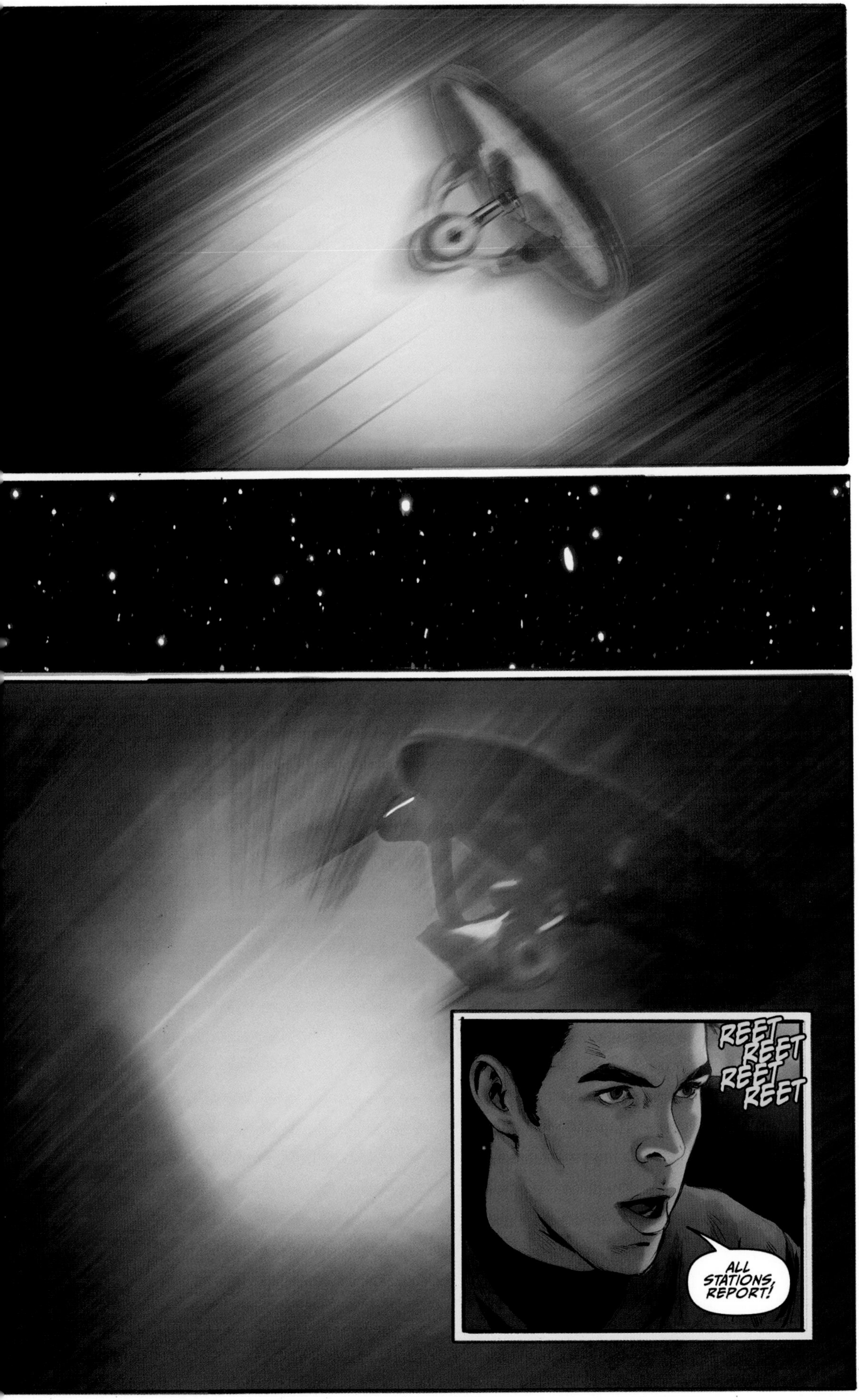
REEET REEET REEET REEET
ALL STATIONS, REPORT!

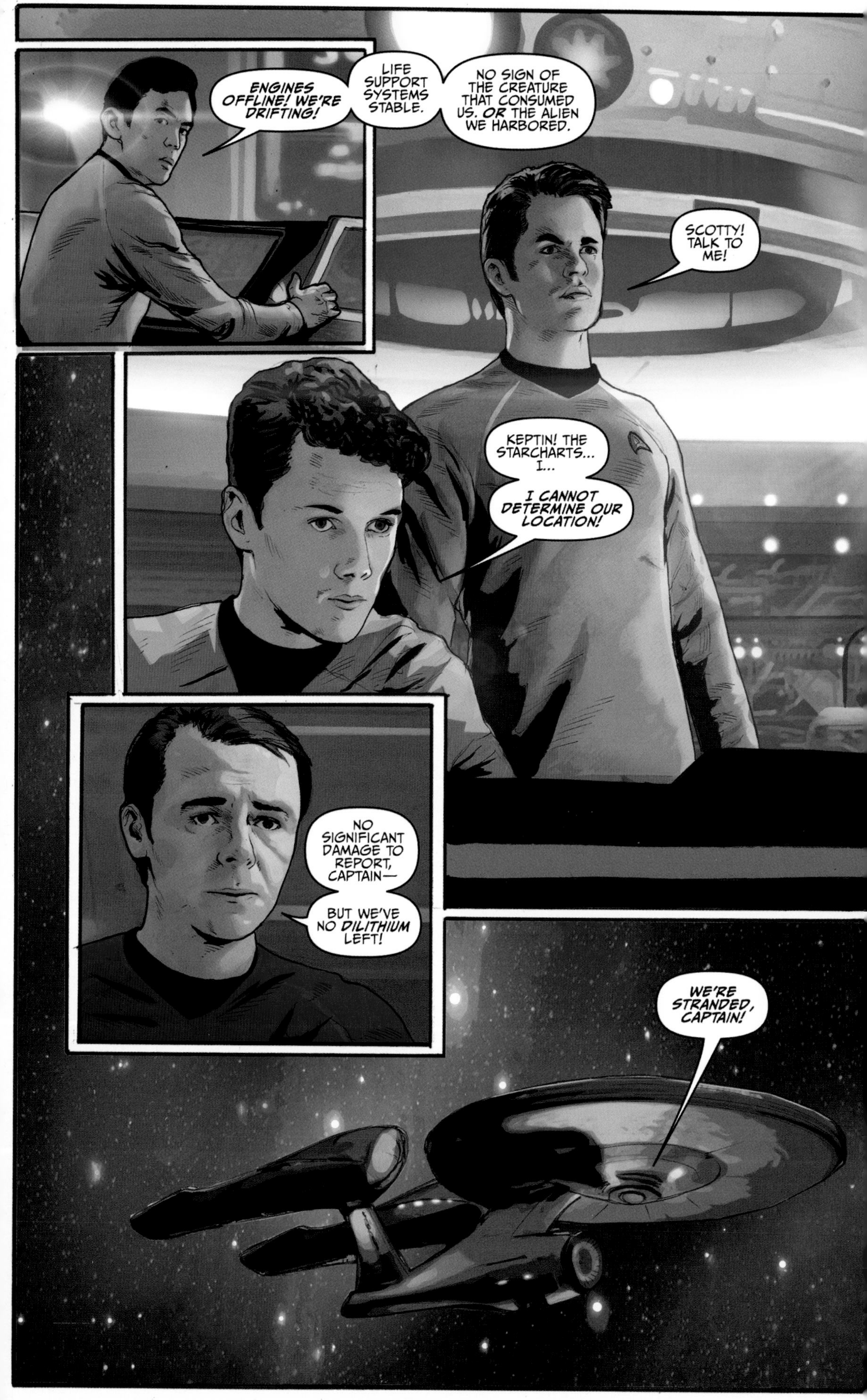
ENGINES OFFLINE! WE'RE DRIFTING!
LIFE SUPPORT SYSTEMS STABLE.
NO SIGN OF THE CREATURE THAT CONSUMED US. OR THE ALIEN WE HARBORED.
SCOTTY! TALK TO ME!
KEPTIN! THE STARCHARTS... I...
I CANNOT DETERMINE OUR LOCATION!
NO SIGNIFICANT DAMAGE TO REPORT, CAPTAIN—
BUT WE'VE NO DILITHIUM LEFT!
WE'RE STRANDED, CAPTAIN!

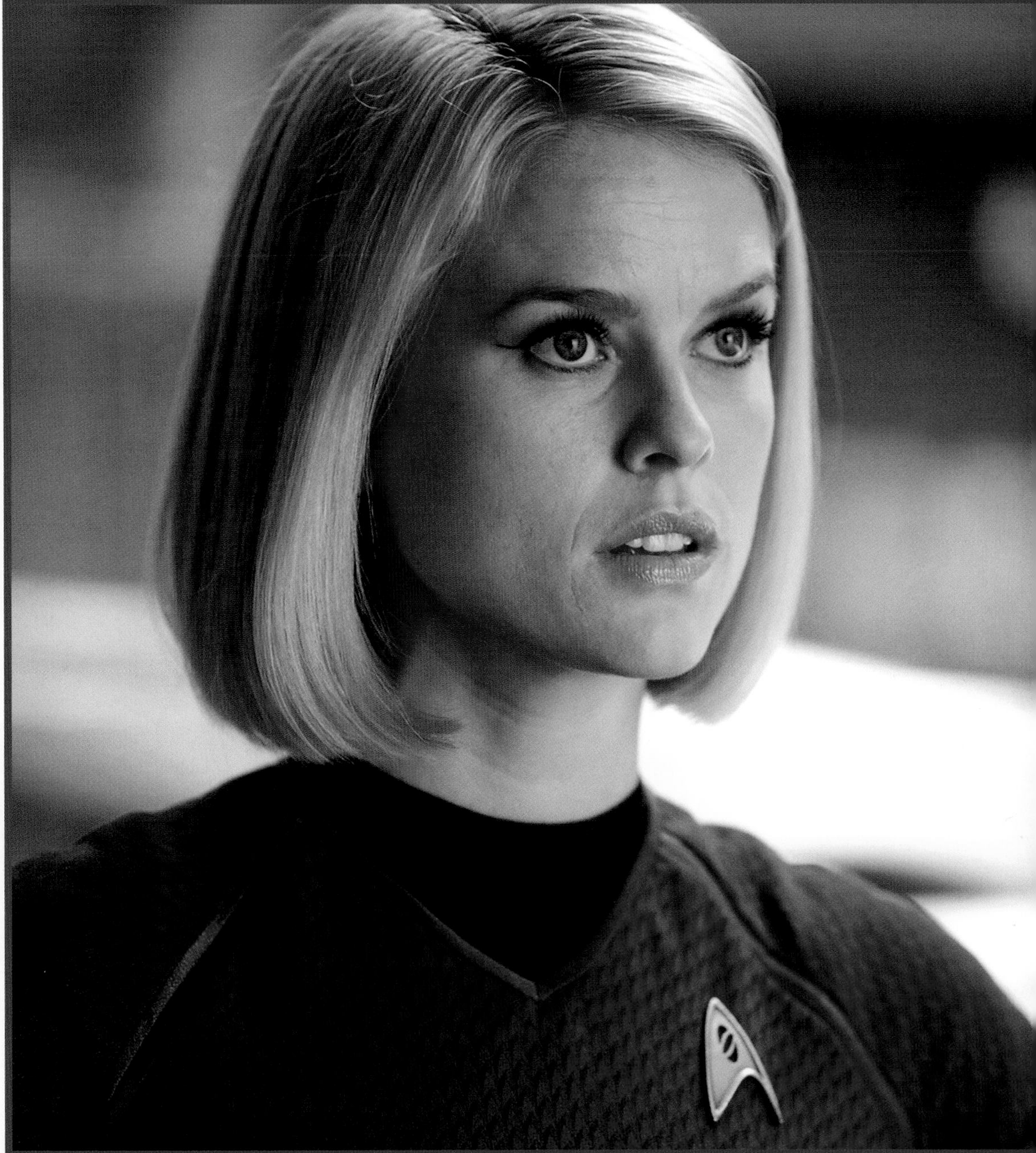

EURYDICE

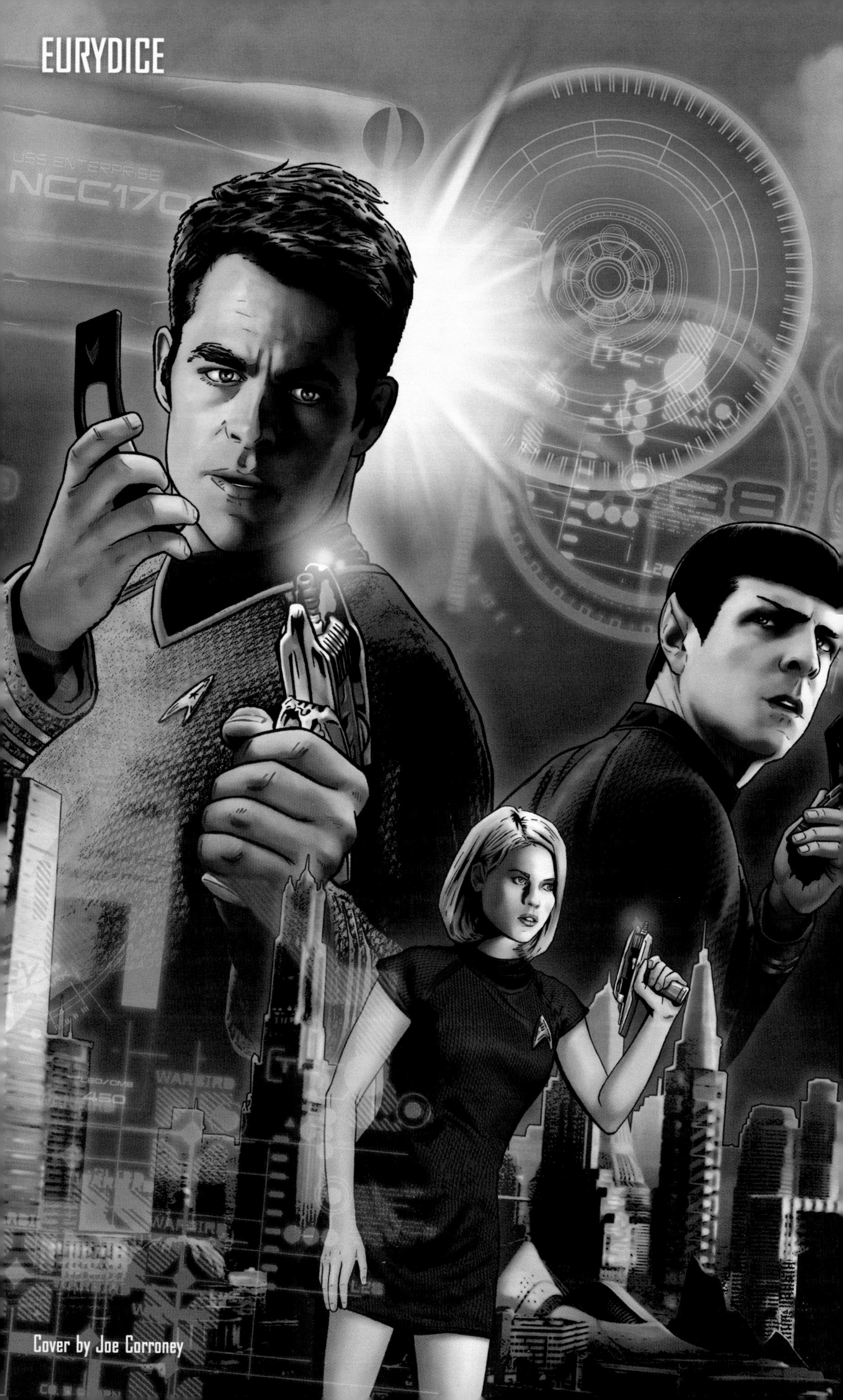
USS ENTERPRISE

Cover by Joe Corroney

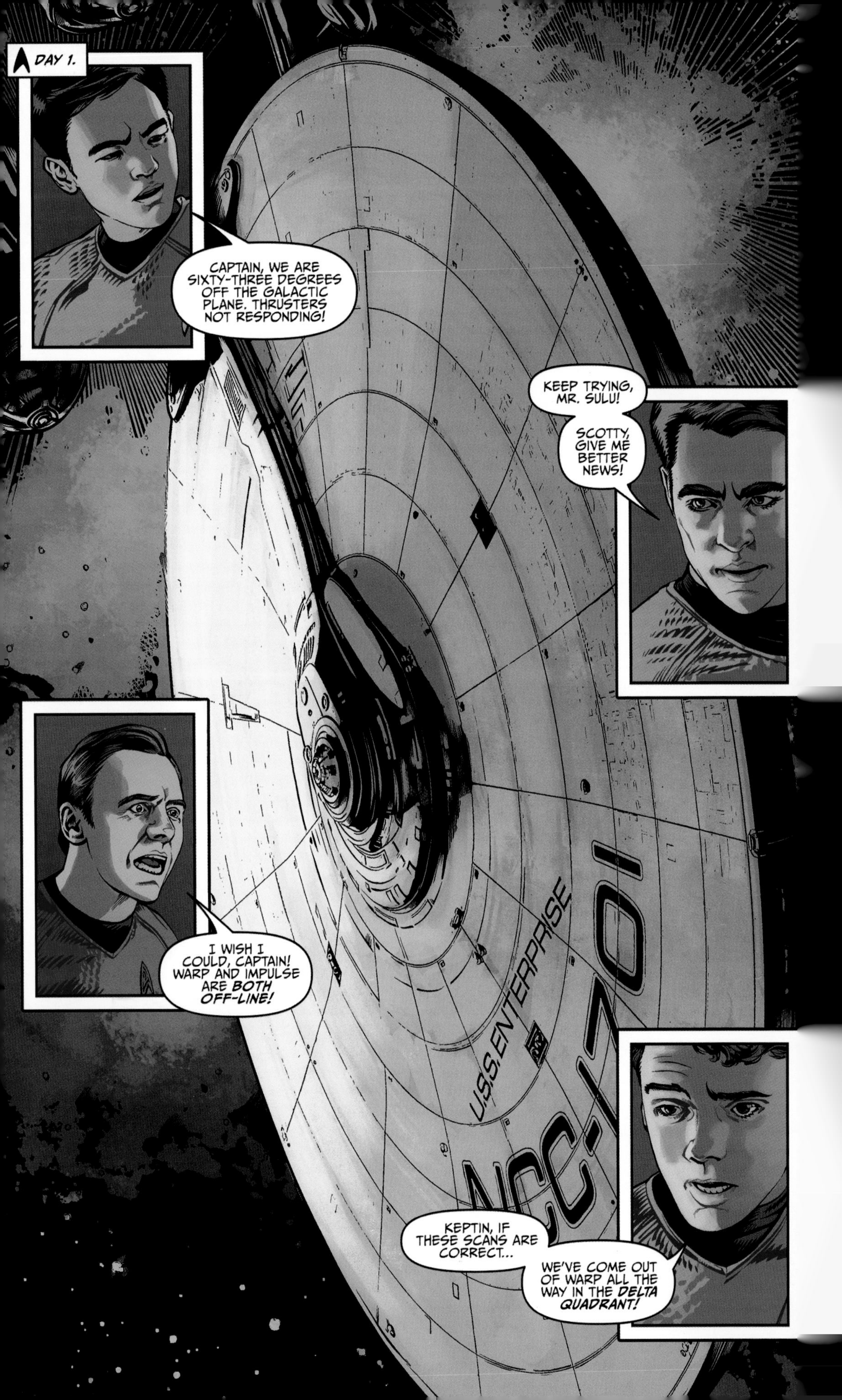
DAY 1.
CAPTAIN, WE ARE SIXTY-THREE DEGREES OFF THE GALACTIC PLANE. THRUSTERS NOT RESPONDING!
KEEP TRYING, MR. SULU!
SCOTTY, GIVE ME BETTER NEWS!
I WISH I COULD, CAPTAIN! WARP AND IMPULSE ARE BOTH OFF-LINE!
U.S.S. ENTERPRISE
NCC-1701
KEPTIN, IF THESE SCANS ARE CORRECT...
WE'VE COME OUT OF WARP ALL THE WAY IN THE DELTA QUADRANT!

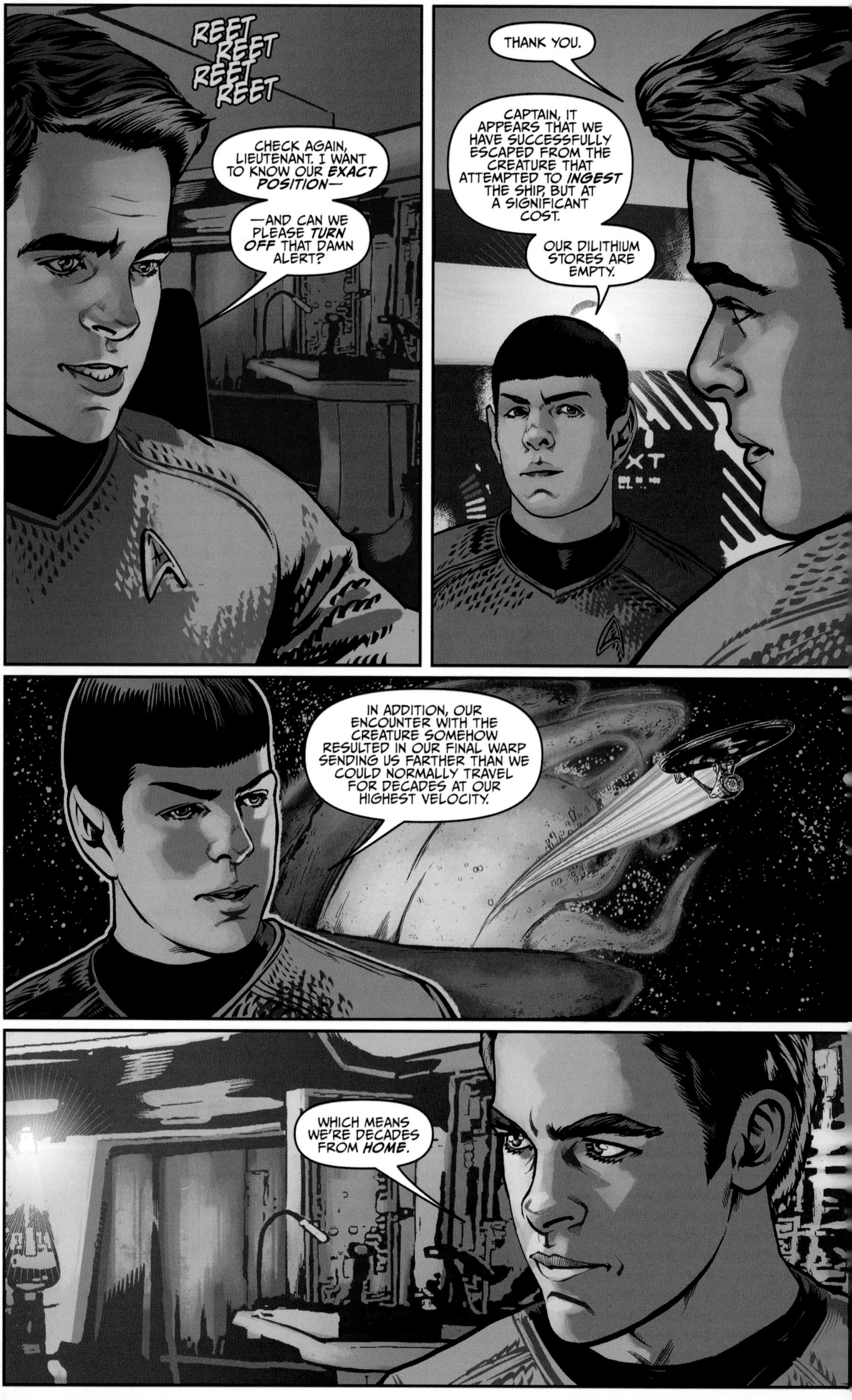
REET REET REET REET
CHECK AGAIN, LIEUTENANT. I WANT TO KNOW OUR EXACT POSITION—
—AND CAN WE PLEASE TURN OFF THAT DAMN ALERT?
THANK YOU.
CAPTAIN, IT APPEARS THAT WE HAVE SUCCESSFULLY ESCAPED FROM THE CREATURE THAT ATTEMPTED TO INGEST THE SHIP, BUT AT A SIGNIFICANT COST.
OUR DILITHIUM STORES ARE EMPTY.
IN ADDITION, OUR ENCOUNTER WITH THE CREATURE SOMEHOW RESULTED IN OUR FINAL WARP SENDING US FARTHER THAN WE COULD NORMALLY TRAVEL FOR DECADES AT OUR HIGHEST VELOCITY.
WHICH MEANS WE'RE DECADES FROM HOME.

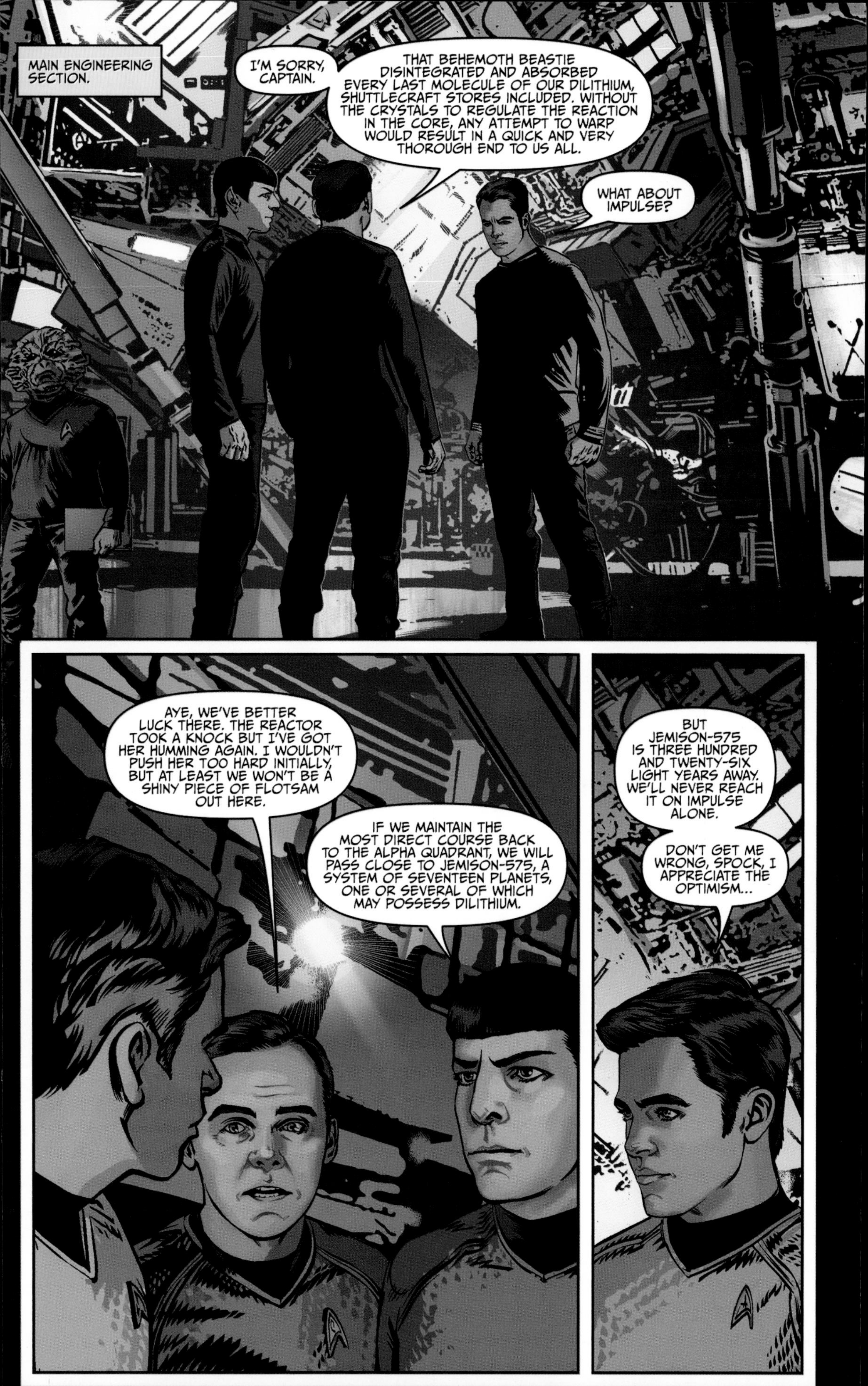
MAIN ENGINEERING SECTION.
I'M SORRY, CAPTAIN.
THAT BEHEMOTH BEASTIE DISINTEGRATED AND ABSORBED EVERY LAST MOLECULE OF OUR DILITHIUM, SHUTTLECRAFT STORES INCLUDED. WITHOUT THE CRYSTALS TO REGULATE THE REACTION IN THE CORE, ANY ATTEMPT TO WARP WOULD RESULT IN A QUICK AND VERY THOROUGH END TO US ALL.
WHAT ABOUT IMPULSE?
AYE, WE'VE BETTER LUCK THERE. THE REACTOR TOOK A KNOCK BUT I'VE GOT HER HUMMING AGAIN. I WOULDN'T PUSH HER TOO HARD INITIALLY, BUT AT LEAST WE WON'T BE A SHINY PIECE OF FLOTSAM OUT HERE.
IF WE MAINTAIN THE MOST DIRECT COURSE BACK TO THE ALPHA QUADRANT, WE WILL PASS CLOSE TO JEMISON-575, A SYSTEM OF SEVENTEEN PLANETS, ONE OR SEVERAL OF WHICH MAY POSSESS DILITHIUM.
BUT JEMISON-575 IS THREE HUNDRED AND TWENTY-SIX LIGHT YEARS AWAY. WE'LL NEVER REACH IT ON IMPULSE ALONE.
DON'T GET ME WRONG, SPOCK, I APPRECIATE THE OPTIMISM...

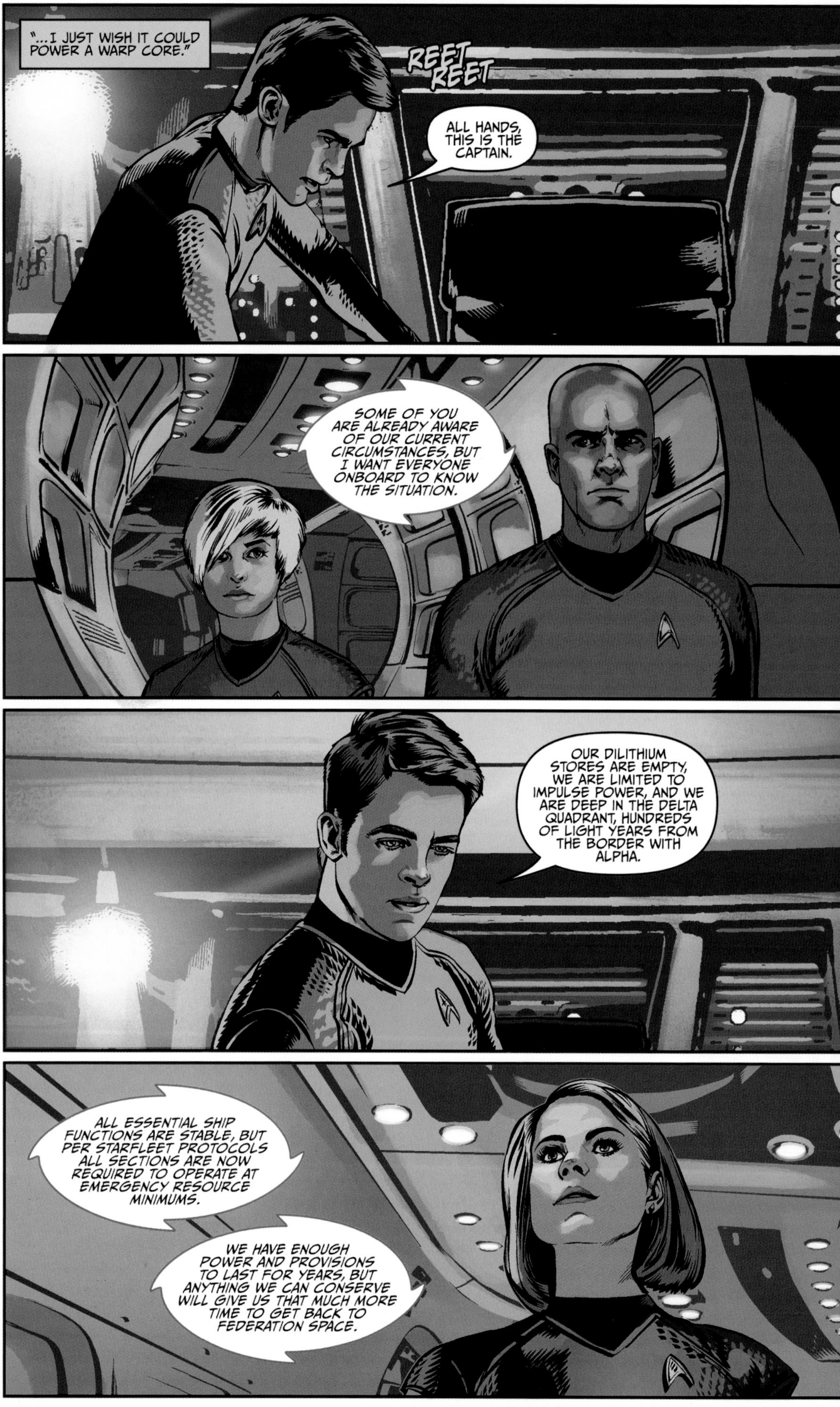
"...I JUST WISH IT COULD POWER A WARP CORE."
REET REET
ALL HANDS, THIS IS THE CAPTAIN.
SOME OF YOU ARE ALREADY AWARE OF OUR CURRENT CIRCUMSTANCES, BUT I WANT EVERYONE ONBOARD TO KNOW THE SITUATION.
OUR DILITHIUM STORES ARE EMPTY, WE ARE LIMITED TO IMPULSE POWER, AND WE ARE DEEP IN THE DELTA QUADRANT, HUNDREDS OF LIGHT YEARS FROM THE BORDER WITH ALPHA.
ALL ESSENTIAL SHIP FUNCTIONS ARE STABLE, BUT PER STARFLEET PROTOCOLS ALL SECTIONS ARE NOW REQUIRED TO OPERATE AT EMERGENCY RESOURCE MINIMUMS.
WE HAVE ENOUGH POWER AND PROVISIONS TO LAST FOR YEARS, BUT ANYTHING WE CAN CONSERVE WILL GIVE US THAT MUCH MORE TIME TO GET BACK TO FEDERATION SPACE.

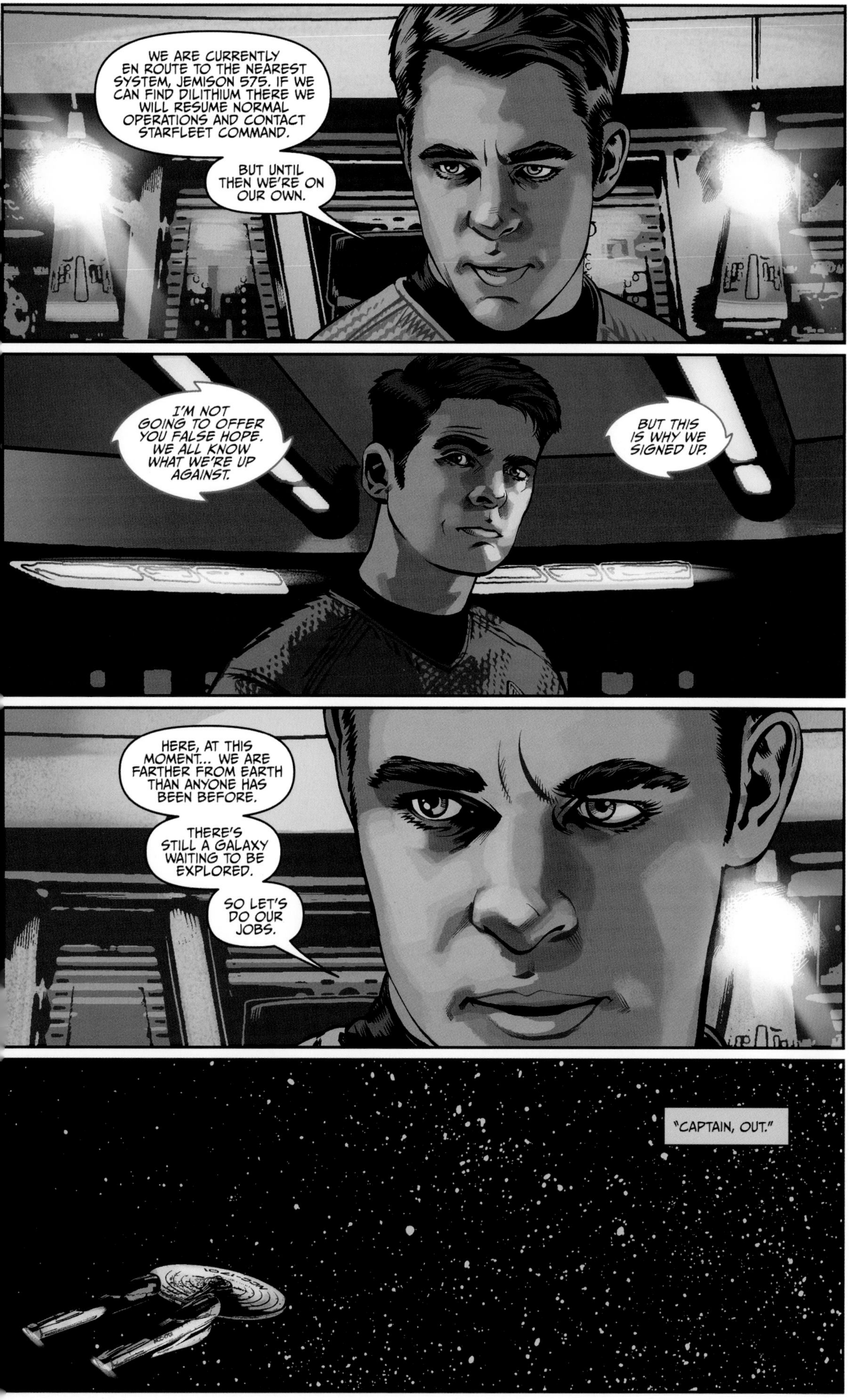
WE ARE CURRENTLY EN ROUTE TO THE NEAREST SYSTEM, JEMISON 575. IF WE CAN FIND DILITHIUM THERE WE WILL RESUME NORMAL OPERATIONS AND CONTACT STARFLEET COMMAND.
BUT UNTIL THEN WE'RE ON OUR OWN.
I'M NOT GOING TO OFFER YOU FALSE HOPE. WE ALL KNOW WHAT WE'RE UP AGAINST.
BUT THIS IS WHY WE SIGNED UP.
HERE, AT THIS MOMENT... WE ARE FARTHER FROM EARTH THAN ANYONE HAS BEEN BEFORE.
THERE'S STILL A GALAXY WAITING TO BE EXPLORED.
SO LET'S DO OUR JOBS.
"CAPTAIN, OUT."

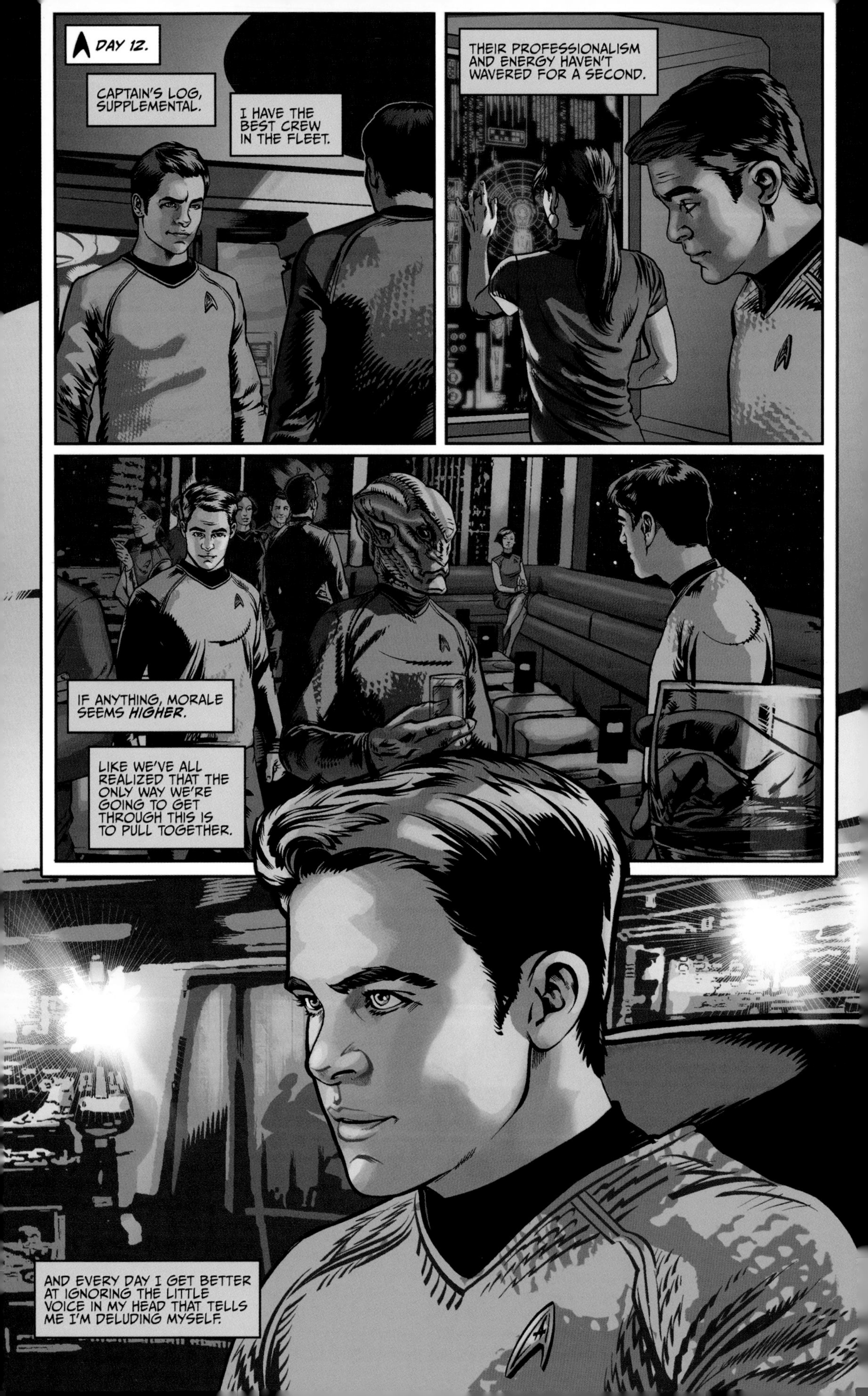
DAY 12.
CAPTAIN'S LOG, SUPPLEMENTAL.
I HAVE THE BEST CREW IN THE FLEET.
THEIR PROFESSIONALISM AND ENERGY HAVEN'T WAVERED FOR A SECOND.
IF ANYTHING, MORALE SEEMS *HIGHER*.
LIKE WE'VE ALL REALIZED THAT THE ONLY WAY WE'RE GOING TO GET THROUGH THIS IS TO PULL TOGETHER.
AND EVERY DAY I GET BETTER AT IGNORING THE LITTLE VOICE IN MY HEAD THAT TELLS ME I'M DELUDING MYSELF.

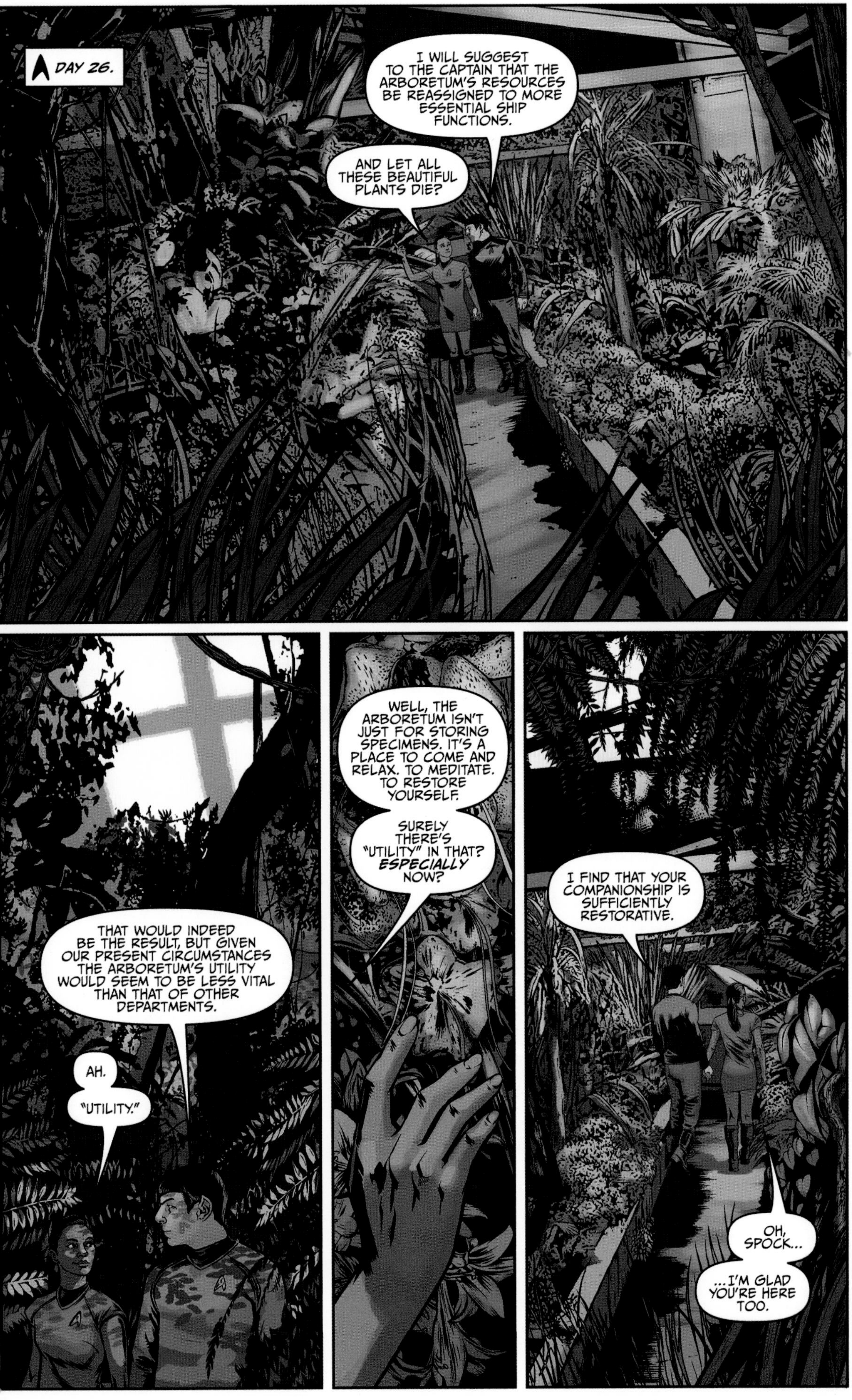
DAY 26.
I WILL SUGGEST TO THE CAPTAIN THAT THE ARBORETUM'S RESOURCES BE REASSIGNED TO MORE ESSENTIAL SHIP FUNCTIONS.
AND LET ALL THESE BEAUTIFUL PLANTS DIE?
THAT WOULD INDEED BE THE RESULT, BUT GIVEN OUR PRESENT CIRCUMSTANCES THE ARBORETUM'S UTILITY WOULD SEEM TO BE LESS VITAL THAN THAT OF OTHER DEPARTMENTS.
AH.
"UTILITY."
WELL, THE ARBORETUM ISN'T JUST FOR STORING SPECIMENS. IT'S A PLACE TO COME AND RELAX. TO MEDITATE. TO RESTORE YOURSELF.
SURELY THERE'S "UTILITY" IN THAT? ESPECIALLY NOW?
I FIND THAT YOUR COMPANIONSHIP IS SUFFICIENTLY RESTORATIVE.
OH, SPOCK...
...I'M GLAD YOU'RE HERE TOO.

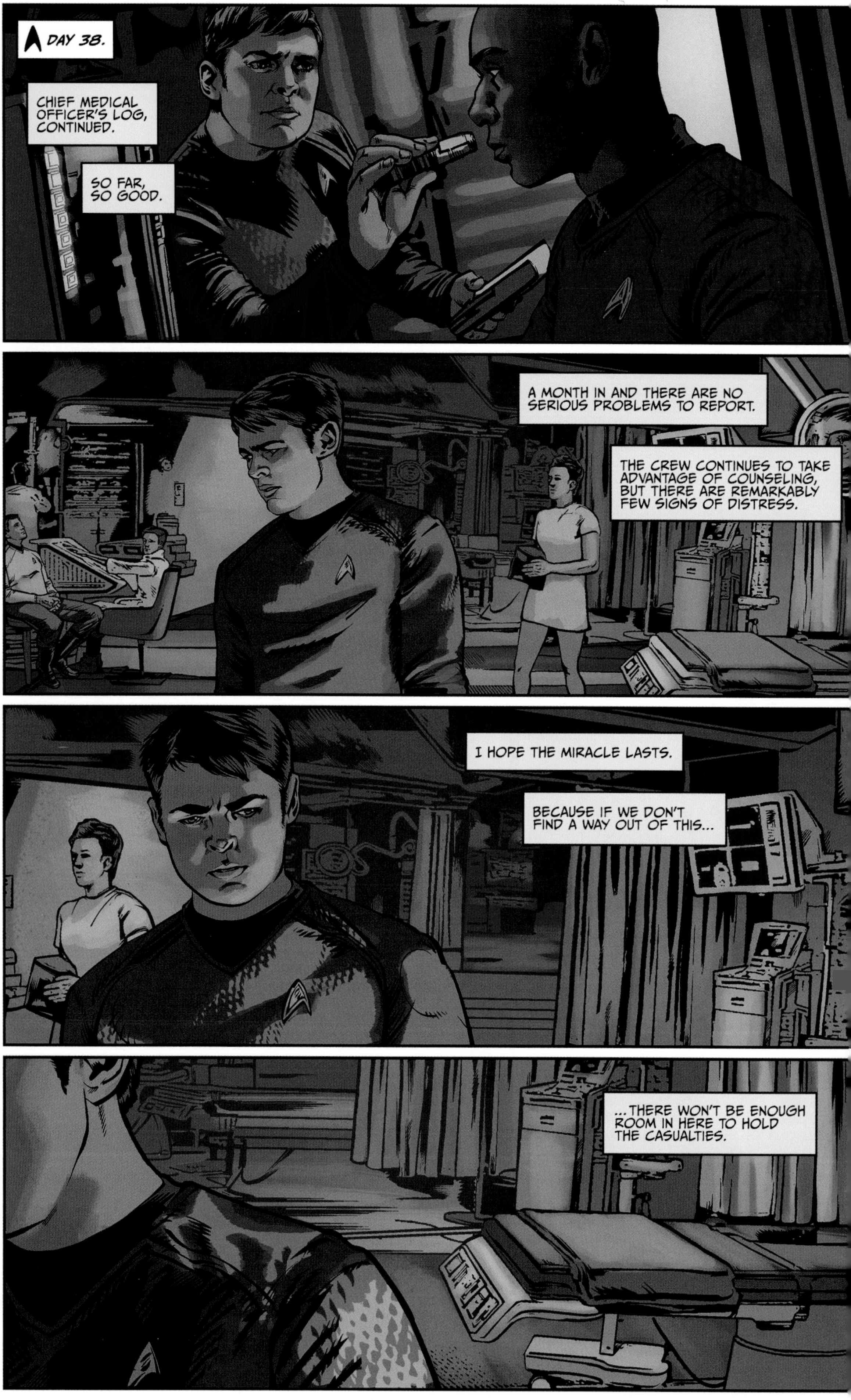
DAY 38.
CHIEF MEDICAL OFFICER'S LOG, CONTINUED.
SO FAR, SO GOOD.
A MONTH IN AND THERE ARE NO SERIOUS PROBLEMS TO REPORT.
THE CREW CONTINUES TO TAKE ADVANTAGE OF COUNSELING, BUT THERE ARE REMARKABLY FEW SIGNS OF DISTRESS.
I HOPE THE MIRACLE LASTS.
BECAUSE IF WE DON'T FIND A WAY OUT OF THIS...
...THERE WON'T BE ENOUGH ROOM IN HERE TO HOLD THE CASUALTIES.

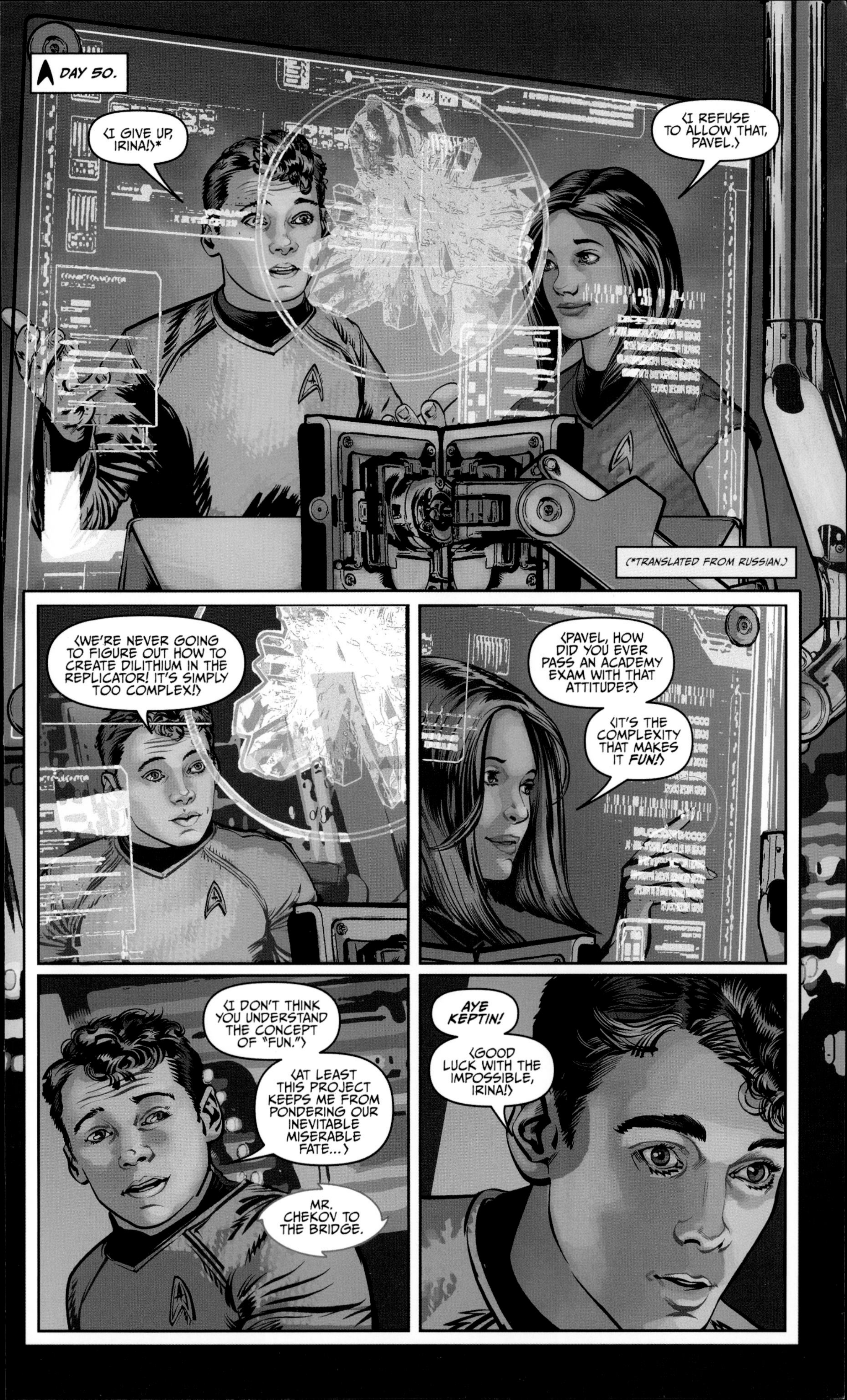
DAY 50.
⟨I GIVE UP, IRINA!⟩*
⟨I REFUSE TO ALLOW THAT, PAVEL.⟩
(*TRANSLATED FROM RUSSIAN.)
⟨WE'RE NEVER GOING TO FIGURE OUT HOW TO CREATE DILITHIUM IN THE REPLICATOR! IT'S SIMPLY TOO COMPLEX!⟩
⟨PAVEL, HOW DID YOU EVER PASS AN ACADEMY EXAM WITH THAT ATTITUDE?⟩
⟨IT'S THE COMPLEXITY THAT MAKES IT *FUN!*⟩
⟨I DON'T THINK YOU UNDERSTAND THE CONCEPT OF "FUN."⟩
⟨AT LEAST THIS PROJECT KEEPS ME FROM PONDERING OUR INEVITABLE MISERABLE FATE...⟩
MR. CHEKOV TO THE BRIDGE.
AYE KEPTIN!
⟨GOOD LUCK WITH THE IMPOSSIBLE, IRINA!⟩

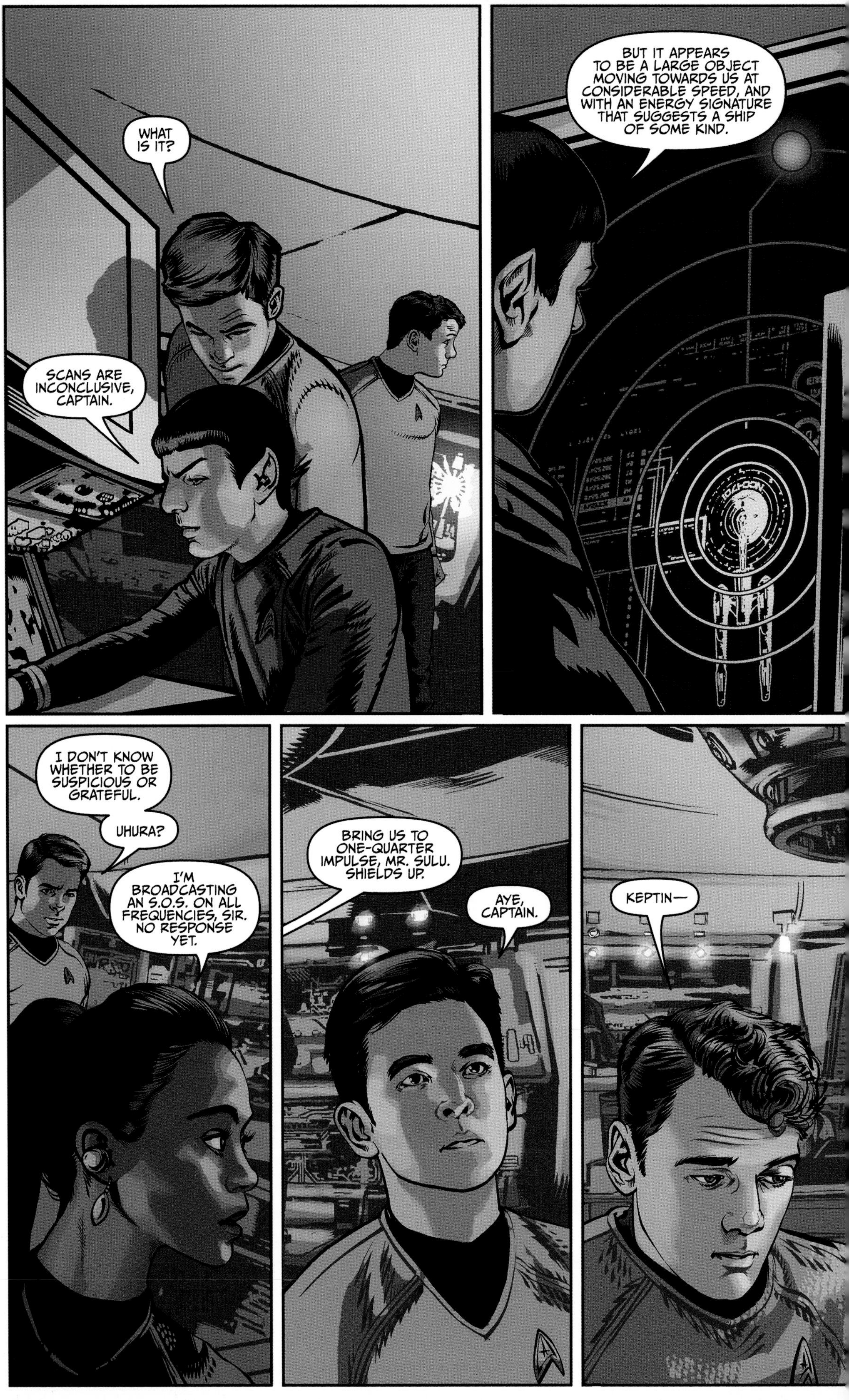
WHAT IS IT?
SCANS ARE INCONCLUSIVE, CAPTAIN.
BUT IT APPEARS TO BE A LARGE OBJECT MOVING TOWARDS US AT CONSIDERABLE SPEED, AND WITH AN ENERGY SIGNATURE THAT SUGGESTS A SHIP OF SOME KIND.
I DON'T KNOW WHETHER TO BE SUSPICIOUS OR GRATEFUL.
UHURA?
I'M BROADCASTING AN S.O.S. ON ALL FREQUENCIES, SIR. NO RESPONSE YET.
BRING US TO ONE-QUARTER IMPULSE, MR. SULU. SHIELDS UP.
AYE, CAPTAIN.
KEPTIN—

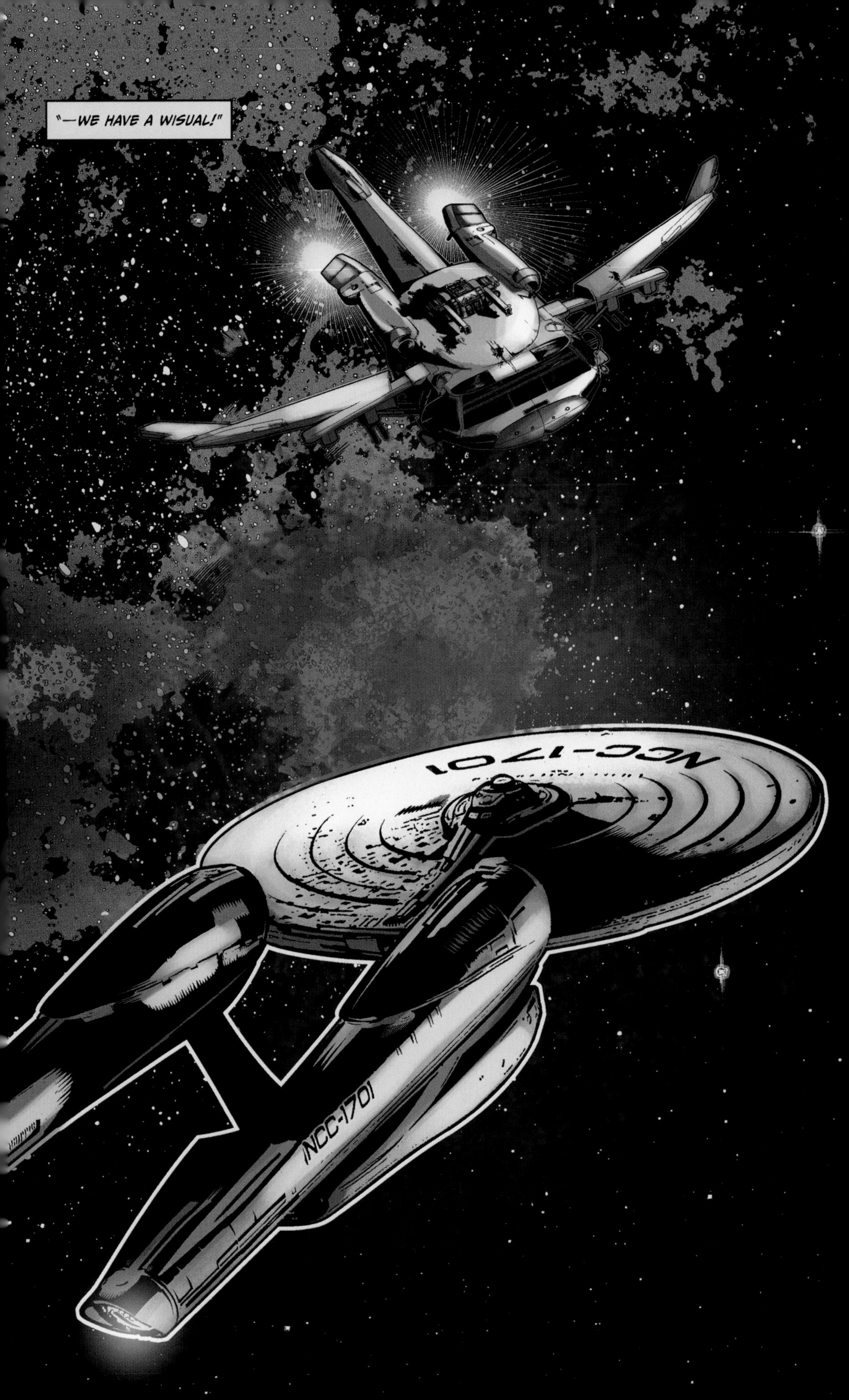
"—WE HAVE A WISUAL!"
NCC-1701
NCC-1701

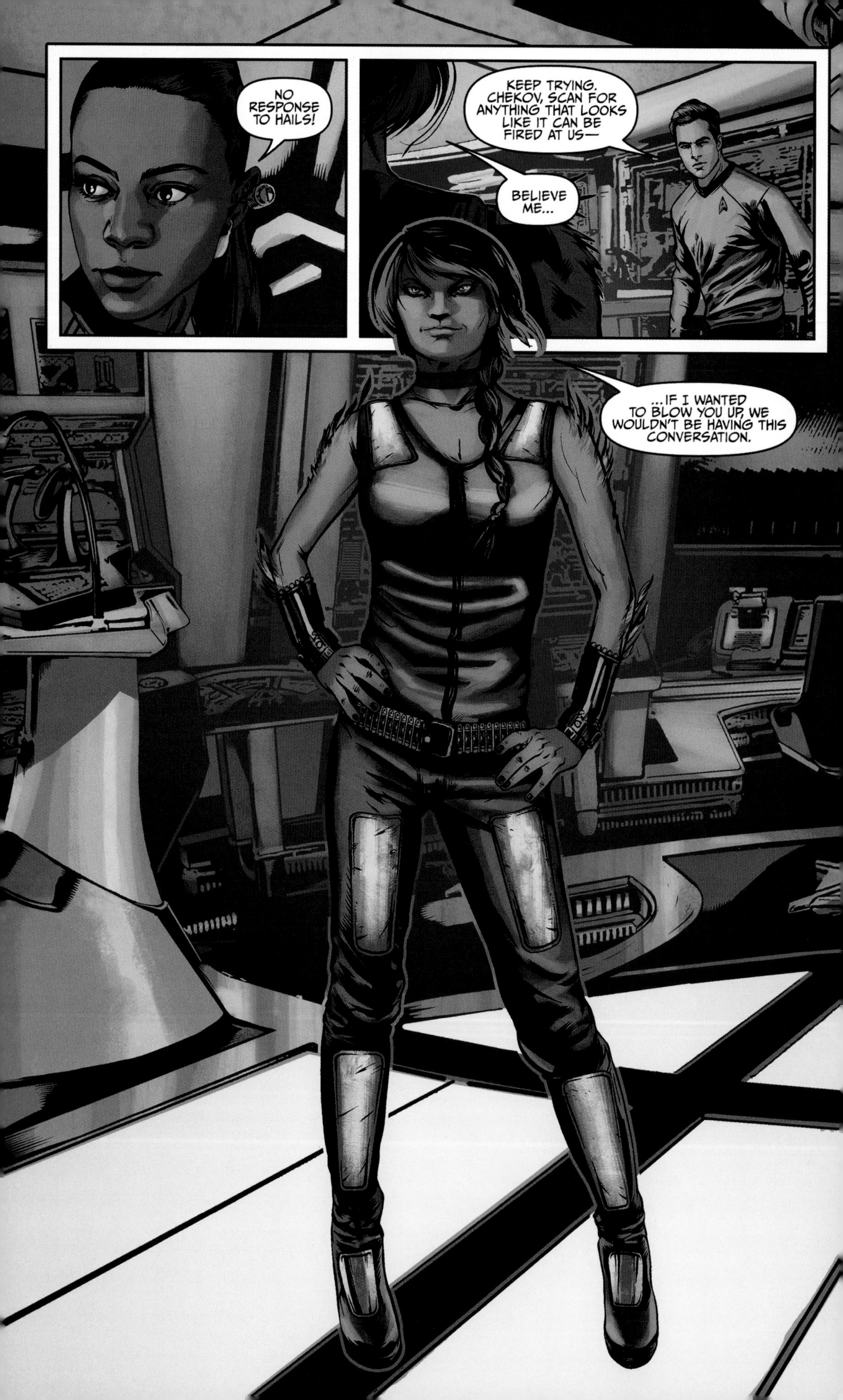
NO RESPONSE TO HAILS!
KEEP TRYING. CHEKOV, SCAN FOR ANYTHING THAT LOOKS LIKE IT CAN BE FIRED AT US—
BELIEVE ME...
...IF I WANTED TO BLOW YOU UP, WE WOULDN'T BE HAVING THIS CONVERSATION.

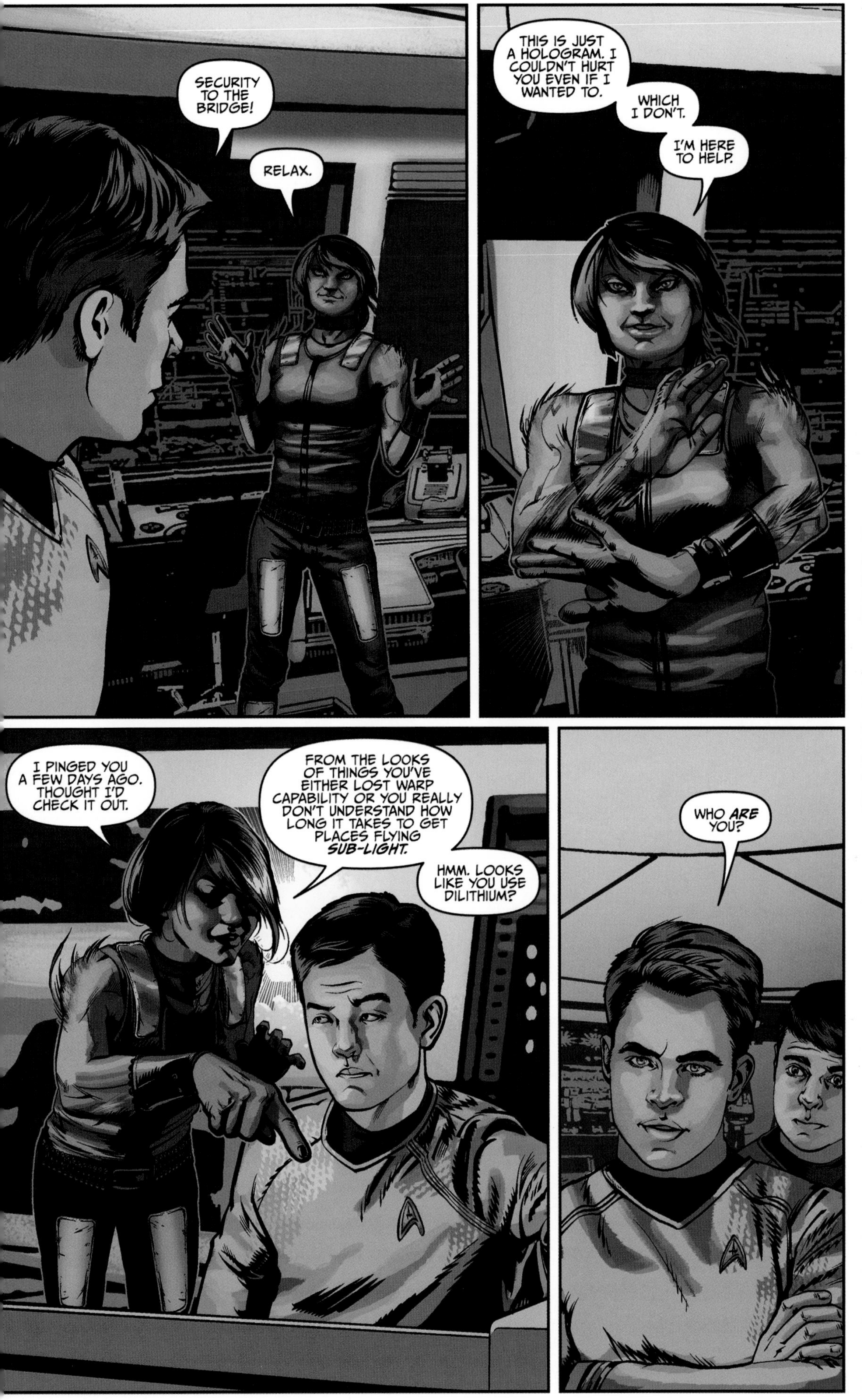
SECURITY TO THE BRIDGE!
RELAX.
THIS IS JUST A HOLOGRAM. I COULDN'T HURT YOU EVEN IF I WANTED TO.
WHICH I DON'T.
I'M HERE TO HELP.
I PINGED YOU A FEW DAYS AGO. THOUGHT I'D CHECK IT OUT.
FROM THE LOOKS OF THINGS YOU'VE EITHER LOST WARP CAPABILITY OR YOU REALLY DON'T UNDERSTAND HOW LONG IT TAKES TO GET PLACES FLYING SUB-LIGHT.
HMM. LOOKS LIKE YOU USE DILITHIUM?
WHO ARE YOU?

I'M *EURYDICE.* SAVIOR OF DEEP SPACE.

"SAVIOR"...?

WELL, MOSTLY SALVAGE. USUALLY SHIPS IN A LOT WORSE SHAPE THAN YOURS.

BELIEVE ME, IT'S ALWAYS NICE TO FIND ONE THAT'S NOT FULL OF *CORPSES.*

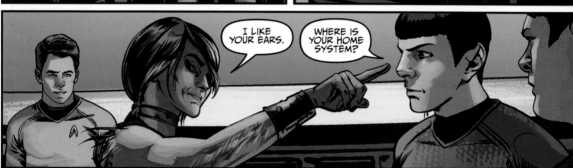

I LIKE YOUR EARS.

WHERE IS YOUR HOME SYSTEM?

SPACE IS HOME.

BUT IF YOU MEAN THE PLACE I RAN AWAY FROM AS SOON AS I WAS ABLE TO HIT "IGNITION," IT'S CALLED *HEXEL SEVEN.* THANKFULLY VERY FAR FROM HERE.

WHAT ABOUT YOU? NEVER SEEN YOUR TYPE BEFORE.

I'M CAPTAIN JAMES T. KIRK OF EARTH. THIS SHIP IS THE *U.S.S. ENTERPRISE.* WE'RE ON AN EXPLORATORY MISSION ON BEHALF OF THE UNITED FEDERATION OF PLANETS.

THAT'S A MOUTHFUL.

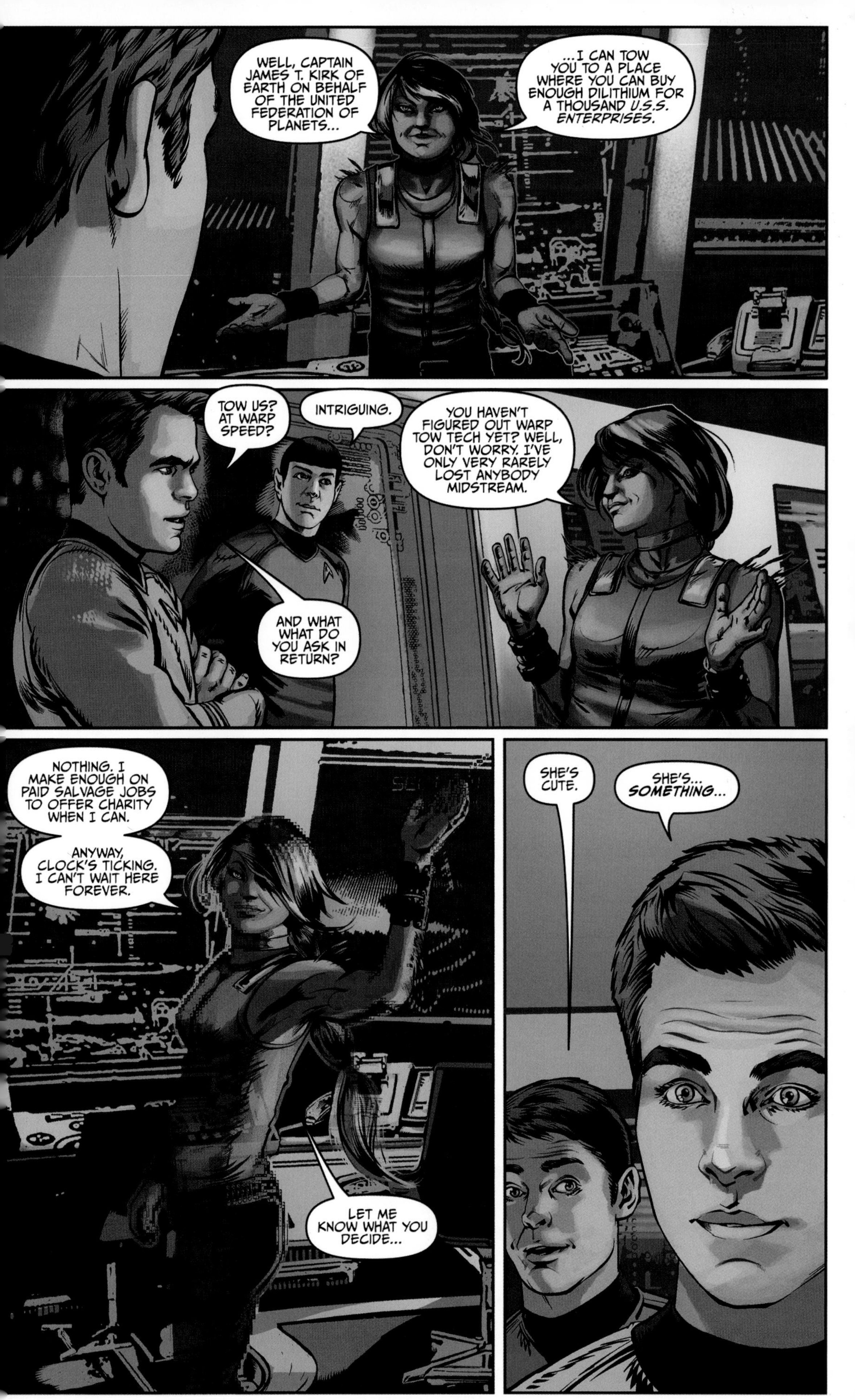
WELL, CAPTAIN JAMES T. KIRK OF EARTH ON BEHALF OF THE UNITED FEDERATION OF PLANETS...
...I CAN TOW YOU TO A PLACE WHERE YOU CAN BUY ENOUGH DILITHIUM FOR A THOUSAND *U.S.S. ENTERPRISES.*
TOW US? AT WARP SPEED?
INTRIGUING.
YOU HAVEN'T FIGURED OUT WARP TOW TECH YET? WELL, DON'T WORRY. I'VE ONLY VERY RARELY LOST ANYBODY MIDSTREAM.
AND WHAT WHAT DO YOU ASK IN RETURN?
NOTHING. I MAKE ENOUGH ON PAID SALVAGE JOBS TO OFFER CHARITY WHEN I CAN.
ANYWAY, CLOCK'S TICKING. I CAN'T WAIT HERE FOREVER.
LET ME KNOW WHAT YOU DECIDE...
SHE'S CUTE.
SHE'S... ***SOMETHING...***

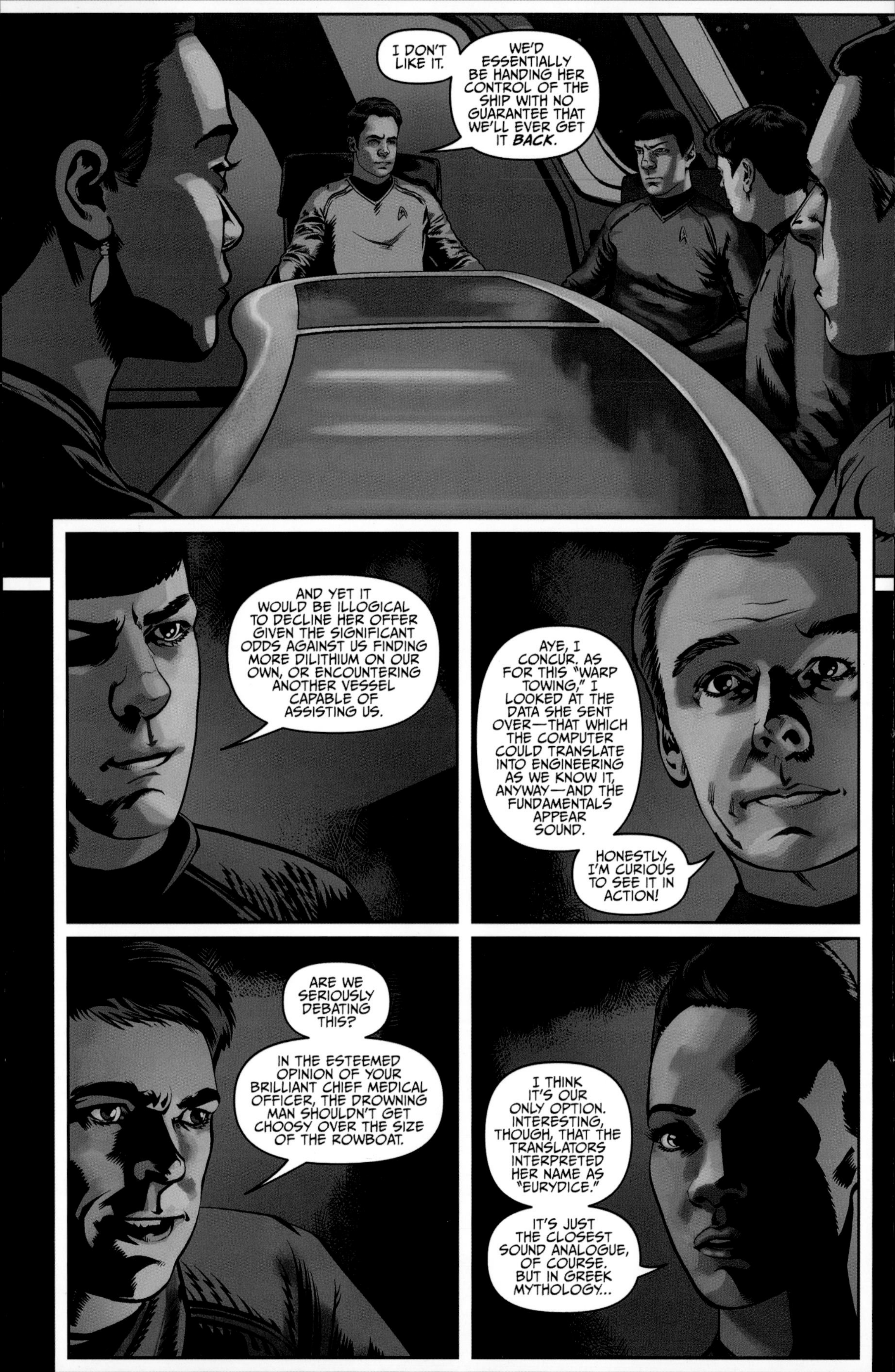
I DON'T LIKE IT.
WE'D ESSENTIALLY BE HANDING HER CONTROL OF THE SHIP WITH NO GUARANTEE THAT WE'LL EVER GET IT *BACK*.
AND YET IT WOULD BE ILLOGICAL TO DECLINE HER OFFER GIVEN THE SIGNIFICANT ODDS AGAINST US FINDING MORE DILITHIUM ON OUR OWN, OR ENCOUNTERING ANOTHER VESSEL CAPABLE OF ASSISTING US.
AYE, I CONCUR. AS FOR THIS "WARP TOWING," I LOOKED AT THE DATA SHE SENT OVER—THAT WHICH THE COMPUTER COULD TRANSLATE INTO ENGINEERING AS WE KNOW IT, ANYWAY—AND THE FUNDAMENTALS APPEAR SOUND.
HONESTLY, I'M CURIOUS TO SEE IT IN ACTION!
ARE WE SERIOUSLY DEBATING THIS?
IN THE ESTEEMED OPINION OF YOUR BRILLIANT CHIEF MEDICAL OFFICER, THE DROWNING MAN SHOULDN'T GET CHOOSY OVER THE SIZE OF THE ROWBOAT.
I THINK IT'S OUR ONLY OPTION. INTERESTING, THOUGH, THAT THE TRANSLATORS INTERPRETED HER NAME AS "EURYDICE."
IT'S JUST THE CLOSEST SOUND ANALOGUE, OF COURSE. BUT IN GREEK MYTHOLOGY...

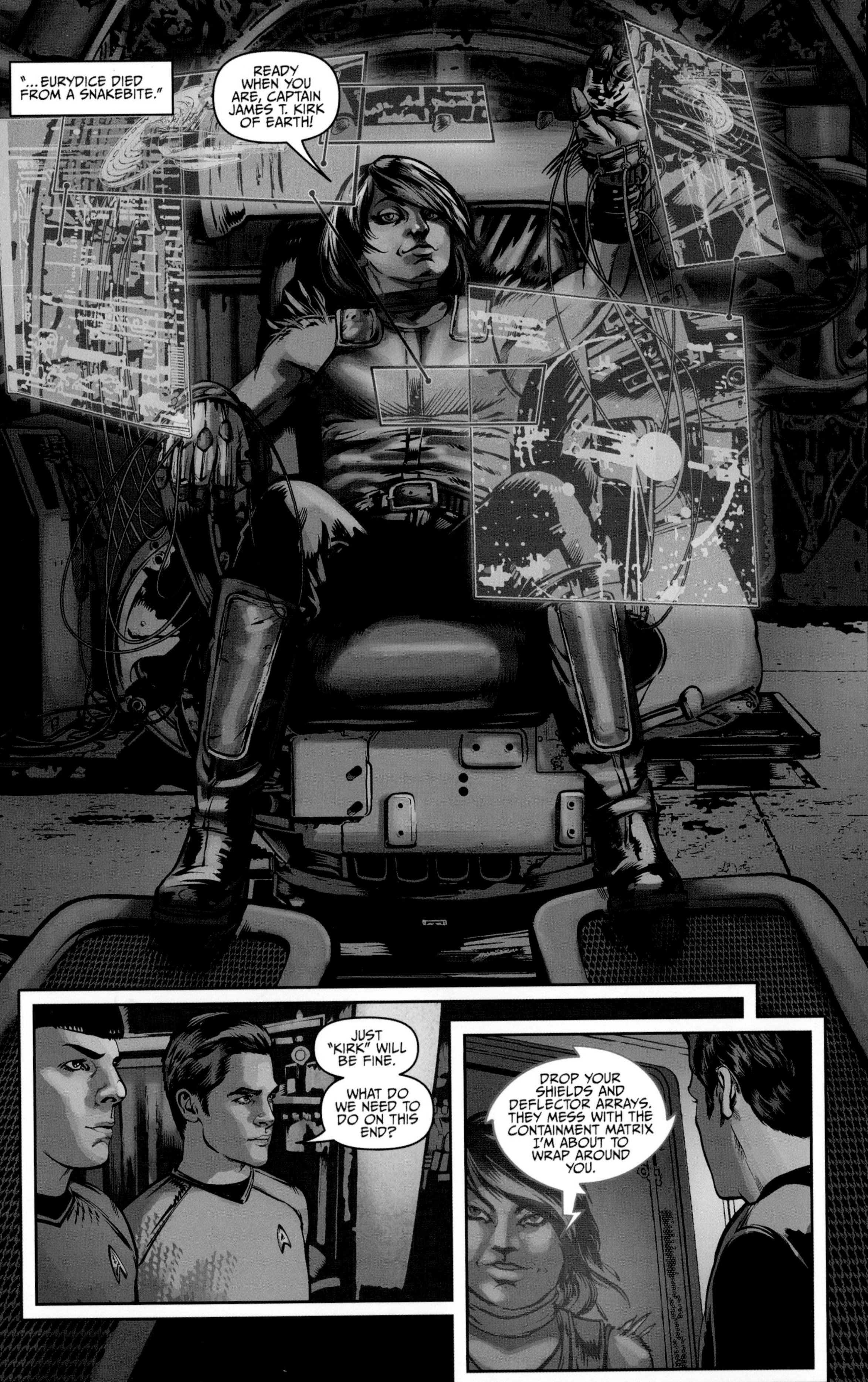
"...EURYDICE DIED FROM A SNAKEBITE."
READY WHEN YOU ARE, CAPTAIN JAMES T. KIRK OF EARTH!
JUST "KIRK" WILL BE FINE.
WHAT DO WE NEED TO DO ON THIS END?
DROP YOUR SHIELDS AND DEFLECTOR ARRAYS. THEY MESS WITH THE CONTAINMENT MATRIX I'M ABOUT TO WRAP AROUND YOU.

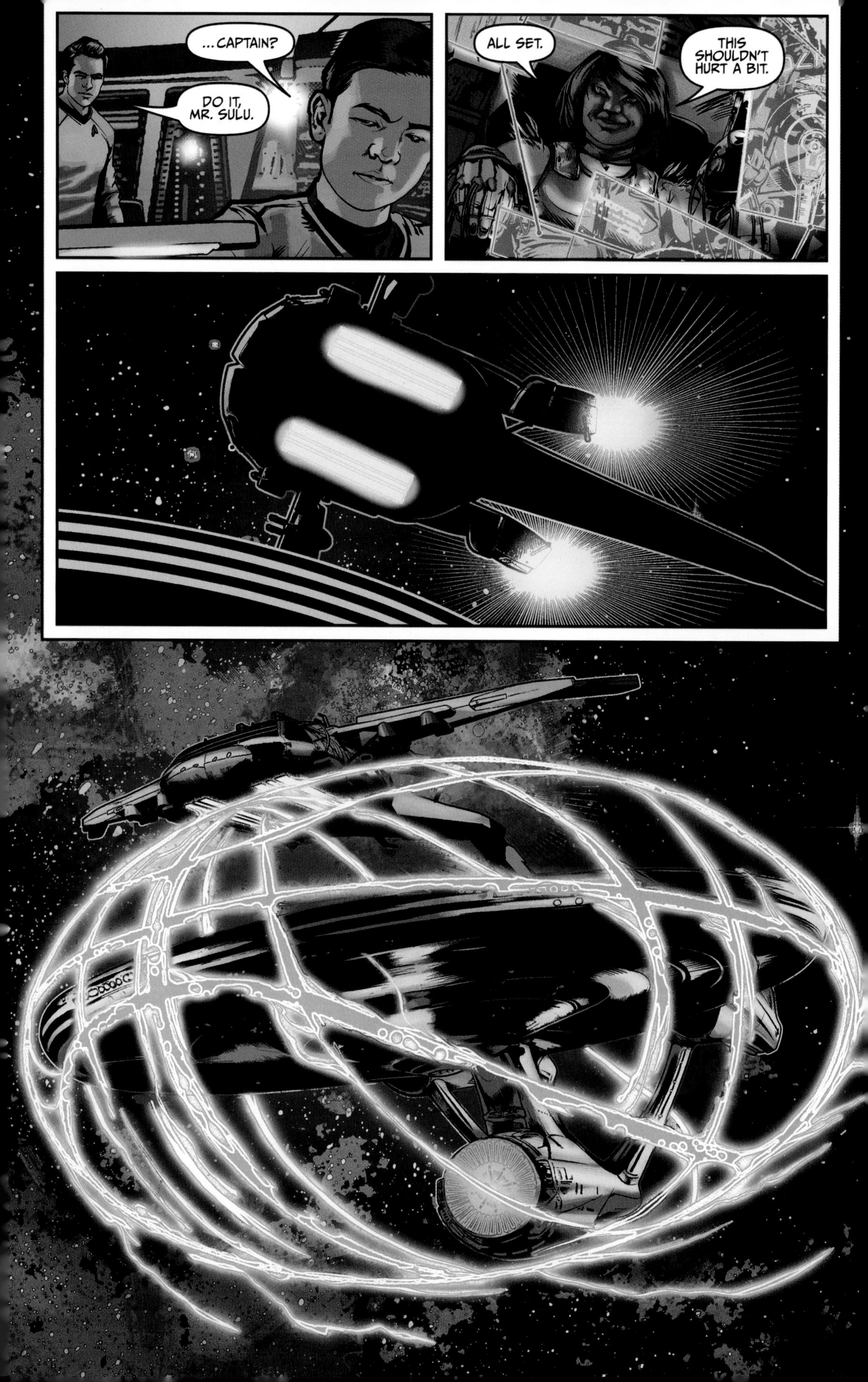
...CAPTAIN?
DO IT, MR. SULU.
ALL SET.
THIS SHOULDN'T HURT A BIT.

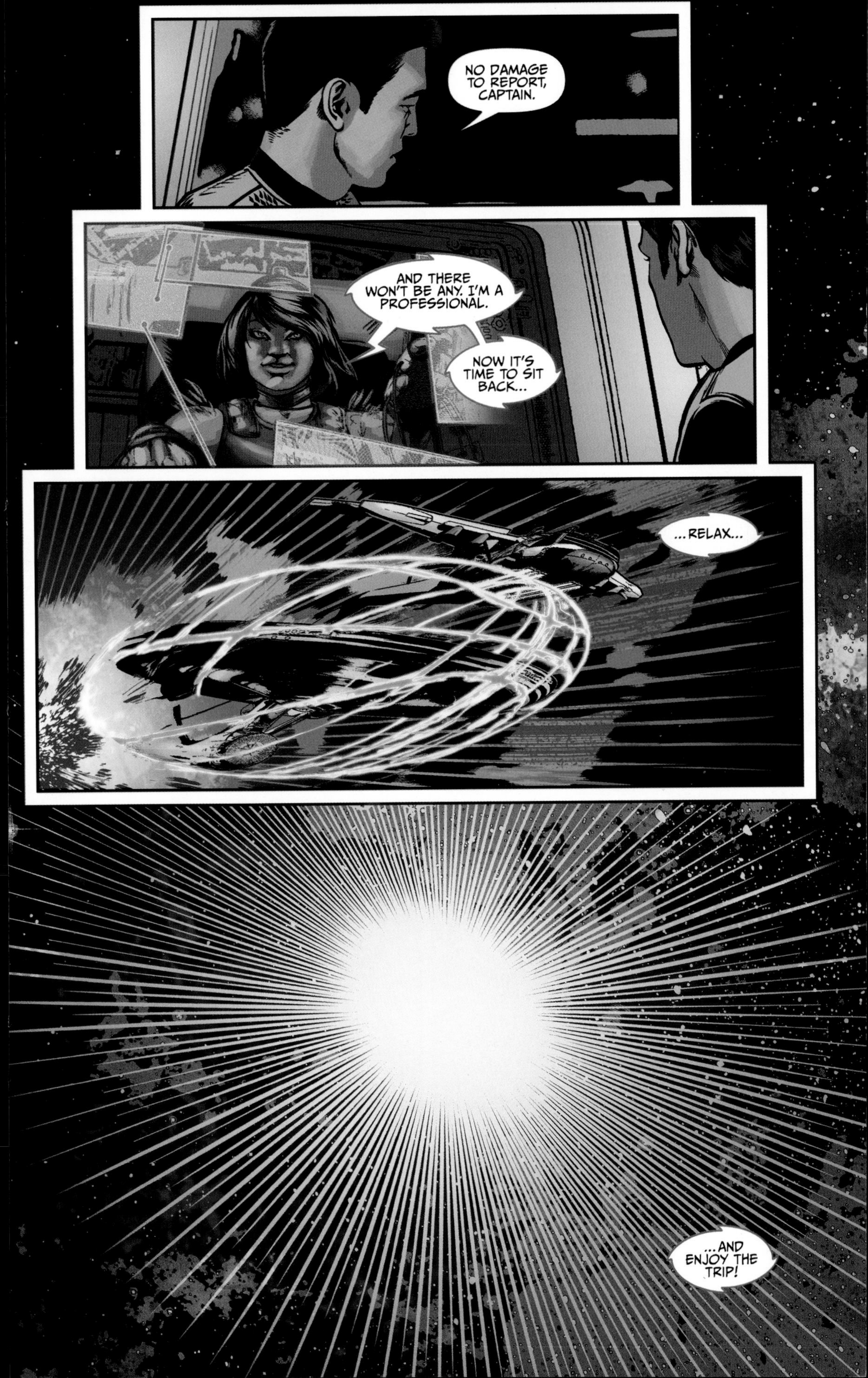
NO DAMAGE TO REPORT, CAPTAIN.
AND THERE WON'T BE ANY. I'M A PROFESSIONAL.
NOW IT'S TIME TO SIT BACK...
...RELAX...
...AND ENJOY THE TRIP!

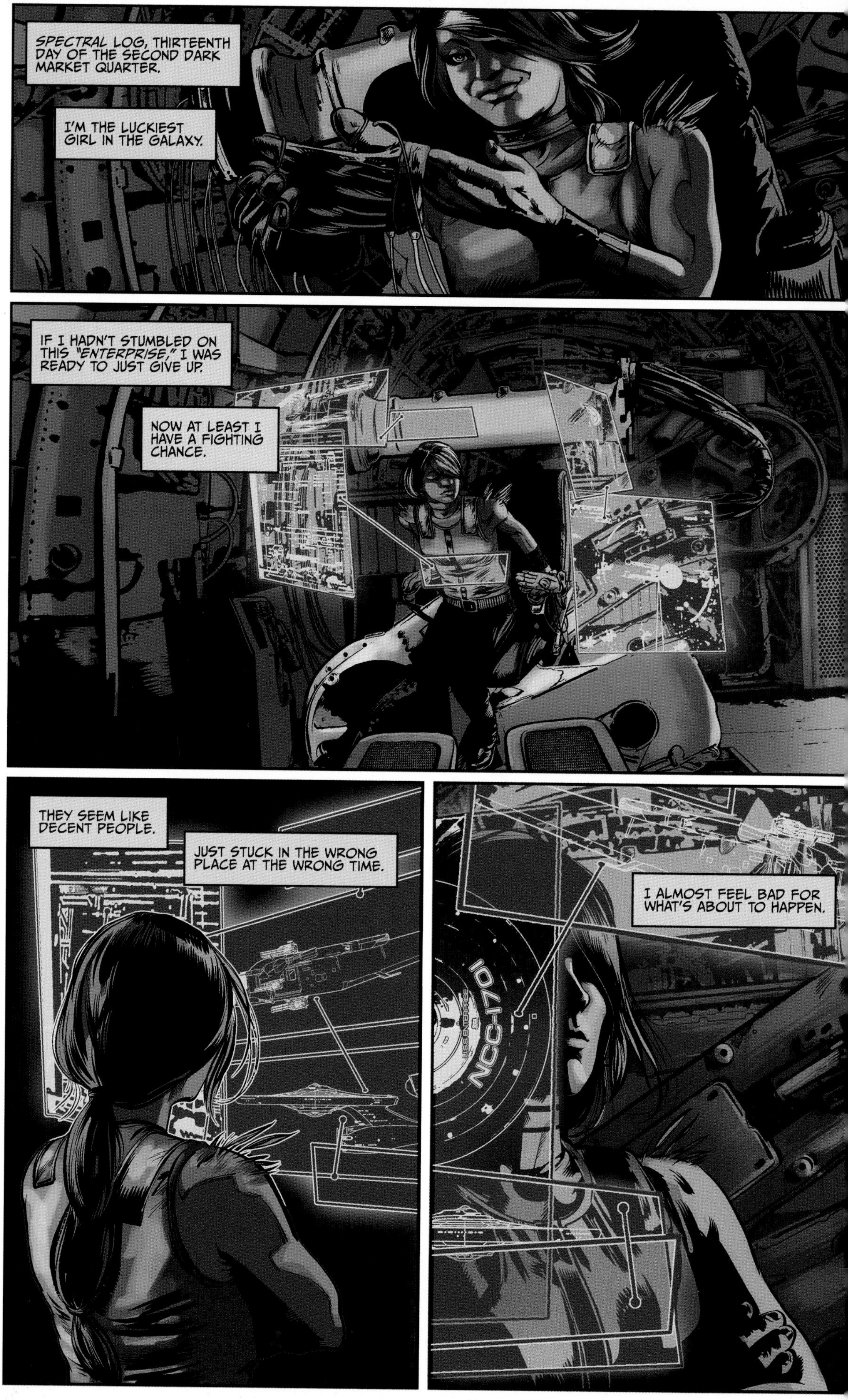
SPECTRAL LOG, THIRTEENTH DAY OF THE SECOND DARK MARKET QUARTER.
I'M THE LUCKIEST GIRL IN THE GALAXY.
IF I HADN'T STUMBLED ON THIS "ENTERPRISE," I WAS READY TO JUST GIVE UP.
NOW AT LEAST I HAVE A FIGHTING CHANCE.
THEY SEEM LIKE DECENT PEOPLE.
JUST STUCK IN THE WRONG PLACE AT THE WRONG TIME.
NCC-1701
I ALMOST FEEL BAD FOR WHAT'S ABOUT TO HAPPEN.

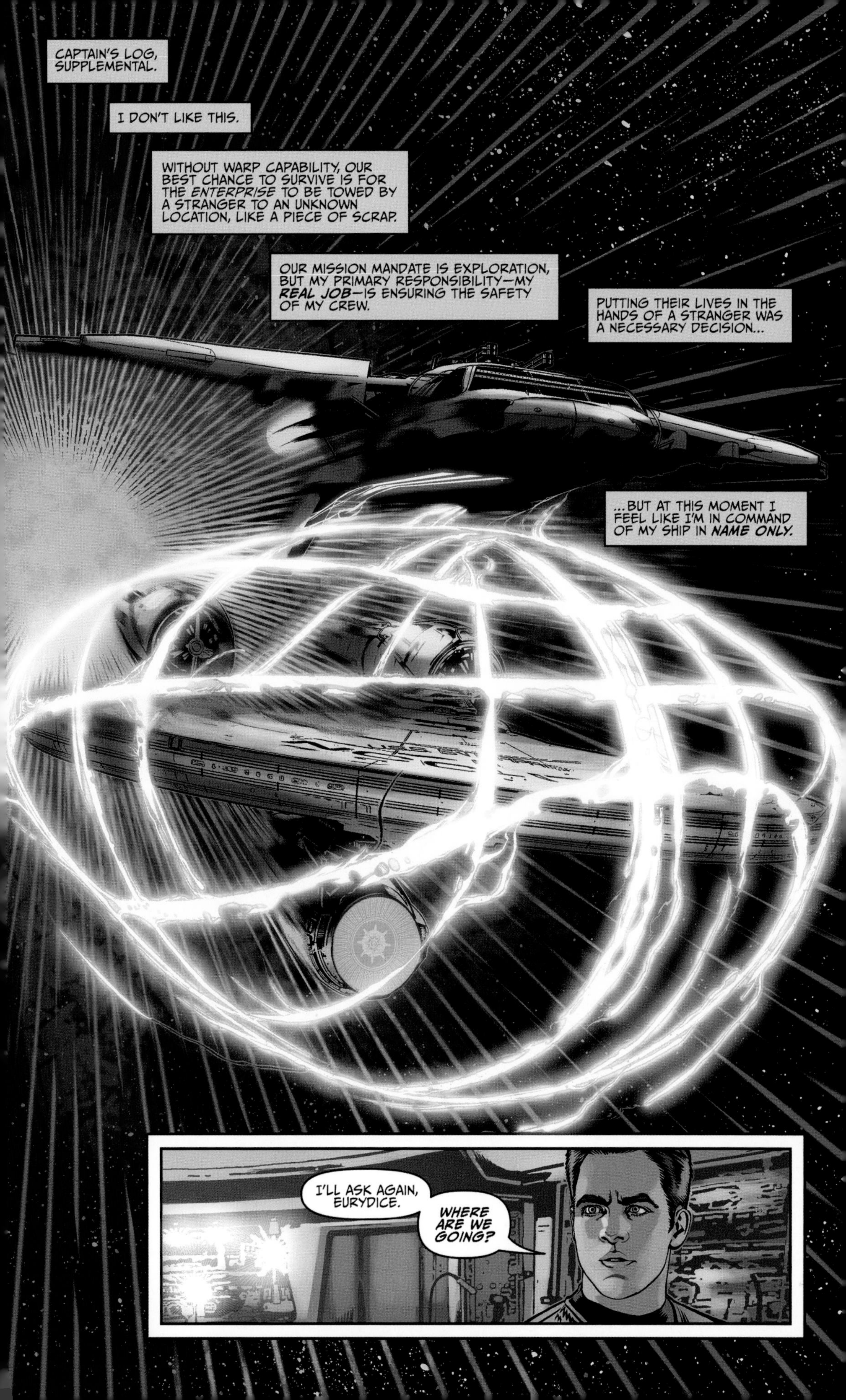
CAPTAIN'S LOG, SUPPLEMENTAL.
I DON'T LIKE THIS.
WITHOUT WARP CAPABILITY, OUR BEST CHANCE TO SURVIVE IS FOR THE *ENTERPRISE* TO BE TOWED BY A STRANGER TO AN UNKNOWN LOCATION, LIKE A PIECE OF SCRAP.
OUR MISSION MANDATE IS EXPLORATION, BUT MY PRIMARY RESPONSIBILITY—MY ***REAL JOB***—IS ENSURING THE SAFETY OF MY CREW.
PUTTING THEIR LIVES IN THE HANDS OF A STRANGER WAS A NECESSARY DECISION...
...BUT AT THIS MOMENT I FEEL LIKE I'M IN COMMAND OF MY SHIP IN ***NAME ONLY.***
I'LL ASK AGAIN, EURYDICE.
WHERE ARE WE GOING?

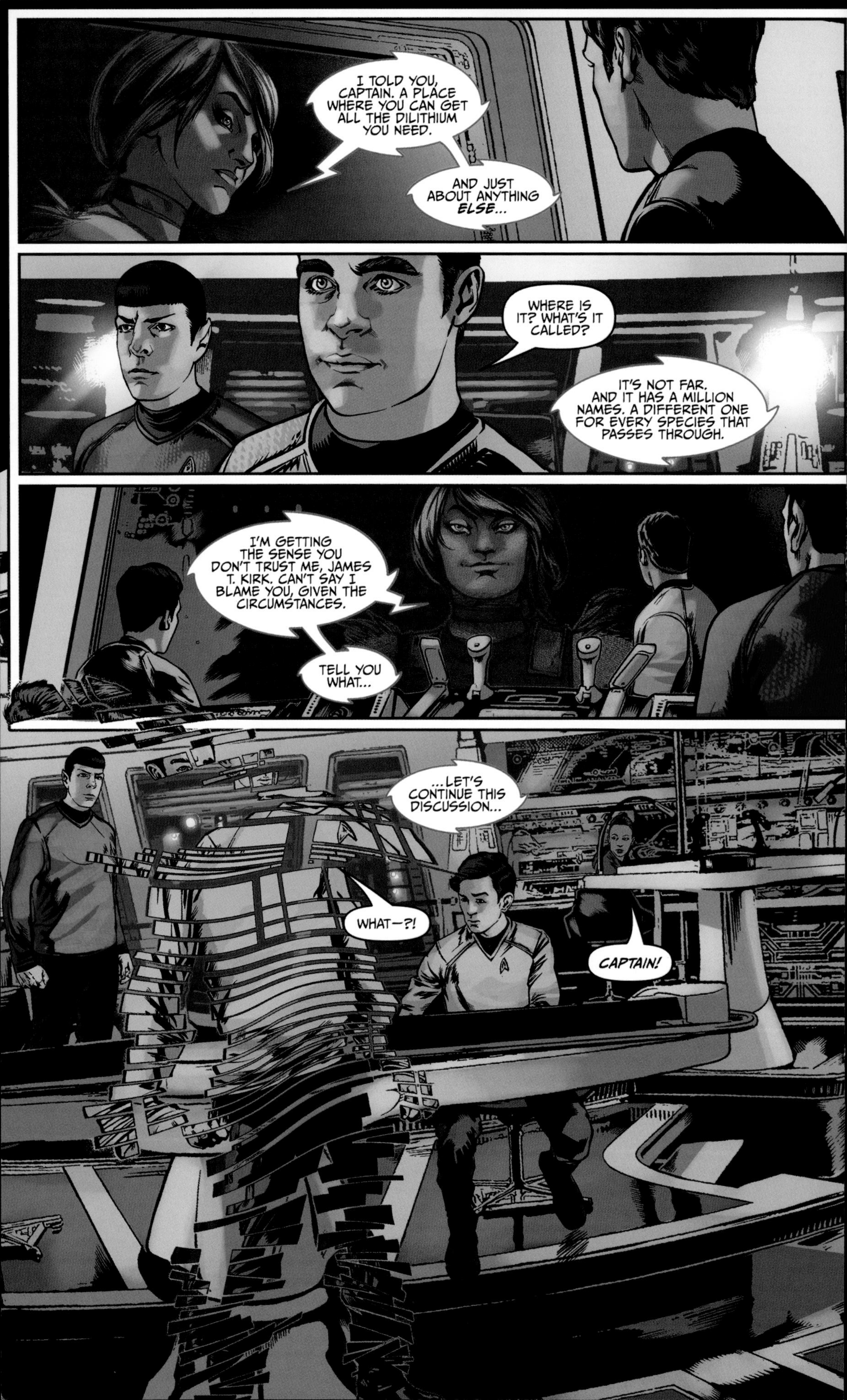
I TOLD YOU, CAPTAIN. A PLACE WHERE YOU CAN GET ALL THE DILITHIUM YOU NEED.
AND JUST ABOUT ANYTHING *ELSE*...
WHERE IS IT? WHAT'S IT CALLED?
IT'S NOT FAR. AND IT HAS A MILLION NAMES. A DIFFERENT ONE FOR EVERY SPECIES THAT PASSES THROUGH.
I'M GETTING THE SENSE YOU DON'T TRUST ME, JAMES T. KIRK. CAN'T SAY I BLAME YOU, GIVEN THE CIRCUMSTANCES.
TELL YOU WHAT...
...LET'S CONTINUE THIS DISCUSSION...
WHAT—?!
CAPTAIN!

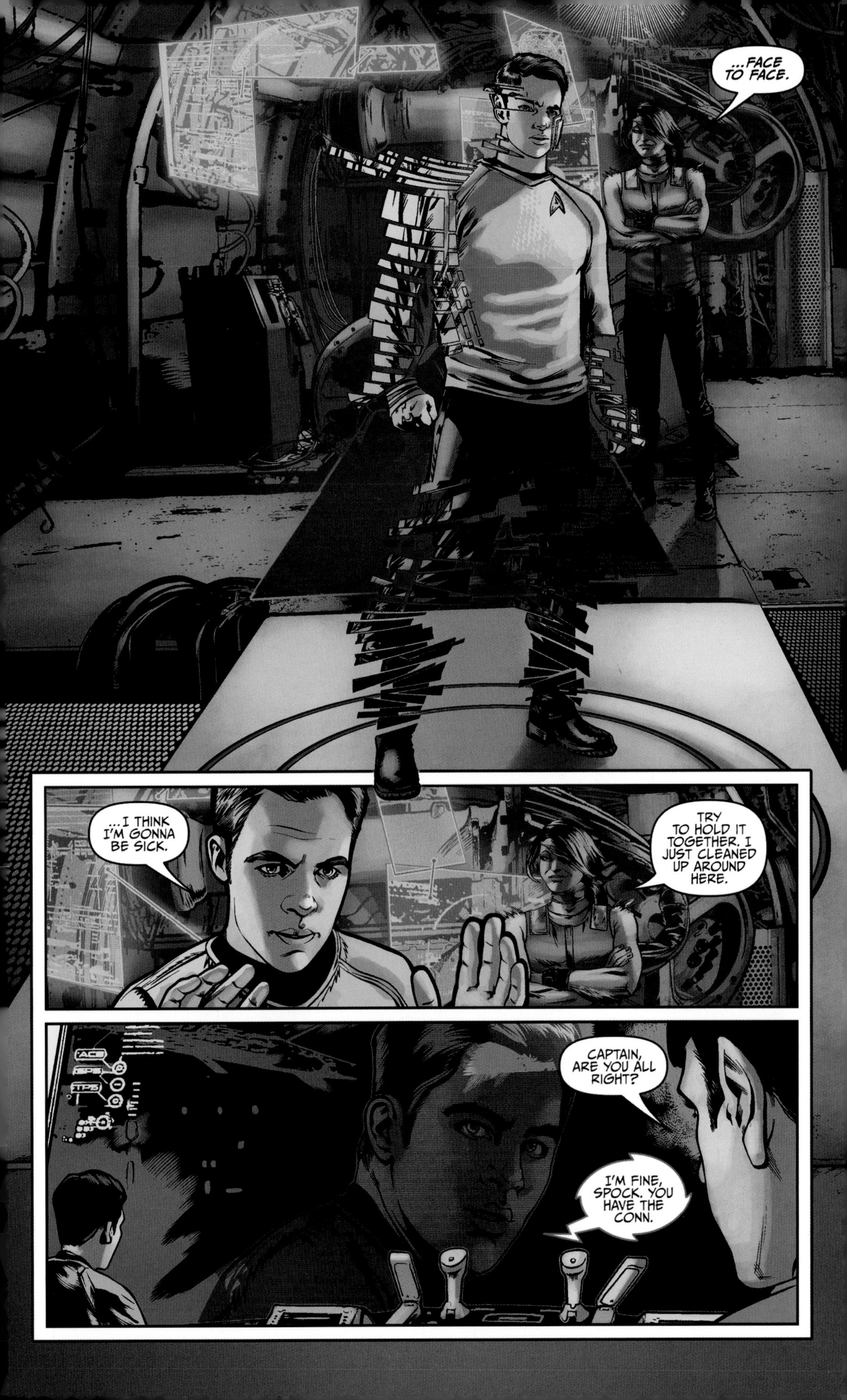
...FACE TO FACE.
...I THINK I'M GONNA BE SICK.
TRY TO HOLD IT TOGETHER. I JUST CLEANED UP AROUND HERE.
CAPTAIN, ARE YOU ALL RIGHT?
I'M FINE, SPOCK. YOU HAVE THE CONN.

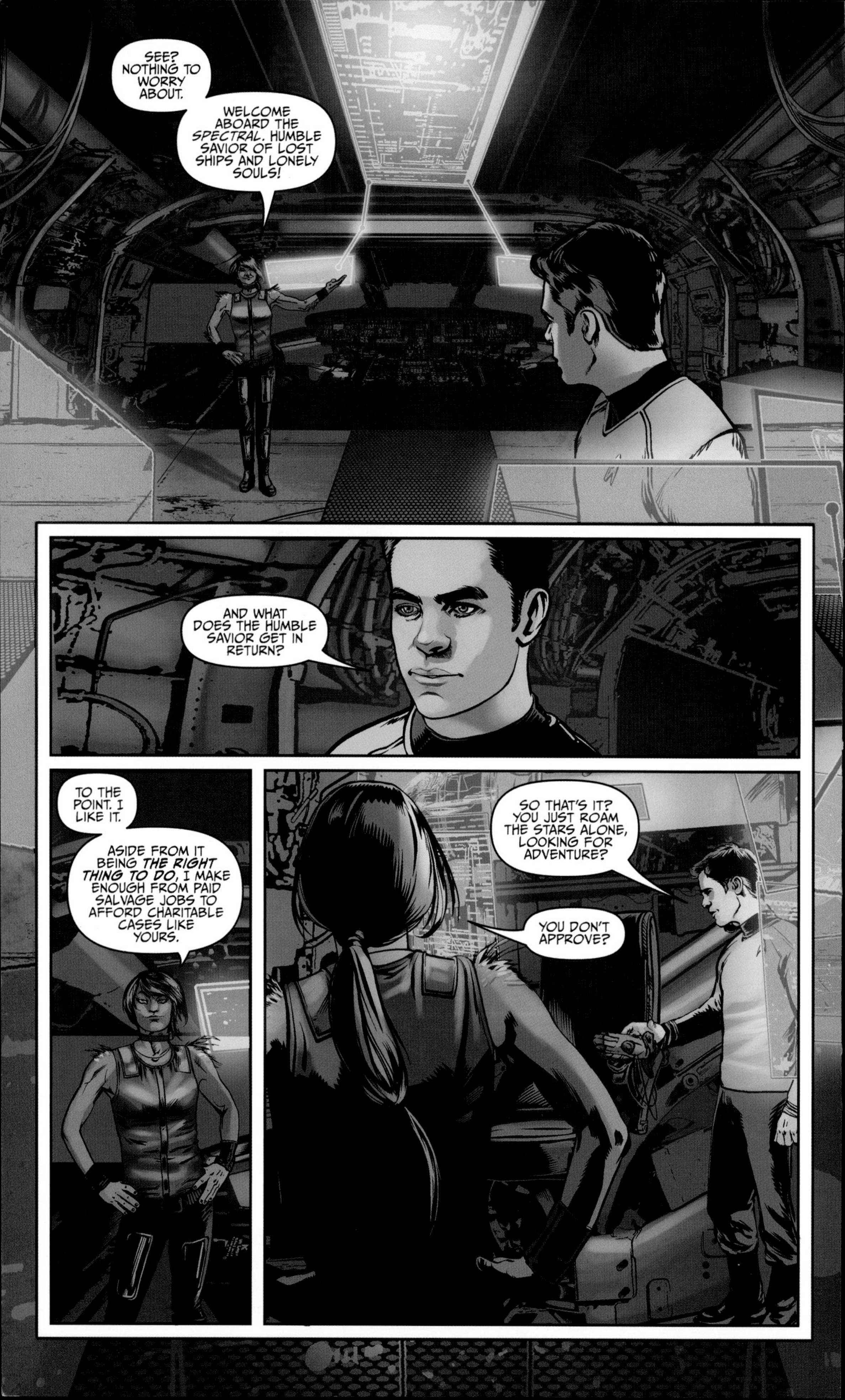
SEE? NOTHING TO WORRY ABOUT.
WELCOME ABOARD THE *SPECTRAL*. HUMBLE SAVIOR OF LOST SHIPS AND LONELY SOULS!
AND WHAT DOES THE HUMBLE SAVIOR GET IN RETURN?
TO THE POINT. I LIKE IT.
ASIDE FROM IT BEING ***THE RIGHT THING TO DO***, I MAKE ENOUGH FROM PAID SALVAGE JOBS TO AFFORD CHARITABLE CASES LIKE YOURS.
SO THAT'S IT? YOU JUST ROAM THE STARS ALONE, LOOKING FOR ADVENTURE?
YOU DON'T APPROVE?

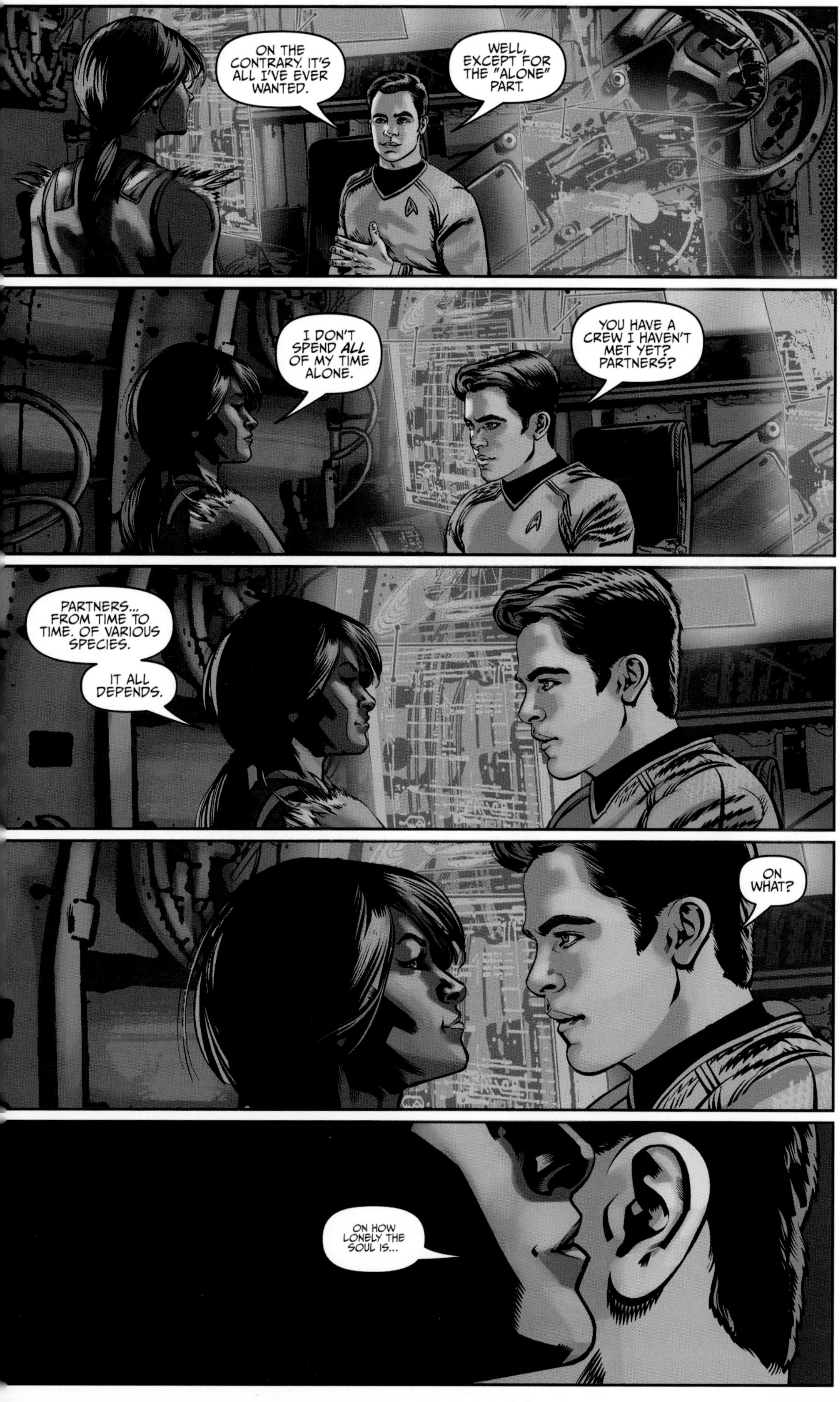
ON THE CONTRARY. IT'S ALL I'VE EVER WANTED.
WELL, EXCEPT FOR THE "ALONE" PART.
I DON'T SPEND *ALL* OF MY TIME ALONE.
YOU HAVE A CREW I HAVEN'T MET YET? PARTNERS?
PARTNERS... FROM TIME TO TIME. OF VARIOUS SPECIES.
IT ALL DEPENDS.
ON WHAT?
ON HOW LONELY THE SOUL IS...

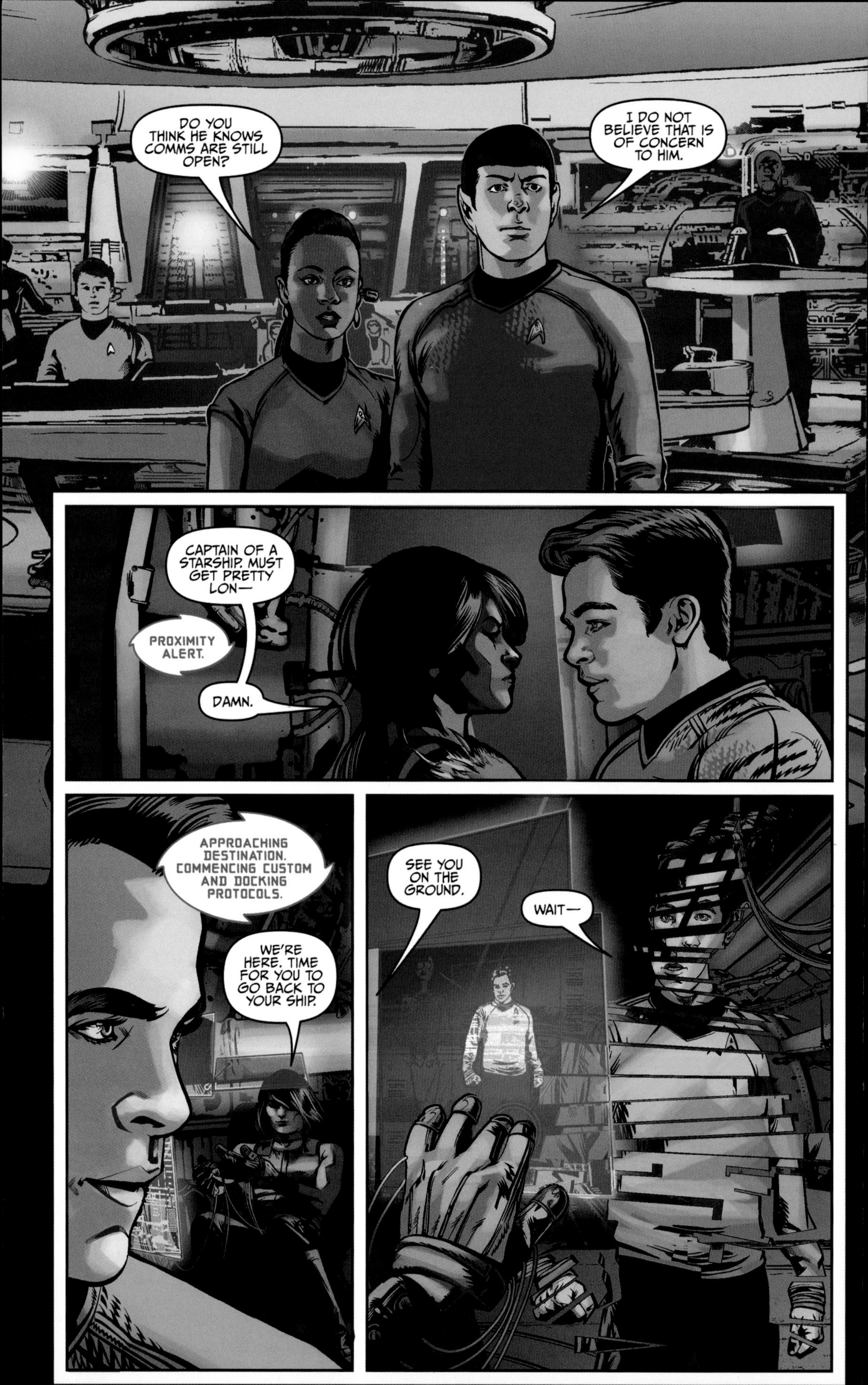
DO YOU THINK HE KNOWS COMMS ARE STILL OPEN?
I DO NOT BELIEVE THAT IS OF CONCERN TO HIM.
CAPTAIN OF A STARSHIP. MUST GET PRETTY LON—
PROXIMITY ALERT.
DAMN.
APPROACHING DESTINATION. COMMENCING CUSTOM AND DOCKING PROTOCOLS.
WE'RE HERE. TIME FOR YOU TO GO BACK TO YOUR SHIP.
SEE YOU ON THE GROUND.
WAIT—

FASCINATING.

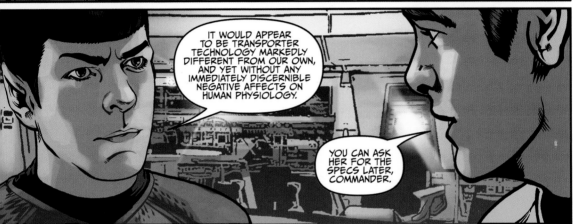

IT WOULD APPEAR TO BE TRANSPORTER TECHNOLOGY MARKEDLY DIFFERENT FROM OUR OWN, AND YET WITHOUT ANY IMMEDIATELY DISCERNIBLE NEGATIVE AFFECTS ON HUMAN PHYSIOLOGY.

YOU CAN ASK HER FOR THE SPECS LATER, COMMANDER.

MR. SULU, REPORT!

WE'RE COMING OUT OF WARP NOW, CAPTAIN.

WE ONLY CARE ABOUT ONE ASTEROID.

THE *BIG* ONE.

KEPTIN! WE ARE APPROACHING WHAT LOOKS LIKE AN *ASTEROID FIELD!*

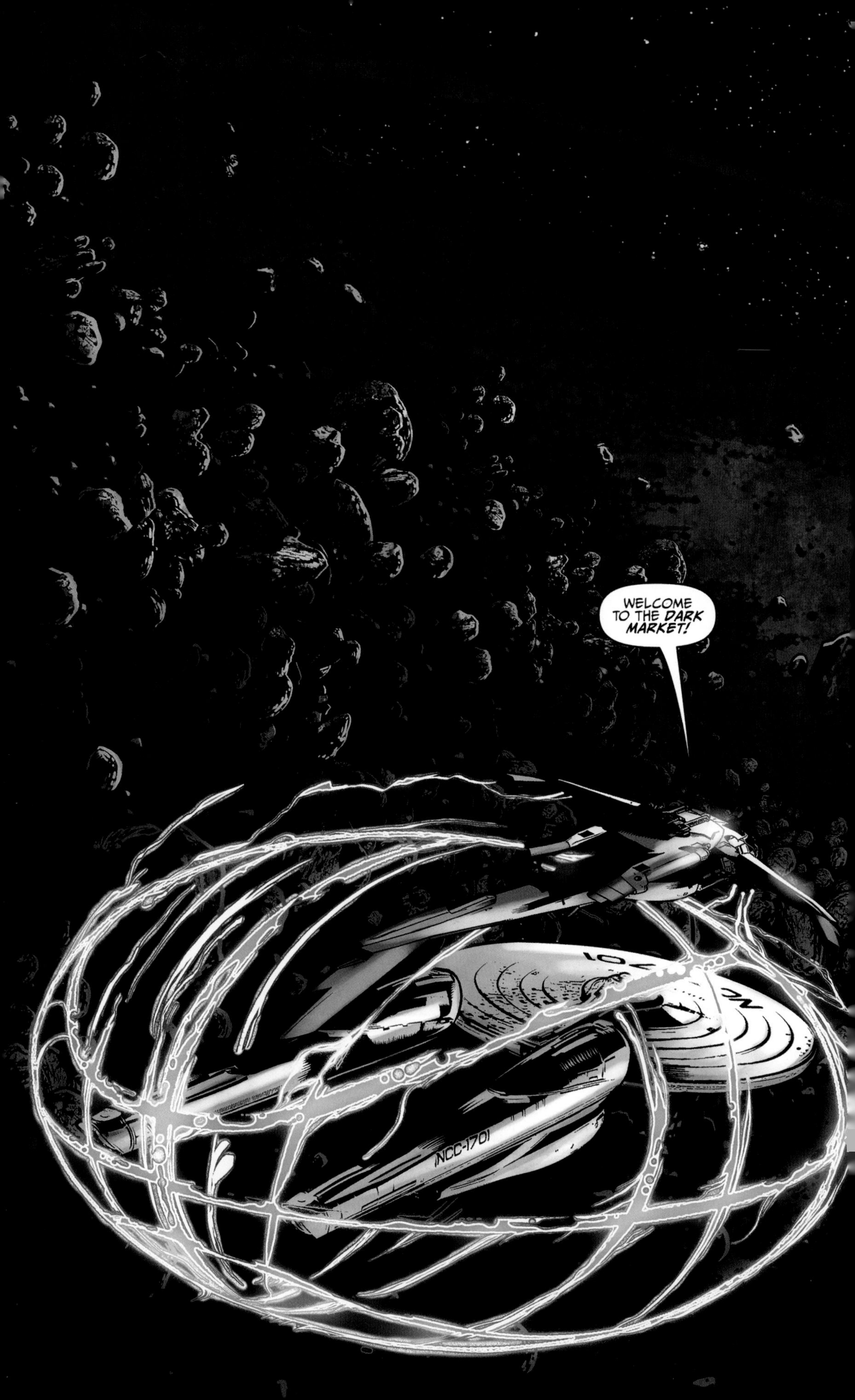
WELCOME TO THE DARK MARKET!
NCC-1701

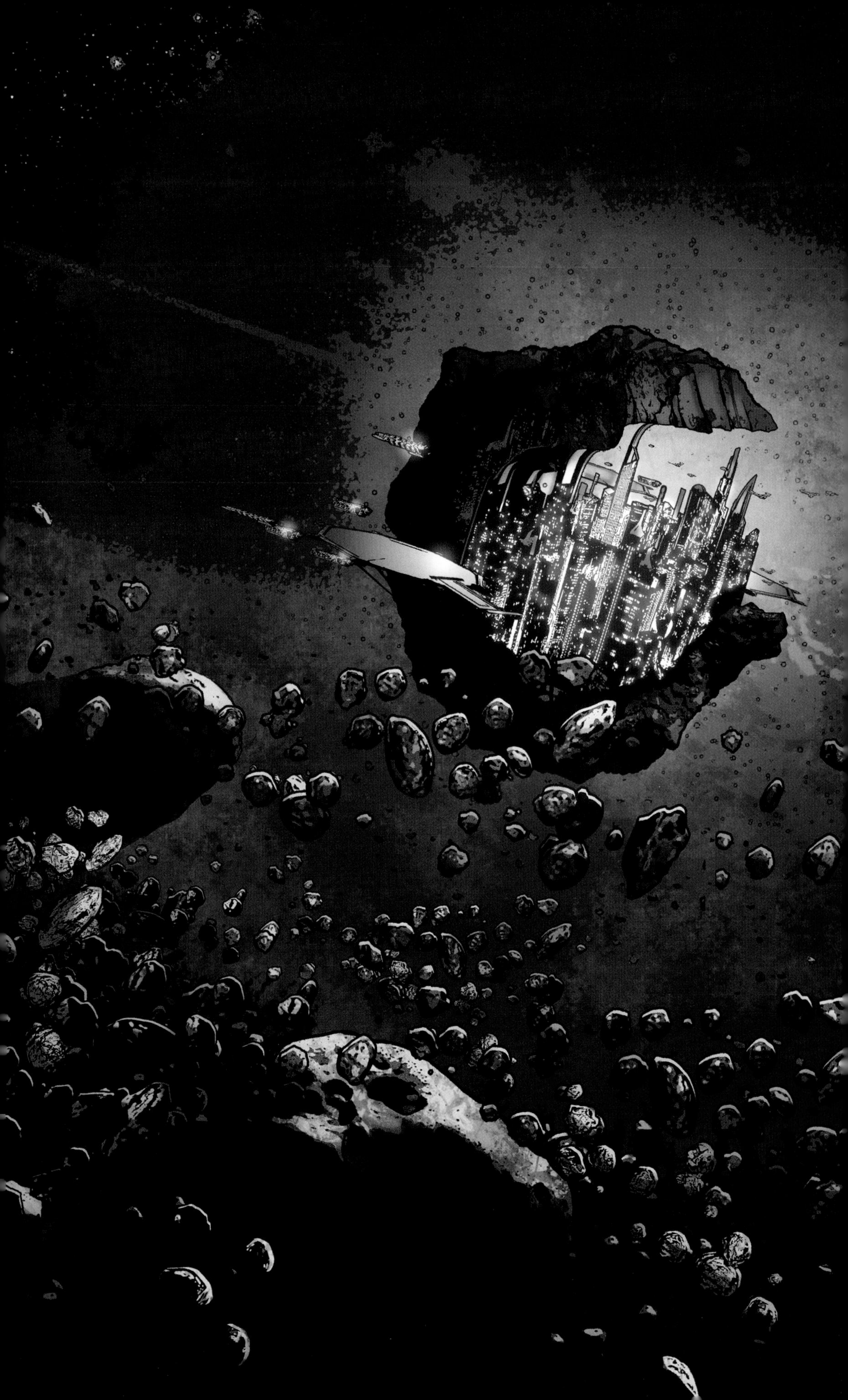

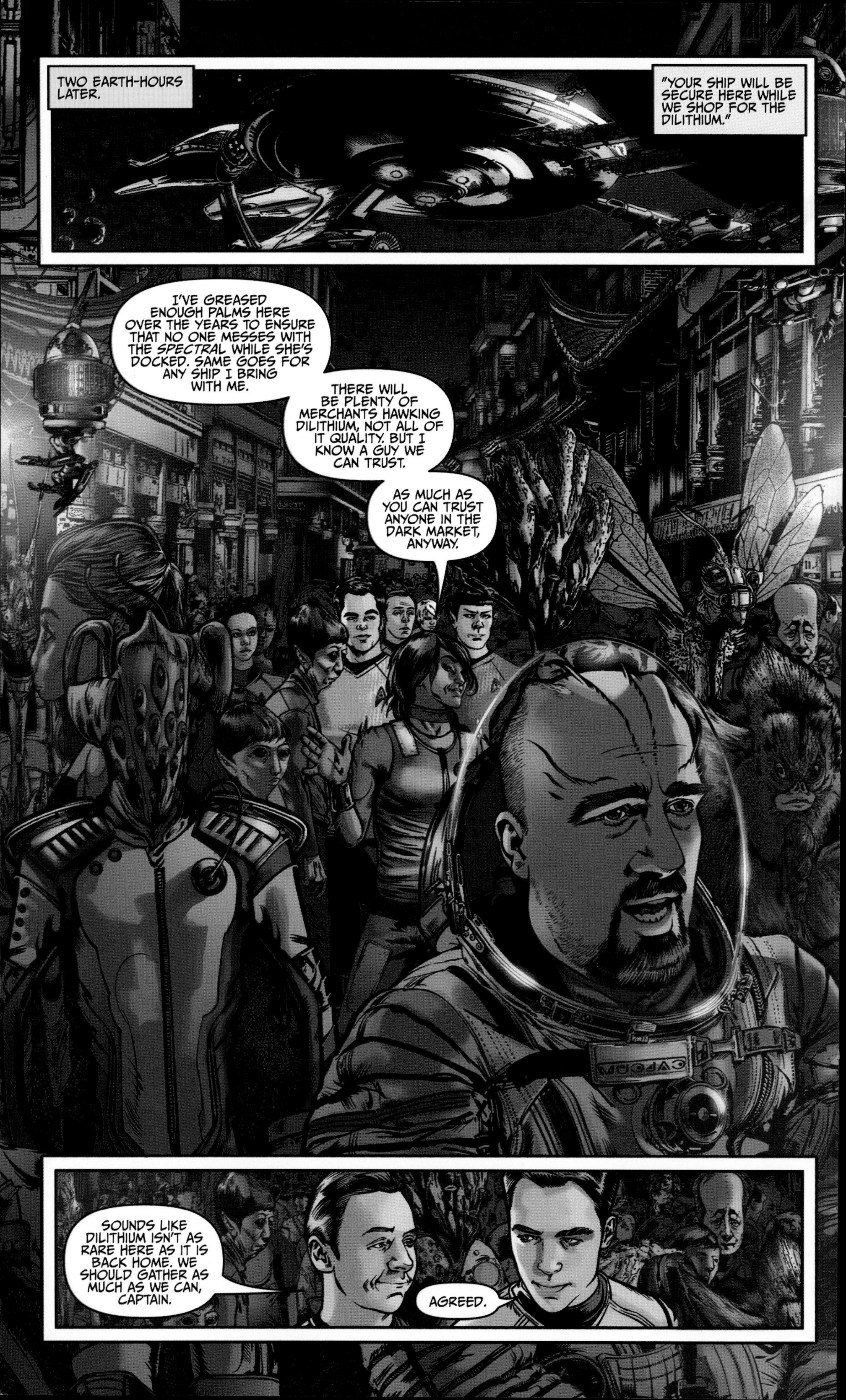

TWO EARTH-HOURS LATER.
"YOUR SHIP WILL BE SECURE HERE WHILE WE SHOP FOR THE DILITHIUM."
I'VE GREASED ENOUGH PALMS HERE OVER THE YEARS TO ENSURE THAT NO ONE MESSES WITH THE *SPECTRAL* WHILE SHE'S DOCKED. SAME GOES FOR ANY SHIP I BRING WITH ME.
THERE WILL BE PLENTY OF MERCHANTS HAWKING DILITHIUM, NOT ALL OF IT QUALITY. BUT I KNOW A GUY WE CAN TRUST.
AS MUCH AS YOU CAN TRUST ANYONE IN THE DARK MARKET, ANYWAY.
SOUNDS LIKE DILITHIUM ISN'T AS RARE HERE AS IT IS BACK HOME. WE SHOULD GATHER AS MUCH AS WE CAN, CAPTAIN.
AGREED.

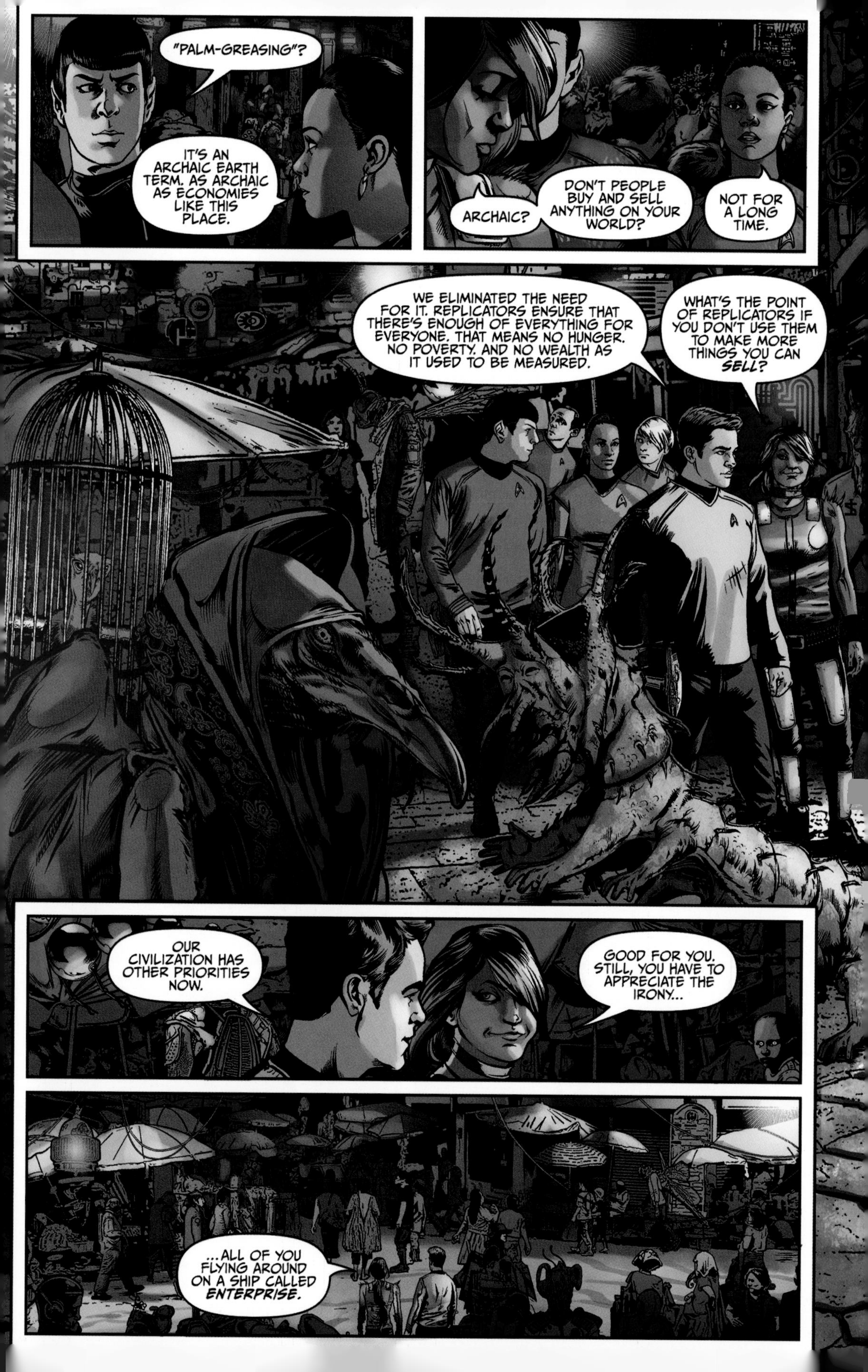
"PALM-GREASING"?
IT'S AN ARCHAIC EARTH TERM. AS ARCHAIC AS ECONOMIES LIKE THIS PLACE.
ARCHAIC?
DON'T PEOPLE BUY AND SELL ANYTHING ON YOUR WORLD?
NOT FOR A LONG TIME.
WE ELIMINATED THE NEED FOR IT. REPLICATORS ENSURE THAT THERE'S ENOUGH OF EVERYTHING FOR EVERYONE. THAT MEANS NO HUNGER. NO POVERTY. AND NO WEALTH AS IT USED TO BE MEASURED.
WHAT'S THE POINT OF REPLICATORS IF YOU DON'T USE THEM TO MAKE MORE THINGS YOU CAN *SELL*?
OUR CIVILIZATION HAS OTHER PRIORITIES NOW.
GOOD FOR YOU. STILL, YOU HAVE TO APPRECIATE THE IRONY...
...ALL OF YOU FLYING AROUND ON A SHIP CALLED *ENTERPRISE*.

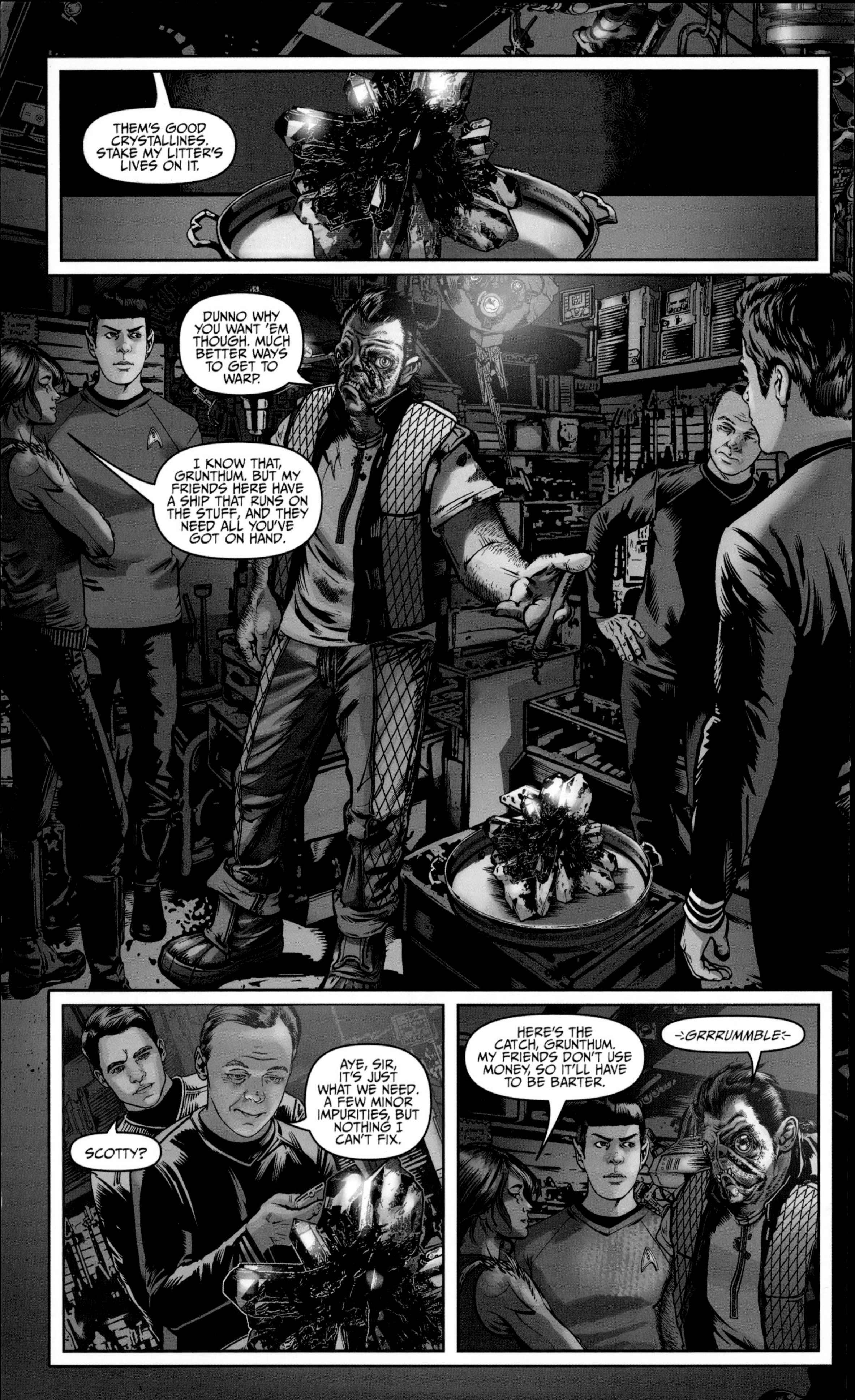
THEM'S GOOD CRYSTALLINES. STAKE MY LITTER'S LIVES ON IT.
DUNNO WHY YOU WANT 'EM THOUGH. MUCH BETTER WAYS TO GET TO WARP.
I KNOW THAT, GRUNTHUM. BUT MY FRIENDS HERE HAVE A SHIP THAT RUNS ON THE STUFF, AND THEY NEED ALL YOU'VE GOT ON HAND.
SCOTTY?
AYE, SIR, IT'S JUST WHAT WE NEED. A FEW MINOR IMPURITIES, BUT NOTHING I CAN'T FIX.
HERE'S THE CATCH, GRUNTHUM. MY FRIENDS DON'T USE MONEY, SO IT'LL HAVE TO BE BARTER.
-GRRRUMMBLE-

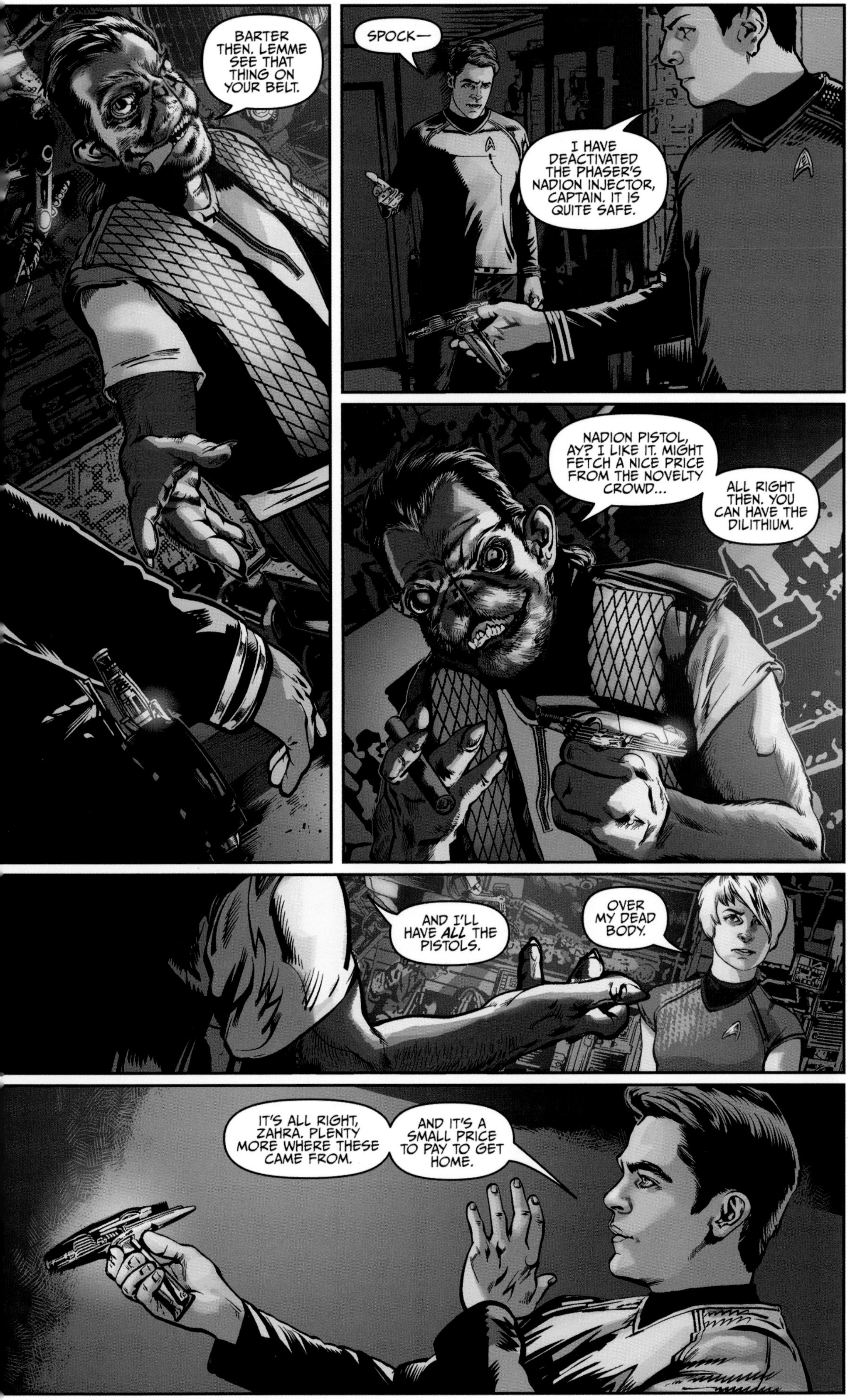
BARTER THEN. LEMME SEE THAT THING ON YOUR BELT.
SPOCK—
I HAVE DEACTIVATED THE PHASER'S NADION INJECTOR, CAPTAIN. IT IS QUITE SAFE.
NADION PISTOL, AY? I LIKE IT. MIGHT FETCH A NICE PRICE FROM THE NOVELTY CROWD...
ALL RIGHT THEN. YOU CAN HAVE THE DILITHIUM.
AND I'LL HAVE *ALL* THE PISTOLS.
OVER MY DEAD BODY.
IT'S ALL RIGHT, ZAHRA. PLENTY MORE WHERE THESE CAME FROM.
AND IT'S A SMALL PRICE TO PAY TO GET HOME.

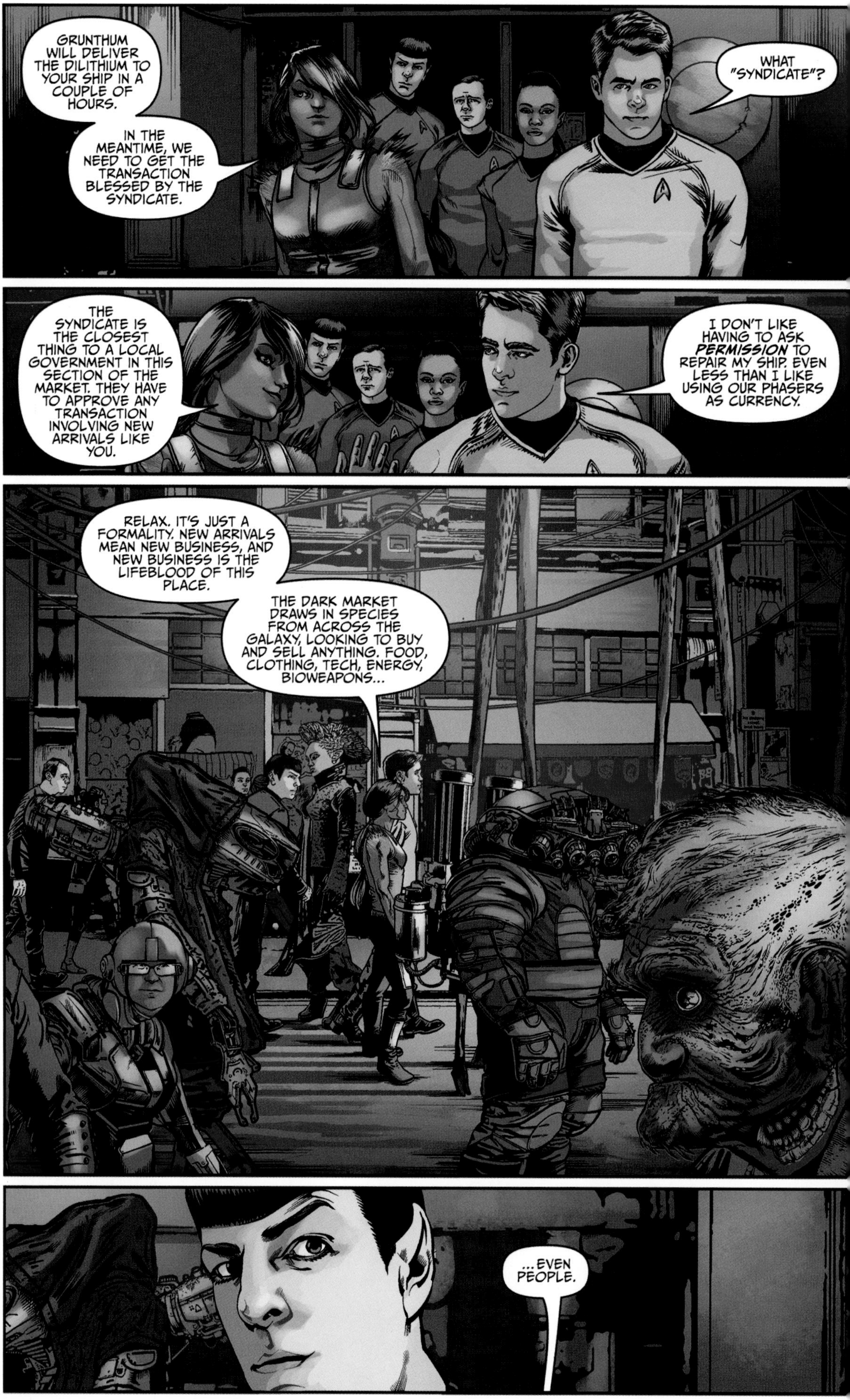
GRUNTHUM WILL DELIVER THE DILITHIUM TO YOUR SHIP IN A COUPLE OF HOURS.
IN THE MEANTIME, WE NEED TO GET THE TRANSACTION BLESSED BY THE SYNDICATE.
WHAT "SYNDICATE"?
THE SYNDICATE IS THE CLOSEST THING TO A LOCAL GOVERNMENT IN THIS SECTION OF THE MARKET. THEY HAVE TO APPROVE ANY TRANSACTION INVOLVING NEW ARRIVALS LIKE YOU.
I DON'T LIKE HAVING TO ASK *PERMISSION* TO REPAIR MY SHIP. EVEN LESS THAN I LIKE USING OUR PHASERS AS CURRENCY.
RELAX. IT'S JUST A FORMALITY. NEW ARRIVALS MEAN NEW BUSINESS, AND NEW BUSINESS IS THE LIFEBLOOD OF THIS PLACE.
THE DARK MARKET DRAWS IN SPECIES FROM ACROSS THE GALAXY, LOOKING TO BUY AND SELL ANYTHING. FOOD, CLOTHING, TECH, ENERGY, BIOWEAPONS...
...EVEN PEOPLE.

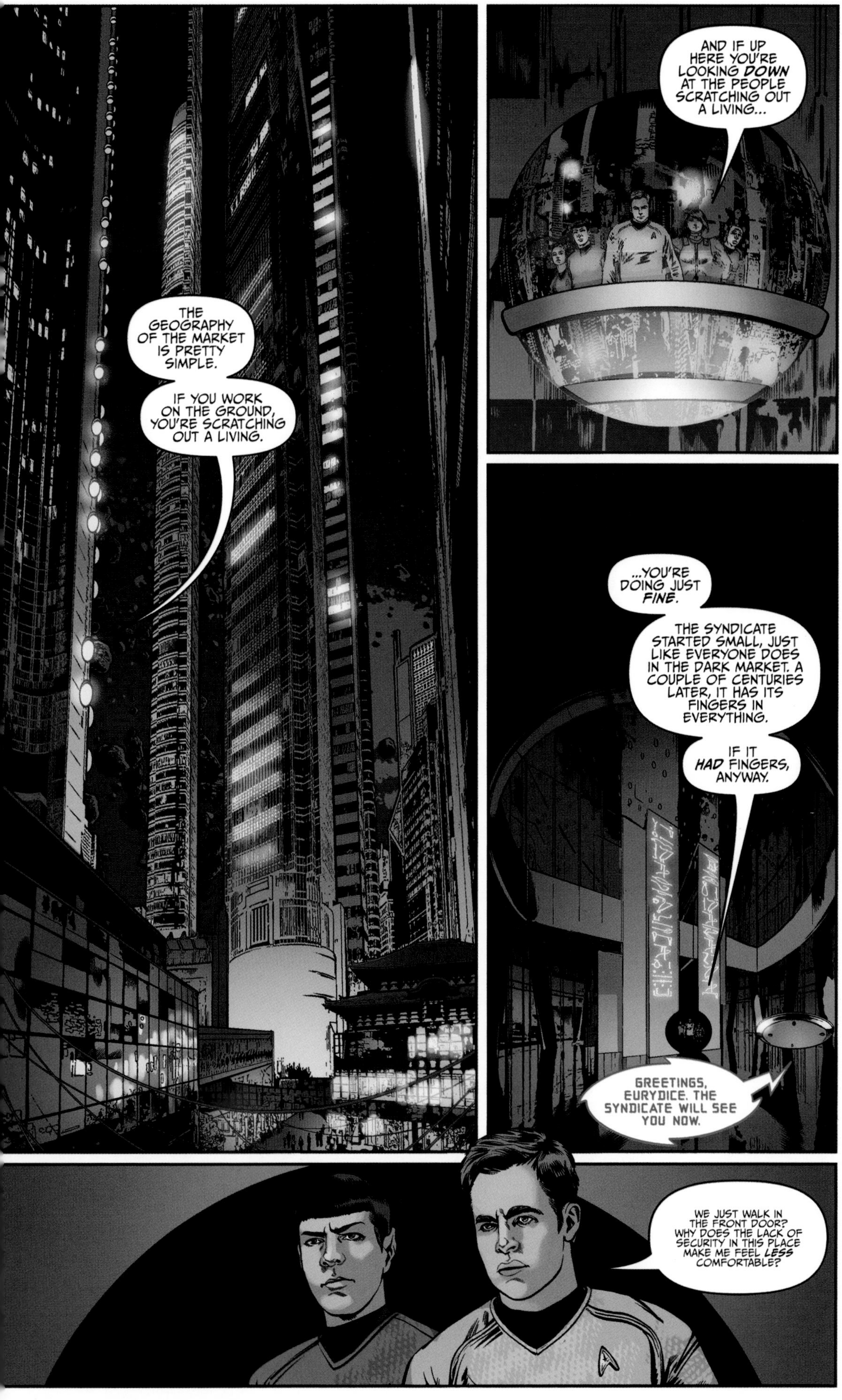
THE GEOGRAPHY OF THE MARKET IS PRETTY SIMPLE.
IF YOU WORK ON THE GROUND, YOU'RE SCRATCHING OUT A LIVING.
AND IF UP HERE YOU'RE LOOKING *DOWN* AT THE PEOPLE SCRATCHING OUT A LIVING...
...YOU'RE DOING JUST *FINE*.
THE SYNDICATE STARTED SMALL, JUST LIKE EVERYONE DOES IN THE DARK MARKET. A COUPLE OF CENTURIES LATER, IT HAS ITS FINGERS IN EVERYTHING.
IF IT *HAD* FINGERS, ANYWAY.
GREETINGS, EURYDICE. THE SYNDICATE WILL SEE YOU NOW.
WE JUST WALK IN THE FRONT DOOR? WHY DOES THE LACK OF SECURITY IN THIS PLACE MAKE ME FEEL *LESS* COMFORTABLE?

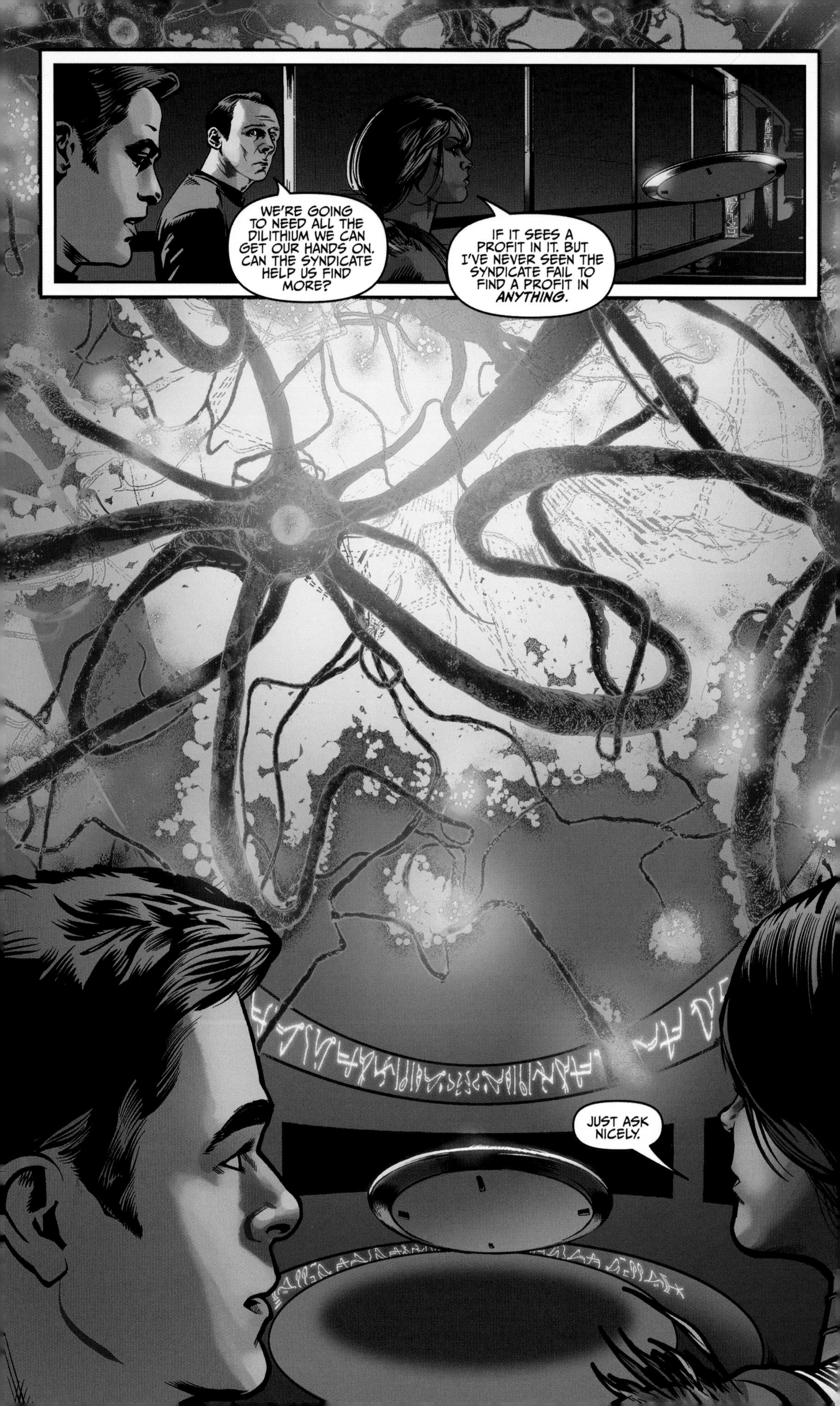
WE'RE GOING TO NEED ALL THE DILITHIUM WE CAN GET OUR HANDS ON. CAN THE SYNDICATE HELP US FIND MORE?
IF IT SEES A PROFIT IN IT. BUT I'VE NEVER SEEN THE SYNDICATE FAIL TO FIND A PROFIT IN *ANYTHING*.
JUST ASK NICELY.

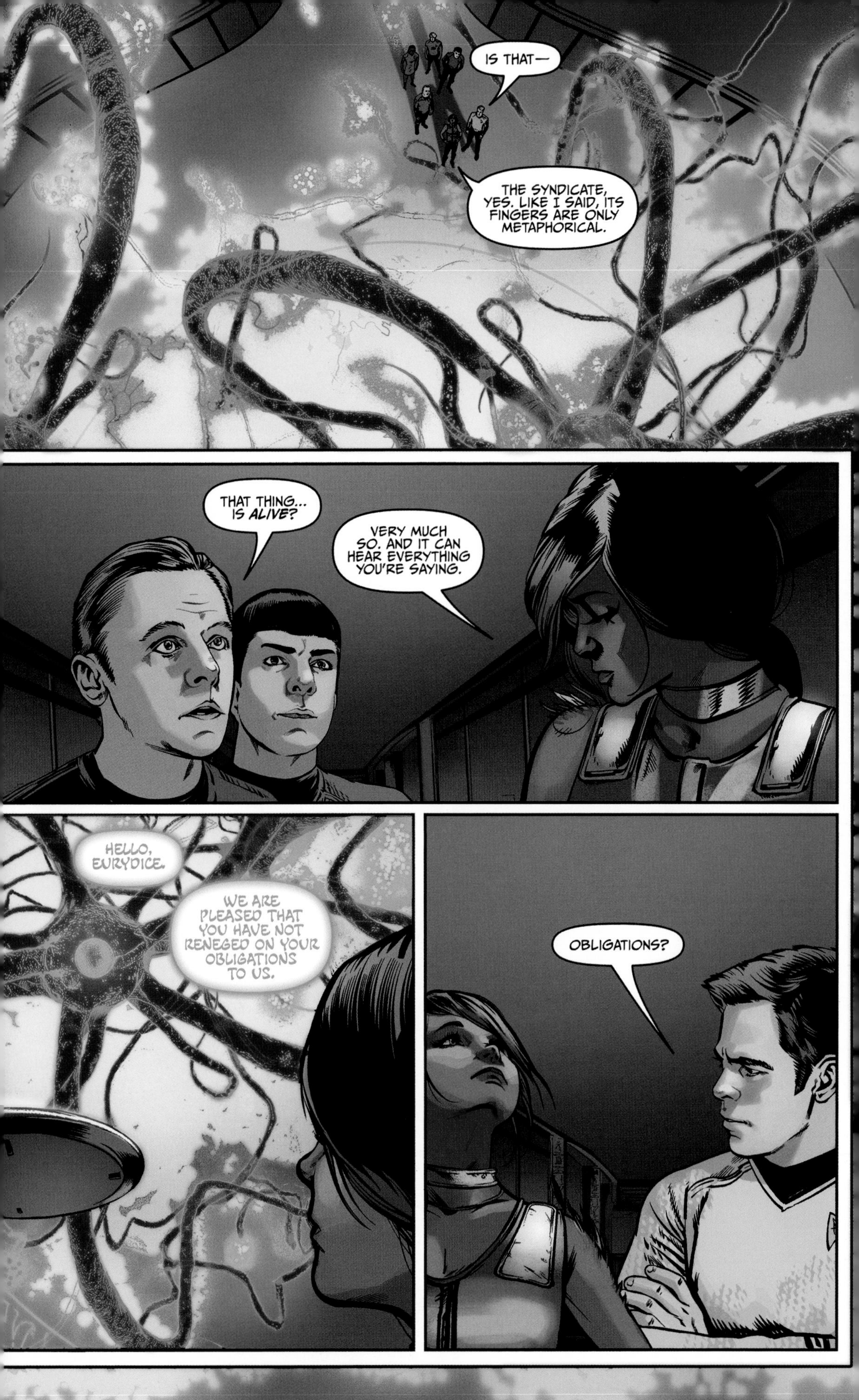
IS THAT—
THE SYNDICATE, YES. LIKE I SAID, ITS FINGERS ARE ONLY METAPHORICAL.
THAT THING... IS *ALIVE*?
VERY MUCH SO. AND IT CAN HEAR EVERYTHING YOU'RE SAYING.
HELLO, EURYDICE.
WE ARE PLEASED THAT YOU HAVE NOT RENEGED ON YOUR OBLIGATIONS TO US.
OBLIGATIONS?

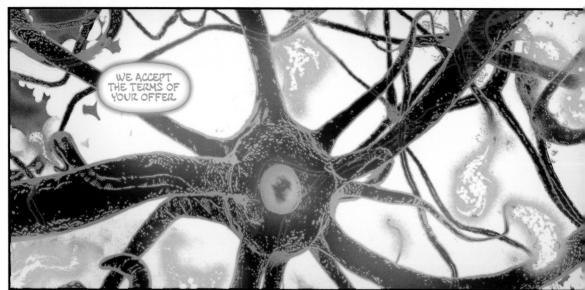

WE ACCEPT THE TERMS OF YOUR OFFER.

GOOD. WE'D LIKE TO CONTINUE COLLECTING AS MUCH DILITHIUM AS WE CAN.

WE ARE NOT SPEAKING OF THE DILITHIUM TRANSACTION.

IT IS BUT ONE OF BILLIONS WE HAVE OBSERVED IN THE MOST RECENT CYCLE.

WE ARE SPEAKING OF OUR AGREEMENT WITH EURYDICE.

I THOUGHT YOU SAID WE NEEDED THIS THING'S *APPROVAL.*

I NEEDED TO GET YOU UP HERE SOMEHOW. AND WITHOUT ANY WEAPONS ON YOU.

I'M SORRY, KIRK.

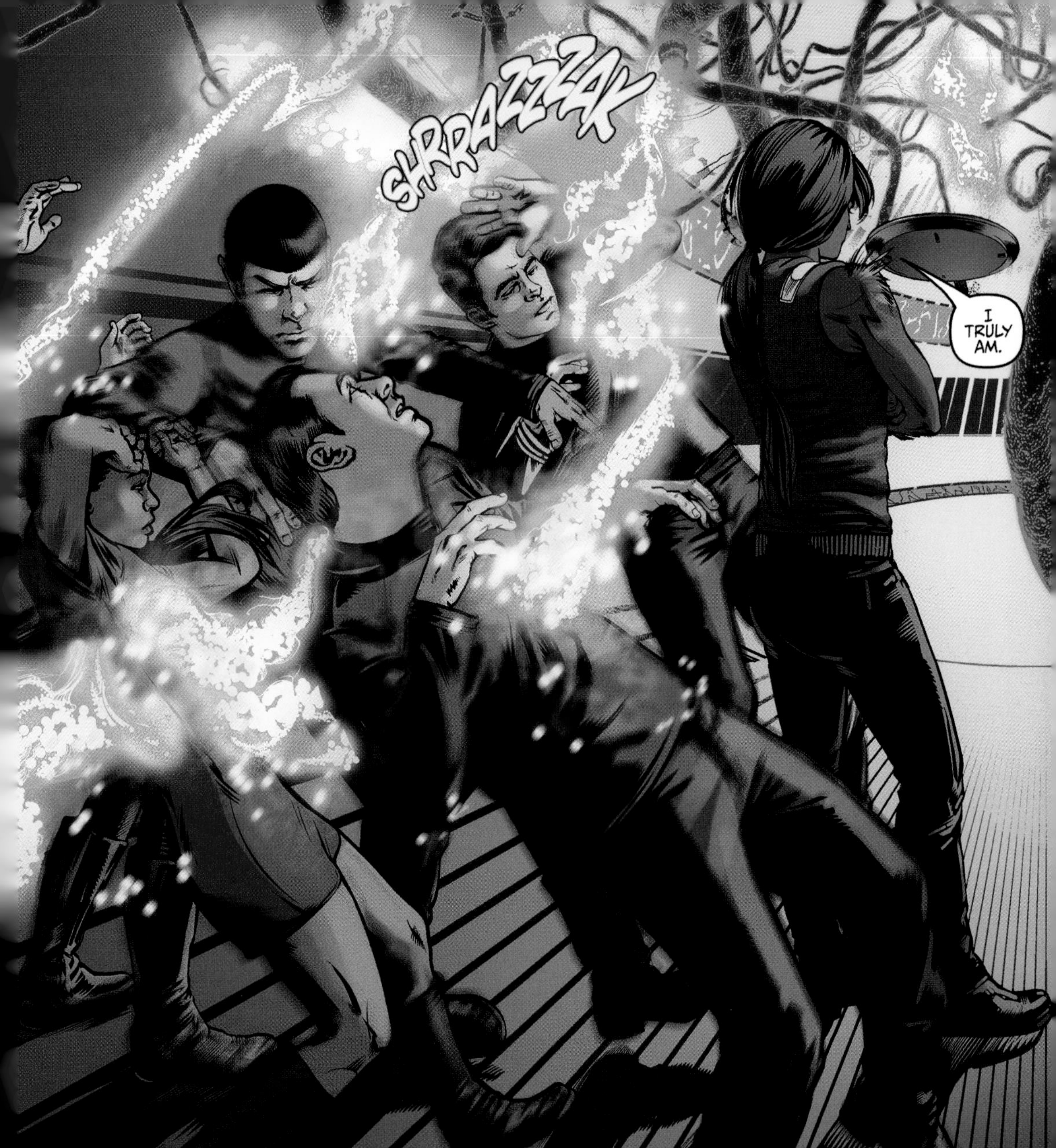
SHRRAZZZAK
I TRULY AM.

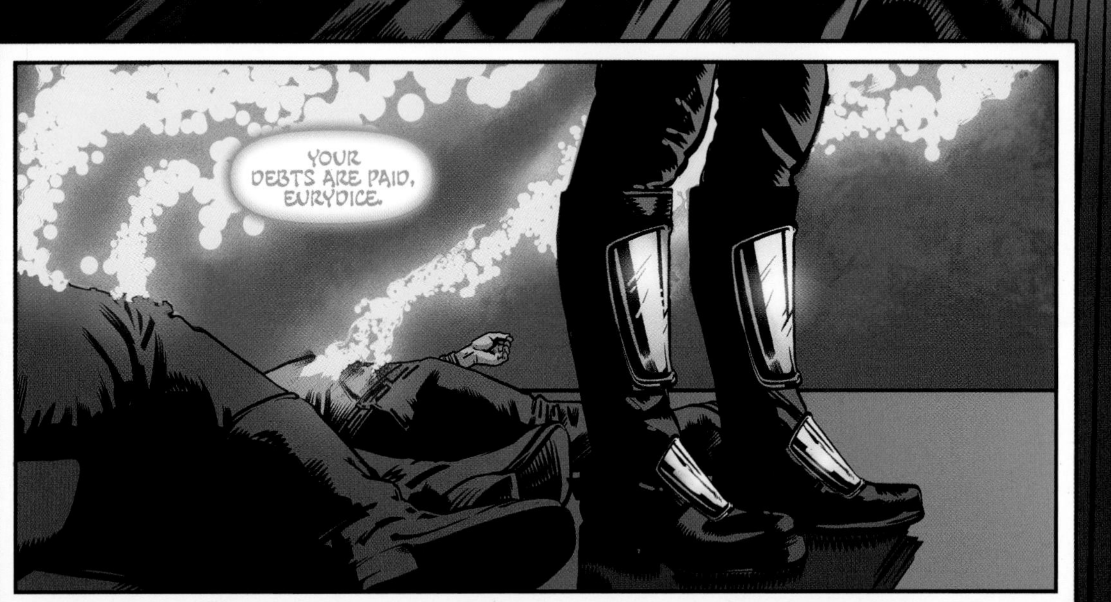
YOUR DEBTS ARE PAID, EURYDICE.

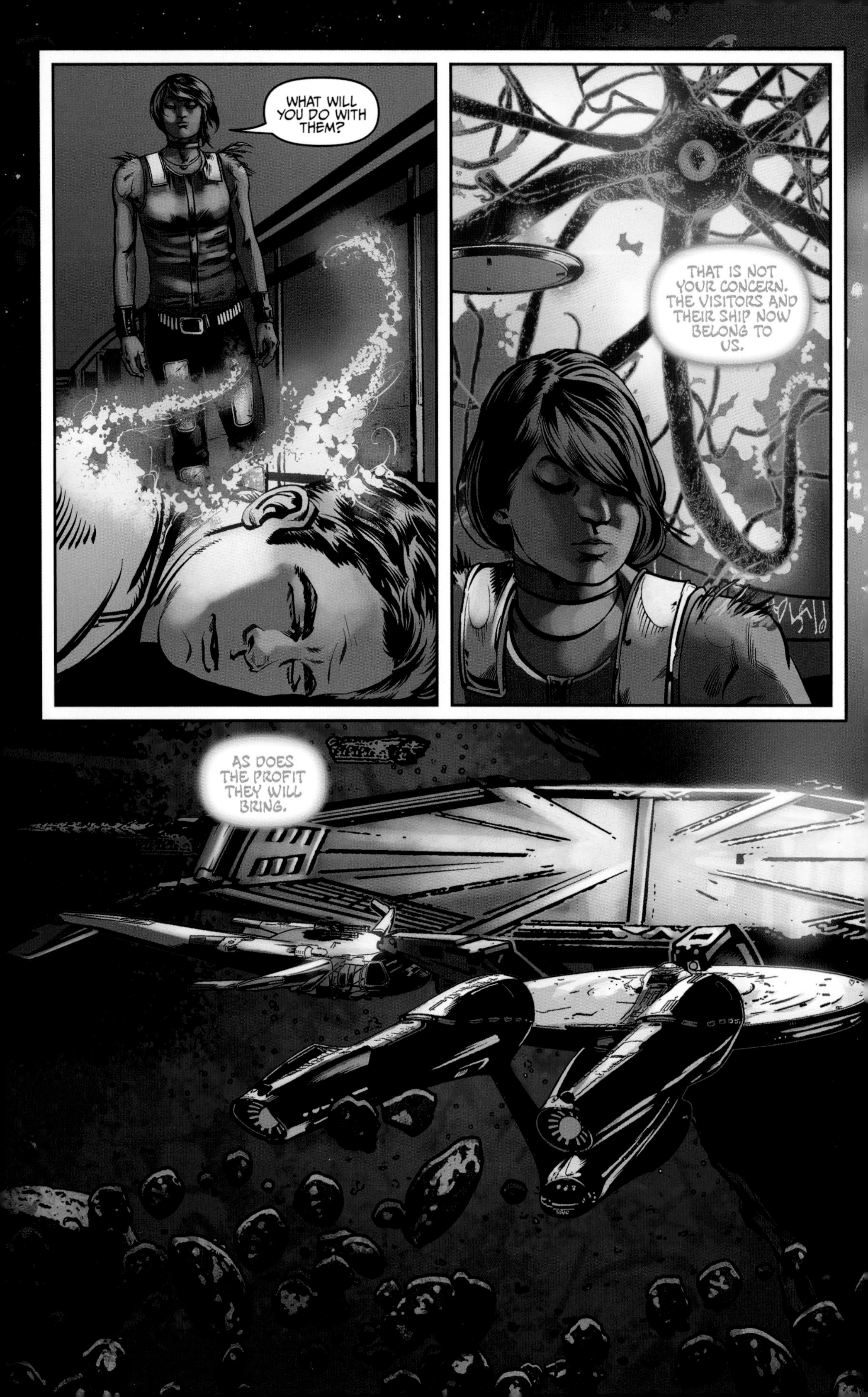
WHAT WILL YOU DO WITH THEM?
THAT IS NOT YOUR CONCERN. THE VISITORS AND THEIR SHIP NOW BELONG TO US.
AS DOES THE PROFIT THEY WILL BRING.

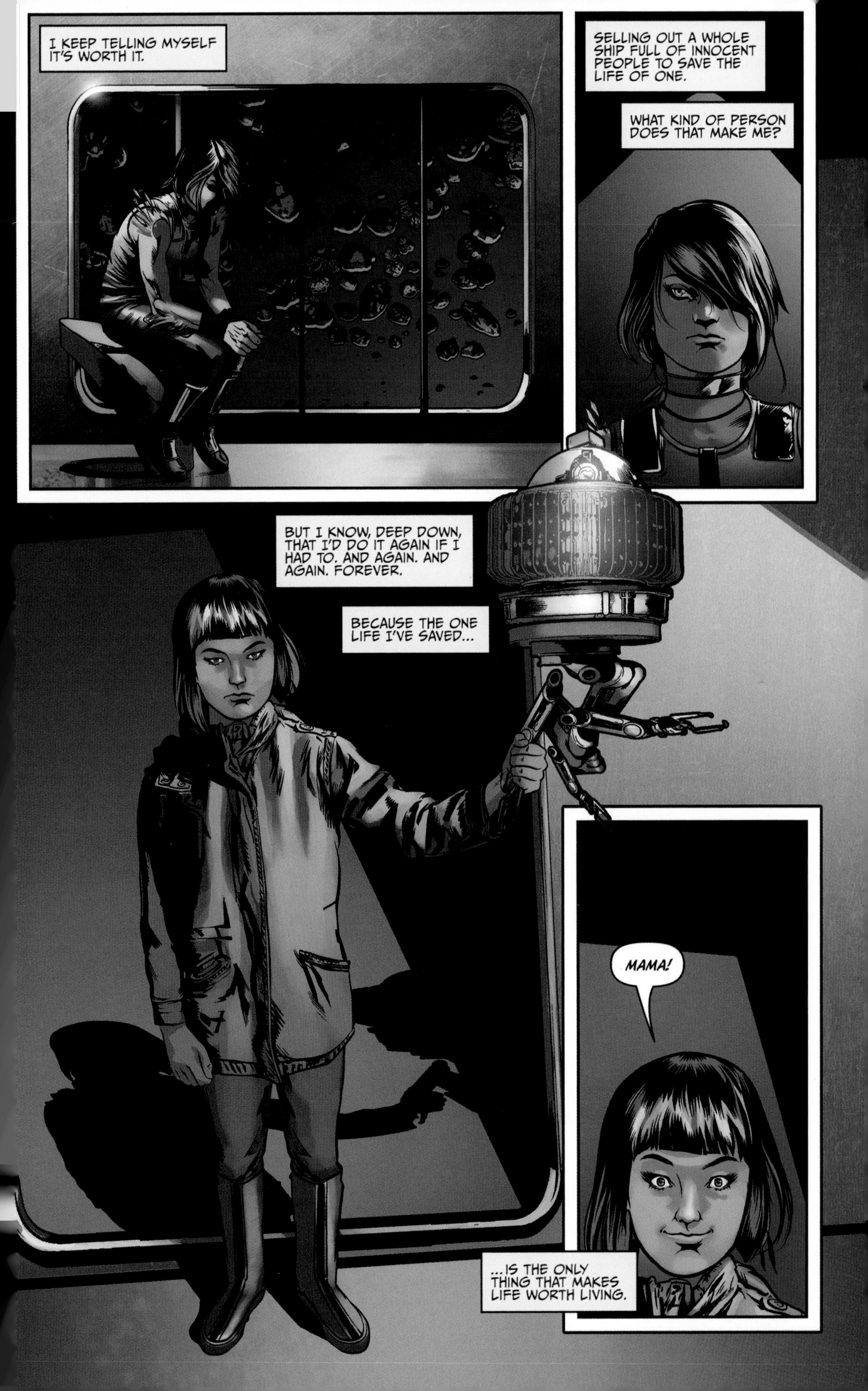
I KEEP TELLING MYSELF IT'S WORTH IT.
SELLING OUT A WHOLE SHIP FULL OF INNOCENT PEOPLE TO SAVE THE LIFE OF ONE.
WHAT KIND OF PERSON DOES THAT MAKE ME?
BUT I KNOW, DEEP DOWN, THAT I'D DO IT AGAIN IF I HAD TO. AND AGAIN. AND AGAIN. FOREVER.
BECAUSE THE ONE LIFE I'VE SAVED...
MAMA!
...IS THE ONLY THING THAT MAKES LIFE WORTH LIVING.

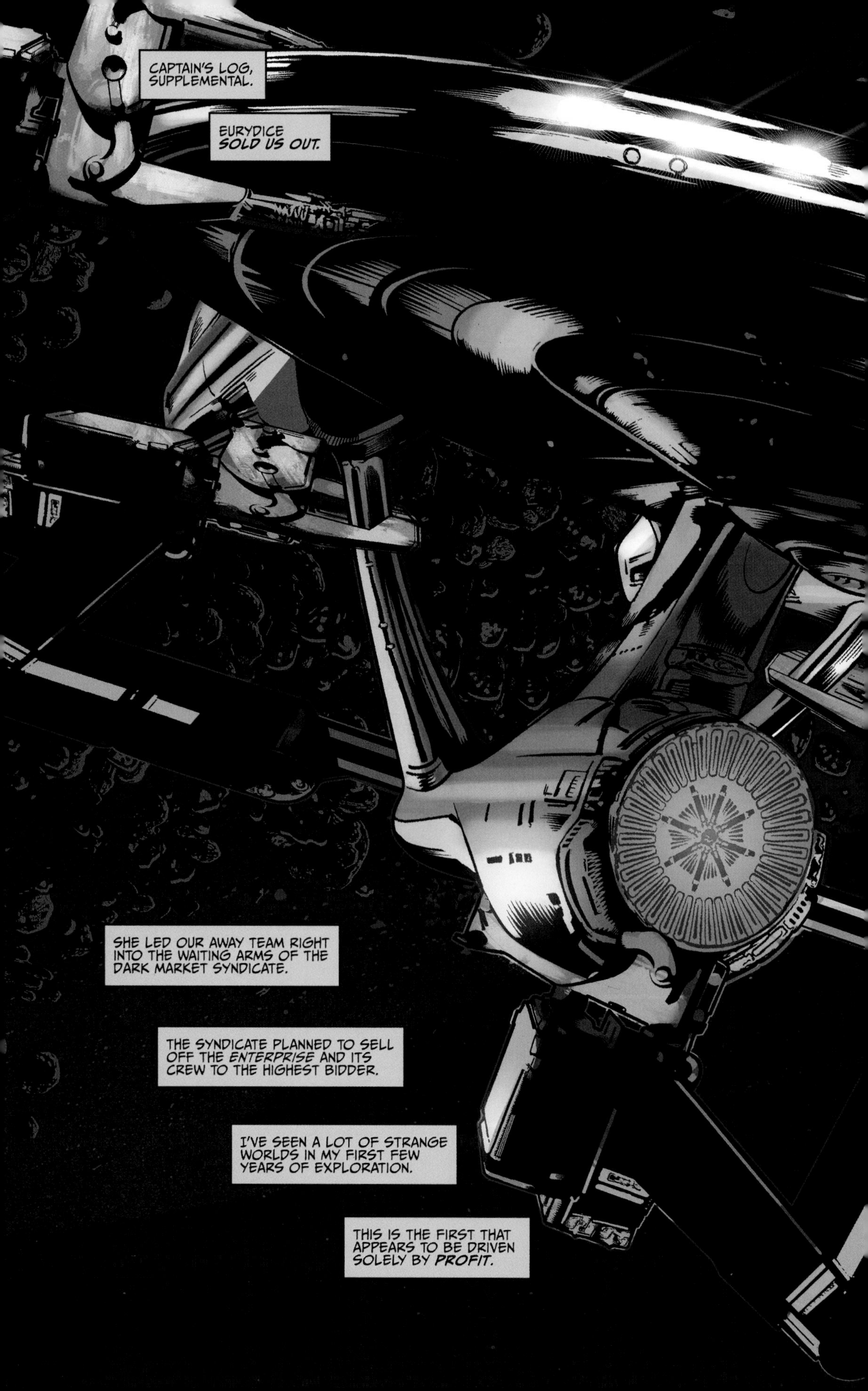
CAPTAIN'S LOG, SUPPLEMENTAL.
EURYDICE *SOLD US OUT.*
SHE LED OUR AWAY TEAM RIGHT INTO THE WAITING ARMS OF THE DARK MARKET SYNDICATE.
THE SYNDICATE PLANNED TO SELL OFF THE *ENTERPRISE* AND ITS CREW TO THE HIGHEST BIDDER.
I'VE SEEN A LOT OF STRANGE WORLDS IN MY FIRST FEW YEARS OF EXPLORATION.
THIS IS THE FIRST THAT APPEARS TO BE DRIVEN SOLELY BY *PROFIT.*

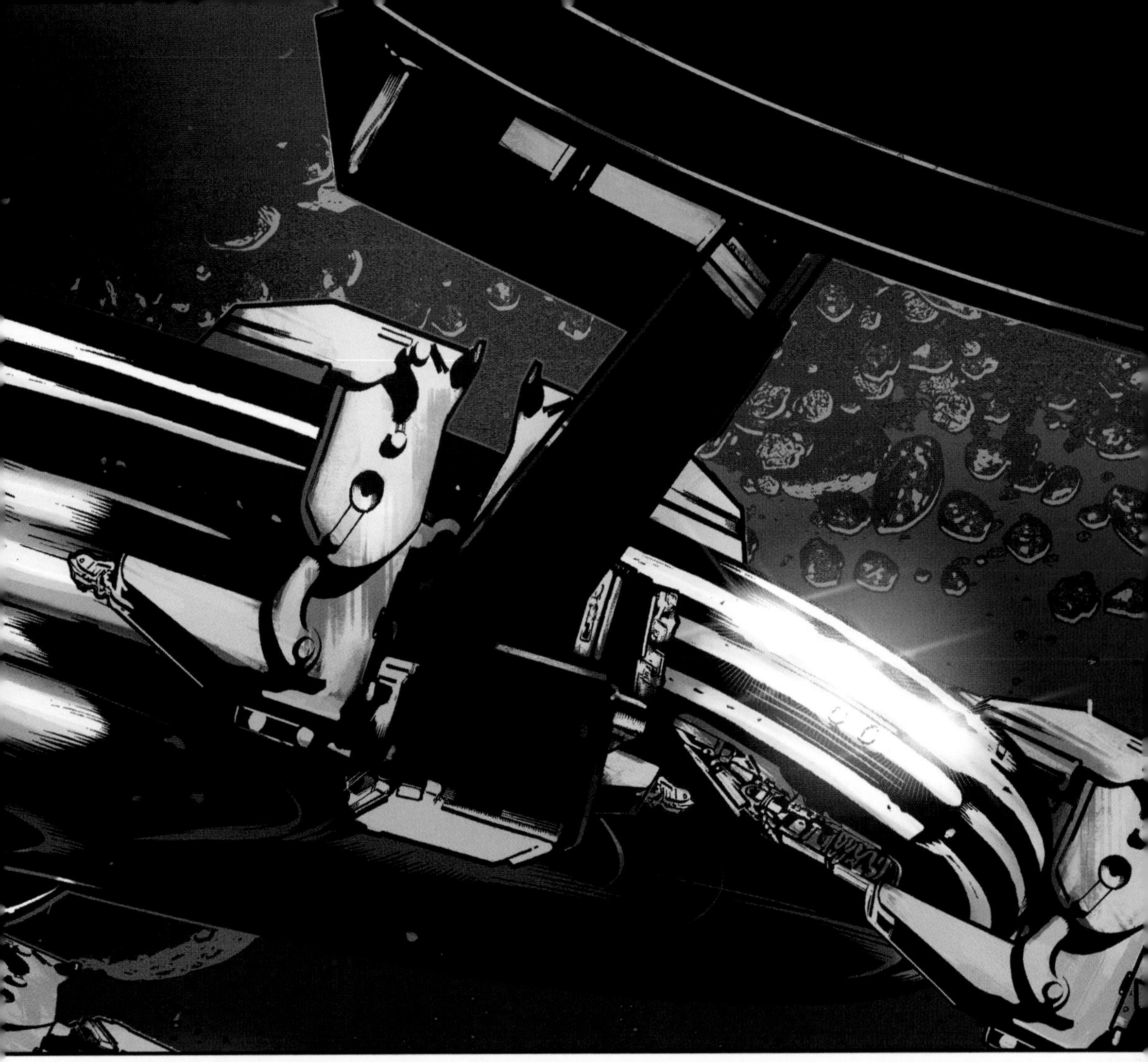

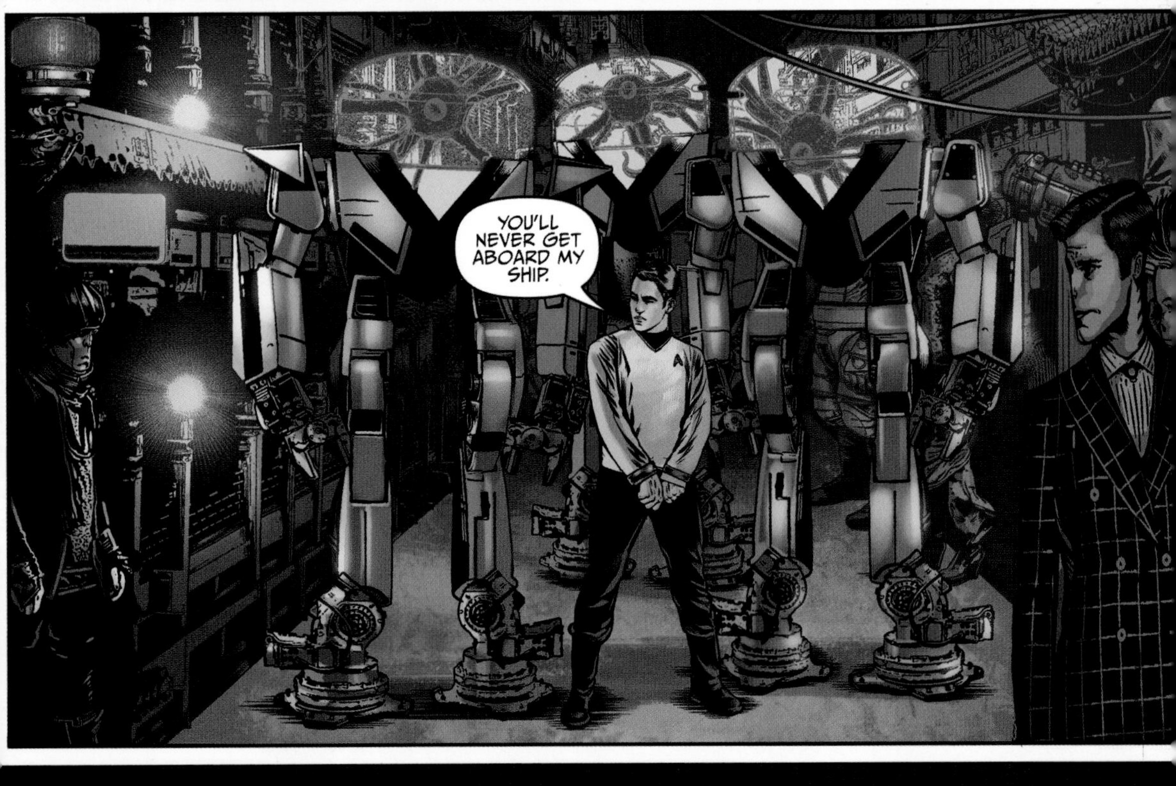
YOU'LL NEVER GET ABOARD MY SHIP.

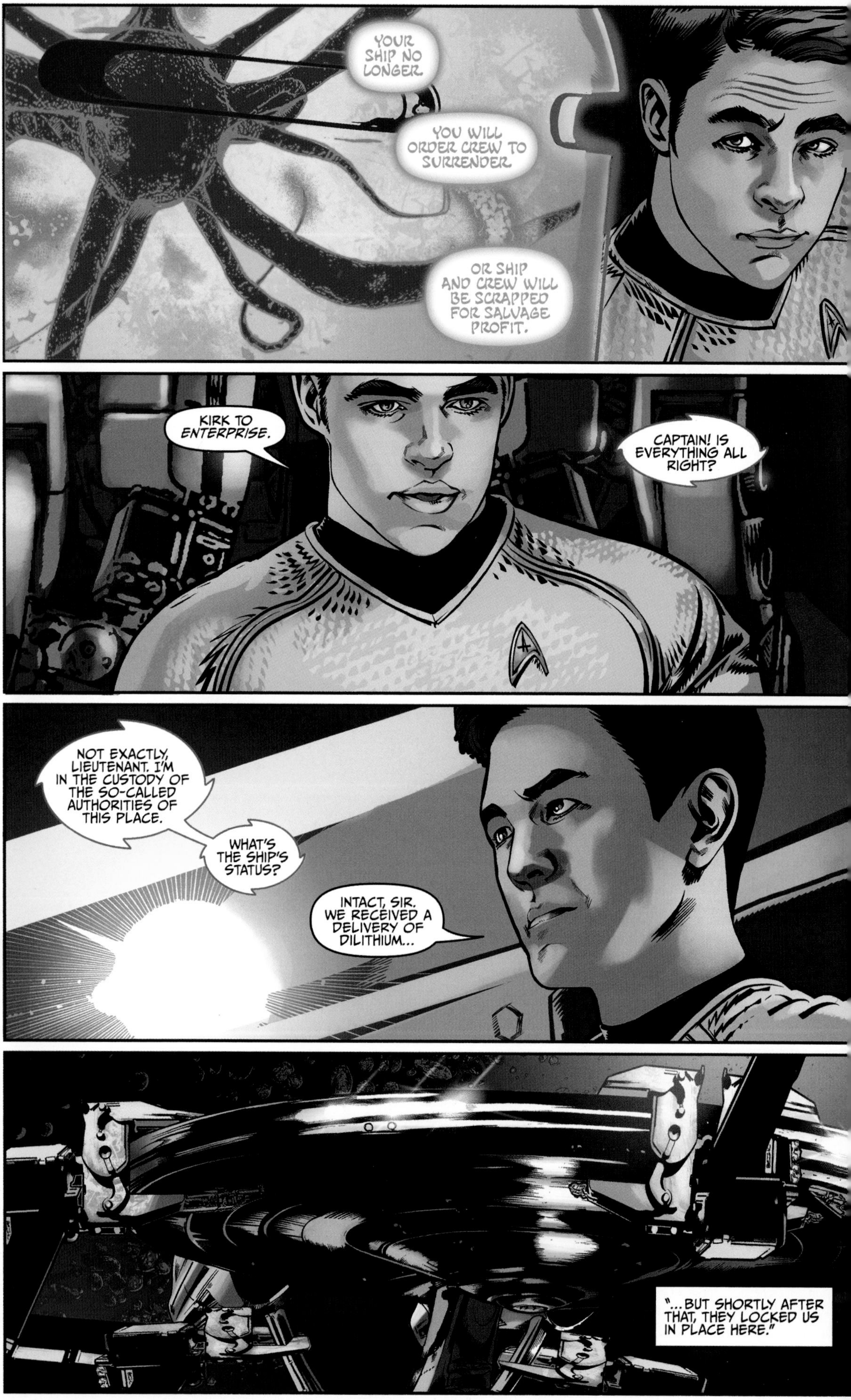
YOUR SHIP NO LONGER.
YOU WILL ORDER CREW TO SURRENDER
OR SHIP AND CREW WILL BE SCRAPPED FOR SALVAGE PROFIT.
KIRK TO ENTERPRISE.
CAPTAIN! IS EVERYTHING ALL RIGHT?
NOT EXACTLY, LIEUTENANT. I'M IN THE CUSTODY OF THE SO-CALLED AUTHORITIES OF THIS PLACE.
WHAT'S THE SHIP'S STATUS?
INTACT, SIR. WE RECEIVED A DELIVERY OF DILITHIUM...
"...BUT SHORTLY AFTER THAT, THEY LOCKED US IN PLACE HERE."

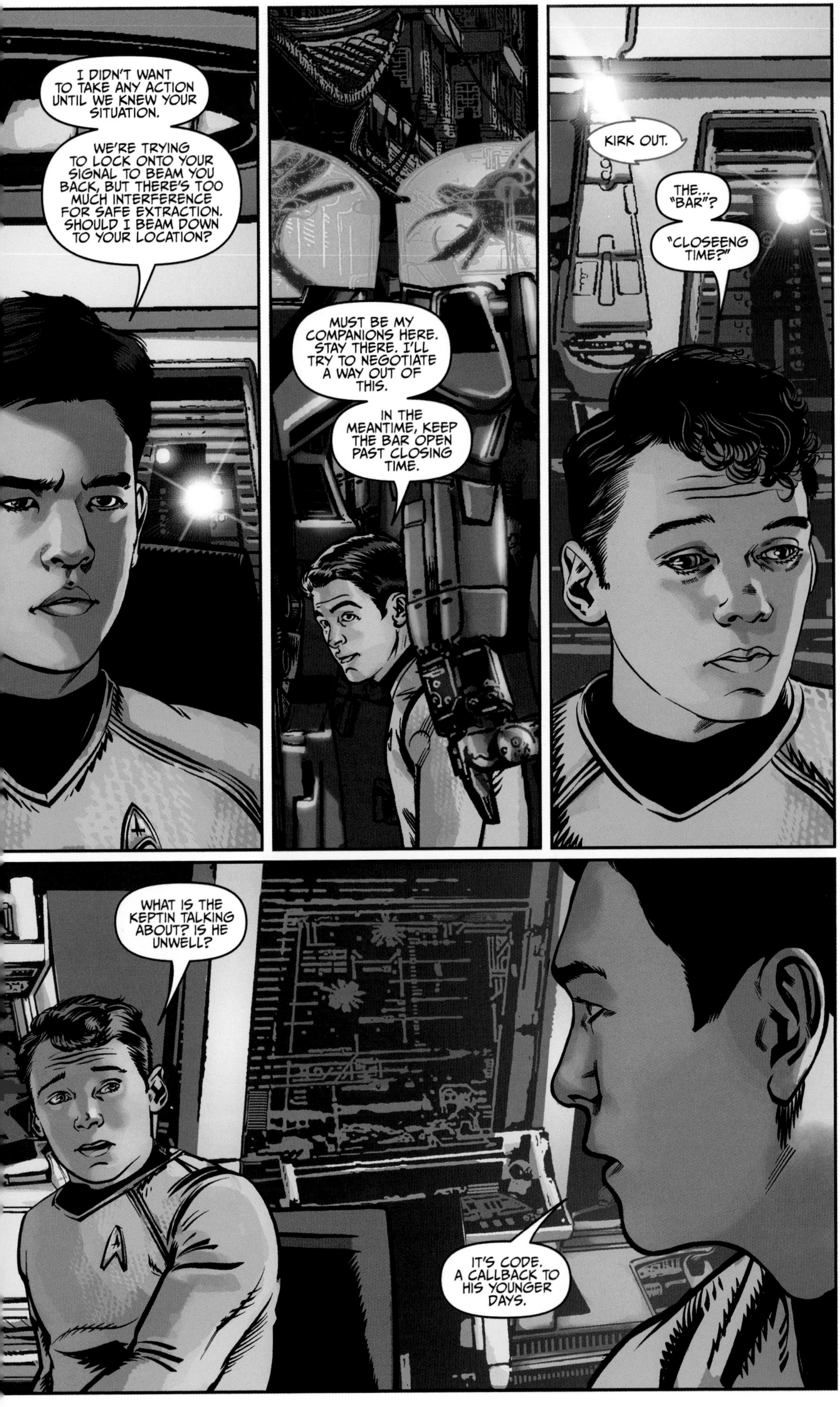

I DIDN'T WANT TO TAKE ANY ACTION UNTIL WE KNEW YOUR SITUATION.
WE'RE TRYING TO LOCK ONTO YOUR SIGNAL TO BEAM YOU BACK, BUT THERE'S TOO MUCH INTERFERENCE FOR SAFE EXTRACTION. SHOULD I BEAM DOWN TO YOUR LOCATION?
MUST BE MY COMPANIONS HERE. STAY THERE. I'LL TRY TO NEGOTIATE A WAY OUT OF THIS.
IN THE MEANTIME, KEEP THE BAR OPEN PAST CLOSING TIME.
KIRK OUT.
THE... "BAR"?
"CLOSEENG TIME?"
WHAT IS THE KEPTIN TALKING ABOUT? IS HE UNWELL?
IT'S CODE. A CALLBACK TO HIS YOUNGER DAYS.

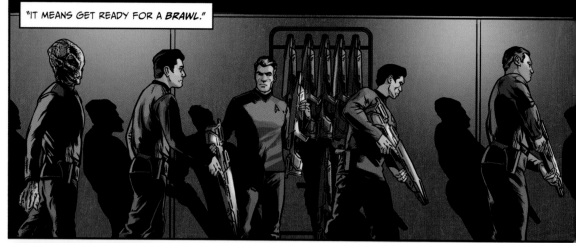

"IT MEANS GET READY FOR A *BRAWL*."

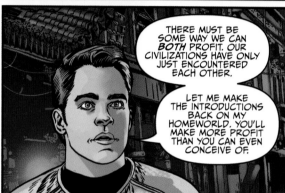

THERE MUST BE SOME WAY WE CAN *BOTH* PROFIT. OUR CIVILIZATIONS HAVE ONLY JUST ENCOUNTERED EACH OTHER.

LET ME MAKE THE INTRODUCTIONS BACK ON MY HOMEWORLD. YOU'LL MAKE MORE PROFIT THAN YOU CAN EVEN CONCEIVE OF.

...PROFIT...

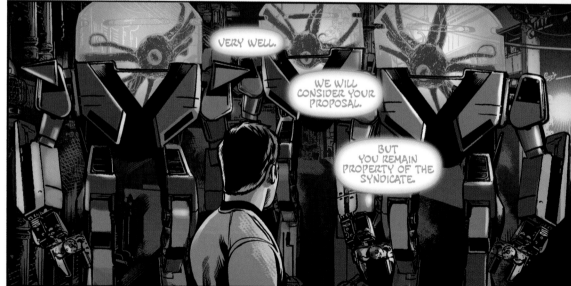

VERY WELL.

WE WILL CONSIDER YOUR PROPOSAL.

BUT YOU REMAIN PROPERTY OF THE SYNDICATE.

OKAY THEN. FIRST POINT OF NEGOTIATION: WHERE IS THE REST OF MY *TEAM*?

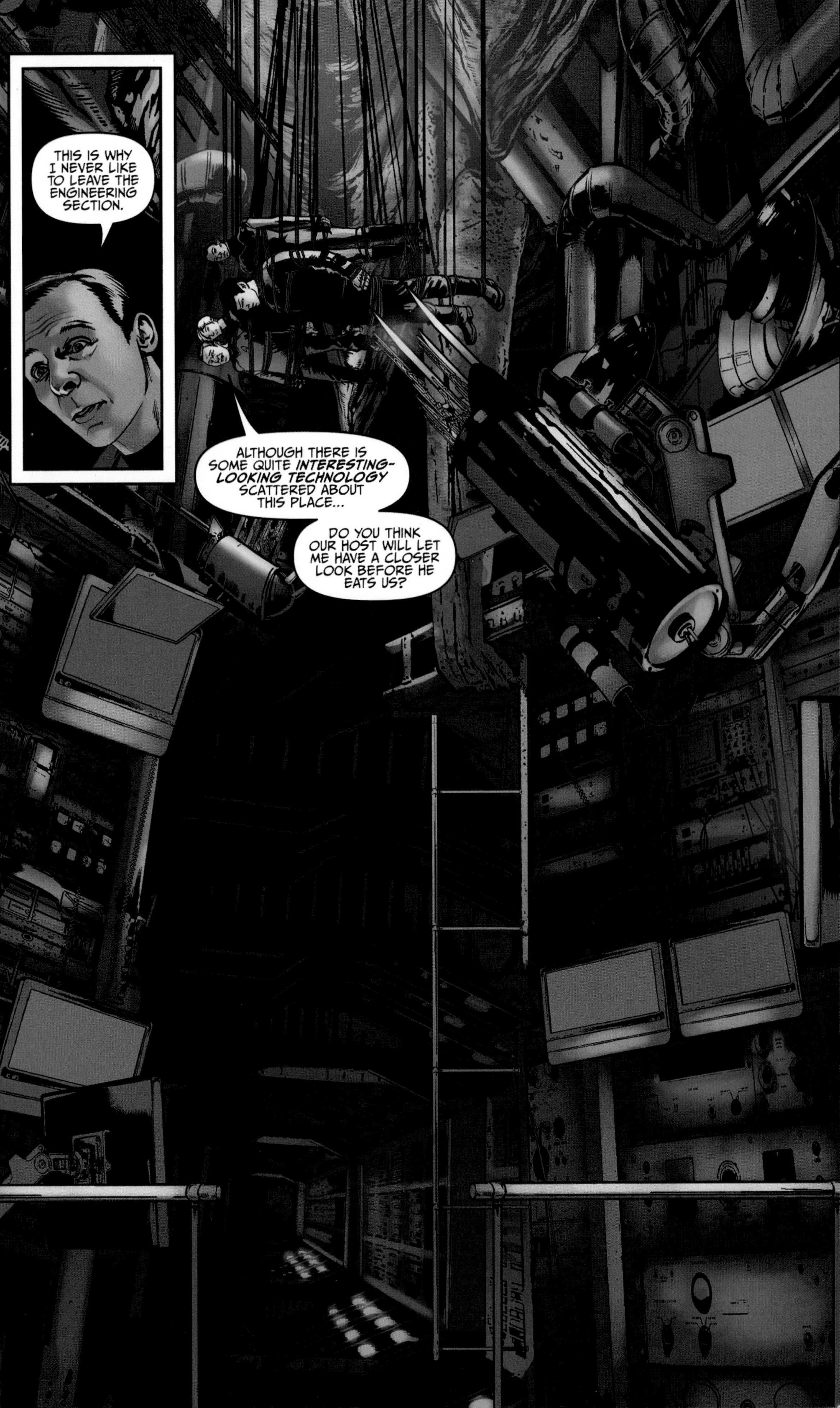
THIS IS WHY I NEVER LIKE TO LEAVE THE ENGINEERING SECTION.
ALTHOUGH THERE IS SOME QUITE *INTERESTING-LOOKING TECHNOLOGY* SCATTERED ABOUT THIS PLACE...
DO YOU THINK OUR HOST WILL LET ME HAVE A CLOSER LOOK BEFORE HE EATS US?

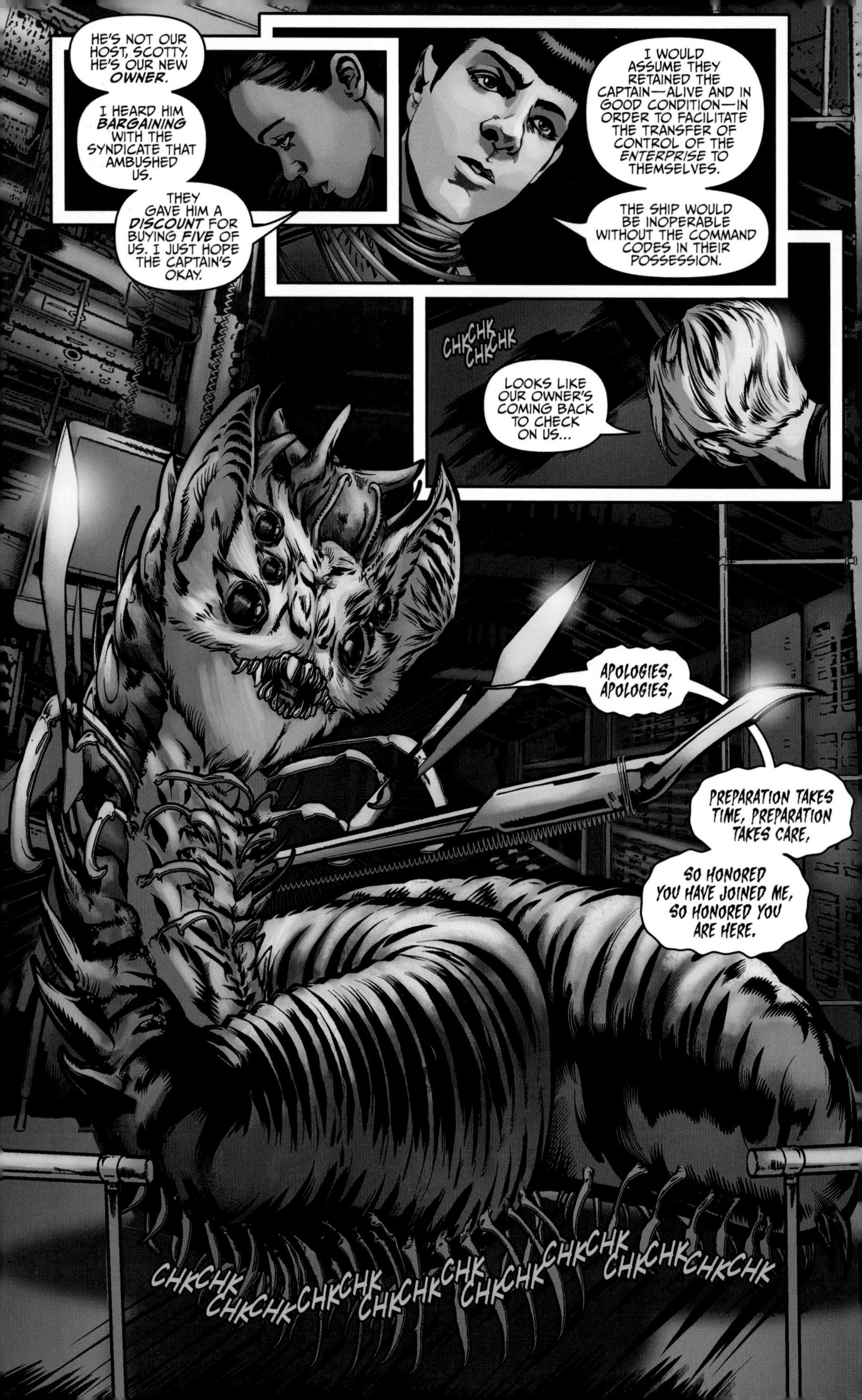
HE'S NOT OUR HOST, SCOTTY. HE'S OUR NEW OWNER.
I HEARD HIM BARGAINING WITH THE SYNDICATE THAT AMBUSHED US.
THEY GAVE HIM A DISCOUNT FOR BUYING FIVE OF US. I JUST HOPE THE CAPTAIN'S OKAY.
I WOULD ASSUME THEY RETAINED THE CAPTAIN—ALIVE AND IN GOOD CONDITION—IN ORDER TO FACILITATE THE TRANSFER OF CONTROL OF THE ENTERPRISE TO THEMSELVES.
THE SHIP WOULD BE INOPERABLE WITHOUT THE COMMAND CODES IN THEIR POSSESSION.
CHKCHK CHKCHK
LOOKS LIKE OUR OWNER'S COMING BACK TO CHECK ON US...
APOLOGIES, APOLOGIES,
PREPARATION TAKES TIME, PREPARATION TAKES CARE,
SO HONORED YOU HAVE JOINED ME, SO HONORED YOU ARE HERE.
CHKCHK CHKCHKCHKCHK CHKCHKCHK CHKCHKCHKCHK CHKCHKCHKCHK

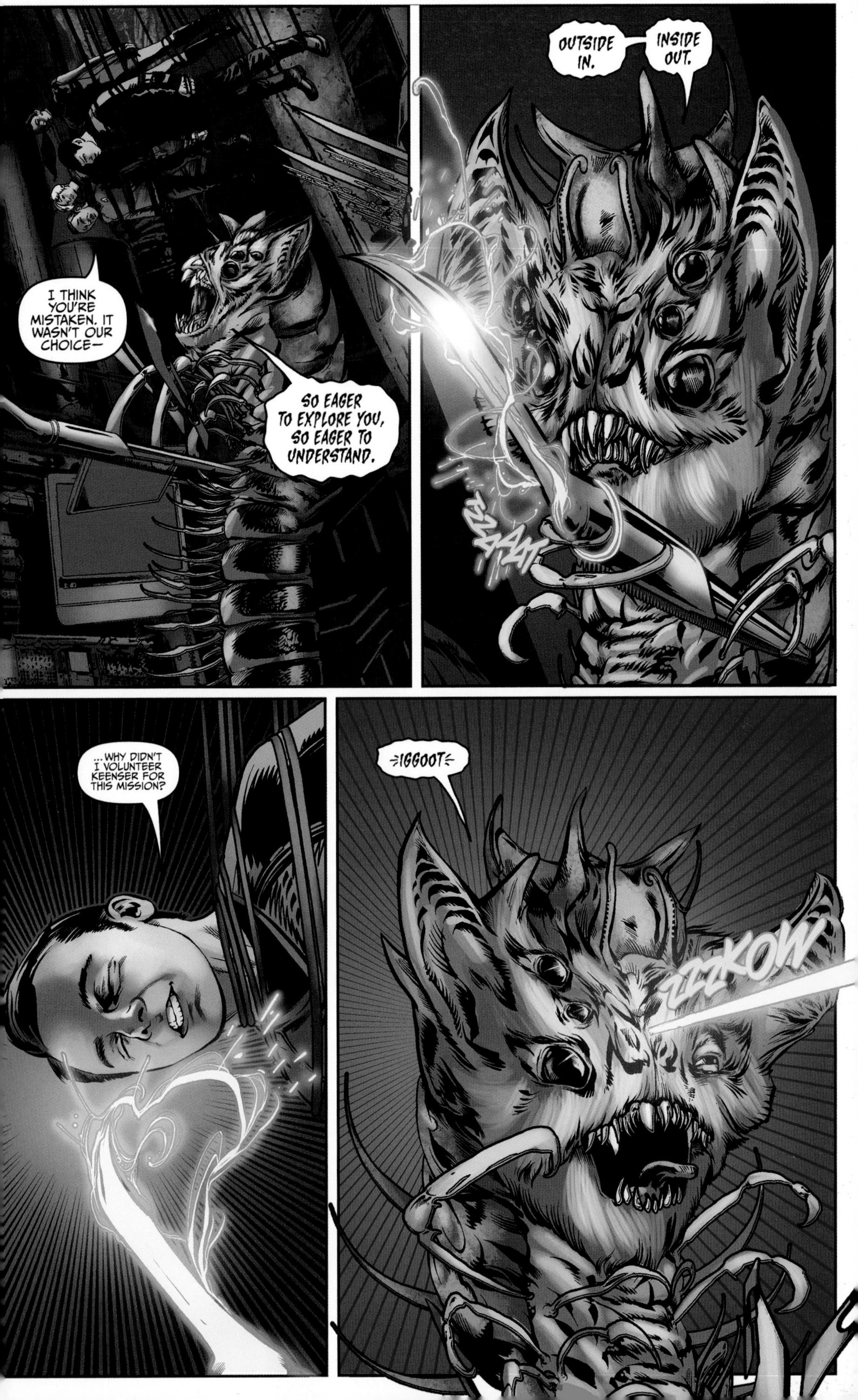
I THINK YOU'RE MISTAKEN. IT WASN'T OUR CHOICE—
SO EAGER TO EXPLORE YOU, SO EAGER TO UNDERSTAND.
OUTSIDE IN.
INSIDE OUT.
...WHY DIDN'T I VOLUNTEER KEENSER FOR THIS MISSION?
IGGOOT
ZZZKOW

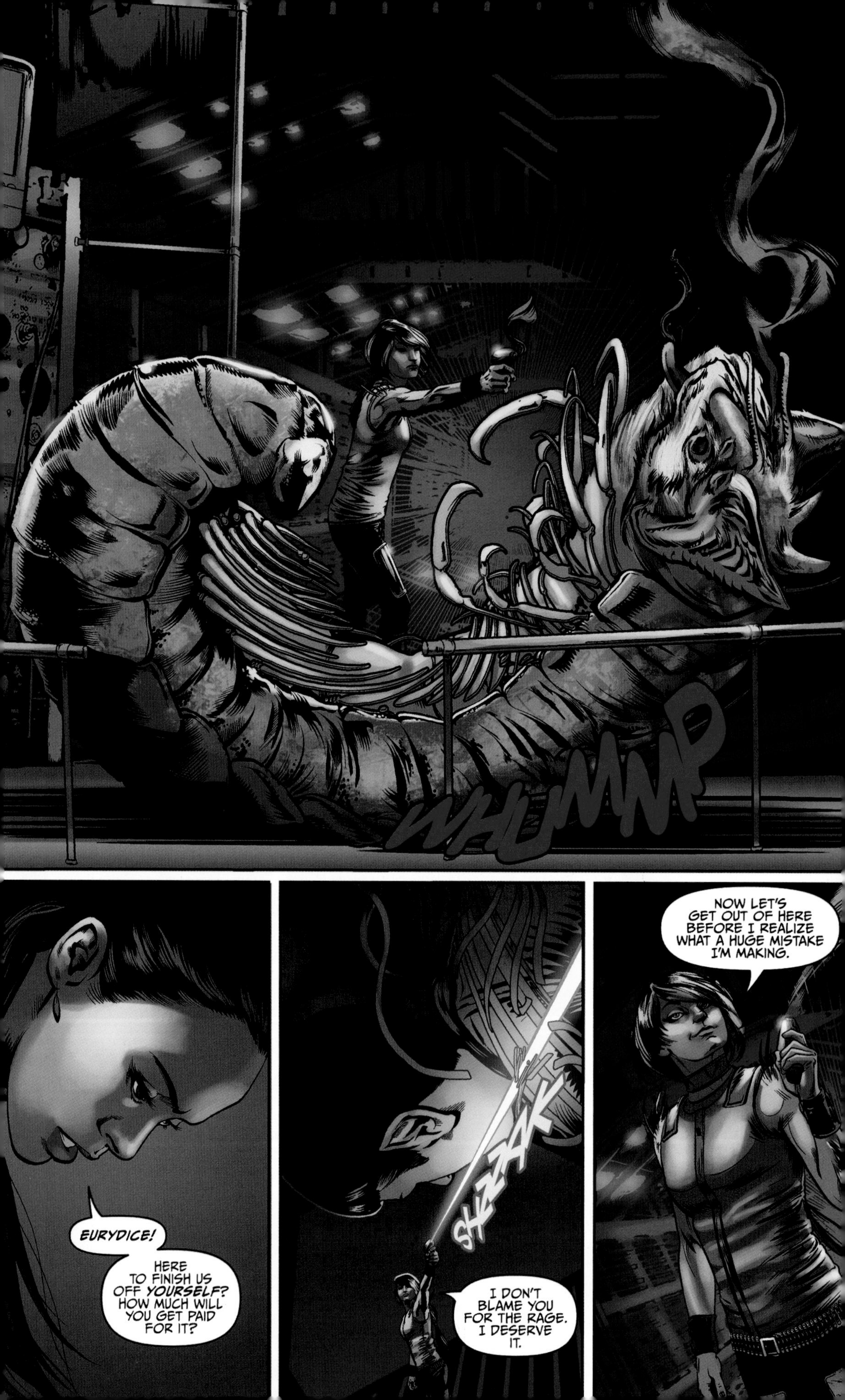
WHUMMP
EURYDICE!
HERE TO FINISH US OFF *YOURSELF*? HOW MUCH WILL YOU GET PAID FOR IT?
SHZZAK
I DON'T BLAME YOU FOR THE RAGE. I DESERVE IT.
NOW LET'S GET OUT OF HERE BEFORE I REALIZE WHAT A HUGE MISTAKE I'M MAKING.

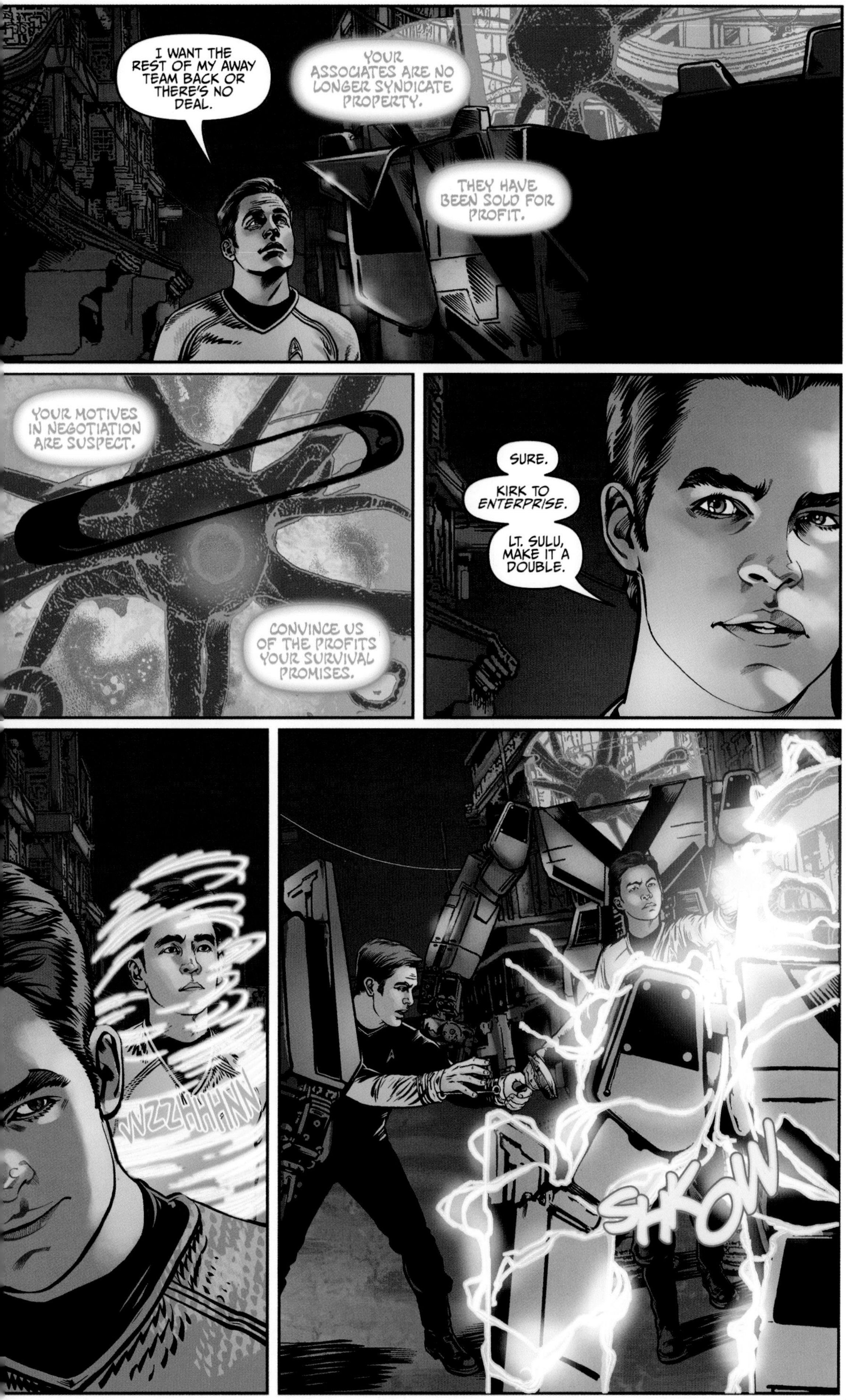
I WANT THE REST OF MY AWAY TEAM BACK OR THERE'S NO DEAL.
YOUR ASSOCIATES ARE NO LONGER SYNDICATE PROPERTY.
THEY HAVE BEEN SOLD FOR PROFIT.
YOUR MOTIVES IN NEGOTIATION ARE SUSPECT.
CONVINCE US OF THE PROFITS YOUR SURVIVAL PROMISES.
SURE.
KIRK TO *ENTERPRISE.*
LT. SULU, MAKE IT A DOUBLE.
WZZHHHNN
SHKOW

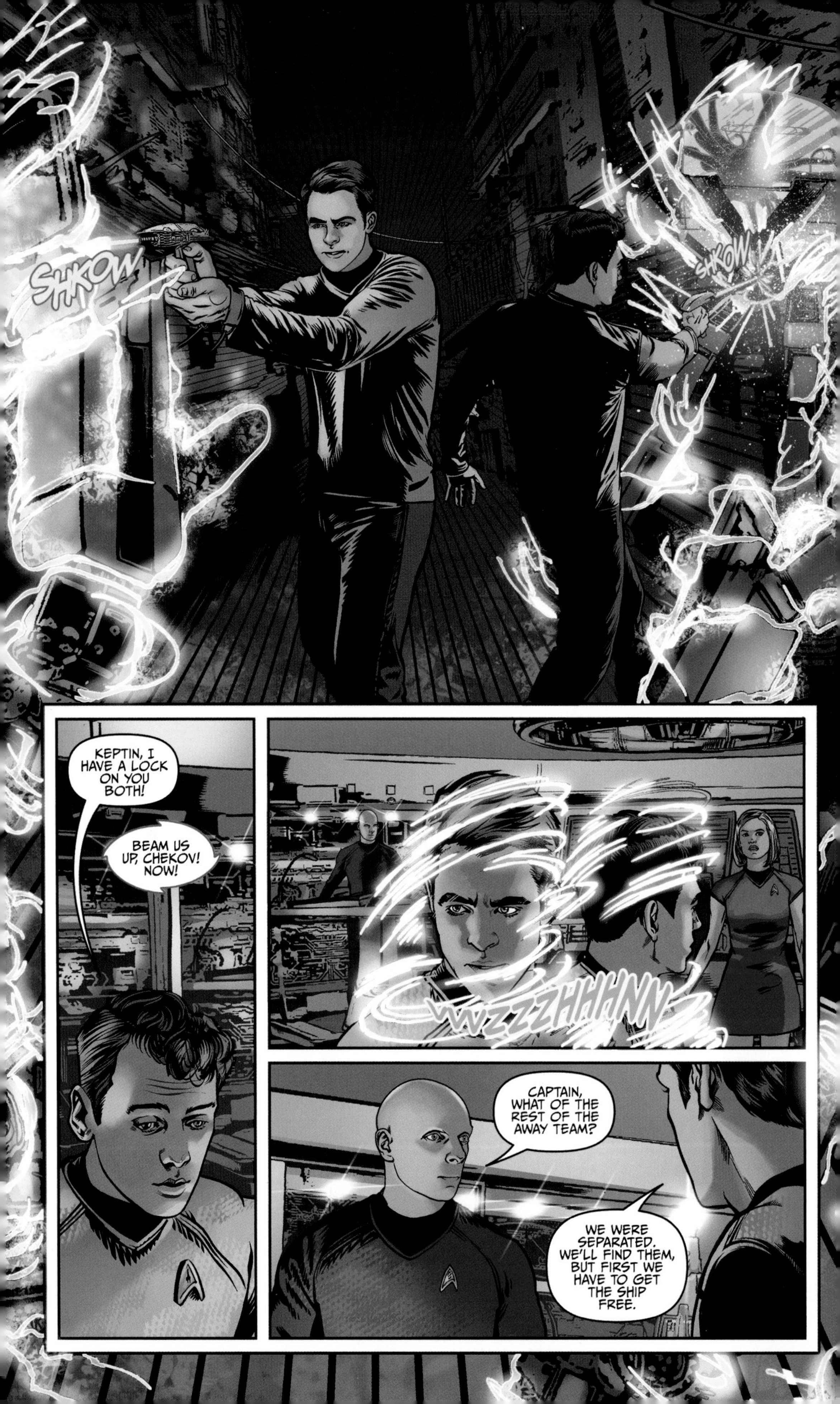
SHKOW
SHKOW
KEPTIN, I HAVE A LOCK ON YOU BOTH!
BEAM US UP, CHEKOV! NOW!
VVVZZZHHHHNN
CAPTAIN, WHAT OF THE REST OF THE AWAY TEAM?
WE WERE SEPARATED. WE'LL FIND THEM, BUT FIRST WE HAVE TO GET THE SHIP FREE.

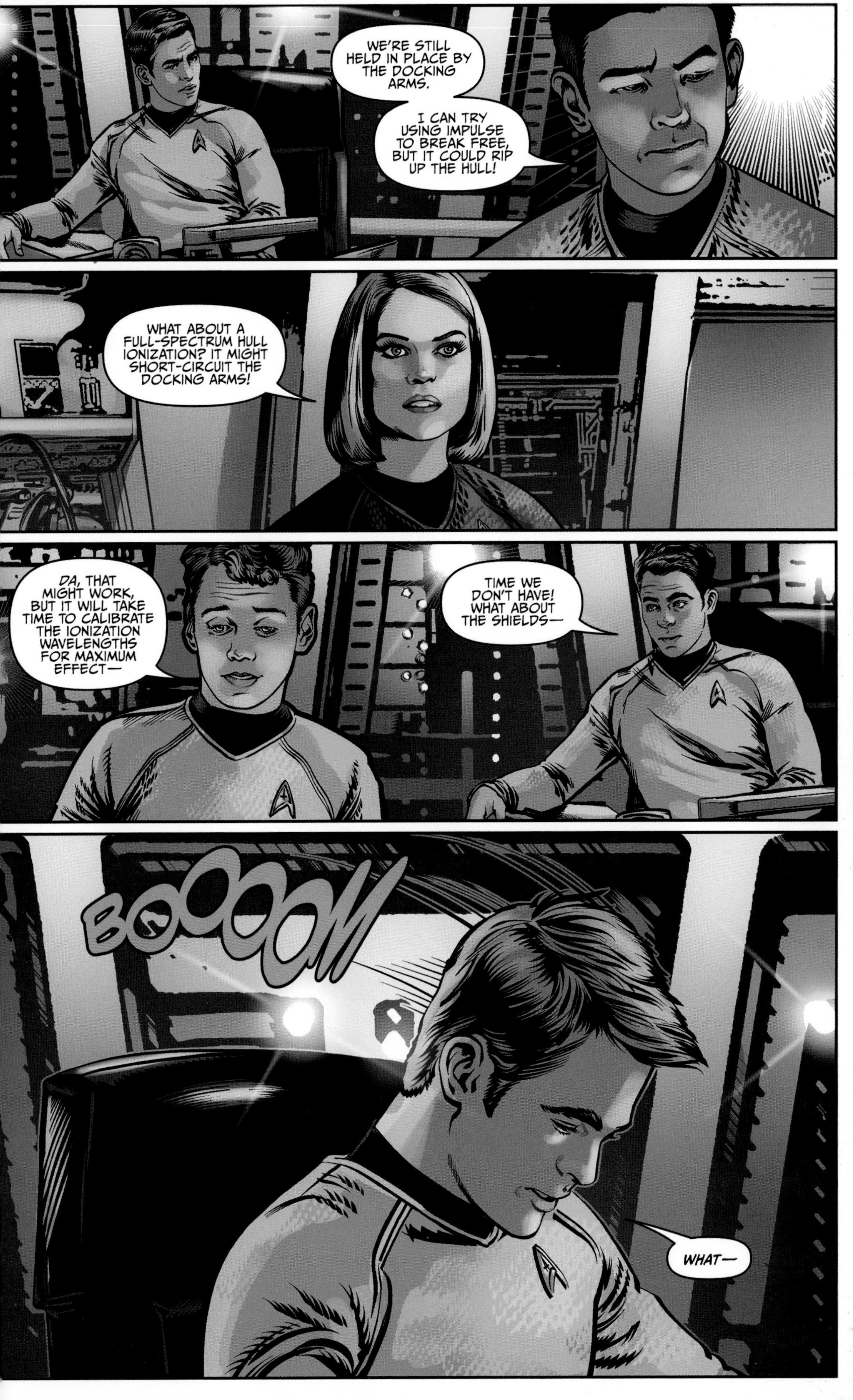
WE'RE STILL HELD IN PLACE BY THE DOCKING ARMS.
I CAN TRY USING IMPULSE TO BREAK FREE, BUT IT COULD RIP UP THE HULL!
WHAT ABOUT A FULL-SPECTRUM HULL IONIZATION? IT MIGHT SHORT-CIRCUIT THE DOCKING ARMS!
DA, THAT MIGHT WORK, BUT IT WILL TAKE TIME TO CALIBRATE THE IONIZATION WAVELENGTHS FOR MAXIMUM EFFECT—
TIME WE DON'T HAVE! WHAT ABOUT THE SHIELDS—
BOOOOM
WHAT—

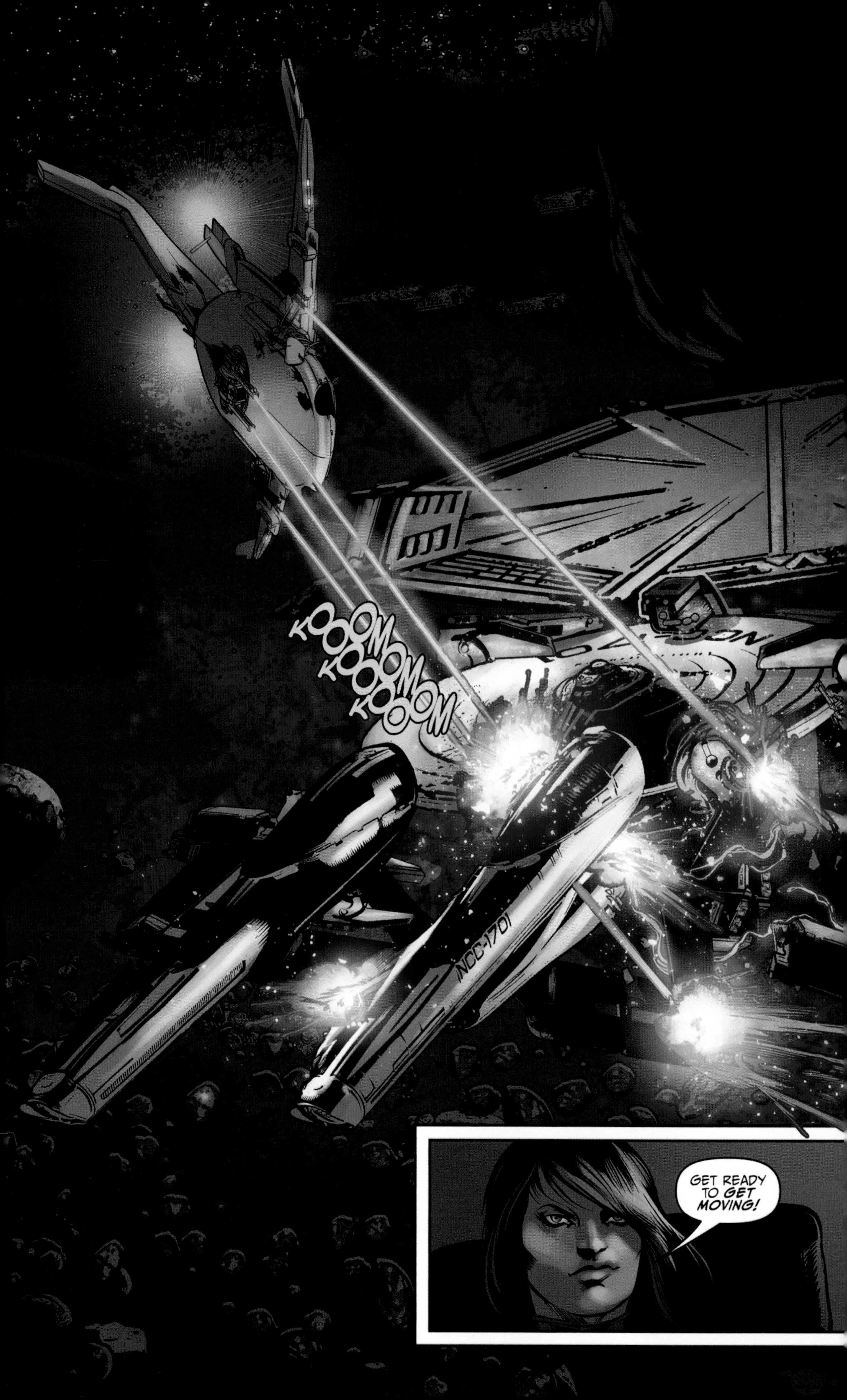
KOOM KOOOM KOOOM
NCC-1701
GET READY TO GET MOVING!

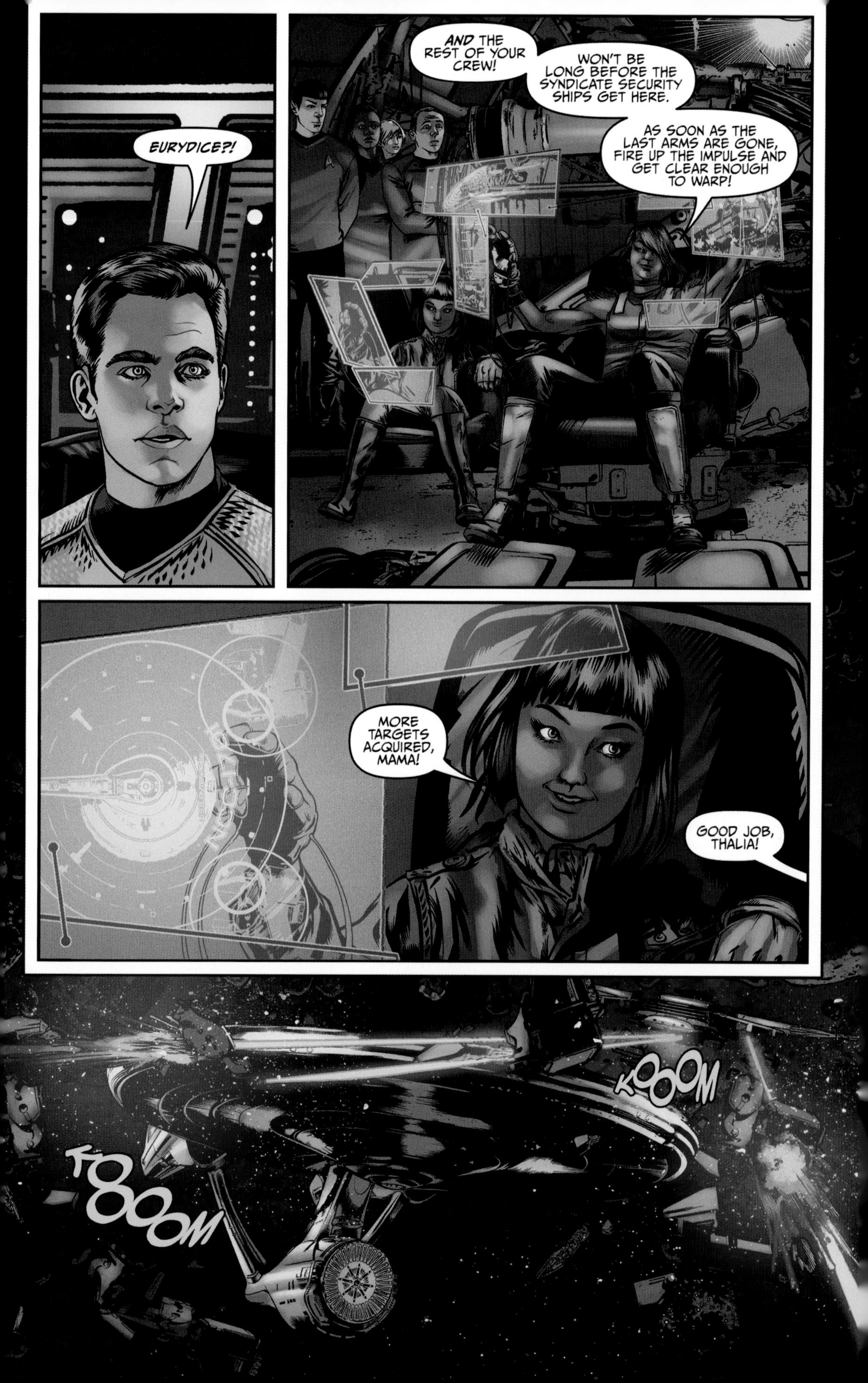
EURYDICE?!
AND THE REST OF YOUR CREW!
WON'T BE LONG BEFORE THE SYNDICATE SECURITY SHIPS GET HERE.
AS SOON AS THE LAST ARMS ARE GONE, FIRE UP THE IMPULSE AND GET CLEAR ENOUGH TO WARP!
MORE TARGETS ACQUIRED, MAMA!
GOOD JOB, THALIA!
KOOOM
KOOOM

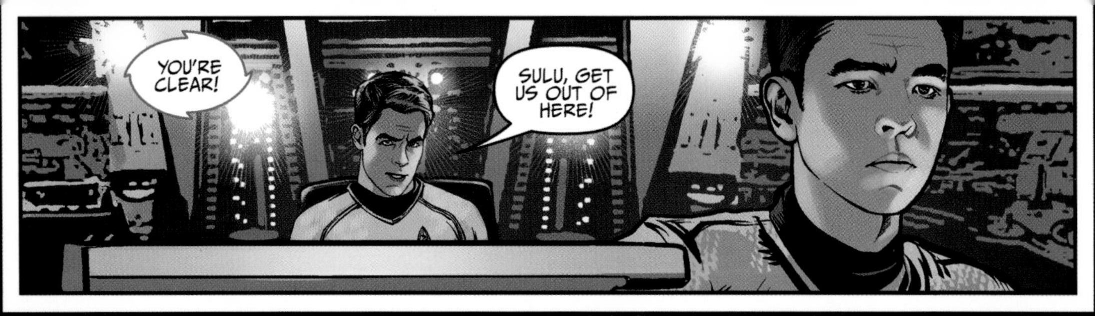
YOU'RE CLEAR!
SULU, GET US OUT OF HERE!

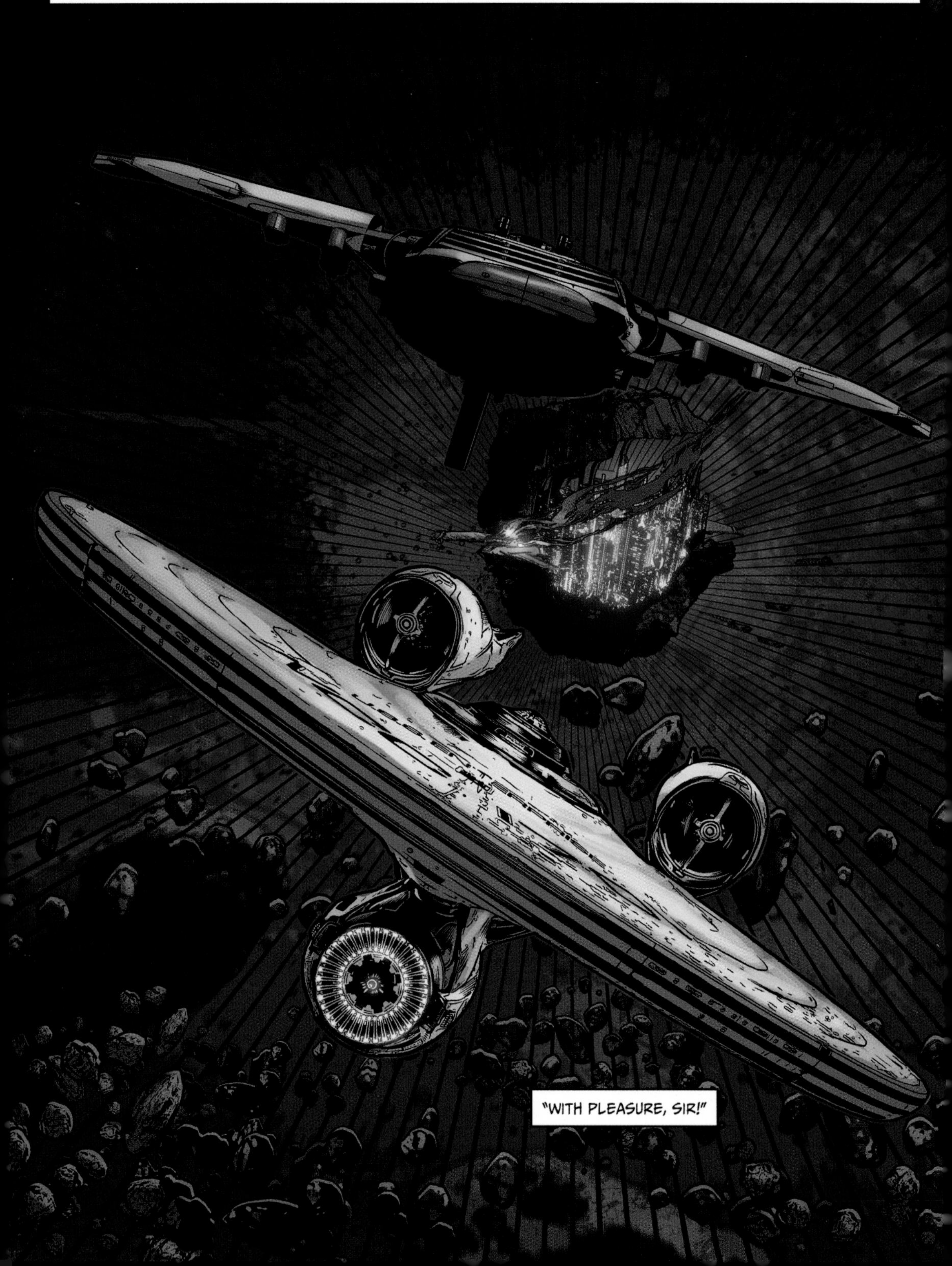
"WITH PLEASURE, SIR!"

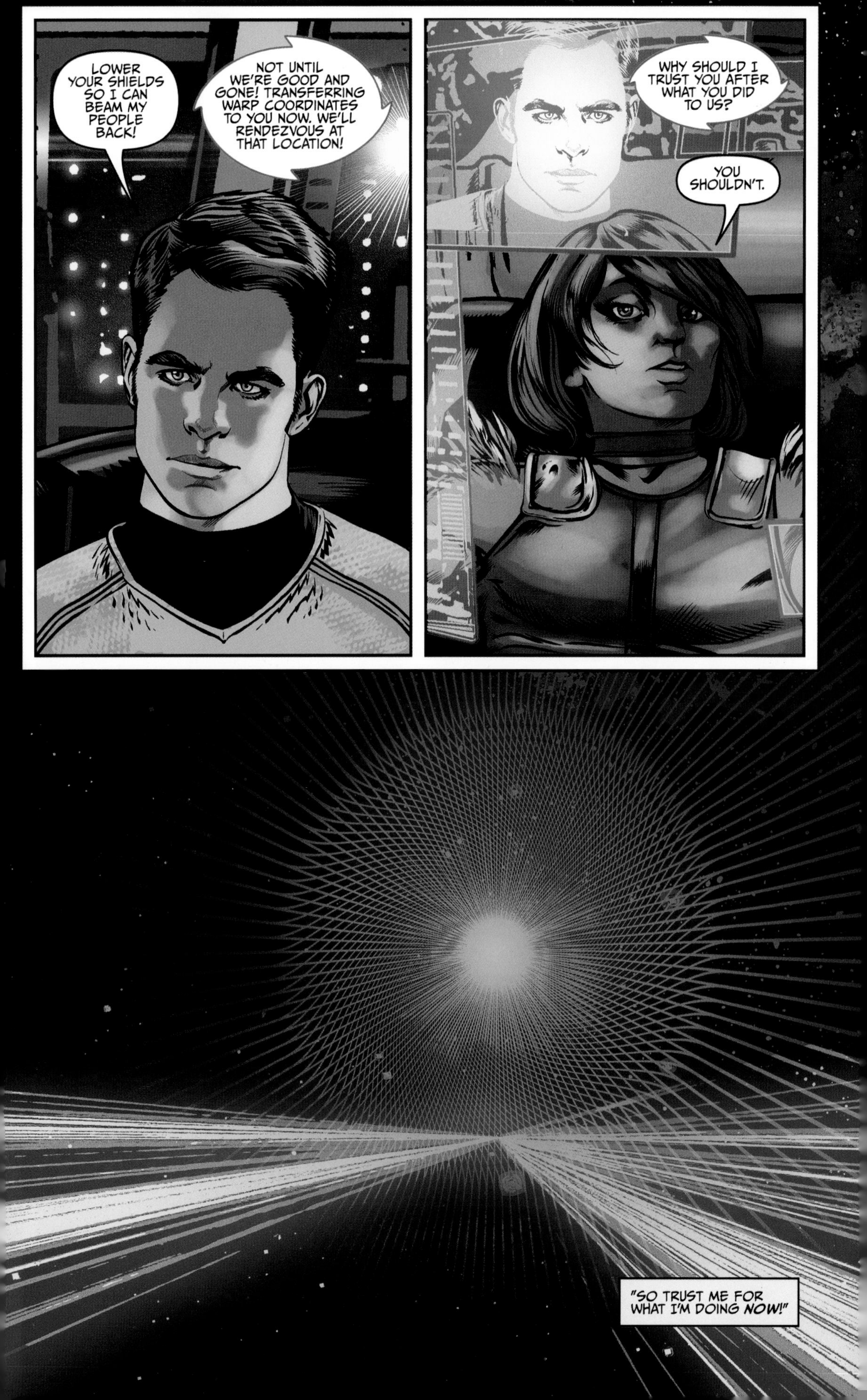
LOWER YOUR SHIELDS SO I CAN BEAM MY PEOPLE BACK!
NOT UNTIL WE'RE GOOD AND GONE! TRANSFERRING WARP COORDINATES TO YOU NOW. WE'LL RENDEZVOUS AT THAT LOCATION!
WHY SHOULD I TRUST YOU AFTER WHAT YOU DID TO US?
YOU SHOULDN'T.
"SO TRUST ME FOR WHAT I'M DOING NOW!"

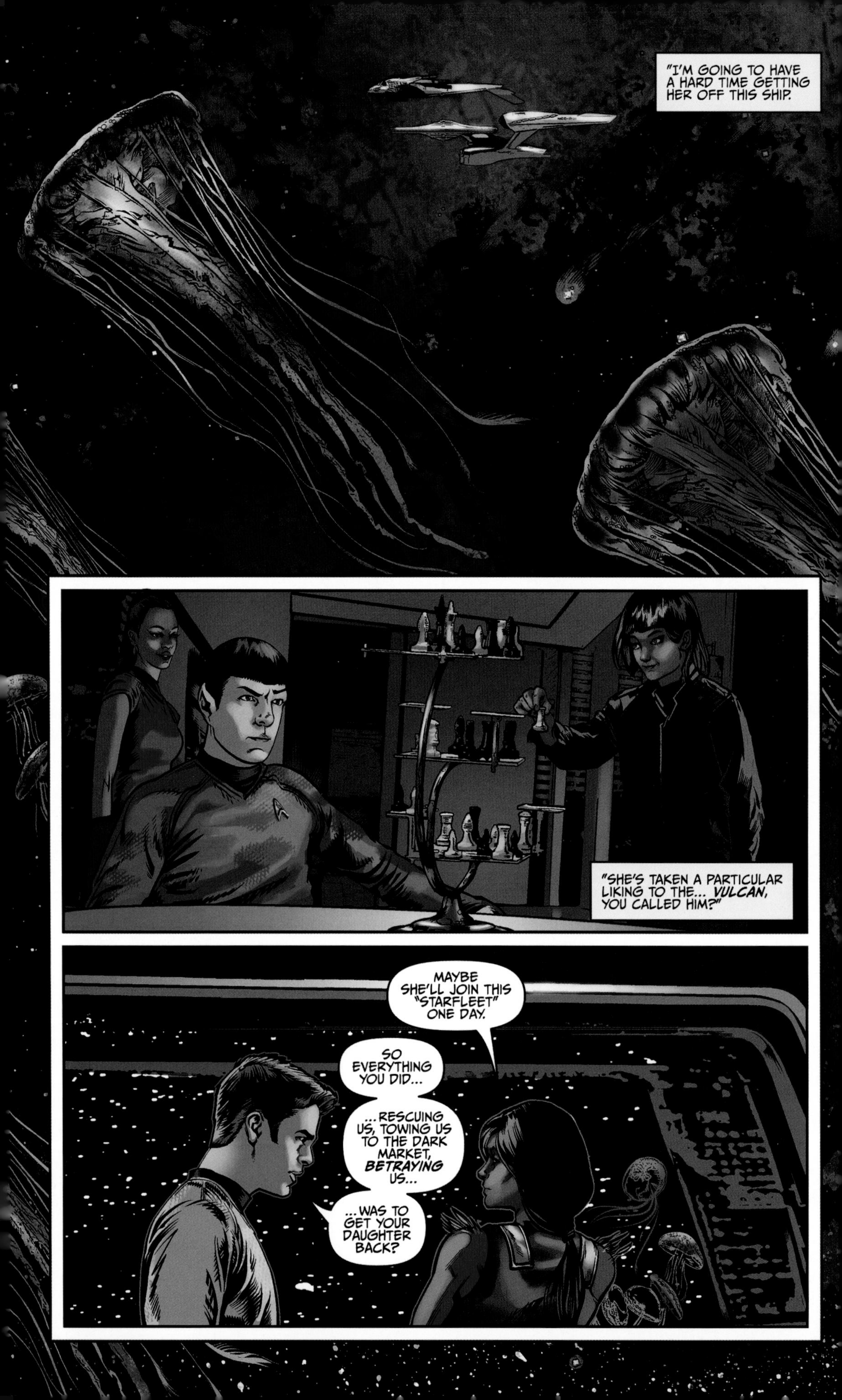
"I'M GOING TO HAVE A HARD TIME GETTING HER OFF THIS SHIP.
"SHE'S TAKEN A PARTICULAR LIKING TO THE... *VULCAN*, YOU CALLED HIM?"
MAYBE SHE'LL JOIN THIS "STARFLEET" ONE DAY.
SO EVERYTHING YOU DID...
...RESCUING US, TOWING US TO THE DARK MARKET, *BETRAYING* US...
...WAS TO GET YOUR DAUGHTER BACK?

FOR YEARS I'D BEEN DOING BUSINESS WITH THE SYNDICATE. YOU CAN'T STAY IN BUSINESS IF YOU *DON'T*.

BUT AS THEY GREW STRONGER THEIR TERMS GREW WORSE. EVENTUALLY I WAS BORROWING FROM THEM JUST TO PAY THE COSTS OF FINDING SALVAGE TO SELL *BACK* TO THEM.

TO MAKE SURE I PAID MY DEBTS, THEY TOOK MY DAUGHTER.

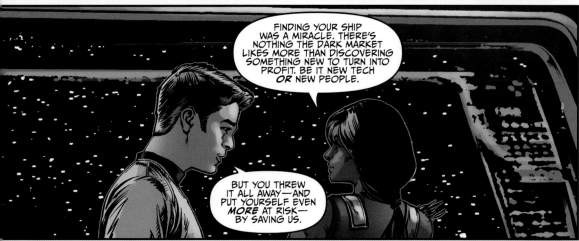

FINDING YOUR SHIP WAS A MIRACLE. THERE'S NOTHING THE DARK MARKET LIKES MORE THAN DISCOVERING SOMETHING NEW TO TURN INTO PROFIT. BE IT NEW TECH *OR* NEW PEOPLE.

BUT YOU THREW IT ALL AWAY—AND PUT YOURSELF EVEN *MORE* AT RISK— BY SAVING US.

I'VE BEEN A FUGITIVE BEFORE. THAT STRESS IS NOTHING COMPARED TO THE GUILT I FELT AFTER I TURNED YOU IN.

I KNOW JUST HOW *DARK* THE MARKET CAN GET, KIRK. WHATEVER LIVES YOU HAD LEFT TO LIVE WOULD HAVE ENDED... *BADLY*.

SO WHERE DO YOU GO NOW? HOW WILL YOU SURVIVE IF YOU CAN'T DO BUSINESS IN THE MARKET?

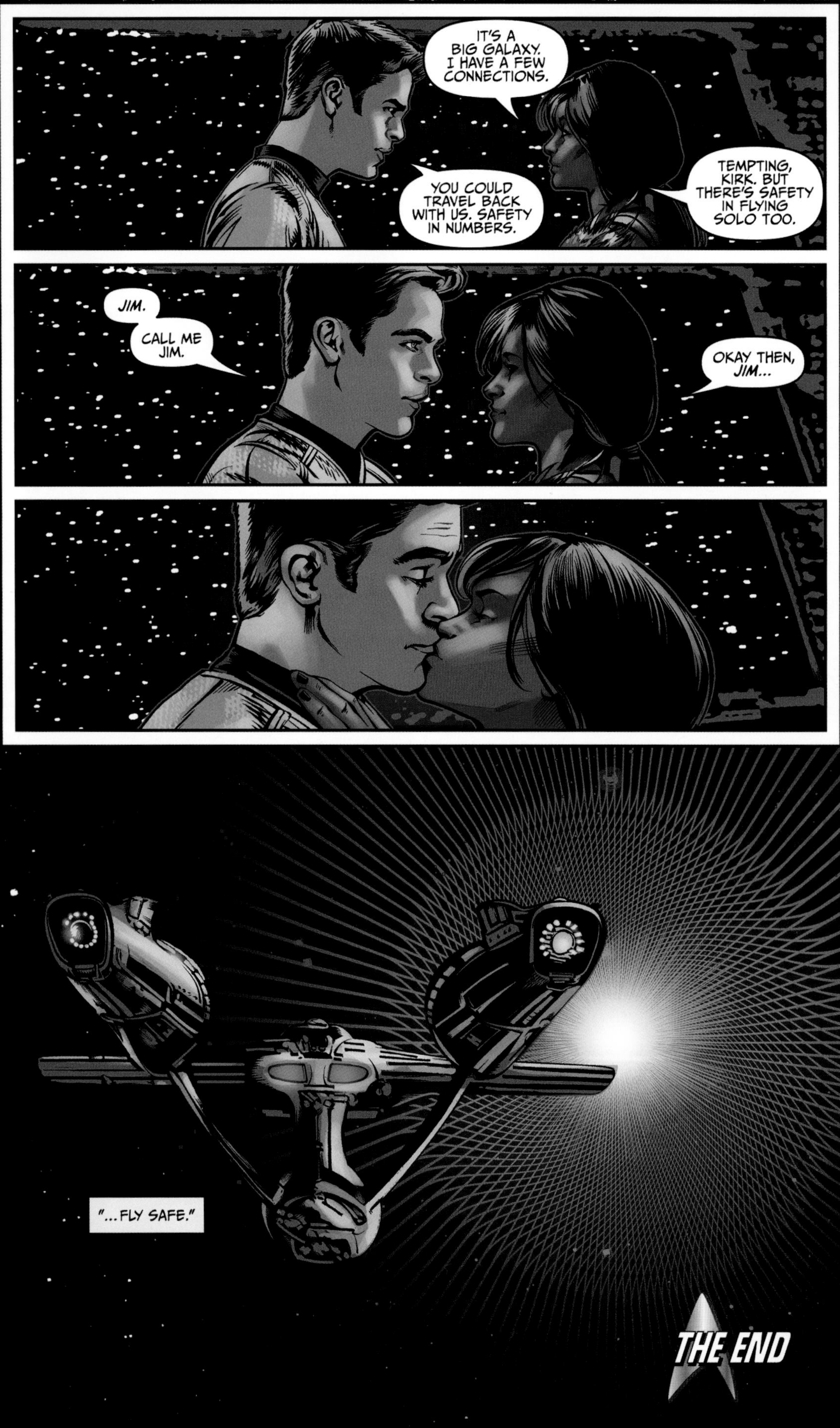
IT'S A BIG GALAXY. I HAVE A FEW CONNECTIONS.
YOU COULD TRAVEL BACK WITH US. SAFETY IN NUMBERS.
TEMPTING, KIRK. BUT THERE'S SAFETY IN FLYING SOLO TOO.
JIM.
CALL ME JIM.
OKAY THEN, JIM...
"...FLY SAFE."
THE END

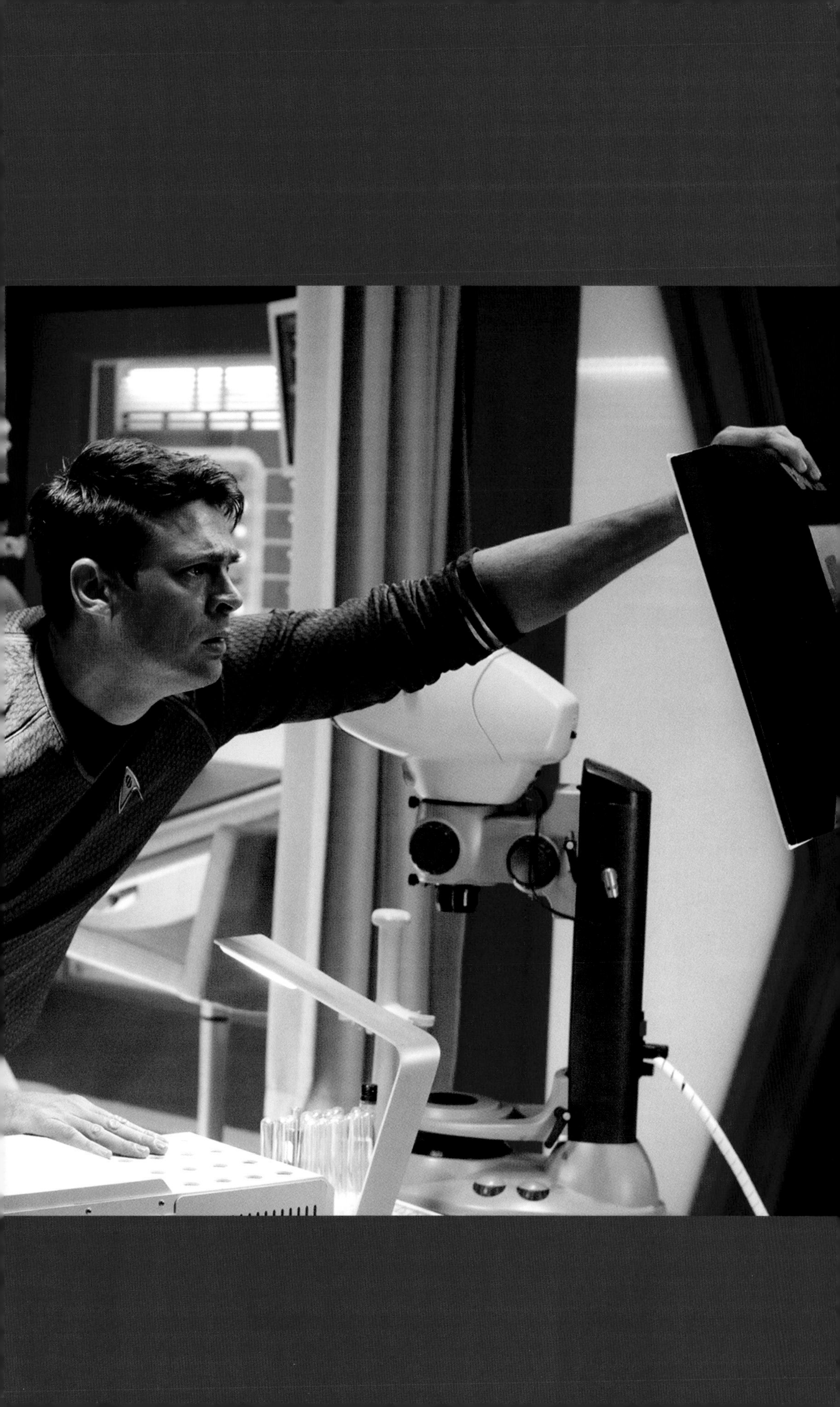

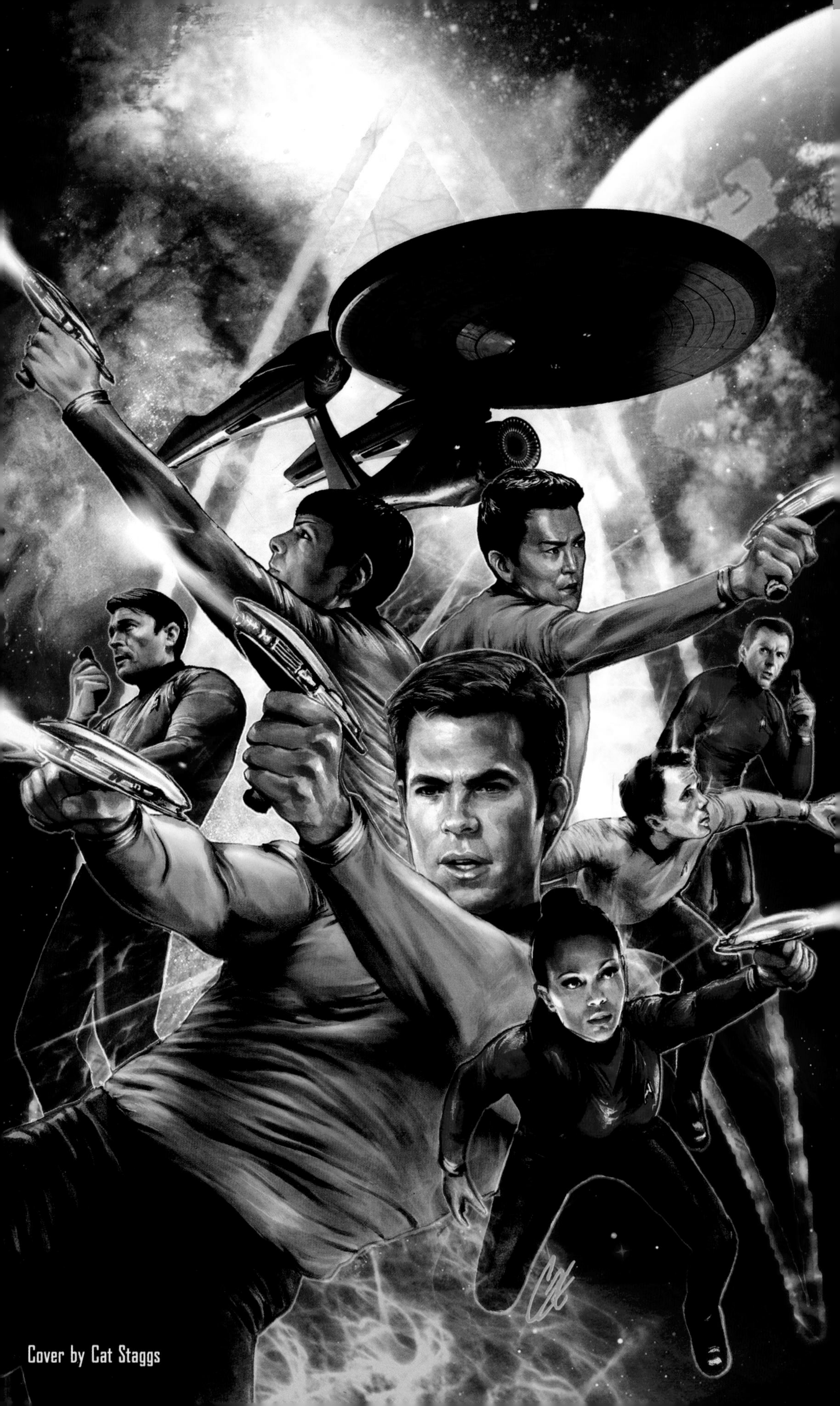

Cover by Cat Staggs

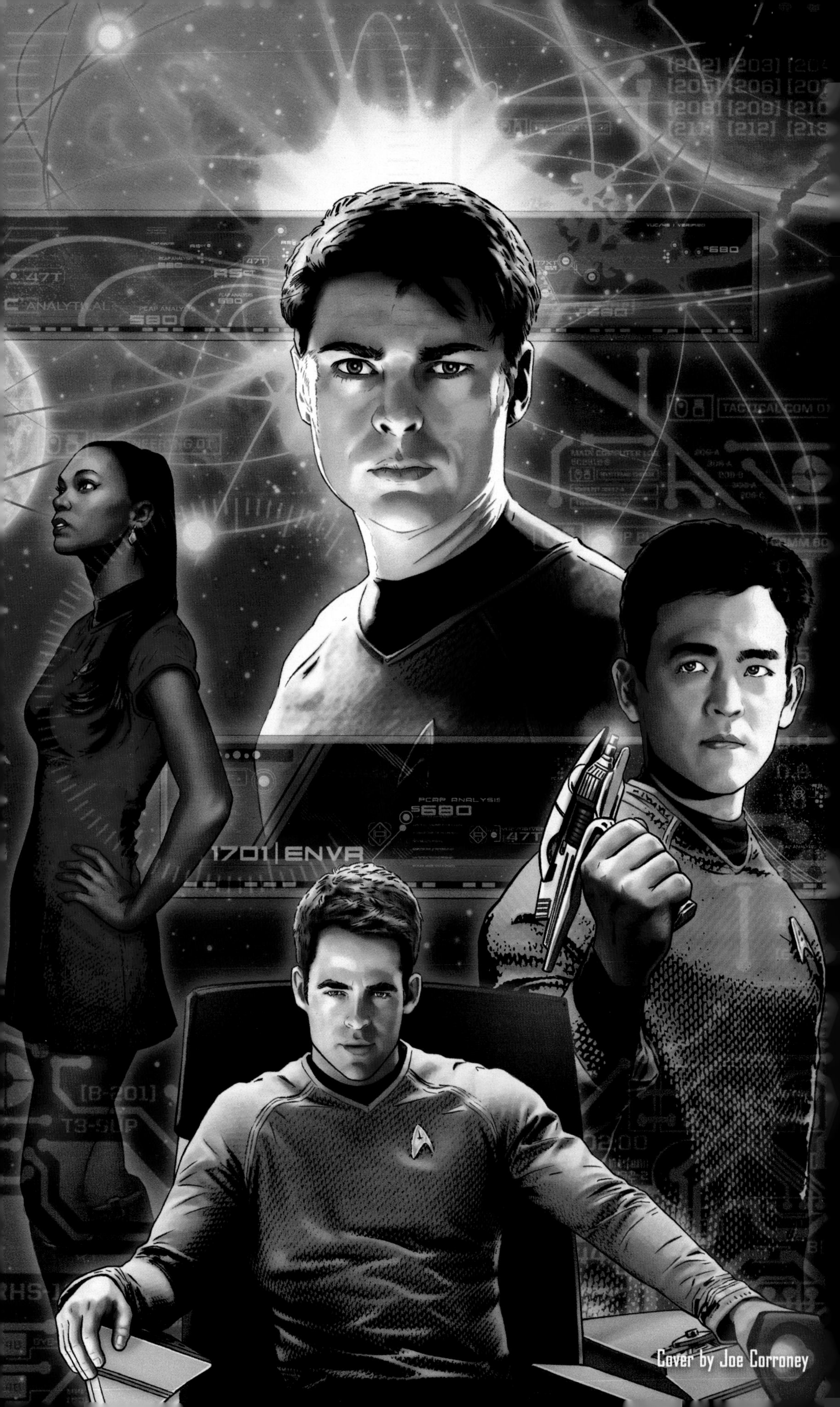

1701 | ENVR
PCAP ANALYSIS
680
TACTICAL COM 01
[B-201]
T3-SUP

Cover by Joe Corroney

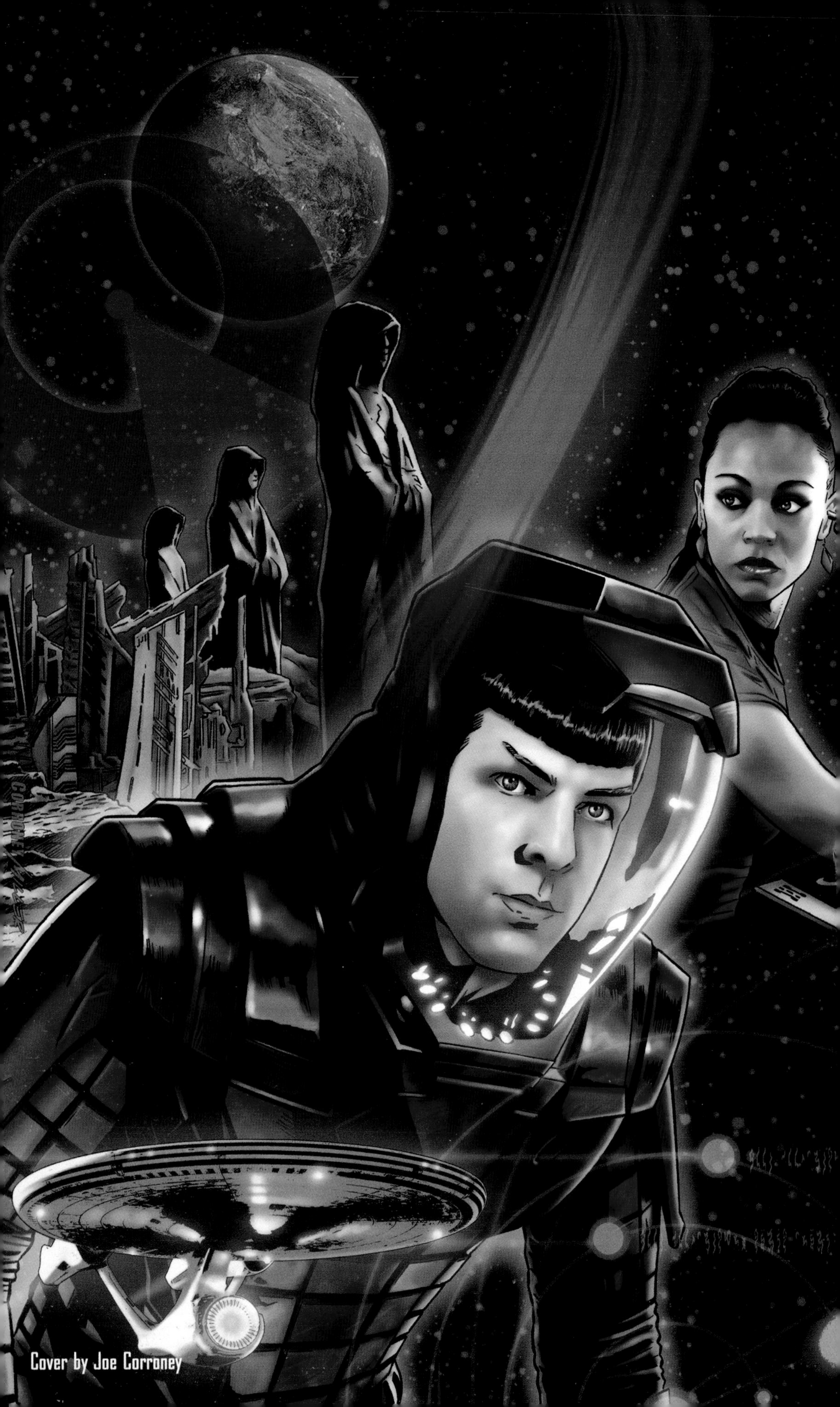
CORRONEY
Cover by Joe Corroney